Storm Echo

Storm Echo

A PSY-CHANGELING TRINITY NOVEL

NALINI SINGH

BERKLEY
New York

BERKLEY
An imprint of Penguin Random House LLC
penguinrandomhouse.com

Library of Congress Cataloging-in-Publication Data

Names: Singh, Nalini, 1977- author.
Title: Storm echo / Nalini Singh.
Description: First edition. | New York: Berkley, 2022. | Series: A psy-changeling trinity novel ; 6
Identifiers: LCCN 2022000421 (print) | LCCN 2022000422 (ebook) |
ISBN 9780593440674 (hardcover) | ISBN 9780593440698 (ebook)
Classification: LCC PR9639.4.S566 S76 2022 (print) | LCC PR9639.4.S566 (ebook) |
DDC 823/.92—dc23/eng/20220107
LC record available at https://lccn.loc.gov/2022000421
LC ebook record available at https://lccn.loc.gov/2022000422

Printed in the United States of America
1st Printing

Storm Echo

Scarab Queen

THE PSYNET.

A psychic network that spans the globe.

A network without which the Psy race cannot survive.

To sever the PsyNet link of another is to commit murder.

No rational person would ever do that to their fellow Psy.

But the Architect is not rational.

The Architect dreams of total dominion over not just the Psy race, but humans and changelings, too.

And the Architect has within her grasp the cooperation of hundreds of tormented minds brimming with violent psychic power.

The Architect and her Scarabs.

Are about to change the history of the Psy race.

There will never be any going back.

Chapter 1

The child has severe attachment issues. It is not Silence. He is simply psychologically damaged to the extent that he may never be able to form an attachment to another on any level. As such, his loyalty to the family cannot be guaranteed. He is a risk.

—Private PsyMed report on Ivan Mercant, age 8 (20 June 2059)

3 May 2083

IN TERMS OF age, Ivan fell in the older cadre of Ena's grandchildren. Younger than Canto, older than Silver and Arwen. He'd also always been the one who gave the family the least trouble—no trouble at all really. Canto was as stubborn as a bull and Silver had a steely spine, and neither ever bent for Ena unless they wished to do so.

As for Arwen, gentle, empathic Arwen could be obstinate in his own way. Like water running over stone. Slow and persistent until the edges of the rock were no longer so sharp and the water had carved a new channel without the rock ever being aware of the change.

Ivan, in contrast, was more wont to say yes than no. Ask any of the other three and they'd never use the words "obstinate" or "stubborn" in relation to Ivan. One of the teenage members of the family had used the term "chill" to describe Ivan, and when Ena had looked up what that term meant when used in that context, she'd had to agree.

Ivan flowed through life, willing to bend, never opposing Ena . . . and still doing exactly what he wanted and nothing else. It had taken a long time for Ena to realize that the least openly stubborn of her grandchildren was also the most relentless in his quiet will. It was Ivan, after all, who'd never studied at the tertiary level, despite Ena's strong desire that he do so; and it was Ivan who'd chosen to walk a path she'd initially forbidden him from pursuing.

Ivan did as he pleased . . . but he did have one vulnerability.

"Ivan?" she said now, as she watched him pack the final items for his journey to San Francisco. She rarely intruded in the suite he kept at the family compound, but with him leaving today, it was well past time to have this conversation. "Is all well?"

"Of course, Grandmother." He unzipped a side pocket of his holdall, then reached for a small and flat black bag that could contain either his toothbrush and soap—or a weapon.

There was no way to know when it came to Ivan.

"Are you certain?" She remained in the doorway, for she would not push into the private area of his bedroom—though she knew Ivan wouldn't rebuff her. That was the problem, and why she asked so little from him. Because Ivan would give it to her. He went his own way when it came to his life and the choices he made, but should Ena ever request he do a task, he'd do so without hesitation.

Whether it was to put a bullet in someone's head or to allow her in his space.

That was Ivan's only vulnerability.

"I'm fine," he said, zipping up that pocket. "Why do you ask?"

"You've been different since you returned from that training course in Texas." Close to a year and a half ago. She hadn't been sure at first, and Ivan had somehow slid out of any conversations where she tried to bring it up, and then he'd vanished from her sight for various duties. "Did something happen?"

The most minute pause in his efficient movements. So small that likely not even Canto, Arwen, or Silver would've noticed, and they were the closest to Ivan aside from Ena. But Ena had always looked at Ivan with more careful eyes than she had his cousins. They'd all needed her in one way or another, but Ivan . . . he was the one least likely to verbalize or openly show that need.

He'd learned too young that asking for help was useless. No one would ever come. She'd tried to overwrite that ugly lesson, but it had been too long embedded by the time Ena came into his life. All she'd been able to do was make sure she responded to his unspoken needs—and hope that one day, he'd learn that she would *always* respond if he asked her for anything.

Now he closed the final tab on his holdall and turned to face her, those eyes of pale blue shot with darker shards striking against his black hair and the cool white of his skin. "Just the cut I received on my calf," he said, "and that's long since healed." Slipping the strap of the holdall over his shoulder, he walked to join her in the doorway.

"Are you certain, Ivan?" Ena didn't budge; she hadn't held this family together through the cold reign of Silence by being weak of will, and she wasn't about to let Ivan obfuscate this. Because the thing was, Ivan never lied to her. He just somehow managed to give her only as much information as he wanted.

Canto had been known to mutter that Ivan was more like Ena than any of them: a Mercant who kept his own counsel and who shared information only when he decided it was time.

Ena respected that. But how he'd been of late . . . as if the light inside him had dimmed . . . that disturbed her on a level beyond flesh and bone. Because Ivan's light had almost been snuffed out once. She'd had to cup her hands around it for years, protecting it from the winds of pain and the storms of scars, until the light was strong enough to survive on its own.

He held her gaze, so much quiet power in him that it hummed in the air, then glanced away. "I can't talk to you about this, Grandmother." His eyes returned to her. "It's not a thing about which I can speak."

There it was, that inviolable core he'd always kept separate from everyone, even Ena. She'd never been able to work out whether it was conscious or a result of wounds inflicted long before he was this powerful man who could hold his own against the world.

There was no point pushing him. Not when he'd given her an unusually forthright response. That alone told her that whatever had happened, it'd had a profound impact on him.

She stepped back so he could exit the bedroom. As she fell in beside him on his walk to leave the suite, she said, "You know I'll always be here if you change your mind."

Opening the door, he paused, met her eyes again. "I know, Grandmother."

Then he walked out, her grandson tall and strong and deadly. She hadn't wanted the latter for him, had wanted him to have a life of calm and peace. But Ivan would not have it. He would not allow her to choose for him a life in the light . . . because he believed he'd been born to walk in the dark.

15 MONTHS EARLIER

Chapter 2

The child's attachment to the family unit—and associated loyalty—is absolute. His ability to form bonds with those outside this small circle remains an unknown, but it is my view that when he does form any such bond, it will be one without boundaries—he does not appear to have the capacity to limit his loyalty once given.

—Private PsyMed report on Ivan Mercant, age 14 (9 November 2065)

IVAN BRACED HIS hand against the tree trunk, the forest hushed around him, then looked down at the cut on his calf. He'd tied a tourniquet above the cut, but the bleeding showed no signs of stopping. If he hadn't known better, he'd have said the fall onto the sharp edge of rock had severed a major artery.

But he did know better—he'd done enough first-aid courses, had enough knowledge of anatomy and of his own body, to judge this wound as disabling but not dangerous. It should, however, have stopped bleeding by now. If it kept up like this, he'd have to call for assistance and drop out of the training course for the day.

If there was one thing Ivan preferred never to do, it was to ask for help. His reticence was bad enough that he was conscious it could end up a fatal flaw, but even knowing that, he had to be on the edge of endurance before he'd reach for a helping hand—because sometimes, being aware of a problem wasn't enough to fix the reason it existed.

Ivan had instead used this awareness to make himself as self-sufficient as possible. It was why he'd taken those first-aid courses when he was the furthest thing from a healer that anyone could imagine. It was also why he'd made an effort to learn basic computronic engineering, as well as gaining a flight certification.

Languages had never been a problem for him, probably because of how many he'd been exposed to as a small child, but he'd made the conscious effort to become fluent in three aside from the Russian and English used interchangeably within the family.

Some would call him obsessive. Ivan called it being prepared.

He'd have made the perfect mercenary had Grandmother not asked him to put his skills to use overseeing the family's overall security instead. The title of security specialist was still one that sat awkwardly on his shoulders, but if there was one person on this Earth to whom he would never say no, it was Ena Mercant.

His grandmother had earned the right to ask of him what she wished.

But his title didn't change what he was—a born killer. A born monster. Not even Grandmother, with her indomitable will and ruthless devotion to the family, could change that. All she'd been able to do was redirect him into a task that was about protection rather than violence. And it was for that reason that he was in this dark green landscape.

Deciding once again that, bleeding or not, the cut wasn't enough to halt his participation in the tracking course, he continued on through the heavily forested region still dripping with the last vestiges of the rain that had fallen a couple of hours earlier; the raindrops cradled in the leaves shone like jewels in the dull winter sunlight that managed to pierce the canopy.

This wasn't his natural milieu; he was a creature of the city. But any gaps in his knowledge could lead to holes in the family's security systems and procedures. Especially now, with the changelings turning into major power players. Ivan didn't intend to be caught flat-footed, needed to know of exactly what a changeling predator might be capable.

So here he was in Texas, on a course run by a small wolf pack. RockStorm might be small, but their course was highly respected in mercenary circles. Of which Ivan was still a part, even if all his kills were off the books and done for reasons that had nothing to do with monetary payment.

To the outside world, Ivan Mercant was an urbane city dweller with a sophisticated haircut and a wardrobe full of bespoke suits. Even the vast majority of his mercenary contacts only knew his alternate identity, but those contacts were the reason he'd been accepted into this course. RockStorm only took on Psy trainees who'd been vetted and recommended by other trusted changelings—the wolves weren't out to train the enemy.

It was a tiger named Striker who'd hooked him up with Rock-Storm, vouching that Ivan wasn't violent against changelings except in defense of his family. The latter was a more than acceptable qualification to the pack-minded race. Attack one changeling and you made an enemy of their entire pack.

It also didn't hurt that Ivan had once helped out a vulnerable herd of deer who'd been having a problem with a Psy conglomerate. He hadn't done it to earn brownie points, had put a bullet in the head of each of the governing board for the simple reason that their operation was a cover for a drug manufacturing plant—and Ivan would destroy anyone who pumped out that poison.

And so here he was, wounded and in an alien environment.

Today's task was simple: to make it from point A to B without any assistance but for the navigational markers provided by the landscape, and to find water and food on his own.

Ivan would've been fine except that he'd been caught in a sudden rockfall that had propelled him onto a sharp edge of stone. His own fault. He'd been overconfident and, as such, hadn't considered all factors—including the genesis of the pack's name: RockStorm.

He wouldn't make that mistake a second time, would remember that nothing was predictable in the wild.

His leg trembled.

Examining the wound, he spotted a bluish discoloration around the tourniquet. Not good. He stopped, scanned his surroundings with his telepathic senses, and when he received no pings that indicated another mind in the vicinity, decided to take a seat on the leaf-littered ground so he could better check his leg.

He'd already cut his pants leg up one side and torn off fabric to use for the tourniquet, so he had no issue seeing the injury. No signs of the redness and swelling that might indicate the onset of infection, but it was obvious he had to call it a day. He might be dogged when set on a task, but no one had ever accused him of stupidity.

That was when he heard a stir in the trees, the leaves rustling in a pattern that wasn't natural—because it was coming closer. He scanned again, hit a mind. That was the entirety of his knowledge. He knew the mind was there, but it was a blank wall to him.

Changeling.

A rare few humans did have minds that opaque, but it was standard with changelings, and he was in changeling territory. Likely, one of the wolves had been assigned to keep rough track of Ivan and had come looking for him when he didn't pass by a particular navigational marker.

He still shifted so he could rapidly access the small gun he had in a special holster designed to lie flush against the base of his spine. A lot of people just tucked their guns into their belts. Great way to shoot themselves or lose the guns. This particular gun was a sleek model barely on the market.

Ivan had used it to end the life of a whimpering man last night. Was he sorry? No. Not about that man, or about all those who'd come before him. Grandmother worried he was turning into a psychopath, but Ivan's PsyMed results always came back clean. He wasn't a psychopath; he had very firm moral lines. It was simply that they didn't always coincide with those of the civilized world.

But the person who emerged from the trees with a woven basket held to one side was neither an enemy who needed to be shot nor a hard-nosed wolf trainer in combat fatigues. Tall, her curves lush, she had hair of midnight that rippled down her back in a cloud and mid-brown skin that glowed under the faint winter sunlight that penetrated the canopy.

A scar, old and taut, bisected her right eyebrow, ran over her eyelid, and down her cheek before trailing off toward her ear. But it circled back across her neck, or perhaps that was a different scar.

Her clothing couldn't be further from fatigues: she wore an ankle-length dress of vivid aqua with a swirly skirt that had a white frill around the bottom. Her cardigan was the same white, but the clusters of gemstones that dangled from her ears were all the hues of the world, with no regard at all to her dress.

Ivan found himself staring, it seemed so impossible that she existed in this time and place. He was concerned he was hallucinating. That would mean he *did* have an infection.

"I knew I smelled blood!" Striding over to him on long legs, a stern frown on her face, she put down her basket with a bad-tempered grumble that was very real. "I'm going to have to talk to the wolves about this," she said as she began to undo his tourniquet. "They can't just keep releasing helpless people into the wild!"

Ivan preferred to keep people at a distance, but somehow, he'd not only allowed her this close without protest, he'd then let her grumble at him—however, this he couldn't let go. "I'm far from helpless."

She didn't bristle or startle at the ice in his tone, her attention on sanitizing her hands using what looked—oddly—like a medical wipe. "And I know what I'm doing, so hush and let me concentrate."

No one told Ivan to hush.

But since her hands were confident and competent on his leg as she examined the injury, he held his silence . . . and watched her with a fascination he hadn't felt in a long, long time. Not since he was a child perhaps. He couldn't remember. All he knew was that this woman who'd appeared out of the rain-soaked forest intrigued him in ways he'd have believed impossible only two minutes earlier.

She wasn't a wolf, he knew that in his gut. She didn't move like any of the wolves he'd met. Neither was she a bear. He'd seen enough bears in Moscow to be certain of that. But she was definitely changeling. Aside from the wall of her mind, she was too comfortable in these surroundings to be human or Psy.

It fit her, the wild.

Having removed the tourniquet, she made an aggravated sound at the renewed bleeding, then reached into her basket . . . to come out with a tiny bottle of disinfectant. Ivan was no longer so certain he hadn't hallucinated her. What kind of woman wore makeup that made her eyelids shimmer and her lips glossy, then walked around a forest with a basket of miniature medical supplies?

"It's going to hurt," she said, then kind of . . . petted him on the other leg, as if to comfort him.

Right before she poured the disinfectant on the wound.

Fuck. Oh yeah, this was fucking real.

Gritting his teeth, he rode the burn without a sound. When the pain finally began to ebb, he looked up to see her retrieving a very small suturing device from her basket. "You're lucky whatever cut you didn't hit bone," she said. "It looks like you cleaned out the wound, and the disinfectant will have finished the job—it's powerful stuff. So I can seal it."

A glance at him, her eyes as dark as the rich soil of the forest—and as unknowable. "I don't have any numbing gel though, just a single shot of anesthetic that'll make you dozy."

Ivan's entire self recoiled. "There's no need for it." Psy minds didn't do well with drugs as a rule, but that wasn't why Ivan refused to use any drug that might influence his thought processes. "I can regulate my pain responses." Grandmother had made sure he'd learned how. "I'm ready."

The woman with the healer's hands raised an eyebrow. "Psy? Thought so. Or you could've been a grumpy wolf, I suppose. They like to snarl a lot."

"I. Am. Not. Grumpy."

A lithe shrug. "Okay, cutie pie. Now think happy thoughts."

Ivan was yet agog over that statement when she began stitch-stapling with quick, efficient hands. He clenched his gut, gritted his teeth again. Pain regulation wasn't a cure-all. It just meant he wouldn't pass out. She'd also sealed half the wound while he'd still been trying to process the way she'd addressed him.

Clever.

His breathing was harsh by the time she'd finished, his heart rate accelerated, but he knew she'd taken care to be gentle in the scheme of such things. "Thank you," he managed to get out while she took a small disinfectant wipe from her basket and wiped down the wound.

Inhaling another ragged breath, he said, "Do you always carry first-aid supplies?"

"Yes. One of my teachers was a paramedic who said the worst he ever felt was when he couldn't help a wounded friend because he lacked a few basic supplies. He gave us a limited list of absolutes—and told us to get tiny versions we could carry in pockets or purses." She held up a glittery silver bag roughly the size of her palm. "My everyday medical kit. Everything fits if packed just so."

Opening up a thin packet of transparent bandage strips that she'd retrieved from the glittery bag, she put them all down his stitched leg in a neat pattern. "There," she said, sitting back on her heels. "You'll survive even if you plan to be an idiot and finish whatever ridiculous thing the wolves have you doing."

As she began to pack up the used medical supplies into a thin plas packet marked with a biohazard symbol, he realized the rest of the Basket of All Things was filled with edible items foraged from the forest. Mushrooms, fresh green tips from plants he couldn't name, what looked to him like wild nuts. "Are you an herbalist?"

"No." She used another wipe to sanitize her hands, tucked it into the plas bag, then sealed up the bag and put it in the basket. "But I know green spaces and wild places." A lingering stroke of the tree trunk before she rose.

When he followed, he braced himself against the tree with one hand so he could test his weight on his leg. It held. Didn't even hurt much. "You did an excellent job."

A snort. "Try not to split it open." Spinning on her heel, a whirlwind of color and life, she began to walk away.

Ivan called after no one. Asked no one for anything. But he said, "Wait! What's your name?"

A look over her shoulder, her eyes liquid pools of mystery. "You can call me Lei."

Then she was gone, moving so fluidly into the forest that he had no chance of tailing her, not in his current state. Changeling, definitely changeling. But after Ivan made it to the end of the course—because apparently he *was* an idiot—the wolf lieutenant in charge of him had no idea who Ivan was talking about when he mentioned Lei.

"A paramedic?" Jorge Herrera frowned. "None of our healers or other trained medical personnel match your description. And Rock-Storm's small enough that I'd know if we had a lovely dark-eyed visitor." A grin. "I'm single and in my prime, after all."

"I'm certain she was changeling."

Jorge rubbed a jaw heavy with dark stubble against brown skin. "Yeah, she might be. The part of the forest you were in at the time is public land outside our pack's territorial boundaries. Open for everyone to use. No other packs real close to us, though, so I'm guessing she's probably visiting a human friend or family member."

The wolf lieutenant shrugged. "Guess she'll have to be a mystery, your nurse."

Ivan said nothing, but he was a Mercant. Information, data, connections, those were the foundations of his family. He'd find her. *Had* to find her, the compulsion to see her again a pulsing beat in his blood.

For the first time in his life, Ivan Mercant *wanted* something . . . someone.

Chapter 3

The neurological changes are permanent. Long-term effects remain unknown.

—Private report by Dr. Jamal Raul on Ivan Mercant,
age 17 (8 August 2068)

IVAN KNEW HE was spoiled when it came to access to data. Side effect of growing up in a family of spies. Grandmother did not approve of Ivan and his cousins' use of that term, far preferring to state that their family was in the business of intelligence.

In other words, a family of spies.

However, given the limited information he had on Lei and the large areas changelings could traverse on foot, pinpointing her identity was proving to be difficult. Changelings were more off-grid than humans or Psy, so he couldn't even look through lists of changeling healers in an effort to narrow down the possibilities.

The packs just didn't put that type of information online, and as those of Ivan's race had long ignored the changelings, there was no information floating around in the PsyNet for him to mine.

He still couldn't stop looking. He took on the task with the same obsessive attention that had left him with multiple complementary skill sets. Complementary to his mind, anyway. Being a dead shot with any handheld weapon on the planet was as critical to him as knowing how to take apart a computronic or mechanical device to diagnose a problem.

The world was a place where things cracked and shattered—and where bad people existed. Those like Ivan were born to eliminate the others from the board so the softer, gentler creatures could exist. Creatures like her.

Cutie pie.

Grumpy.

Try not to split it open.

Their short conversation ran over and over in his mind, until he did the only thing he could—he missed a day of training, which was out of character for him in the extreme, and went back to the spot where he'd met her. Ridiculous to assume it would work when the forest was a sprawling wilderness that went on for miles, but he had to try.

He put his nascent forest tracking skills to use and tried to follow her path, but she'd been too light on her feet, had left no real mark that he could discern. Halting in the center of a small clearing when it became clear he'd never be able to track her, he looked around . . . and saw mushrooms exactly like the ones she'd had in her basket.

He crouched down, touched his finger to one.

Would Lei come back for more?

Since it was all he had, he settled in to wait, back against the trunk of a large tree and eyes on the myriad greens and browns of the forest. Ivan could be patient. According to his grandmother, he had the gift of quiet.

He'd never told her how he'd developed it, all the hours he'd spent in lonely silence while his mother "rested," hadn't even spoken of it to the PsyMed specialist Grandmother had handpicked for him, but he thought she'd guessed. It wasn't a difficult thing to deduce once you knew his history.

He supposed it was the one good gift his mother had left him.

Nowhere near enough to balance out the far more twisted gift inside his mind, but something at least.

The hours crawled past, and though he had plenty to keep him busy on the PsyNet, he ignored the vast psychic space in favor of watching the forest shift and stir. Waiting for her.

But she didn't come back that day.

Or the day after.

He had no reason to return for a third day, especially when Jorge warned him that his absenteeism put him in danger of being kicked off the course. Ivan had never not completed what he'd begun. That was who he was: tenacious and relentless to the point of obsession.

Except now he had a different focus.

He went to the clearing . . . and there she was, stepping out of the forest in an ankle-length dress the color of autumn leaves and sunsets, her hair in a long braid, and a familiar basket on her arm. Small metal leaves hung from her ears, delicate as her skin.

"Oh." She halted, her eyes widening as she caught sight of him seated by the mushrooms. "Did you hurt yourself again?"

He shook his head. "I came to see you."

A blink, a hint of color on her cheeks, her feet shifting.

"Let me check your leg," she said at last, and strode over.

He didn't resist when she pushed up the leg of his black combat pants with a gentle touch. A frown on her forehead and her braid falling over one shoulder, she examined the healing wound with care.

This close, he could see that her scar was ragged. Most likely not done by a knife. A claw? A piece of broken glass? If it was the result of violence, if another had hurt her with malice, he'd end them. A woman who went around tending to wounded strangers would've never done anything to deserve such violence.

Ivan was dead certain on that point.

"It doesn't hurt," he told her as he fought not to touch the softness of her hair, the urge an unfamiliar one. "It's started to itch." Anyone who'd ever had a cut heal over knew that to be a good sign.

"Excellent." After rolling down the leg of his pants, she tilted her head in a way that felt oddly familiar but that he couldn't pin down. "You really came to see me?" A softness to her voice.

"Yes." Why would she be so startled at the idea? She was the most fascinating person he'd ever met, her skill evident and her presence unforgettable.

"Oh." She smoothed her hands over her thighs. "The thing is, you're ridiculously pretty. Doesn't this bother you?" Gaze intent on his, she touched her fingers to her scar.

"I realize I have an aesthetically pleasing appearance." It was simply another tool he used when necessary—add a layer of beauty and people would ignore the most obvious danger, refuse to see the monster stalking them. "The only thing that bothers me about your scar is that someone might've given it to you. Who was it?"

She stared at him, blinked. "Car crash," she said slowly, watching him as you might a feral animal. "When I was a child. No one you need to kill."

He gave a curt nod. "As for the other—you're beautiful. That's undeniable fact. Dark eyes, lush lips, flawless skin, thick and soft hair. You also have the correct facial proportions."

Her lips twitched before she threw back her head and laughed, the sound full and warm, and her eyes not quite human when she looked at him—but it was only a slight shift, not a full one.

Compelled by the faint edge of gold shot with light, he said, "What kind of changeling are you?"

Mischief in her smile. "Figure it out," she said, this wild creature who'd emerged out of the forest and enraptured him without warning. "Want to walk with me after I gather the mushrooms?"

When he nodded, she shifted position to pick a few mushrooms from nearby. "Do you like these?"

"I've never eaten any." Consuming food for taste, for enjoyment, was still a new concept to Psy who'd grown up under the Silence Protocol.

"Nutrient drinks and bars are a far more efficient source of nutrition than discrete food items, though certain such items were part of the accepted Silence diet." Items that had always been bland, or had been made that way for the Psy. Because any sensation was a risk to a protocol designed to eliminate all emotion from their race.

"Food isn't just about nutrition!" It was a gasp. "Food is about joy, about family, about delighting the taste buds." Sitting up from her bent-over position, she said, "I'll make you a caramelized mushroom tart. Bet you like it. What's your name, mystery man who thinks I have the correct facial proportions for beauty?" Laughter in her voice again.

"Ivan."

"Ivan," she said with a smile. "I like your accent. Can't quite place it. It feels like it could be from so many places."

"I've worked off the rough edges in my accent over the years." It was far easier for a spy to blend in if they didn't stand out in ways specific and memorable. "I live in Moscow right now," he found himself telling her, though he wasn't a man who shared personal information with anyone.

"Oh, I've always wanted to visit there—it's meant to be beautiful." With that, Lei stood up. "Come on. I don't need lots today."

Rising, he fell into step beside her. She was tall enough to reach his shoulder, and he wasn't a short man. The height suited her, everything about her suited her. Most of all the quicksilver emotions on her face, the smile that never quite left her lips. She was . . . radiant. "Do you visit the forest every day?"

A shake of her head. "I've come to see a friend of mine—yesterday, she wanted to rummage through garage sales. I've never done that before."

Ivan wasn't even sure what that was, but he wanted to hear her talk, so he asked her about it, and she regaled him with stories of dusty barns and literal garages, quirky sellers who priced everything at a dollar and others who wanted full "as new" prices for mismatched sets of cutlery or incomplete sets of retro DVDs.

It felt like a glimpse into another universe.

"I bought three small planters shaped like pouncing cats," she confessed. "They're painted funny colors and they weren't expensive, but I like silly, pretty things."

Ivan had no concept of silly and pretty, but he didn't want her to go quiet, didn't want her smile to fade, so he said, "One of the humans in my apartment complex has a cat who's often in the shared green space. I watch her when I'm outside—she can spend entire hours napping in the sun, then move like a flash with zero buildup."

A glance from under her lashes. "Do you like cats?"

"Pets weren't a concept under Silence."

Husky laughter that turned into giggles she couldn't seem to stop.

Ivan didn't understand joy. He'd never been Silent—that ship had sailed the first time the drug entered his mother's bloodstream while he lay cradled inside her womb, his mental pathways warped before they could form—but the tools of Silence suited him. He preferred to keep his distance from the world, and from the ties of emotion.

Such things led only to weakness and to loss and pain.

The sole place he'd failed was with his family. They'd become part of him through their steadfast refusal to give up on the boy who didn't fit, but even Grandmother couldn't erase his childhood. He would forever be the monster the drug had created—there was no way to alter that. And the monster didn't comprehend joy.

But it sighed listening to her laugh. "What's so funny?"

"Tell you later," she said, her smile a sparkle in her eyes. "I want to show you a gorgeous waterfall—it's this way."

He let her lead him, even though he'd already explored the area.

But he'd never seen the natural formation through her eyes. She pointed out how the spray captured rainbows, and how the water was as clear as glass, the stones beneath polished to a smooth shine.

"I like swimming," she told him. "But not in water this cold." Dipping a toe in after slipping off her shoe, she shivered. "Makes my fur bristle."

At that moment, her gaze held a wildness that he could *almost* identify, but then it was gone, and she was putting her shoe back on. "I have to meet my friend. We're going to the theater—she bought the tickets two months ago."

Ivan was considered smooth and sophisticated by the vast majority of people he met, the mask one he'd long perfected, but he found he couldn't put it on with her. It was as if it didn't exist, as if he could only interact with her in his rawest form.

"Will you meet me again?" he asked with no effort to hide his need to see her.

A long look, no smile now, just an intensity of focus.

He didn't breathe until she said, "I'll come tomorrow night."

Ivan didn't know what to offer her, how to make sure she didn't change her mind. "I found a small cave while I was exploring. It has the imprint of a fossil."

"Really?" She rose up on her tiptoes, rocked back, her expression alight. "Oh, we can go see that."

And that was exactly what they did the following night, spending an hour on a gentle walk there, and an hour on the walk back. It was full dark on a moonless night, but he had a flashlight . . . and he was fairly certain Lei could either see in the dark or close to it. Despite his compulsive need to know her, he didn't aggressively dig for more information.

She was . . . important to him, and they were too new, too fragile, for him to risk fracturing it. It was disturbing to him to admit that she'd walked right past his defenses as if they didn't exist, but he couldn't make himself be sorry about it. Not when she existed, this bright and wild creature who seemed to like him.

Just him. No mask. No sophistication. No Mercant power. Just Ivan.

"I can't come tomorrow night," she told him at the end of their time together, her teeth sinking into her lower lip. "I promised my friend I'd spend the time with her."

That—the importance of keeping promises—was a thing Ivan did understand. "Do you have time in the afternoon?" It was easier to ask this time, with less risk of rejection. "I only have half a session tomorrow." The morning was meant to be brutal, the afternoon intended for rest and repair.

That dazzling smile that did things to him that should've been impossible. "Yes. I was just going to forage for wild herbs to make a special oil. I could do that another day."

"We could do that together." Ivan just wanted to be with her; the activity was irrelevant. "You can teach me what to look for."

That strangely familiar tilt to her head, a sparkle in the eyes he could see in the glow thrown off the flashlight. "Meet me at two thirty, then . . . cutie pie." She was gone the next second, her laughter lingering behind her.

He dreamed of her that night, woke sweat-slick and with a racing heart at the thought that he'd imagined her. It took pulling up his sweatpants to look at his stitches to convince himself that she wasn't an illusion. She existed . . . and she liked him. Enough to spend time with him.

Would she still like him if she knew what he was? If he told her of the thing that lived in his head? Of the damage done to his neural pathways that meant he'd never quite be "normal"?

Chapter 4

User 231i: No one goes after a Mercant and survives. Even if the assassin succeeds in eliminating the mark, the rest of that family would then hunt the assassin with unremitting focus, make their life a constant race for survival. Only an idiot would target them.

User 47x: Can confirm. Remember user 6nvy? Some CEO wanted Ena Mercant out of the picture and 6nvy decided to ignore our advice. Ena is still alive and kicking. Can't say the same for the CEO, and 6nvy has never again posted here after taking that job. My guess is that they're six feet under in some remote location, never to be discovered.

—Conversation on anonymous bulletin board reputed to be utilized by mercenaries and assassins (unconfirmed)

WOULD LEI STILL *smile at him if he showed her the truth of himself?*

Ivan stared at the wall in front of him, his gut tight as he pushed aside the question. He knew the answer and he didn't want to face it. So he didn't. Not today. But driven by his increasing panic at the inevitable—because not telling her the truth wasn't an option—he aced the session that morning, which was about hand-to-hand combat with a highly trained changeling armed with claws and teeth.

He'd watched the wolves the entire time he'd been with them, learned how fast they could move, how flexible they could be—and he utilized all his knowledge against his opponent. When that opponent shifted without warning, coming at him in full wolf form, he handled that, too.

The wolf—Flint—clapped him on the back in the aftermath. "Bloody hell, Ivan. You ever want to join a pack, I think our alpha would happily accept you as a lieutenant." He wiped off the blood at the corner of his mouth, winced. "At least I got a few claws into you."

Ivan touched his aching ribs. "More than a few." It had been far from an easy battle.

Flint's teeth gleamed, the predator in his eyes pleased. "We'll do it again in a few days. I'll be more prepared next time."

Ivan had zero doubts about that. This was why he was doing the training. Because the teachers were good and pushed both themselves and their students. But he was glad to be away in time to shower, then make his way to the forest clearing to meet Lei.

He wished he'd brought more sophisticated clothing so he could look better for her, but aside from a rough winter jacket, all he had were pairs of basic combat pants, T-shirts, and two sweaters of fine wool.

Not that Lei seemed to notice anything about his clothing when she walked into the clearing. A scowl immediately hitting her face, she put down her basket and ran over to him. "What have you done to yourself?"

He'd forgotten about the black eye until that moment. And the cut on his cheekbone. Oh, and he'd caught a swipe of a claw across his throat now that he thought about it. "Hand-to-hand combat," he said. "Training."

"*Training?*" She sounded like she was gritting her teeth. "You did this on purpose?"

"I need to learn how to handle myself against changelings."

Shoving back the sleeves of her navy blue cardigan, she put her hands on her hips, against the deep pink of her dress, and glared at him. "Tell me who did this. I want to talk to them about their training methods."

He had the strange sense that she'd do exactly that, march up and tell Jorge off to his face. So whatever animal she was, it wasn't one that was scared of wolves. Or of dominants. But he didn't get an impression of dominance off her—now that he'd been around the wolves long enough, he'd begun to intuit the power differentials. It wasn't obvious to him as it clearly was to changelings, but it wasn't opaque, either.

So he could tell that Lei wasn't a dominant. But neither did she radiate the same feel as a submissive. He'd only met one submissive to date, as the wolves were incredibly protective of their more vulnerable packmates, and this submissive had just been dropping off Flint's phone, which he'd forgotten at home. But that young male hadn't met Ivan's eyes except in short bursts. He *had* met Flint's gaze, however, the deep trust between them obvious.

Lei, on the other hand, had never hesitated to look Ivan in the eye. "I'm okay," he said to her. "It's all surface wounds."

Folding her arms, she tapped her foot. "What about the gash on your leg? Did you tear that open?"

He was very glad to be able to say, "No. I got it sealed." A Rock-Storm nurse had turned up and done the repair, while marveling at Lei's neat stitching. "The nurse was very complimentary of your skills."

She sniffed, her nose a little up in the air. "Hmm." Then she picked up her basket and they went herb hunting, while the frost of her temper lingered in the air.

Since Ivan had no idea what he was doing, mostly he just watched and listened to her. When she showed him a plant, he looked for it, and had a hundred percent success rate with identifications.

"That's amazing," she said an hour later, the frost long thawed. "Your memory must be incredible."

"Just trained," he said. "Memory skills come in handy in a family of spies."

A burst of startled laughter. "Really? A family of spies?"

"Intelligence is our business," he said. "Might as well be our family motto."

"Do you have one? A family motto?"

He didn't hesitate in answering. This was no secret he was bound to keep. It just wasn't well-known. Dig deep enough, far enough back, and you'd find it. "*Cor meum familia est*. My heart is family."

She sat back on her heels, her eyes shining. "Oh, how wonderful." Hands fisting on her thighs, she said, "But isn't that against the rules with Psy? I don't know too much about your people but I've picked up bits and pieces, and that motto . . . well, it's so poignant."

"Yes, it's against the rules—or was before the recent change in our leadership," he said, the fall of the emotionless Silence Protocol yet too new for the knowledge to have settled inside him. "Too much inherent emotion."

"So how did it survive?"

"Ancestors took it off public-facing buildings and off the crest that goes on outward-bound items, and the rulers of the time thought that meant we got rid of it." He found a clump of an herb she'd wanted. "Stupid, really. Should've been obvious the family was as tight as before."

Lei's lips curved as she accepted the herbs he'd picked for her. "I like your family already. My parents were like that with me—just all in, you know?"

He'd caught the past tense, probed with all the gentleness he had inside him—and when it came to Lei, he had unexpected depths of it. "They're gone?"

She nodded. "A long time ago. We were caught in a hurricane. The winds flipped my father's car while he was trying to drive us out."

Ivan would've frowned if he hadn't long ago learned to control external indications of his internal responses.

Weather tracking had advanced to the nth degree since the ravages of the twentieth and early twenty-first centuries. Hurricanes and cyclones were now often accurately predicted a considerable time out from the event, and all cities had structures built to act as shelters for massive numbers of people, since authorities had realized it made more sense to ride out the situation in place than try to evacuate millions of people, many of whom had nowhere to go. The shelters were built to withstand even the most deadly categories of storm—and had done so multiple times.

Even those who chose to remain in their homes had plenty of time to prepare.

Fatalities from being caught out in the elements *during a storm* were extremely rare. But he didn't ask why her family had been driving on the road when everyone else was hunkering down. He knew the answer. He'd lived the answer. A minority of people always fell through the cracks, either because society forgot them, or because of unforeseen circumstances—or because they weren't capable in a way that couldn't be predicted or ameliorated.

Ivan's mother wouldn't have had the capacity to get him to a shelter had the news of a storm broken while she was walking the petals of the crystalline flower. He'd have stayed where he was, a child with no knowledge of the storm winds about to smash the city.

Instead, he focused on the rest of her words. "You had a good childhood?"

"A happy one," she told him, the sadness of her old and faded. As if she'd come to terms with the loss long ago. "My papa spoke fluent Spanish and English, while my mama was only fluent in English—but she'd retained just enough knowledge of French that the three of us spoke in a mishmash of French, English, and Spanish. And every so often, she'd add in a Māori word she'd learned from her grandma before she passed away."

A smile breaking through the sadness. "It was like a secret language all our own. My father would say 'te amo, my belle' to my mother, and she'd pretend to swoon, then call him by a funny French endearment, like 'my little quail.' I have terrible Spanish grammar because I keep trying to mix it up."

From the light in her gaze, it was clear to Ivan that she didn't care about her imperfect language skills. "We traveled a lot. I'd been to most corners of this continent by the time I was ten."

"Your pack didn't mind?"

A slight fading of her expression, her attention suddenly tightly concentrated on the herbs she held. "My mom and dad were loners. Two loners who fell in love and had a baby. Pack life wasn't for them."

But what about their child?

Ivan didn't ask that question, either. He knew *exactly* how hard the loss of her parents, her only foundations, would've been for Lei. "My father was never in my life—I don't even know his identity," he said, telling her a fact that would get him blacklisted among the vast majority of Psy families should he go looking for a genetic match for a procreation agreement.

It mattered nothing to him, since he had no intention of passing on his genetic material. "I was raised by my mother as a child. She died when I was eight."

Her fingers flexing open as if without her conscious control, Lei dropped the herbs in her hand. "Oh." A softness to her as she turned to look at him, she said, "Then you know."

"Yes." He'd never forget that sensation of being moorless, without even the fragile and fractured anchor that had been his lifeline. "What was your favorite place to travel to that you remember?"

A frown, then she clicked her fingers. "The Amazon rain forest. We had to get permission from the local packs to travel there—but wow, I'll never forget it. A kind of green that's so rich it's beyond description, the songs of the birds, the sounds of the other animals. We shifted and ran and ran, so many scents in the air."

As he listened, she told him more stories of her family's adventures, of hours and days on the road, of nights spent under the stars, of vistas endless and breathtaking. No mention of anyone else. Not even friends met and made along the way. Only Lei's parents and Lei.

"They left you with extraordinary memories," he said after she finished a story about a winter trip where her father had built a snow cave for them to spend the night in.

"Yes." A pause, her voice quieter when she said, "I just wish they'd planned better for what would happen if they weren't there one day."

So much pain in those words that even his stunted emotional core hurt. "Did you end up in foster care?"

"A short time." A tight smile. "Then my grandfather came for me."

It was clear from her tone that her experience with a grandparent hadn't been the same as Ivan's. He didn't want to cause her more pain, so he didn't ask why. Rather, he let her choose the route of their conversation, and what she chose was to get up. "I want a reed that usually grows near waterways. I think I hear a stream."

Ten minutes later, Ivan was looking carefully for that reed when flecks of water hit the side of his face. He glanced up, saw she was intent on her own search, and realized she must've flicked the water on him by accident somehow.

Wiping off the small droplets, he returned to his search.

More water hitting the side of his face.

He turned . . . to see her looking innocently at a stone she'd picked up from the stream. "Isn't this pretty?" she said, holding it to the light.

Ivan didn't say anything, but he watched her out of the corner of his eye as he pretended to return to his search. She put the stone down, seemed to be looking for the reed again . . . then glanced over with a grin and flicked him again.

He snapped his head toward her and leaped.

Giving a laughing scream, she abandoned her basket and ran, her hair streaming behind her and the skirts of her dress a dazzling flag of color through the trees. He was highly trained and extremely fit, and he took the obstacles in his path with ease—but she was a change-ling, this her natural ground.

It ended up an even match, until the two of them stood on opposite sides of a tree, each moving left and right as they attempted to outsmart one another. He jumped to the other side. But she'd already done the opposite and they were back in their same positions.

Her grin was wild and not at all human or Psy. It was changeling. Primal and full of delight. And he realized this was play. She was playing with him. He'd never believed he knew how to play, though he could fake it, but this felt as natural as his skin and his breath.

This time when he jumped, she was laughing too hard to avoid him, and he could've grabbed her . . . but he paused only inches from her, a sudden awkwardness between them as they stared at one another. A pulse beat in the hollow of her throat, a rapid little butterfly that echoed his own erratic heartbeat.

Heat made her skin glow, and he wanted badly to touch, wanted badly to have that right. But the frozen moment went on too long, until she looked down and brushed off her skirts. "I should get home."

Clouds blotted out his private horizon, but he walked back with her and picked up her basket. "Will you come tomorrow?" he asked, even though all he wanted to do was grab hold of her and make her stay.

Not rational, that wasn't rational. It would also scare her.

A look from below her lashes as she accepted the basket. "Evening picnic?" It was a husky question. "It'll be dark, but I can borrow a string of charged solar lights from my friend. And you can try my mushroom tart."

He nodded. He'd have said yes to anything she suggested. "What shall I bring?"

"Just yourself, cutie." That tilt of the head again, her smile secretive. "I'll see you tomorrow." A quicksilver movement that caught him by surprise, her lips brushing his jaw in a fleeting kiss before she was gone in a waft of the most delicate perfume, a wild creature he couldn't hold.

Shaken, he raised a hand to the place she'd touched, hovered over it. He didn't know what was happening to him, how she'd walked right inside his defenses and made a place for herself . . . but it was done and he wasn't sorry. What he had to do now was figure out how to make her stay even after she knew all he'd done and all he was: a predator whose mind ate the souls of others, leaving them empty, dead husks.

Chapter 5

Your neurological profile remains unchanged from earlier scans. The abnormal variation in your pattern appears to have settled into its adult form.

—Dr. Jamal Raul to Ivan Mercant (2 January 2071)

ARWEN WAS WAITING outside Ivan's cabin when he reached home early that evening, having called up Flint for a couple of hours of extra hand-to-hand training. Not a fight this time, rather a slower exploration of the differences between Psy and changeling in this context. The often amused wolf had been as interested as Ivan, the two of them oddly well suited as training partners.

"Finally!" Arwen rose from the rickety bench on the porch, settling the cool gray of his perfectly fitted suit jacket around himself. "I thought you'd never get back."

Ivan wasn't the least surprised to find his cousin haunting his doorstep. Ivan had been out of touch for over a week. His entire family was made up of fiercely independent individuals, but they were powerful because they were also a unit. As such, they kept in regular contact— or as Canto termed it, provided "proof of life." Especially when they were on their own in unfamiliar surroundings.

Most people, however, would've just given him a call or sent him a message.

Not Grandmother. And not Arwen.

"Why didn't you go inside?" Ivan said as he pushed open the door.

"Are you kidding?" Arwen poked his salon-perfect dark head cautiously through the doorway. "Who knows what booby traps you've laid."

"This is just a place to crash. Nothing here I want to protect." He went to make a nutrient drink. "You hungry?"

"Not for that," Arwen muttered with a shudder. "I eat real food now."

Arwen had always been different, gentler, kinder, more vulnerable. Because Arwen was an empath, and he'd made the family better simply by existing. It was difficult to be evil when an empath was trying to give you his toys when he thought you were sad, and crying because you'd gotten a scratch or a cut.

Ivan didn't know how Arwen could be that open to the world and survive—it was a point on which he, Canto, and Silver agreed. They'd always done everything in their power to shield outwardly suave Arwen.

Reality was that the man had no sense of self-preservation when it came to caring for the people who were his own; if Ivan needed it, Arwen would cut off his own arm and give it to him. It was who he was. Good. Just good in a way Ivan had never been nor ever would be. But Lei . . . yes, she had the same radiant center as his cousin.

Ivan would spill blood without compunction to protect her.

Because a world that held empaths also held monsters.

Gut tight at the thought of what was coming, what he had to tell her, he turned to lean back against the small counter—to see Arwen making a face at the painting that hung on the wall.

"This is so cliché country classic that it might as well come with the tinny music they put in those kitschy greeting cards," he pronounced with a shudder.

Yet Ivan had witnessed this same man sit quietly beside a home-less person, accept a cup of tea from a dirty hand. Arwen was a con-tradiction in terms, but one thing never changed: the kindness within. Fashion and décor might be the target of his scorn, but he'd never turn that rapier judgment on a person.

Ivan's empath cousin didn't know about Ivan's homicidal little hobby, could never know about it. Some stains were too dark, needed to be worn only by the one affected. Grandmother, of course, had figured it out—but Ena Mercant was made of grit and stone and will. She'd han-dled it even if she continued to disagree with his stance on the matter.

Ivan thought some people needed killing. So he took care of it. The end.

"Where did you find this place?" Arwen muttered as he continued to walk around the small space. "Log Cabins United?"

"Private rental. Closest spot to the RockStorm den I could locate." He drank half the glass of nutrients. "Arwen?"

Arwen was poking hesitantly at the dusty coat of what looked to be a stuffed hamster. "Oh, thank goodness. It's fake." He exhaled. "Though . . . I suppose you wouldn't want to be in changeling territory and have actual stuffed animals mounted on plinths."

He turned, hands on his hips, his jacket pushed back. "I'll have to make sure I check up on you more often or next thing I know, you'll be wearing checked shirts and camo pants and singing 'Yee-haw I'm a mountain man.'"

Sometimes, Ivan wondered what media Arwen consumed that he could come up with those statements. "I need advice."

Slightly widened eyes.

Ivan had never, not once, said those words to the family empath. And Arwen, to his credit, had never pushed him—though Ivan had sensed long ago that Arwen was distressed around him. Not the dis-tressed of repulsion, but the distressed of knowing something was wrong and being unable to do anything about it.

Poor Arwen, unable to fix a member of his beloved family.

"You can ask me anything, Ivan," his cousin said now. "I'm a vault when it comes to private talks." His expression was solemn, nothing in it of the apparently shallow man who'd decried the cabin's décor.

Ivan inclined his head; he knew that the Arwen who'd tried to help him by giving him his toys still lived in the sophisticated man that child had become. "I'm . . . fascinated by a woman." That was the only word that felt right. "I can't stop thinking about her. I dream of her."

Arwen's eyes got progressively wider. "Really?" It was a whisper. "Who?"

Ivan ignored the question, not yet ready to share Lei in any shape or form. "I've never had a reaction like this to anyone." A near compulsion to be with her, to look at her, to hear her voice, to . . . make her smile. "I missed training on the small chance I'd see her."

"Okay, I need to sit down." Arwen gave the ratty old armchair a jaundiced look but took it, then blew out a breath. "It sounds like the beginning of something important." He looked up, a gentle smile on his lips. "Your shields are sky-high, cousin. You barely even let family in. She must be special to get through your defenses."

Ivan pushed aside the nagging voice that told him he couldn't afford to allow anyone beyond his defenses. He was stable, had been stable for nearly two decades. Assuming she accepted him once she knew the truth of him, he was in a position to take this risk, embrace the laughter and the warmth that had stepped unexpectedly into his life. He'd never looked for it, never wanted it, but he couldn't turn away now that it had found him.

Now that she'd found him.

"She is special," he said simply. "I don't know how to be in any kind of a romantic relationship. I'm not good at bonding." The words were in his medical file, which he'd accessed as an adult. He agreed with them.

Arwen's lips tugged up. "Ivan, I know that if I ever needed help, I could call on you and you'd turn up, ready to coolly, calmly, extract me from trouble."

He held up a hand when Ivan would've spoken. "You don't have to be warm and fluffy to bond with people—you just have to be there, loyal and present. It helps if you're ready to do things that give them joy, but I don't have to tell you that. It wasn't Grandmother who got me that introduction to the best tailor in Moscow."

"Family is different." He'd grown up with Arwen, had known that he'd appreciate the introduction to the master craftsman. "I don't know anything about her. I don't know how to make her happy."

Arwen's smile deepened. "That's the best start. The fact that you want to make her happy. Now just listen to her, and you'll learn what delights her, what brings her joy."

Ivan thought of how she'd laughed and colored a little as she'd told him she liked "silly, pretty things," considered his mental file of her colorful earrings and dresses, the way she'd had little threads of sparkle in her hair today.

He nodded slowly. Maybe he could do this, could actually have a chance at normality in a way he'd never before believed. Because he had a gift for noticing things. Most Mercants did; a side effect of growing up in a family of spies. "Thanks, Arwen."

Arwen's smile held none of the snooty elegance he could do so well; it was innocent in a way Ivan had never been. At least not as far as he recalled. Perhaps he'd been the same as Arwen as a very young infant, but it was unlikely. He'd already had the crystalline flower in his mind, had already walked its noxious petals.

"I'm so delighted for you." Rising, Arwen walked over but stopped before making physical contact; he knew Ivan was even less comfortable with that than most Psy. "You deserve happiness."

Ivan stared at his cousin with the glass of nutrients partway to his mouth. It was uncanny, how Arwen could say things out of the blue that cut right to the heart. Not until that moment had Ivan so clearly understood that he'd always believed he *didn't* deserve any kind of a good life. Not given the ugliness of what lived in his mind.

But he'd reached thirty-two years of age without hurting anyone, and his shields were airtight. The faceted crystal spider was contained. Silence had fallen. He'd never felt any compulsion to take the drug that had stolen his mother. And . . . Lei existed.

There was no reason for him to walk away. Not yet. Not when there remained a chance that she might not reject him once he showed her the spider that slept inside him.

SHE brought one of her colorful little cat planters to the picnic. The blue and pink striped creature, formed as if it was about to pounce, fit easily on the palm of Ivan's hand. There was a tiny chip on one paw that spoke of its unknown history, and the hole in the cat's back was so small that he asked Lei what plant could possibly thrive within.

Laughter in her expression, she held up her hands, palms up. "I don't know. It'll be fun to find out. Tell me what you decide."

"What?"

She ducked her head a fraction, her unbound hair sliding over the shoulder of the vibrant red-violet dress that she'd paired with a denim jacket. "I brought it for you." A quick look up. "It's silly, isn't it? I'll take it back. Sorry, I shouldn't have—"

He kept it out of her reach. "No. You said I could have it."

Dropping her half-raised hand, she looked at him with eyes that were big and oddly soft. Vulnerable, he realized. As vulnerable as Arwen's. And he knew she truly was afraid he wouldn't want the gift.

Parting those soft lips, she said, "You like it?"

He brought it back down, looked at it again. "Yes." It was a thing he'd never thought to have in his life, but he would now protect it with everything he had. Because she'd given it to him. "Thank you."

Her smile was dawn breaking across the sky; it made his heart twist in ways he didn't understand. He didn't smile back. He didn't know how to smile in truth, had only ever put it on as a mask and he couldn't wear a mask with her—but she didn't seem to mind.

"I packed a whole bunch of things for our picnic, not just the tart." Her joy was a welcoming fire flickering against him, warming places that had been cold for an eternity.

When she handed him small bites to try, he did so without argument. The flavors were explosions of sensation on his tongue, an overload of input. He must've betrayed some response because she laughed—the kind of laugh that said this was a shared amusement. He knew that even though he had never laughed.

"Try this instead," she said, offering him another tidbit.

He took it, but waited. "You, too." Ivan didn't know about relationships like this, but he knew he wanted to take care of her, keep that happiness on her face.

When her smile dimpled the roundness of her cheeks, he realized this wasn't so difficult after all. Arwen was right; he could figure it out if he only listened. So he did exactly that, content—more than content—to stay quiet as she spoke about what she'd got up to with her friend, how she'd made the tart, and myriad other topics. Her mind was a quicksilver place, bright and enthusiastic.

But she wouldn't allow him to listen alone. No, she asked him questions, wanted to know about him as much as he wanted to know about her. He answered with honesty; he would not lie to her, would not steal her by hiding the scars on his mind and psyche.

"I'm part of an unusual PsyNet family," he said. "My cousin turned up yesterday to check that I wasn't dead, after I fell out of contact for a week. I guess you could call us a pack."

Laughter, but hidden within the sparkle was a thread far darker and less joyful. "That's exactly how a pack should be—a strong, cohesive, loving unit."

"Is your pack not that way?"

"No. I'm visiting with my friend partially because I needed space to come to a decision." She swallowed. "I'm thinking about leaving the pack."

Pack was the core of changeling life. Even Psy knew that. For Lei to be considering a permanent break, particularly given the lack of stability in her past, things had to have gone terribly wrong. "Have you decided?"

"No." She twisted her lips. "I love my packmates, but—" An exhale. "Is it okay if we don't talk about this anymore? I'm not being sly by not telling you details about my pack. I will. I just . . . I need time apart from them, even in my own head."

"Just tell me one more thing—are you safe there?" Unspoken was that if she wasn't, he'd handle it.

A blink, her pupils expanding. "Yes," she whispered, then raised her hand as if to touch his face.

When he didn't shift away, she brushed her fingertips over his skin, and the contact was a tactile punch that rocked him. He tightened his abdomen, held his breath, not about to flinch and cause her to believe he didn't want her touch. He did. But his body wasn't used to it, didn't know how to process the sensations.

Dropping her hand, she said, "You're a dangerous man."

Ivan gripped the wrist of his left hand with his right, squeezed. "Yes."

"Have you killed?" A soft question.

Chapter 6

The infection is in the Net . . . we're all vulnerable to breathing in the poison if we come too close to it.

—Vasic Zen, Tp-V, Arrow Squad (January 2082)

GIVING A CURT nod, Ivan said, "Many times. There can be no forgiveness for some crimes, execution the only appropriate punishment."

No flinch. No withdrawal. "Changelings have the same law." Hugging her arms around her raised knees, she said, "But meting out death, it changes a person." A look at him. "Each life taken darkens a piece of your soul."

He should've just nodded and let it go, but nothing was simple with this woman who was like a dream become flesh and blood. "I feel no remorse, Lei." It was a compulsion, to show her all of himself and see if she ran. Far better to do it now, when she was nearly a mirage, a dream he could one day forget, than to wait until she'd become part of the fabric of his very being.

Though . . . he had the sense that it was already too late. It had been too late the day she'd walked out of the forest, the embodiment of a promise he'd never dared imagine for himself. "I think of my targets as vermin who need to be eliminated."

Huge eyes looking at him with care, as if she was trying to see the truth or the lie in his words . . . but she still didn't run. "Tell me," she demanded with unexpected sternness. "Tell me of the last person you targeted and why."

Squeezing his wrist even harder, Ivan gave another short nod. He'd started this and he'd finish it. "A Psy who used his money and influence to 'clean' the streets around his home. He hired a group of thugs to beat homeless people and addicts to death. His thugs then incinerated their bodies in a commercial furnace."

Breath coming faster and a golden ring around her irises, Lei said, "How did you find out?"

"Because I speak to people most don't." He'd left the street behind a long time ago, had never thought to return, but it got into your bones, the street. So he'd decided to use his contacts for good—though some might not see it that way.

"Tell me about another target," she said.

So he did. Three more times. At the end of which, tears were rolling down her cheeks, and she was shaking her head. "Ivan, no. I can't argue with you that they were evil, that the world is a better place with them gone, but it hurts you to see yourself that way. As an assassin, a killer."

Ivan shook his head. "It doesn't hurt me. I don't feel anything at all—it's a job. I do it. Then it's over." He didn't dare touch her, but he refused to break their locked gazes. "I need you to tell me if any of this is a deal breaker. I need to know now, before . . ." *Before I give you more pieces of myself.*

As if she'd heard the silent coda, she said, "It's too late." A whisper, her fingers rising to touch his cheek again. "You're inside me already." Her palm flattened on his cheek, her lips soft and parted. "It should feel too fast, but it doesn't. It feels exactly as fast as it should be."

"There's more," he continued, dogged in his determination to show her the darkest recesses of his soul. "I have a psychic ability that can enslave people. It lives inside a cage in my mind but should I let it out, it'll ensnare other minds in its web and suck them dry."

"Yet you don't use it, do you? Because you believe in good and evil, and you choose to be good."

"I'm not—"

"Stop trying to chase me away." Words that were a breath, the warmth of her soaking into his skin and through to the chilled heart of his soul. "I'm not going anywhere."

Ivan didn't know about intimate physical contact, not from experience. But he'd seen others kiss. And now he understood why. He wanted to taste her breath, taste her lips, *know* her. So he bent his head toward her, waiting, watching to see if she'd pull back.

She didn't.

She met him halfway.

Breath on breath, lips on lips, it was too much sensation to process, but he didn't care. Staying motionless, he let her lead the kiss. He let her teach him. By the time he put his hand on her—curving it around the side of her rib cage—his heart rate was erratic, his vision hazed.

Breathless, she pulled back, and her eyes, they weren't in any way human. A pale kind of tawny with golden edges and a slightly elongated black pupil. Eyes full of a wild light. He could've run a quick PsyNet search, come up with a short list of animals who bore such eyes, but she was showing herself to him piece by piece, and now that he knew she wasn't going to run, he could be patient, could wait until she was ready to reveal all of herself.

"That was . . ." She lifted trembling fingers to her lips. "I never saw you coming, Ivan."

He went to lean in, take another kiss, but she shifted position without warning, busying herself putting away the picnic. A flush rode her cheekbones, a jitteriness to her every action.

"Did I do something wrong?" he asked, not sure how things had gone awry.

She froze. "No, God, no." A shuddering exhale. "I just . . . I'm overwhelmed." A haunted look. "I think I know who you're meant to be for me, and I'm not ready. Not now, not when I'm already so lost and confused and screwed up."

Leaning in, she brushed her lips over his in a jolt of pure adrenaline. "But overwhelmed or not, I'll never run from this, from *us*. I'll be back tomorrow night, and I'll tell you about me. Promise."

Ivan nodded. "I'll be here."

And he was. But Lei never came.

He waited until long after dark, through the hours of the night, all the way to daybreak, unwavering in his belief that she wasn't a woman who broke her promises. He even came back the next night.

It took until the third dawn for him to accept that she'd decided against him after she'd had time to think about what he'd told her—about the blood that stained his hands, the lives he'd taken . . . and the evil that lived in his brain.

She had every right to make that decision.

He still searched for her. And only then realized how little he knew about her. He didn't know her animal or the name of her friend, or even the city in which she made her home.

As he packed up his gear on the afternoon of the third day, having finished the first block of the course with an ease fueled by loss, he found himself staring at the little cat she'd given him.

Silly and pretty and a physical symbol of memory.

He told himself to leave it behind, that he didn't need a reminder of rejection, yet still he wrapped it carefully in an old and soft T-shirt, then wrapped it again in his spare sweater before tucking it neatly in the center of his clothing.

A memory of her fingers against his cheek, the shine in her eyes as she'd said, *It's too late. You're inside me already.*

It had felt so real, so authentic, as had the kiss that had altered the foundations of his life. He'd never forget her, would never stop searching for her, this he knew. If only to ask why she hadn't just told him she was walking away.

"Because you're a killer, Ivan," he said to himself. "She's afraid of you." And she was right to be afraid—because he *was* a killer. But he would never have hurt her. Never. He would've done everything in his power to protect her.

Walking out of the cabin, he put the bag in the back passenger-seat footwell of the rugged SUV he'd hired for this trip, then went back and locked up the cabin, after which he dropped the key in the lockbox secured to the outside. As the metal clanged on metal, he felt the same hollowness within himself. Foolish, it had been foolish to dare to believe he could hold a creature so lovely and bright in his blood-soaked hands.

The sound of her laughter, the feel of her lips, it haunted him as he drove through the sugary coating of snow that had fallen over the past couple of days. Snow was rare in this region, but it did happen—and the weather had turned bitter the past few days, as if his mood had thrown itself on the world.

Every flash of color was a surge of pain, every woman he glimpsed a torrent of hope. It was stupid. He was a Mercant. He knew exactly how easily a person could disappear if they wanted to disappear. Especially when they had a whole life into which to vanish. A life about which he knew nothing.

He'd done a search on her eyes after all, had come up with multiple options.

The reasoned part of him knew not to follow any of those trails. She'd made her choice. He needed to respect that or he risked becoming like some of the people he hunted, those for whom choice was a privilege they withheld from their prey.

Yet his obsessive need for her was a roar in the back of his brain.

Find her, it said. *Keep her.*

Neck muscles tight, he clenched his fingers on the steering wheel. "No," he said aloud. "I will not take that which isn't freely given." He hadn't needed anyone to teach him that lesson—he'd learned it as a child on the streets, had witnessed how it broke a person to have no choice but to submit.

His mother had been a slave to the drug. Others had taken advantage of that need while he watched, unable to do anything. Too small to save her. Too small to even understand what was happening.

Never would he put another woman in the same position.

He drove on, away from a broken promise that had shattered his stone-cold heart . . . and right into a field of death. It was late afternoon of the following day when he came upon the carnage. He could've driven on, had no duty to be there, but this wasn't about duty.

He stopped, got out, looked at the faces of the cleanup crew.

Each and every one of the team appeared exhausted—hardly a surprise, given the waves of horrific insanity that had hit their race over the past weeks, the outbreaks so random that there was no way to prepare for them. Ivan had kept an eye on the news the entire time he'd been on the course, ready to respond with an assist should it be required. But he'd been too far away from this one to help during the event itself.

It was the least he could do to assist with the cleanup.

Because the recovery part of this particular operation was long over. It had been forty-eight hours since the Psy in this settlement lost themselves to the urge to do murderous violence. Many affected by this insidious disease turned on themselves, but others threw their inexplicable rage outward.

Ivan found the woman in charge, volunteered his services. Perhaps the assistance offered by a random Mercant wouldn't have been accepted at any other time, his family's reputation for hoarding secrets and unearthing skeletons too strong. But this was no secret. This was just death, and he was a strong man with the capacity to help put bodies in bags and haul them to the morgue trucks.

That the cleanup was still in progress two days after the massacre was an unspoken indicator of resources stretched to the limit. He hadn't realized it was this bad, or he'd have come much earlier. The entire settlement would've been a putrid pit had they not been in the heart of winter. A dusting of white covered the bodies around him, creating silent sculptures unchanged from the moment of death.

A small, furred body, glimpses of black and gold below the white.

Crouching down, he brushed away the snow with a gloved hand, his breath visible puffs in the air. It was extraordinary, how changelings could have such a different mass in their human form as opposed to their animal one. In human form, this small feline had likely been a full-grown adult.

"All ocelot bodies go in that truck," the mortuary attendant told him, pointing to a truck parked away from the others. "Survivors want to deal with their own dead."

Ivan nodded, unsurprised by the need of the pack to see to the respectful burial of their lost packmates. "Neighbors caught in the crossfire?"

"Yes, the ocelot pack's main residential area butts up against this settlement." The attendant indicated a line of trees on the other side of the wide parklike strip that held the vast majority of the bodies; it had functioned as this small township's outdoor recreation area. Now it was their temporary grave.

As the attendant knelt down beside another ocelot body, Ivan picked this one up on his own. It was heavier than it looked—another thing that set changelings apart from ordinary animals. Their bodies weren't built the same.

"No question that the infected Psy attacked their neighbors, and the cats tried to defend themselves," the attendant added as he made a note on the datapad he was using to track the dead. "Significant number of ocelot casualties."

"Why haven't the survivors already retrieved the bodies?" Changelings took care of their own; he'd witnessed that multiple times with the bears in Moscow. No wounded or otherwise incapacitated bear was ever left on their own. The idea of a pack leaving its dead out in the open like this . . . no, it didn't sit right.

"Majority of the pack is dead," was the sobering response. "The others are injured. We offered an assist, but they're adamant they'll bury their dead without help."

Ivan asked no more questions until after he'd put both dead ocelots in the truck with their brethren. Not all the changelings were in their animal form. A number were in human form—but had been identified as ocelot from identification found on their bodies, or from signs of a semi-shift: claws unsheathed, eyes frozen in their other form by death, patches of fur on their skin.

The latter he'd never even heard of, so he had to assume it to be an artefact of severe trauma, a malfunction in the changeling ability to shift. Those found in full human form with no visible sign of changeling status would be identified later, using whatever resources were available. If he had to guess—and with the bodies so well preserved—he'd say the pack would send a survivor to look through the dead.

Changelings didn't like to share fingerprints or DNA data with the Psy.

That task done, he returned to the attendant who'd been assigned as his partner, and they continued on in their grim work. The other man was able to immediately identify the Psy casualties using a fingerprint or DNA database. Ivan's family made it a point to keep their information off those databases, but most Psy took the tracking for granted. The same with many humans—not so much on the DNA, but with fingerprints.

When another attendant came to consult with Ivan's partner, Ivan carried on. He could handle the smaller bodies on his own, and the attendant had paired his device with Ivan's phone so Ivan could run the IDs.

Despite everything, he still wasn't ready to see bodies so small he could carry two or three at once.

But of course, children had called this place home, too.

"They're just as dead," he told himself, keeping things chillingly pragmatic. That was how he functioned with anyone but Lei, was the reason *he* wasn't insane: a wall of cold sophistication that separated him from the wider world.

He pulled that ice around himself now. He was no use to the dead if he couldn't do what needed to be done, if he saw in these small bodies a whisper of what might've been for a small boy born into a pitiless life some three decades ago.

After ID'ing and logging the first child's body, he got a small body bag from one of the boxes situated throughout the area of the massacre. It was a matter of two minutes to return, put the body gently in the bag, write the ID on the tag, and carry it with care to the refrigerated truck.

"Sleep well, little one," he found himself saying though he knew it was foolish; this child's ears would never again hear anything.

He still treated the body with utmost care, even climbing inside the truck so he could position the body on the top shelf.

Where nothing would crush that small, cold form.

Then he continued on. Body after body.

It was in the most churned-up part of the park area that he found her. She was buried under five other bodies, and invisible to his gaze. He'd been planning to ID the bodies he could see, then call over his partner to help get them in body bags, as the deceased were all adult males. Because while Ivan was far stronger than suggested by his lithe frame, the dead had a dark weight to them.

Then the background telepathic scan he ran at every moment, a low-level security tactic that was second nature, suddenly snagged, hitting a mind that was a wall. Not shielded. Naturally opaque. Only changeling minds felt like that.

Memory crashed into him, of the last time he'd hit a mind that closed.

Suffocating the wave of emotion that threatened to surge past the ice, he glanced toward the forest that bordered this settlement, assuming he had an ocelot watcher—but the line of trees was too far, not captured even on the far edge of his scan. He took in the area again. To his knowledge, every other worker here was Psy, and the civilian survivors had been evacuated for the duration of the cleanup.

That left only one possibility—a living changeling mind among the dead.

Chapter 7

We were once knights to a king, our loyalty unbreakable. We serve no kings now, but we continue to live with honor. Family, fidelity, integrity. That is what it means to be a Mercant.

—Ena Mercant to Ivan Mercant (circa 2061)

IMPOSSIBLE, SAID THE most logical part of Ivan's brain, but—as proven by his attempt to bond with Lei—he was far more than simply that part. His mind had been blown wide open in childhood, the memories he held a kaleidoscope of sweet madness. And it was that part of him that had him in motion the instant he realized he was looking for a living mind.

It was possible the survivor had been frozen into a suspended state, as had occurred in the past with people who fell into ice-cold bodies of water . . . or they'd been insulated from the cold by the bodies on top of them. Just enough warmth to keep their heart pumping.

He began to slide aside the male bodies in the closest pile one by one, not being as gentle as he should've been. If he was wrong, so be it. If he was right . . .

Then there she was, a long-legged form crumpled inside an ankle-length dress of vibrant pink-red that had twisted around her, her denim jacket torn almost to shreds. She was covered in blood that had dried to a viscous thickness, her hair a tumbled black stuck to the side of her face with more dried blood.

At least one of her arms and her left leg were clearly shattered. Bruises and cuts swelled and broke her face, and the warm brown of her skin was now flat and edged with blue where it wasn't bruised a sickly green.

None of it mattered.

He *knew* her.

"Lei," he whispered, his voice sandpaper and his hand trembling as he forced himself to check her pulse.

Ice against his fingertips, a cold whisper that this place belonged to the dead. Except . . .

Thud . . . thud . . . thud . . .

The pauses between beats were dangerously long. Even as he processed the horror of finding his sparkling Lei so broken and hurt, he was scooping her up in his arms. He had to tug to release her from the earth. Jarring her broken bones didn't matter, not when her life was at stake. She was barely clinging to the world, the dull speed of her pulse a countdown to death.

A small ax lay below her, its blade pointing up . . . and slick with fresh blood. It had been embedded in her back, he realized, just as wet fluid began to seep from her back and onto his arm.

I have a survivor! Blasting the telepathic message on a wide band as he tucked her body against his chest, he ran toward the small ambulance parked at the top of the site. It was there for the cleanup crew, the medics dispensing water and nutrients, as well as handling any minor injuries. *Heavy bleeding from deep cut to the back! Multiple broken limbs, severe bruising, possible fractured facial bones!*

The female paramedic had just snapped open the stretcher when Ivan reached her. Placing Lei on the white surface, he stepped back so the paramedic could press a scanner to her neck.

Flatline.

"I felt her pulse. And she's bleeding." Ivan didn't imagine things—and he fucking wasn't about to give up on Lei. "Check again!"

The paramedic obeyed, got another flatline.

It had to have been bare seconds since Lei's last heartbeat. Falling back on the chilling precision of the pragmatic half of his brain, Ivan smashed into her mind using his telepathic energy. Psy couldn't enter changeling minds—but they could smash them open. But a true hit tended to cause irreparable harm to the mind in question, which wasn't his aim at all.

He would *never* hurt Lei.

He modulated the blow to be powerful but not deadly.

Powerful enough to shock and startle.

A faint gasp, her eyelids fluttering even as a strange clawing jolt burned through him—as if his telepathy had been reflected back—before Lei went still. But it was enough. The paramedic got to work, together with a colleague who'd just made it to them, events moving at rapid-fire speed.

"Wait!" Ivan yelled out after they'd loaded Lei into the ambulance and he saw there wasn't enough space for him to join the paramedic in the back. "Her name is Lei! She's a changeling!"

The driver nodded to acknowledge the words as he pulled his door shut. Then the vehicle was backing up to turn onto the road, its lights flashing.

"You have her ID?" his partner asked him, datapad in hand and chest heaving from his frantic run to reach Ivan. "I need to record it."

Ivan stared after the retreating vehicle, Lei's blood a metallic scent stuck to his gloved hands and jacket. "She's not dead."

"I'll add her to the rolls of the survivors. Families are searching for their lost members."

"No ID," Ivan said, thinking of her cold, cold skin, so unlike the firelight of the woman who'd kissed him. "I know her." Little pieces of her that he'd never forget. "First name: Lei. She's changeling."

"Ocelot?"

"I don't know, but that's the strongest possibility." Inside his mind, a bruise throbbed. The clawing echo of the blow he'd struck, deep psychic grooves in his mind. That recoil hadn't been normal. Had been psychic . . . but not quite.

"Ocelots will ID her if she's one of them," his partner stated, then—shoulders slumping—turned back to the field of the dead. "Finding her, it will help maintain morale . . . but there are so many more bodies to load."

Ivan had been preparing to head to his vehicle, follow the ambulance—follow Lei—to the hospital, but he knew then that that wasn't the choice Lei would want him to make. She'd helped an injured stranger for no reason except that it was the right thing to do. And the right thing to do at this moment was to give what respect he could to the dead, to make sure they didn't spend another night out in the cold.

Lei was in good hands and, given the gravity of her wounds, would be taken directly into surgery. He'd go to her after he completed this dark task; he'd stay by her side so no one could hurt her while she was vulnerable and unconscious. He'd watch over her until she opened her eyes and told him to leave.

Because she would.

This massacre had taken place roughly two days ago, but Lei had chosen not to meet him an entire day earlier. She'd made her decision—and that decision was a future without Ivan Mercant.

Chapter 8

"Soleil Bijoux Garcia. Ah, Arturo, such a long name you've given your niñita!"
"That's for later, when she's all grown up. Right now, she's my sweet Leilei; aren't you, mi princesa? Papa loves you."

—Conversation between Arturo Garcia and
Yariela Castaneda (7 August 2056)

SOLEIL WAS ON the edge of a dark gray horizon, the light fading glimmer by final glimmer when it hit her. A demanding bolt of energy that jolted her entire body and turned the horizon to white fire.

A sharp gasp that almost hurt, cold air shards in lungs that had already been shutting down . . . and then her cat leaped. She didn't know to where until she found herself with her claws hooked into a cool black space electric with silvery currents of energy that curved around her in a protective wall.

I know the scent of this place. Oh, it's him. Of course it's him.

Such an odd thought, one her wounded mind couldn't hold.

Her cat wanted to bat its paws at the wild currents of silver, but it had to cling on, knew that to let go would be the end of everything.

It would fall into the gray horizon. It would . . . die. The knowledge came not from the primal half of her nature but from the half that was human. It understood death, had seen far too much of it before her body fell under an unseen and vicious blow.

No.

A repudiation of death.

She had promises to uphold, that she knew, though she could no longer see the full shape of those promises, her mind dull and heavy as her body directed all its energy into keeping her alive.

I'm hurt bad.

A sluggish realization.

Fighting not to fall into the nothingness, she clung on to the electric space, allowed it to protect her, and as she did so, she saw flashes of a dingy room with dull-colored carpet, the deep blue waters of an ocean crashing against rocks, the elegant face of an older woman who had the eyes of an alpha, a pair of powerful hands with squared-off nails and cool white skin.

She stared at those hands, saw them flex inward, squeeze.

The image flashed out of existence, to be replaced by a glimpse of bodies in the snow. She jerked away from that, and to another face. This one of a young man with eyes the haunting shade of silvery morning light—the tilt at the corners gave him an almost feline appearance. Her cat liked that.

He was pretty. But kind. So kind that she felt it in her heart.

His black hair was straight and cut with neat precision. It suited his square jawline and high cheekbones. His expression was gentle and familiar, though she didn't know him. She was certain of that.

Those hands once more, now sheathed in black gloves.

They flexed again, this time to pull a thin wire taut in between.

This one, he wasn't kind. He was dangerous. A predator.

She should've been afraid. She wasn't.

Now the image in front of her was of a small room with walls of palest green, a plant in the corner, and a desk set up by the window. On it lay a datapad that held equations from a child's textbook.

Everything collapsed, highways of crystalline flowers exploding in her brain, their colors infinite. Beautiful. So beautiful. Her mind began to fade at the edges again, the flowers blurring, but this time, she knew the fading wasn't death. It couldn't be. Because when the cat released its claws and pounced back into the mind that was her own, it brought with it a shimmering necklace of crystalline lightning awash with colors beyond colors.

Wrapping that lightning around itself, her cat curled up inside her, ready to heal.

The lightning crackled a pure silver as it created a shield around her brain. She sighed as she fell into the dark. She knew he'd protect her. The man with death in his hands. He'd keep her safe.

Chapter 9

I've met someone, Farah. Someone wonderful.

—Soleil Bijoux Garcia to Farah Khan (5 February 2082)

EXHAUSTION HIT IVAN with the force of a tidal wave ten minutes after he left the site. And it wasn't the bodily exhaustion of hard work; if he didn't know better, he'd have said he'd maxed out his psychic power, was on the verge of a dangerous mental flatline. Except that made no sense—even the jolt he'd given Lei had used only the most minor percentage of his psychic reserves.

His state got so bad that he had to pull off the night-cloaked highway and intake three nutrient bars before he could function again. Even then, he knew he was unsafe to drive. He was as likely to crash the vehicle and kill himself as make it to the hospital.

Ivan Mercant *did not* nap.

He didn't today, either. This sleep was demanding and too deep, left him feeling leaden and drugged when he finally clawed his way out of it some five hours later, the world yet dark. He was starving, hungrier than he could remember being since he was a child.

He ate and drank so many nutrients in the ensuing ten minutes that he cleaned out his entire stock and had to stop at an automated convenience store to pick up more. It was as if he were a bottomless void. The food just vanished into him and it wasn't until a half hour later that he felt in any way stable.

He'd already called the hospital to check on Lei. They couldn't locate her. Too many wounded coming in, he was told. Too much confusion. No matter. He'd find her when he got there.

He arrived twenty minutes later, walked straight into the patient area. It was amazing, the places you could get into if you simply acted like you belonged. No one asked him what he was doing there, and he was able to check every single room, put his eyes on every single patient.

He'd left his gift in the vehicle, knowing Lei couldn't use it yet.

It was a dress he'd purchased after he spotted a clothing outlet in the small automated mall that housed the convenience store. Automations in that vein had never quite taken off as predicted—even in majority-Psy areas, which was interesting in itself—but they worked in lonely places like this, with passing motorists glad for a place to find essentials no matter the time of day or night.

The clothing store's stock had been limited, but he'd managed to find an ankle-length dress in a bright lemon yellow that seemed as if it would speak to Lei's sense of color and style. She was always bright, Lei. Sunshine in human form. He'd tried to replace her denim jacket, too, but the store didn't have that in stock, nor anything else that might suffice, so he'd made a note to get that later.

As he went to check out, the automated service station had offered him a list of other suggested purchases, and he'd indicated yes to all of them. It had then presented him with a small box that was labeled as containing underwear, a toothbrush and toothpaste, a generic skin cream, and a small makeup palette for "midrange" skin tones. He'd figured she might be able to use the eye powder.

Lei liked putting sparkle on her eyelids.

Some might see his gift as a bribe, a way to nudge his way back

---

into her life. It wasn't. He'd do anything for her to choose him; to gain her attention by stealth, by taking advantage of her when she was hurt and defenseless . . . no, it would break him. He'd always know that it was all false.

Too soon. Too fast. But it had happened. He'd bonded to her with the same obsessive focus that had kept him functional and alive this long.

Now he had to learn to live without her.

As for the gift, Ivan simply valued the power of being clean and having clothes of your own. Those were the first things Grandmother had given him after she brought him home; he could still remember standing in front of the mirror after a bath, touching his hand carefully to the brand-new shirt that no one else had ever before worn—and that Grandmother had told him no one could take from him.

His, it was just his.

Even if Lei didn't like the dress, it would give her some non-institutional clothing into which to change. But though he went through the entire multi-level hospital room by room, patient by patient, he couldn't find her. There was no woman with her long limbs and specific pattern of injuries.

"We've been transferring a lot of patients," a harried human nurse told him when he queried her, deep grooves marking the ebony skin of her face. The medical net she wore over the tight curls of her hair told him she must've just come out of a surgery. "Massive number of injured due to recent events."

Though she was clearly tired, she went to a computronic monitor and said, "I can look up your friend for you."

"She was brought in as Lei, last name unknown, from the site adjacent to the SkyElm ocelot pack. Identified as changeling, most likely ocelot."

The nurse input the information, frowned. "I have a Lei here, but notes say she wasn't ID'd as an ocelot. SkyElm alpha himself came in to ID the unknowns an hour after she was brought in, and he didn't recognize her."

Ivan tried to make sense of that; all he could come up with was that Lei had been passing through on her way home to her own pack and had stepped in to help. It was what she did, who she was. "Does it say where she was transferred?"

"It should." A minute later, after bringing up multiple different pages one after the other, she sighed. "I'm sorry, it looks like someone screwed up and didn't note the details of her transfer. We're sending patients across the country—sometimes, in the rush to get a patient onto a jet-chopper, the record trail gets broken."

The nurse brought up another document. "No female patients listed as DOA or expired in the past eighteen hours, so you don't have to worry about that. She's alive, just at another hospital. I'm sure she'll get in touch with you as soon as she's able."

Ivan nodded. "Thank you," he said, and called Canto the instant he walked out of the hospital and into the cold and dark gray winter light. If anyone could locate Lei, it was his eldest cousin; Canto had an intelligence network so vast it reached every corner of the globe.

But even Canto couldn't follow an invisible thread. "Medical records are in chaos," he told Ivan two hours later. "Malware attack attributed to a fringe group inspired by Pure Psy—it's wiped a ton of data."

Ivan was well aware of the pro-Silence fanatics. "Can it be retrieved?"

"Unknown. Depends on whether the organizations have uninfected backups. I'll set up an automatic alert to scan for any patient who fits the description you've given me."

Canto didn't know the truth of who Lei was to Ivan; he believed Ivan just felt a responsibility for the woman he'd rescued. That wasn't out of the ordinary for a Mercant. Legend had it they'd once been the loyal knights to a king—Mercants looked after the people under their care.

Canto's scan, however, never bore any fruit. Canto was used to finding data, and he pushed the limits for Ivan, breaking into multiple secure databases. All for naught. "I'm sorry, Ivan," he said weeks later. "The malware infection was so bad that many hospitals wiped their entire systems, then put up SnowDancer-DarkRiver-designed firewalls."

The SnowDancer wolves and the DarkRiver leopards had within their ranks a team that built the best computronic shields on the planet. They were meant to be impregnable. And though Ivan knew his cousin was the best of the best, he still found other hackers to test those firewalls. Each and every one failed to get through.

Ivan had also activated his network of contacts, but they all came up empty. There were too many hospitals, infirmaries, and recovery centers in play. And those had never been his family's specialty—they just didn't have enough connections in the medical sphere.

Ivan continued to search—and the claw marks in his brain continued to throb. He needed to see that Lei was safe and well. He knew what it was to awaken among the dead. If he'd believed in hope, he'd have hoped that she had no memories of her time buried beneath those five bodies.

Weeks turned into months into a year, and still, he couldn't find any trace of her. When he asked the RockStorm wolves if anyone had left a message for him with them, they answered in the negative. Lei could've found him if she'd wanted to—because he had to believe that she was alive and healed by now. That she hadn't tried was a message all its own.

Ivan had to stop searching for her.

If he didn't, he'd turn her into prey . . . and become as big a monster as those he hunted. It was time to let her go.

PRESENT DAY:

10 AUGUST 2083
SAN FRANCISCO

Chapter 10

Changeling law is clear. The penalty is death.

—Lucas Hunter, alpha of DarkRiver (June 2082)

SOLEIL TOOK CARE to keep her breathing even and her actions unremarkable as she walked through the colorful bustle of San Francisco's Chinatown. It was difficult when the scents of predators far bigger and stronger than her surrounded her on every possible side. She'd known San Francisco was a leopard town, but she hadn't actually *understood* until she set foot past its borders.

Beside her, Farah shivered. "My fur's standing up."

"Shh." Soleil shot her best friend a quelling glance, even though, of the two of them, Farah wasn't the one most likely to get them busted. "There're sharp ears everywhere. Think human thoughts."

Farah crossed her eyes at Soleil.

Soleil almost laughed, but her heart was beating too fast, fear a slick coat on her skin. The worst of it was that it wasn't only the leopards she could scent all around her. Another scent—darker, heavier, with a different bite to it—wove through the air. Even though she'd never before scented its like, she knew it had to belong to the wolves.

There were too many threads of it for it to be any other predatory changeling, and the leopards' powerful alliance with the wolves was well-known in changeling circles.

Any other predatory changeling who dared cross the border into this territory without permission put their life on the line. While the wolves were said to "shoot first and ask questions of the corpses," the leopards had a softer reputation—which only meant that they might give you time to answer one question before they shredded you with their claws.

The DarkRiver leopard pack took territorial boundaries extremely seriously. Humans and Psy unconnected to a changeling group weren't subject to the same rules—because to the animal that lived within their changeling hearts, humans and Psy weren't a threat. Not to territory anyway.

Soleil had the scars to prove that the other races could do brutal damage.

Farah's understanding gaze, so wise and gentle. "It's okay, Leilei. We made it this far, didn't we?"

Throat thick as she looked away, Soleil said, "Yes."

A *powerful* scent thread, one so dominant that it raised all the tiny hairs on her body. She covered her stumble by pretending it was a loose shoelace and going down on one knee to do it up. Her fingers trembled.

"Has to be the alpha's scent," Farah murmured, though Soleil could no longer see her. "Deadly, aggressive, a warning to outsiders."

Lucas Hunter.

Soleil would be dead within a split second if she came face-to-face with him. As the few surviving members of her pack were dead, young and old and even the cubs. How did this alpha justify their executions to himself? It wasn't as if they'd been a threat to him.

Farah's hand on her shoulder, no weight to it. "Are you sure, Leilei?" Troubled concern. "This anger isn't who you are."

Eyes hot, Soleil rose to her feet without responding. There was no point. Farah was gone. Soleil tried not to think about that, tried not to know why Farah was there at times, gone at others. And why she always wore the same clothes. Soleil wasn't insane. She knew the answer. But she didn't have to accept it. Not yet.

It was instinct to scan the area, ensure that she remained unseen as a changeling. Almost no other predatory changeling could've pulled this off—but Soleil's cat had withdrawn so long ago that she no longer carried its scent.

Human.

She smelled human.

Half a person.

Half a soul.

Her eyes locked with those of a man on the other side of the street. A striking blue—shards of paleness mixed in with vivid cobalt—his irises stood out against the barely sun-touched white of his skin, the black of his neatly combed hair the perfect foil.

Clean, sharp bone structure, square jaw, a height over six-two, he could pull off a suit as easily as he did the blue jeans, simple white tee, and black leather-synth jacket he was currently sporting.

And he was looking straight at her.

Her breathing hitched . . . as claws pricked against the insides of her skin, her cat jolting to a sudden and violent wakefulness. No warning, no reason. It was just there as it hadn't been for over a year, baring its teeth beneath her skin and staring right back at the stranger who made her skin prickle, her breath catch.

Her eyes threatened to semi-shift.

"No, no, no," she whispered even as another part of her sobbed at this sign that she wasn't permanently broken.

One glimpse of her changeling status and it was all over. There were leopards on this street right now. She'd spotted at least two. They didn't appear to be dominants, but that didn't matter. They'd see her as a threat, immediately alert the closest dominant.

Who'd track her down with relentless dedication.

Later, she told her cat.

Ignoring her, it strained at her skin, wanting to pounce on the man across the street as if he were Soleil's favorite cake: marbled strawberry vanilla with fresh cream. A man who looked *less* like strawberry and vanilla she couldn't imagine. And yet she wanted to keep on staring at him, drink him in with an endless thirst.

Perhaps she needed to question her sanity after all.

Her cat snarled inside her.

"No," Soleil muttered again.

Breaking the unwanted eye contact that threatened the only purpose she had left, she slipped to the left of a tall man in conversation with two women. None of them changeling and enough of a group to block the view.

Her heart thudded, her skin hot, her pulse a roar in her ears. And her cat *extremely* aggravated with her, even though she'd made the only rational decision. It was so insistent that they had to get back to the man that she had to grit her teeth and fight consciously—not just to keep her eyes human, but to not turn around and walk right up to him.

Now? she said to that primal part of her. *You decide to wake up now?*

Padding restlessly inside her, the cat lunged at her skin, almost initiating a shift.

Soleil didn't swear. Yariela had brought her up to be ladylike, but she was swearing a blue streak inside her mind—even as she ran frantically through the known nonleopard members of DarkRiver. The blue-eyed man hadn't been changeling, of that her cat was certain.

Psy or human, then.

But not a person who'd been identified as part of DarkRiver by the media. That didn't mean much. While Lucas Hunter was visible in his position both as the head of the pack and as a changeling representative on the Trinity Accord, most of the cats kept a low profile.

The back of her neck itched; she knew that the blue-eyed man who'd awakened her cat was following her. He might have scrambled her neurons, but she had to shake him loose, or it was all over. The only way she could win against DarkRiver was by stealth—alone, she had nowhere close to the strength required to get to the alpha, take her vengeance.

He'd murdered her packmates, destroyed what little had been left after the Psy outbreak. He had to pay.

"Leilei," Farah murmured in her ear. "You know you can't kill. That's not who you are. It'll drive you to madness."

I'm no one, she said silently, even as tears threatened. *Madness would be better than this.* Soleil was all alone, the sole survivor of a pack once called SkyElm.

But Farah wouldn't let her be. "You're my best friend. You wear the brightest colors in the world, laugh until everyone gets the giggles, and cuddle so fiercely that it's a gift. You're not a murderer."

Throwing a glance over her shoulder as Farah's words tormented her, she saw that the blue-eyed man remained on the other side of the street—but he was pacing her.

Her cat stretched in readiness to shove out of her skin, forcing the shift in a way it had never before done. It wanted to go to him with a feral desperation. "No," she said under her breath, her hands fisted to bone whiteness. "Not until—"

That was when the world went to hell, screams splitting the air as people fell to their knees or straight down onto their faces. Bones snapped, blood spilled, and chaos reigned.

IVAN crashed to one knee on the hard asphalt right as he went to cross the street, follow a ghost. The only thing that saved him from a cracked kneecap was instinct born of years of training; he'd slammed his hand against the faux-adobe wall of the café he'd been passing and thrown his body weight that way, absorbing most of the impact with his shoulder, arm, and upper body.

He'd be bruised, but nothing was broken.

All of that had happened in the space of split seconds, his vision going hazy at the same moment. Then his mind began to slide away into a black nothingness that chilled his blood.

He knew what this was: a major PsyNet rupture.

And his mind was caught on the cliff edge. If he didn't anchor himself, he'd slip and fall, his connection to the PsyNet severed with brutal efficiency. At which point, he'd die.

Psy did not survive without a connection to a psychic network.

And reconnection was only possible should the psychic pathways in the brain remain undamaged. Such a violent separation would twist them to unusable knots, brain cells dying in a massive shock wave.

Teeth gritted, he shot out telepathic grappling hooks into the fabric of the PsyNet. Canto had taught him that. His older cousin was an anchor—one of the foundational elements of the PsyNet—and he'd made it a point to teach all his cousins "emergency first aid." Once it became clear it worked, the anchors had disseminated that same information freely out into the PsyNet.

The first rule was to do *anything* you could to hold on.

Ivan wasn't as psychically powerful as his cardinal cousin, but he hit 8.9 on the Gradient on his particular—and eerie—psychic ability. His secondary telepathic ability was a respectable 6.1. When he used the latter to look at the psychic plane, all he saw was horror. The PsyNet was fraying around him, minds blinking out at the speed of light.

Life after life. Gone. Erased.

This wasn't a rupture.

It was too deep, too black, too endless.

No chance of survival or reconnection.

Grabbing another falling mind with a psychic hand in an effort to save it, he channeled even more energy into the grappling hooks . . .

and then he felt it. Something—*someone*—had grasped his hooks and pulled them into such a deep part of the PsyNet that Ivan couldn't even see it.

Anchor.

Not Canto. Not Payal. Not anyone he knew. Just an anchor who'd recognized what he was trying to do and helped him.

Ivan used his newfound stability to literally throw the untethered mind deeper into the PsyNet, where—since he'd caught it before a total break—it would reconnect instinctively. Psy were built to *be* connected to a network. Disconnection was the error.

In front of him in the physical world, a brunette woman who'd fallen to the ground gasped and sat up in a jagged movement. Ignoring her because she was safe now, he grabbed another mind, then another, then another.

At some point, he became aware that all those minds were now linked to him by fine silvery threads. Not unexpected with the continuing erosion of his shields. He'd deal with it later, would cut them free the same way he'd learned to cut his cousins free when he'd inadvertently captured them in his web as a child.

Behind him, the breach in the Net grew and grew, such a massive divide that he knew it couldn't be fixed. That was when he saw it. A mind on the *other* side of the divide about to slide off into the abyss. Into death.

He didn't even think about it, just threw a grappling hook over the fracture and toward that person. It slammed into the mind and was grabbed with scrabbling desperation, while Ivan threw another grappling hook into the piece of the PsyNet closest to the other mind.

The person clinging to him clearly saw what he was doing and was rational enough to switch telepathic lines and "climb" back to safe ground on the other side of the nothingness that was this unsalvageable fracture.

A fine silvery thread floated over the canyon, linking the two of them.

Spider, spider, my beautiful spider.

Ignoring the haunting singsong voice of memory, Ivan grabbed more people on both sides of the growing divide. Part of him knew that he shouldn't have been able to reach that far, not across dead space devoid of psychic energy.

At the same time, he was conscious that he didn't know half of his genetic history—and the half he did know had been compromised and reshaped by a drug that had seeped into the womb and into the cells of the fetus he'd once been.

No one knew what Ivan carried in his mind and in his blood.

He'd also never fully explored his toxic secondary ability. It was thanks to Grandmother that he was classified as a telepath alone— she'd known that any other classification would mark him and make him a target for the Council. That political body might now be gone, but Ivan's ability remained as ruthless and cold as ever. He had no intention of wearing it as a label—but perhaps it had a side benefit he'd never before realized.

Rich iron. Wet.

His nose was beginning to bleed.

Judging it a sign of a minor psychic overload, he continued to grab and throw back as many minds as he could. Even with all that, he never lost his awareness of the woman he'd been following, the compulsion to get closer, find out if it was *her* so strong that it had overridden every other need.

Her eyes were dark, her lips as lush as the ones that had kissed him, her skin a familiar midbrown, and her hair a thick tumble of inky black, her curls so loose they were waves.

But while she had Lei's height, she was painfully thin. Not the thin of genetics. The thin of not enough food. The evidence was there in the lack of light in her skin, the way her features didn't quite fit right.

Hollows existed in her cheekbones, the blades sharp instead of rounded—and she bore no scar on her face. Her clothes were also nothing Lei would've worn: a baggy gray sweatshirt and ill-fitting jeans.

Yet every instinct he had said he'd found her.

Found the woman who'd awakened him . . . then left him in the dark.

The softness of her hair shone under the summer sunshine as she ran into his line of sight to assist a woman who'd crashed hard to the ground, cracking a gash into her skull.

Despite her apparent fragility, she wedged one shoulder under the fallen woman's arm and got her up in a single lift, though the injured woman appeared far heavier than her.

Changeling.

Another piece of the puzzle slotting into place.

His quarry took the Psy woman to the side of the street, set her down gently against a wall. A store owner ran out with a red box stamped with a cross, and the familiar stranger who had to be Lei— unless he'd lost his mind at last—said something before grabbing gauze out of the box and holding it to the side of the woman's head.

The shopkeeper nodded and took over the pressure, while Lei ran back to assist others who'd collapsed in ways that caused injury. Even with most of his mind focused on the Net, Ivan was too compelled by her not to note the way she moved, so fluid and quick and graceful.

The same way Lei had moved when she played with him. This time, however, he had an advantage: he'd been in San Francisco long enough to have seen plenty of leopards in motion. She was a cat. Of what variety, he didn't know, but he would bet that one dazzling kiss on his prey being feline.

Then he saw five minds going over the cliff edge at once as the chasm widened, and turned all his energy into holding them to the world. To life.

Chapter 11

Your mother's heart, my boy, is a fierce beast, ferocious in its will.
Healers are like that.

—Carlo Hunter to Lucas Hunter (2058)

SOLEIL IGNORED THE terror rising at the back of her throat, burning her from the inside as people continued to fall around her, and just got on with it. She didn't think about the fact that she was blowing her cover wide open—she was a healer; to help or not, it wasn't a question.

Her cat had given up its rebellion, was with her every step of the way. They were and would always be one in this. To care, to help, to heal, that was the very nature of Soleil's soul.

She knew deep within that had the cat yet been dormant when the world broke around her, it would've awakened with a clawing jolt. Its retreat had been fueled by the biggest shock any changeling could ever suffer—the loss of the entirety of its pack—but even that traumatic shock couldn't kill the drive that was a healer's heart.

A man went down with a sickening thud to the head that told her it was too late to help him even before she checked on him and found a broken neck. Leaving him with a whispered apology for being too late, she ran to the teenage girls who'd collapsed as a group. All five gasped in a breath right then, their eyes flashing open, pupils expanding to cover their irises.

Soleil's heart pounded, her head jerking toward the man her cat craved. He knelt on the other side of the street, his hand braced against the wall and his eyes obsidian.

No whites, no irises. Just black.

She'd seen Psy eyes do that during the worst day of her existence, the world filled with pain and death. But he wasn't out of control, wasn't violent. The impossibly, ridiculously perfect line of his jaw was set, his body rigid in a concentration so merciless it was a pulse in the air.

Her cat batted at it, delighted by him in a way far too familiar between strangers, but that wasn't important at this moment. He had to be the reason these girls were alive. Of all the Psy in the street, he was the only one who was functional—and those black eyes told a story.

After doing a check on the girls to ensure that they'd sustained no physical injuries, she moved on to the next person, her mind and actions driven by years of practice and study. All the while, the scent of death lingered in her mouth, a whispering echo of terrified screams at the back of her brain.

So much blood.

There'd been so much blood then.

Her pack decimated by Psy driven mad by a psychic infection. The ones who hadn't been intent on murder had clawed out their own eyes, smashed their own heads bloody against walls. And they'd been so quiet, some of them. Horrifically, shockingly quiet as they self-destructed in a fountain of violence.

Soleil had fought to help the ones who'd turned the violence inward, had literally tied one's hands to a bicycle park station to stop her from the clawing. The woman had looked lost . . . then smashed her head into the footpath.

Soleil had heard her skull crack like an egg.

These Psy aren't going mad, she reminded herself as she checked on a broken arm, *they're dying*.

"You'll be fine," she told the man with the broken arm. "Just stay here until the ambulances—"

His skin turned to ice without warning, air escaping his throat in a last rattling gasp.

Cat hissing inside her, Soleil almost dropped his arm.

Almost.

She was sane enough, patched up inside enough, to lay it gently against his rapidly cooling body and think not like a woman broken by loss—but a healer. What had just taken place wasn't normal, how quickly all evidence of life had been sucked out of him, how fast his face had lost color. Whatever was happening to the Psy was catastrophic.

Shoving aside images of the dead piled up on top of her, their bodies going from warm to cold and stiff and hard while she bled out below their weight, she moved on to the next injured individual. She had to run around a crashed vehicle to do so, steam hissing up from its crumpled hood. The driver was dead, his spine twisted into an unnatural shape.

But not far away sat a woman propped up against the pole of a streetlamp, her eyes a dazzling green. Those eyes were trained on Soleil's dangerous stranger.

Blood coated one side of her face from where she must've fallen, but she didn't react when Soleil knelt down with her borrowed first-aid kit. It held nowhere near the supplies in her own healing kit, a kit that had vanished from what had once been her aerie, but it was enough to patch people up, keep them breathing until the paramedics reached them.

"You have a severe gash on your cheek," she told the woman with a confidence that first her parents, then Yariela had nurtured with a warmth that Soleil missed each and every day.

Rummaging in the kit, she picked up a small device. "I have a basic stitch-stapler that I'm going to use on you that should halt the bleeding. I'm sorry, I have no numbing gel."

The woman continued to stare at the stranger. "I can feel him." It came out a rasp. "Inside me. Holding me to life. He's so beautiful. Cold crystal fire."

Her words, her almost slavish focus should've raised every hair on Soleil's body. Instead her cat licked its paw, annoyed at her patient because the stranger was *Soleil's*. Regardless of her unhinged thoughts— her cat disagreed vehemently with that diagnosis—healing came first. So she used the woman's preoccupation to start stapling up the cut.

It took until the third staple for the woman to jolt and wince. "It hurts." Her eyes were suddenly wet, the dreaminess erased by pain.

"I know, but the cut is too deep to allow it to remain open." What she hadn't told the woman was that prior to the stapling, Soleil had been able to see inside her mouth—one entire side of her face had been flapping open.

Looked like the blonde had fallen on a sharp piece of metal pro-truding from the crashed car. It had nearly sliced off half her face. But the stitches would help minimize scarring, and there were cosmetic procedures for later on.

Soleil kept her mind on that track. Medical, healing. The beautiful stranger.

Her cat purred inside her, more than happy to focus on him.

She couldn't allow herself to think about death, about how bodies went hard and cold and began to smell. She couldn't think about how people screamed for help when they were being torn apart. And she couldn't think about how she'd fallen with an ax in her back and blood in her mouth, her face half-buried in rucked-up soil.

The scent of damp earth in her nostrils.

The odor of decomposition.

The crushing weight of body after body.

Shoving the memory away with brutal force, she finished stapling up the woman, her hands slick with blood in the aftermath. She used the medical-strength sanitizer in the kit to quickly clean them before she moved on to the next person. Because this was nowhere close to over. People were still falling, still dying.

That was when she saw the pregnant woman, her body convulsing.

Soleil slammed down next to her, managed to get her into the recovery position, and risked her hand to make sure the woman's airway was clear. The patient seized for another few seconds before shuddering, her breathing ragged.

Her eyes were cloudy with bone-deep fear when they met Soleil's, her ebony skin slick with perspiration. "My baby. *Please.* Help my baby."

Severe contractions rippled under the hand Soleil had put on the woman's stomach. "I'm a healer," she said with firm deliberation, her cat at attention. Birth was her favorite part of healing—but not like this, with the mother coated in pain, in fear. "You just do what I say and your baby will be fine."

Yariela had taught her that birthing mothers responded better to firmness than gentleness. "They need to know that *you* know what you're doing and that you're in charge, chica," the senior healer had said. "Especially when you have such a pretty young face."

Soleil's scarred face had never exactly been pretty, and was haggard these days, but she continued to follow Yariela's advice. "What's your name?" she asked, as she touched her fingers to the woman's wrist to get her pulse. "I'm Soleil. My friends call me Leilei."

The woman swallowed. "Zoula."

"Okay, Zoula, I need you to sit up."

"It's too early." Zoula sobbed as she allowed Soleil to put her into a seated position against the wall of a shop.

"Eight months by my glance." Soleil took her vitals again, didn't like what she was sensing, but kept her tone even and calm. "Survivable even outside a hospital." She pushed up the woman's legs so they were bent at the knee, then pulled off her own sweatshirt to drape it over Zoula's knees to give her a semblance of privacy.

Not that the sobbing, scared woman seemed to care.

"I'm going to remove your underwear," Soleil said, thankful Zoula was wearing a loose dress. "I'll be gentle."

"Please save her," Zoula begged. "*Please.* I love her. I'm allowed to now. Silence has fallen. I'm *allowed* to love my baby." Desperation in every word.

Soleil used a pair of disposable surgical scissors to delicately cut off the woman's underwear but left them below her. Then she turned to a shell-shocked man sitting on the nearby curb. "I need your jacket."

Pale and shaking, he nonetheless immediately peeled it off and handed it over. Folding it, she tucked it around the pregnant woman's bottom. She had no intention of allowing the baby to touch the asphalt, but this would also help protect her gloves and hands from scrapes.

She couldn't risk wasting even an ounce of healing energy.

A gush against her hands, too much blood coming out of Zoula. *Shit.* "You," she said to the man again, making sure her voice stayed steady. "Call emergency services, tell them it's a priority. Pregnant woman in distress. Baby coming." That way, the paramedics would know what they'd be facing with this patient.

The man pulled out his phone with a trembling hand.

Trusting him to complete his task, Soleil returned to her own. "You can do it," she soothed Zoula, who'd gone too quiet. Too much blood loss. Too much trauma. "I have you, and I have your little one."

Five minutes later, with Zoula's eyes fluttering and struggling to stay open, Soleil held a tiny baby covered in the fluids of birth. She'd emerged with startling quickness, as if her mother's body was ejecting her because she had a better chance of survival outside than inside a body that might seize again.

Her cry was thin and angry and welcome.

Cat making a happy rumbling sound in her chest, Soleil placed the baby immediately into Zoula's hands, knowing the contact would be good for them both, then used another pair of sterile scissors from the emergency kit to sever the umbilical cord.

A DarkRiver cat—a white-blond male—who'd run over with a blanket gave Soleil a nod that said he saw her, knew her, and would deal with her later. He covered mother and baby in the warmth of the blanket, while Soleil took care of the afterbirth. She placed it in a large biohazard bag from the kit in lieu of anything else, never taking her attention off her patients.

Zoula was rocking her baby, a new light in her face. "She's alive." A shaken whisper. "Thank you. Oh, thank you."

"You did all the work, Mama," Soleil said, exhaling in quiet relief when an ambulance screamed into the street. It stopped right next to them—thanks to the waving arms of the man who'd given up his jacket.

Soleil waited only until Zoula and her baby were both in the ambulance before she moved on to assist other injured.

Whatever had happened, it was still going on.

And the stranger with the obsidian eyes continued to kneel there, his muscles locked but his eyes scanning the area. Gasps of life followed his attention. That black gaze locked with Soleil's for a fleeting instant, a shock of blazing power and cold control . . . and from her cat, a possessive swipe.

Then he was gone, leaving her cat bad-tempered and the human side of her shockingly aware of him in a way she hadn't been aware of *anything* since her waking. Her breath stuck in her throat, her cat grumpy at not being able to touch him.

Mine, it snarled. *Mine.*

Glaring at her own cat—who stuck up its tail *and* its nose in haughty defiance—she ran toward a changeling couple who were attempting to assist an elderly Psy. All the while, no matter where she was on the street, no matter if she was facing him or had her back to him, she could pinpoint the location of the stranger.

As if inside her was a homing beacon attuned only and perfectly to him.

To a Psy with eyes as black as night.

Chapter 12

With all the collapses of late, all the fractures, the PsyNet is going to tear apart regardless. Better to do it in a controlled fashion.

—Payal Rao, Anchor Representative on the Psy Ruling Coalition & CEO of the Rao Conglomerate (16 June 2083)

KALEB HAD BECOME used to dealing with Net ruptures.

The tears had increased in frequency and destructiveness ever since the rise of the Scarabs—powerful, out-of-control Psy who were a by-product of the fall of Silence. Because the Silence protocol had *worked* for a minority of the Psy race, the rules and attendant shielding mandated by it creating a wall around their minds that had helped contain their chaotic power.

Prior to Silence, these same Psy would've imploded as children, burning up in the inferno of their abilities. But Silence had allowed them to grow to adulthood. And these adult Scarabs were viciously powerful—and on the road to death. The vast majority of Psy minds weren't built to process that much psychic energy, would crash and burn under the weight of it.

But the Scarabs could cause—and were causing—massive damage on the way to self-destruction.

Now this.

"This isn't a rupture," he said to the cloaked mind that stood next to him on the starlit black of the PsyNet. Aden Kai, leader of the Arrow Squad, had responded at the same time as Kaleb—because this break was nothing normal.

"Agreed." Aden's presence was a calm ocean in the chaos. "We can't seal this."

"No." It would be the first time the two of them made no attempt to fix a breach. "We save those who we can, reduce the Net lesion where possible." He'd already been doing so even as they spoke, as had Aden.

Now, decision made, they split off in different directions. He could see multiple other strong minds in his vicinity, could tell the untrained ones from the trained. It didn't matter. Power was power and as the untrained were set on assisting minds to hold on to the Net, they could do no harm.

He targeted his own energy—the brutal energy of a dual cardinal— into sealing the "frayed" edge of the PsyNet. He didn't know how the system would work with that massive black space beyond. The PsyNet had always been a single contiguous network, one that spanned the globe. Today, an entire piece had torn off into an island.

And the moat around that island was growing.

A moat.

That was when he realized the PsyNet remained a contiguous entity—it was already redirecting itself to flow around the island. The PsyNet would surround that island, but the two parts were no longer connected. The blackness that separated them was full of nothing— and it was growing.

That was when he saw it.

A mind flashing bright on the other side—on the edge of the island—before it vanished.

A Scarab burning up in their own power.

Coincidence or cause? He'd find out, and he'd deal with it. At this moment, he had to stop the hemorrhaging of the Net, halt the river of death.

Once, he would've sacrificed these strangers without a thought, but that was before Sahara asked him to save them instead. And for her, even the twisted darkness inside Kaleb would seek the light.

Payal, he said as he worked. *Has the island separated from the main body of the PsyNet on every level?*

The woman who represented Designation A—the very foundation of the network—took several seconds to answer. *Unclear*, she said at last. *Massive surges in the Substrate, tears all over the place. We'll have to assess once things calm. What I can tell you is that we've lost multiple anchors to that island.*

The cold and calculating part of Kaleb—a permanent aspect of his psyche that Sahara saw and somehow accepted—weighed up the potential of what had just happened. An island, complete with anchors.

It was the perfect test on whether such a separation could work.

They hadn't done it when the idea was first broached because of a dearth of anchors—and this event would only magnify the shortage—but if it *did* work, then the long-term plan could be to hold on until they had enough new-generation anchors to action the plan in its entirety.

Update. Payal's crisp psychic voice. *Four anchors lost from the main network. Massive structural damage. Cascade collapse imminent.*

Jaw clenched on the physical plane, Kaleb threw his vast psychic power into holding back the ripple effect. But he still saw a mind hanging *in* the dead space between the PsyNet and the island.

Pausing only for a split second, he checked his senses.

No mistake. There was a mind there, a mind cloaked in stealth that was blowing its cover in bursts of faint silver-shot light as it appeared to assist other minds. Its presence defied every psychic law in existence. Psy minds could only exist in a psychic space—and the moat was pure nothing. No psychic threads. No biofeedback. A perfect blackness akin to the emptiness of space.

But someone was hanging in the middle of the chasm; and since that someone appeared to be an ally, Kaleb shoved the oddity aside to deal with later.

Right now, he had to keep the PsyNet from falling.

Chapter 13

Ready for gentle physiotherapy. Prognosis is good but it will take time, especially her leg.

—Medical notes on Patient: Lei, 5:01 p.m., 9 October 2082

SOLEIL COLLAPSED AGAINST a sidewalk tree hours after the nightmare first began. Her hands trembled, the adrenaline crash hitting hard. She'd used up every ounce of energy in her body at least an hour ago. It didn't matter that she hadn't had to utilize her healing ability—that only worked with those who were pack, and Soleil was a changeling alone, her heart broken.

The pull on her resources had been unremitting regardless, patient after critical patient. It hadn't let up even after help arrived in the form of more paramedics as well as changelings with medical knowledge.

Lucy, a blond SnowDancer wolf who'd introduced herself as a trained nurse, had happened to be close to Chinatown at the time of the incident, and she'd worked side by side with Soleil in the aftermath. Soleil had very much appreciated her calm competence.

Now the two of them sat against this tree that had pushed its roots up through the sidewalk. At any other time, the sight would've made her smile.

"You're like this tree," Farah said from her other side. "Stubborn, beautiful, cracking through all the walls people try to put up." Laughter that hurt Soleil's heart. "I was such a little grump as a cub, and still you became my heart's friend."

"Drink." Lucy's voice, the other woman indicating the bottle of electrolyte-laden water a shopkeeper had thrust into Soleil's hand. "I've almost emptied mine."

Soleil looked down at the bottle, her mind sluggish. And her mind was all she had in her quest for vengeance against a goliath. The realization, fuzzy though it was, was enough to have her lifting the bottle, opening the lid, and pouring the liquid down her throat. As a healer, it was her duty to ensure that she was ready to respond to an emergency. She'd failed once, failed to save any of them. Never again.

Unable to watch the dead now being put into body bags, she looked down at her lap instead, her cat too exhausted to argue with her retreat. Would autopsies be done on these dead when their cause of death was as clear as the cloudless blue of the late-afternoon sky?

The entire planet knew that when groups of Psy collapsed without warning, it had to do with a failure in their worldwide psychic network. Soleil often wondered why the PsyNet had ever been such a big secret to begin with—it wasn't as if humans or changelings could enter that psychic space and do damage. Only Psy minds had the ability to access it.

"Leilei, what are you doing here?" Lucy asked with the ease of a friendship forged in fire. "You know you're breaching our laws."

Soleil picked at the label on her bottle, tiny pieces of confetti to match the ruins of her grief-induced plan of revenge. "Will DarkRiver execute me?"

Brow furrowed below the strands of hair that had escaped her ponytail to stick to her sweat-damp skin, and brownish-hazel eyes holding a wolfish edge, Lucy shot her a mystified look. "You're a healer," she said, as if that was an answer.

Soleil didn't understand, but she suddenly had another priority, her head rising and eyes going directly to the Psy male that her cat was obsessed with—it was as if he'd activated an emitter that lit up the baffling homing beacon in her feline brain.

Her cat prowled to the forefront of her consciousness.

She scowled at its attempts to take over but was glad to see that the stranger had finally eased his at-attention stance. As she watched, he shifted to sit against a wall, his hand braced on the raised knee of one leg and his head pressed back against the wall. He'd taken off his jacket at some point, now wore only the blue jeans and white tee, his feet clad in laced-up black boots.

As if he'd felt her scrutiny, his eyes opened without warning, locked on her. They weren't black any longer but that searing blend of blues that shot ice into her blood—and made her cat rub against her skin, urging her to go closer, sniff at him.

Sniff at him?

Soleil was appalled. Yariela had not raised her to go around sniffing random men. Even Soleil's free-spirited parents would've been taken aback by the idea. But driven by her—insane—cat, she inhaled deeply, as if she might catch his scent on the air, figure out the reason behind her primal response.

What she sensed was fresh blood—and though they were surrounded by carnage, she knew it was his.

Her cat growled. How dare he be hurt?

Struggling to her feet, she said, "It's okay," to Lucy when the other woman began to stand. "Quick job."

Since she'd be shriveling away in a DarkRiver prison soon enough, maybe she'd go and sniff at the pretty and dangerous stranger to satisfy her cat. A small piece of feline wildness in the midst of all this horror, a reminder that her cat had always walked to the beat of its own drummer—though never before had it fixated on a stranger.

First, she opened up the much-better-stocked first-aid kit that a paramedic had provided for her. It was all but empty at this point, but she managed to find a couple of gauze pads. Grabbing them, she made her way across a street filled with the sound of zippers closing over people's faces.

Her stomach lurched. Her cat flinched.

Don't look. Don't think. Don't remember.

The orders a mantra inside her head, she made it all the way to the stranger who hadn't taken his eyes off her. It struck her again, how good-looking he was—ridiculously good-looking. The kind of good-looking that made fools of women.

Her cat snarled, swiped again. *Mine*, it growled.

Too tired to fight the feral beast that was the most primal part of her nature, or to keep her feet, she came down onto her knees in front of the stranger in a barely controlled descent.

Snapping out a hand in a motion almost as fast as a cat, he clasped her upper arm to stabilize her. Soleil saw stars. Actual stars. Pinpricks of dazzling light against a vast blackness. Her cat meanwhile was preening. Any longer and it'd be batting its eyelashes.

The stranger released her when she made a slight pulling-away motion. Her cat was *not* pleased. She was meant to *sniff* him, not reject him. A few strokes of his hand through her fur would also be accept-able.

Mad, she was going mad.

But she stayed. And held up the gauze. "Your nose."

A blink—as if he hadn't noticed the bleed that had barely begun—before he accepted the offer and used the gauze to stanch the blood flow. "Thank you." His eyes were even more striking up close, electric in their attention.

Her own eyes threatened to semi-shift under the force of the cat's will. "It's medicated," she said, a slight roughness to her tone that came from that same cat. "Should help heal any minor trauma."

From what she'd picked up from having lived next to Psy for much of her life, and due to the more open channels of information of late, such nosebleeds in Psy often augured an overuse of power, but that didn't mean the bleed itself wasn't a result of broken blood vessels and the like. In the worst-case scenario, it might be a sign of major brain trauma.

She held up two fingers. "How many?" He was cognizant of his surroundings and had sustained no obvious injuries, the reason why he'd been passed over by the paramedics, but that could be a false impression, his brain bleeding out on the inside.

"Two," he said, continuing to watch her with an unrelenting focus that—in a changeling—would've been a challenge. "I don't have a brain injury."

Soleil's cat wanted to hold the eye contact, wanted to show him that it wasn't a submissive—but the healer in her took priority. Ignoring his self-diagnosis, she continued to run through the procedure for checking his mental acuity and reflexes.

He cooperated with no emotion on his face. Silence, the eerie protocol that had conditioned emotion out of the Psy as children, had fallen—at least according to the Ruling Coalition of the Psy. But compared to the hundred years for which it had held, it had been but a bare heartbeat since the fall.

Many, *many* Psy remained cold and shut off.

Soleil didn't blame them. Feelings were tough even if you'd felt them all your life. How much harder must it be for people who'd been taught to stifle all emotion from childhood?

Soleil had learned to suffocate her sadness and fear as a child. Without Yariela, she'd have grown up to be a brittle creature inside a stony shell. She wondered if this Psy had ever had a Yariela in his life.

"Seven hundred and four," he answered in that same cool tone he'd used throughout, this time in response to a complicated math question.

She fought back a shiver, certain all at once that his voice could soften in ways unexpected that would make her toes curl. Those firm lips, too, could feel warm and— She cut off the hallucinatory direction of her thoughts with a curt shake of her head. *It's just the impact of his face*, she told herself. Pretty enough to make her lose all sense.

"Good," she said after a cough, while her cat licked its paw in lieu of licking him. "If I didn't already know the solution, I wouldn't have been able to answer that one without a calculator."

"I appreciate the concern," he said in a way that was so devoid of emotion it would've been easy to dismiss it as meaningless . . . but she could still feel his eyes on her. Like lasers burning into the side of her face.

"Just doing my job as a healer," she said, her voice a rasp, then shifted to collapse against the wall next to him, their shoulders separated by a bare few inches. Just close enough that she could breathe in his scent. Sniff him.

And oh he smelled good.

SHE *didn't know him.*

And he hadn't made a mistake. This was Lei. Ivan would never mistake those clever eyes, the curve of her lips, the shape of her face, but most of all, the gentle way she had when she helped someone who was wounded.

Ivan didn't need the confirmation, but he could see her scar now, too. She'd covered it up with makeup for reasons of her own, but that makeup had worn off under the stresses of the hours past, revealing the familiar ridged line that marked her skin.

It wasn't pretense, her lack of memory. No one was that good an actor. This was trauma. Could be either physical or mental. Her inju-

ries had been catastrophic, and it wasn't unknown for a survivor of
such terrible wounds to have no memory of events that had occurred
in the weeks leading up to their injury.

Ivan didn't even exist as a ghost for Lei.

The heart he'd thought he'd cut out and buried when she left him
wrenched into a warped shape, twisted and broken. It was all for the
good, he told himself. He was no longer the man he'd been when they
met, could offer her nothing other than a descent into the darkness.

Yet he couldn't stop himself from tracing the outline of her profile,
drinking in her presence with a voracious need that was oh so dangerous. Scored by exhaustion or not, her shoulders slumped, Lei had an
undeniable and marked presence. But her injuries and their aftermath
had left a mark—and those marks weren't only physical.

The Lei he'd known had . . . sparkled.

This Lei was . . . curled inward, all her light hidden from the world.

His hand remained unfisted, flat, but inside, the spider flexed outward in a cool, dark anger. There was so much he didn't know about
Lei, so much she'd never told him before she decided that she didn't
want him after all, but one thing he'd learned today as he'd watched
her move.

"Ocelot," he said, because he had to start somewhere on the feline
family tree.

Her head snapped toward him so fast that it was inhuman—
feline—and her eyes, they weren't deep brown any longer. Slightly
elongated black pupils against pale irises of tawny brown surrounded
by a ring of golden light looked into his own, the animal who was her
other half rising to the surface. He wanted to believe that the cat knew
him, remembered him, but that was magical thinking—and no one
had ever called Ivan anything less than harshly practical.

Eyes going wide, her breath catching . . . then a smile so dazzling
it punched him in the gut. A hard shake of her head . . . before she
lifted her hand to his face.

The spider froze.

So did Ivan.

He allowed her to touch her fingertips to his cheek, punch sensation through him with the force of a bullet fired at point-blank range. Despite the chaos within, he stayed motionless, because to react would be to break the chains keeping him in check.

"I know you." A feline rumble, her claws slicing out to lie against his skin. "Oh, I should've listened to my cat!" Dawning realization, the fleeting emergence of the vibrant colors of her. "Stars in the darkness. Silver threads in my mind. It's *you*."

The bruise inside his brain that had never quite healed pulsed anew, but it didn't hurt. It . . . ached. For her. He wanted to believe she'd remembered everything, and that she'd always meant to come back to him, but she wouldn't be looking at him with such innocence if she knew all of him.

It was better this way, he reminded himself. Far better.

Things had changed for the worse since the kiss that had forever altered him. He was no longer the man who'd dared dream those dreams. No, he was now a monster barely leashed, his time as the Ivan his family knew—and the Ivan that Lei had once known—in a sharp countdown to the end.

But he saw no harm in telling Lei one thing. It might lead her to trust him. Then he could help her, look after her. Because it turned out that not even the monstrous spider inside him could bear to see her suffering.

"I found you in the snow," he said, his voice rough.

What he didn't say was that he'd then lost her. But she was alive, and that was what mattered. She breathed, she existed. And she'd just smiled at him as if he was the most wonderful thing she'd ever seen.

It was a beautiful lie, formed on the foundation of memories lost, bloodstains forgotten, but Ivan wasn't about to reject it. Not when he had so little time left as Ivan, as the man Lei had met in a forest well over a thousand miles from this street. Where she was concerned, he'd take the scraps, hold them as close as a miser with his coins.

"Does your leg cause you pain?" he asked. "It was badly shattered."

"In the cold." Claws brushing against his skin, her breath soft as she leaned toward him . . . before she jerked back with a scowl. "Who are you?" A demand.

"Ivan." A man with a nightmare in his head and one who'd just realized he'd permit her to claw him, permit her to mark him.

As she'd already marked him that cold day among the dead, the bruise not a bruise at all, but the swiping marks of a cat's claws. "What's your name?" he asked, because to call her Lei without introduction would give away far too much.

"Tell me what happened that day," she said instead of answering, slicing back her claws but continuing to stare at him with eyes that were hauntingly beautiful. "I need to know."

Undone by the stark request, the ground shaky under him, he told her all of it. From the moment he'd found her, to the moment he'd "crashed" her mind with his own, jolting her to life.

"My cat knows you," she said. "As if you're inside me." Another scowl, her hand going up to her temple before dropping back down. "Did you leave something inside me?"

"Psy can't influence a changeling in such a way—and if I left something, I would've been able to track it, find you." Instead of being haunted by dreams of an ocelot prowling through his world.

Narrowed eyes. "Something happened that day."

"Yes." Impossible to ignore that when it was taking all his will not to touch her. "But I can't tell you what—though I do think you have it the other way around."

Taking a box of energy bars offered by a shopkeeper who was handing them out to all the rescuers, she opened it and put several bars in his lap. And he thought of their starlit picnic and the food she'd made him try, a moment he'd gone over so many times that the memory was frozen in a glass bauble in his mind.

"Other way around?" she muttered when he didn't continue. "What are you talking about?"

"I think you left something in *me*." A thing of fur and teeth that had haunted him each day since.

Chapter 14

Incidents of Scarab Syndrome continue to rise in the general population.

—Address by Dr. Maia Ndiaye, PsyMed SF Echo, to virtual assembly of medical professionals from the Pacific Islands' United Medical Corps

The Consortium can't function as a cohesive unit without solid leadership. Where is the Architect who sold us this bill of goods?

—Priority question from a member of the Consortium (unanswered)

THE ARCHITECT WHO had become Queen of the Scarabs was pleased. "You have done well," she told those of her children whom she had selected for this task.

They didn't respond, couldn't respond, their minds too busy undertaking the work she'd assigned them. She had her own task, too, the most critical one of them all. Settling back in her office chair on the physical plane, she unleashed the full power of her mind on the psychic one.

And this time, none of the Psy, that old and weak race, could see her.

Chapter 15

Psy, human, changeling, all three races spend their lives searching for and highlighting differences, when the truth is that we are far more alike than we are not.

—Excerpt from "Reflections on Identity" by Keelie Schaeffer, PhD, *Anthropology and Psychology Quarterly* (March 2074)

"WE ALL KNOW healers have an ability analogous to a psychic one."

Soleil stared at him, at this beautiful stranger who'd allowed her to touch him in a way that was far too intimate between people who'd only met once before—while one of them had been unconscious. Contrary to what her cat might believe, that didn't count as a relationship.

Nose in the air, her cat twitched its tail.

"It's Psy that play with minds," she said, and made herself look away from the striking blue of his gaze. "Don't try anything."

"If I could have, I'd have found you," he said again. "I looked for you, but you'd been transferred with no forwarding record. And you weren't listed as a SkyElm ocelot. Were you visiting family there?"

The strange joy of finding out why he felt so familiar shattered as things spiked and twisted inside Soleil. She couldn't answer, her cat, too, going mute within. This was a pain for which neither part of her had any words. It was one thing to know you were unwanted by your pack, another to be so viciously rejected.

Her alpha had disavowed her while she was helpless and broken.

A stir next to her that was electricity in the air. "You need to eat."

Soleil's fingers clenched on the cool red of the energy bar she hadn't opened, her eyes on the vista in front of her. Defeat was a hammer coming down on her shoulders. There was no way she could sneak out of this street, far less sneak up on Lucas Hunter.

Paramedics swarmed the area, as did civilians . . . and many, many members of DarkRiver.

"Oh, Leilei," Farah murmured from beside her. "You know you were never going to spill his blood. You heal. You don't murder."

It was my duty as the sole survivor, she wanted to say, wanted to argue. *There's no one else left to take vengeance, get answers.* But she stayed silent—talking to invisible people was something she usually saved for the third date.

Farah laughed—because that was just her kind of humor.

Stifling a strangled laugh-cry, Soleil swallowed the anguish tearing her apart and forced herself to rip open the wrapper of the energy bar. Forced herself not to think about her best friend's enormous laugh, or of how she'd never again look out from her aerie to see Farah, small and smart and fast, running over to share a piece of wicked gossip.

"Staring at it won't get energy into your body," Ivan said.

Soleil's shoulders stiffened. "Neither will stuffing it someplace small and sunless in yours, but I'd sure feel good after."

Ivan turned to look at her, his gaze unblinking.

Her cat, meanwhile, was cackling. The human side of Soleil was by turns astonished and aghast. She did not go around saying that kind of thing—though she *had* always had a quick-fire temper when someone pushed her buttons. But . . . that temper had gone into deep freeze the day her world fell.

Except, it appeared, for this stranger who'd saved her life.

She probably should have apologized. In no mood to do so, though she knew he'd said nothing that deserved such a scathing response, she took a giant bite of the energy bar, chewed.

Ivan returned to his own bar, his focus on getting it down methodical. She tried not to watch him out of the corner of her eye, but it was impossible. She was aware of his every slight move—from the way his eyes tracked their environment, to the way the strong muscles of his throat moved as he swallowed.

Flickers of stars in her mind, streamers of silver that made her cat pounce.

Whatever he'd done that day on the field, it had linked them in some way. He was difficult to read, but instinct—and common sense—told her he hadn't done it on purpose. What reason would a powerful Psy have to attach himself to a broken changeling?

No matter how she looked at it, she couldn't find a rational answer to that question.

And she realized she was staring at him again, as if he was her personal North Star. His cheekbones were knife blades against the cool white of his skin, his cheeks hollow. His eyes glittered. It would take more than a few nutrient bars to make up for the steep physical price he'd paid to do whatever it was that he'd done.

"How did you keep so many people alive?" she asked.

"Grabbed and threw them back into a stable part of the PsyNet, away from the part that was collapsing under us."

A simple but precise explanation. A Psy on a news show had once described the PsyNet as an endless black sea filled with stars. Today, the stars had screamed as they fell into an abyss.

It was a horrifying image.

He turned to pin her with that icy gaze that made her insane cat want to lick him. "You never told me your name."

"Soleil Bijoux Garcia," she said, because the time for stealth tactics was well and truly over. "My friends call me Leilei." She pointed at him. "You can call me Soleil." Whatever this was, it wasn't friendship.

"Soleil Bijoux," Ivan said, as if testing out the name. "Treasure of the sun?"

A stab inside her, her mother's accented voice singing her a lullaby.

"I'll call you Lei," he said.

Her mouth fell open. "You will *not*. Nobody calls me Lei." But she frowned, angled her head, almost able to hear the faint echo of a voice that had called her exactly that. It stayed frustratingly out of reach, a phantom memory she couldn't capture, part of the monthlong black gap in her mind that she hadn't been able to fill.

If Melati hadn't told her that Soleil had been visiting just before the massacre, Soleil would've never known. But though her friend—a friend she'd made when she was nine and somehow managed to nurture to adulthood—had shown her photographs from that visit to Melati's Texas town, Soleil's brain stubbornly refused to remember.

At times, Soleil could swear that her mind didn't *want* to remember, as if what had happened during that time would hurt her. Yet that made no sense. Melati had said they'd had a fun time together, though she hadn't been able to fill in the hours they'd spent apart while Melati put in a little time on her small business.

Was it Soleil's childhood friend who'd shortened her nickname?

Her cat growled in disagreement.

Frustrated, she left it for now and glanced back at Ivan. "Soleil," she said again, her eyes narrowed. "You will call me Soleil."

No shrug from him in answer to her statement, but he might as well have made the motion, the way his expression shifted with utmost subtlety to tell her he wasn't budging. But what he said had nothing to do with her name. "It looks like DarkRiver's alpha has arrived."

"I know." Soleil had sensed Lucas Hunter long before Ivan spotted him, the animal within her responding to the violent power of a man built to lead a pack. Every tiny hair on her body was standing up, her gut a clenched ball.

Then there he was.

Lucas Hunter, killer of the last surviving members of her pack, crouched down in front of her, his skin a muted gold and his white T-shirt stretched across wide shoulders. His thighs pushed up against the faded blue of his jeans, the black of his hair touching his nape. Eyes of panther green scanned her, the light catching on the clawlike markings that scored the right side of his face. Those markings branded him a hunter, a man designed to bring down even other predators.

That was the moment Soleil accepted that she could've never taken him down, that driven by maddened grief, she'd given no thought to harsh reality.

Lucas wasn't Monroe, weak and selfish and soft from lack of training. Lucas was the epitome of a ruthless alpha. He'd have broken her neck before she put a scratch on him. Because this had never been about a shot in the back—no, she'd wanted to confront him, wanted him to tell her why he'd done a thing so shameful and pointless.

"How badly are you drained, healer?" he said in a deep voice that reached to the innermost core of her changeling heart. "What do you need?"

Her cat couldn't resist the compulsion that was an alpha's power. "Flatline," she ground out.

He wasn't her alpha, but he was still an alpha, his dominance brutal. She *could* have resisted had she been bound to another alpha, another pack. But she wasn't. She was on her own. And a healer on her own could never stand up against an alpha of his strength.

To compare him and Monroe was laughable.

His eyes narrowed, his gaze locking with hers. She wondered if he knew her animal—was that instinct in an alpha? But he didn't ask her that question, just said, "I can't transfer pack power to you without a blood bond."

"I know." That was one of the gifts of being a healer in a pack—the alpha could speed up a healer's recovery by sharing with her the power of the pack, a power that flowed in the veins of an alpha.

Yariela had told her about the energy transfer when Soleil first became her apprentice. "You'll be asked to accept a blood bond when you turn eighteen," she'd said, her face seamed with the lines of a life well lived. "You can refuse, of course, but why would you when it can help you heal?"

But Yariela had stopped mentioning the bond by the time Soleil hit eighteen years of age. They'd both known by then that Monroe wanted her gone. The only reason he'd allowed her to remain was because it mattered to Yariela. And the only reason Soleil had stayed was because she loved Yariela and others in the pack more than she hated Monroe.

But Soleil's adoptive grandmother, her beloved Abuela Yari, was dead now. Lucas Hunter had murdered her. She'd been old, tired, a healer who'd lived her life in service to her pack. What threat could she have possibly posed to this leopard, powerful and deadly?

Her hands fisted, tears hot in her eyes.

A rumble in Lucas's chest. "You're not marked by an alpha. Have you come to ask for sanctuary?"

She stared at him, at this man she'd come prepared to hate. It was an out he was giving her, a way to skate under and around the laws that required she be punished for breaching DarkRiver's territorial boundaries. But if she said yes and he accepted her request for sanctuary, then she knew he'd require a blood bond. A symbol of her commitment to the pack and vice versa.

"No," she said sadly, because she thought she could've liked him if he hadn't committed such a heinous crime. Meeting his gaze, she searched for the evil in the panther green.

Healers weren't submissives, and she'd heard that senior healers could gainsay even their alpha, but those were complex bonds she'd never witnessed. Even Yariela hadn't been able to make Monroe listen. She couldn't imagine how it could be otherwise—especially when Monroe's power had been nothing in comparison to Lucas Hunter's.

This man was lethal beyond anything she could've imagined.

"I ask for no sanctuary," she said, her throat thick. "I ask only for answers." If she was going to die, she'd die having forced him to face the shame of his actions.

Scowl dark, he growled at her again.

And she became aware of Ivan going very, very still next to her.

Lucas's eyes snapped to Ivan at the same time. "I'll deal with you later, Mercant."

Mercant.

She sucked in a breath. Everyone knew that unusual surname. It was that of the icy blonde who headed the Emergency Response Network—EmNet for short. It made total sense to Soleil's cat that her enigmatic rescuer belonged to the same powerful family.

"If you believe I'll sit here and allow you to harm Soleil, it's best you recalibrate your assumptions." Ivan's voice was oddly . . . relaxed. No frost to it as might've been expected—but that did nothing to erase the threat in his words.

He was a cold-eyed predator coiled and ready.

Soleil braced for an alpha's rage. From what she'd seen in her grandfather, then Monroe, alphas did not like being challenged. And while Ivan was no doubt powerful, he was exhausted *and* they were in the heart of leopard territory. A single nod from Lucas was all it would take to bring multiple predators down on Ivan.

"It's fine," she said quickly. "I can look after myself."

Lucas raised an eyebrow with . . . was that *amusement* in his gaze?

Her cat was arching its spine in mortal insult when he said, "Sure, little healer," as if she wasn't five feet nine in her bare feet. "While you fall flat onto your face because you're so wiped."

"I certainly will not," she said, while hoping he didn't notice the tremor in her hands.

"Stubborn. It's like you're all born that way." A grumbling mutter. "Sit. Eat. I'll get nutrient drinks sent over for both of you."

He shoved a hand through his hair, his eyes capturing hers. "I see you." A low and deep murmur that made her cat stand at attention, because those words had been meant for the animal heart of her, not the human part.

"As for you," he said, turning his attention to Ivan, "we'll be having a long-overdue discussion. Until then, look after the little healer."

A hot flare in her gut that razed reason to ash. "I am not *little*."

Lucas pinned her with his gaze. "No," he said slowly. "You're not, are you?" A glance at the bar clutched in her hand. "I said, *eat*."

She hated that his growl affected her. Lifting the bar, she bit off a piece and chewed in angry silence as Lucas rose and went to talk to a tall redhead in jeans and a fitted black shirt who appeared to be checking in with the traumatized humans and nonpredatory changelings in the street.

That redhead was a cat, too, her grace sinuously feline. And despite the stylish cut of her clothing and the cute black boots on her feet, she was a soldier. Soleil could see it in the cool grit in her expression, the lithe musculature of her body. She was also someone senior in the pack hierarchy—that was obvious from the way she interacted with Lucas.

DarkRiver's senior dominants, she realized, were tougher than Monroe had ever been. Forget about Lucas Hunter; the redhead alone could've taken him down.

SkyElm had never stood a chance.

"I can get you out of here." Ivan's voice was a subvocal murmur that shivered over her skin.

Favors always come with a price.

One of the things her father had often said. While it might be true of many adults, it was never true of children. Children didn't keep score. They gave you their treasures just because they thought those treasures might make you happy—even if it was a cookie they'd been waiting to eat.

Soleil missed the children the most.

Her heart hurt.

"Why would you?" she asked this man who was nothing like those innocent souls.

"Because I saved your life," Ivan said, the compulsion to be with her no less powerful than the first time they'd met; Soleil had been written into his life, never to be erased. "It's now mine to protect."

A flash of temper in eyes that were ocelot, not human. "I be—" She slumped over, and it was only by moving with all the speed at his disposal that he managed to catch her before she slammed sideways into the ground. As it was, he stopped her downward motion with her head a bare inch from the asphalt.

Chapter 16

Alpha.
Healer.
Sentinel.
They are the foundations. The firm soil on which we all stand.

—From *A History of DarkRiver* by
Keelie Schaeffer, PhD (continuing project)

SHE WAS INCREDIBLY light, far too light. Changeling bones were heavier than Psy or human, and Soleil was light *with* that factored in. Her shoulder bones—revealed by her tank top—jutted out against her skin, her arms were barely clothed in flesh, and he could feel her ribs against the arm he'd used to stop her from falling.

"Shit." Lucas crouched down in front of her as Ivan straightened her up again, holding her protectively to his side. "I knew she'd burned herself out but I was hoping she had more reserves."

Green eyes landed on Ivan, the alpha's power a thing of claws and teeth, primal in its intensity. "This isn't your fight, Mercant."

Ivan didn't bristle. That wasn't how he functioned. Rather, he did a mental analysis of his psychic reserves, a count of the weapons on his body, and decided he could reach a single small shock device before Hunter decapitated him.

Not good enough.

Yet he didn't release Soleil, driven by a protective urge that had nothing of reason to it. He didn't care. Not when he felt whole for the first time since she'd walked out of his life. "She can't fight for herself right now, so it'll have to be me."

Lucas stared at him for a long moment. "I should gut you, but turns out I can't gut a man who's putting his life on the line to shield a healer." Hidden, unspoken things in that statement, a reference to information Ivan didn't possess.

"I give you my word nothing will happen to her while she's under DarkRiver's care," Lucas continued. "She needs that care. She's showing all the signs of a healer who's gone beyond her limits. What you'd call a flameout."

Of course Hunter knew how to refer to a psychic burn that threatened to collapse a Psy mind for a day or more; the alpha was, after all, mated to a cardinal Psy.

Ivan was yet weighing up whether to trust Lucas's words when the alpha said, "My mother was a healer." His expression grew shadowed. "No one in my pack will ever harm a healer."

Family, Ivan knew, was the core of a changeling pack. And Soleil was not only a changeling but a changeling healer. She had needs about which he knew nothing. In holding on to her, he could cause her irreparable harm.

So, even though allowing her out of his sight made a cold black rage boil within, the spider stretching its limbs in a nightmare fury, he permitted Lucas to gather her up in his arms.

The alpha stood with Soleil held to his chest. "Are you about to flame out?" he asked. "Do you need psychic protection?"

"Why would you help me?" Ivan was, after all, a spy in Lucas's city.

"Because you saved lives today." Grim words, an even grimmer expression. "The information coming out of the PsyNet is fragmented, but one thing is certain—a lot of people died during the incident. According to what we're hearing, most of the Psy in this location should be dead—that they aren't is because of you."

Ivan knew he should look on the Net, check on the situation, but he had little to no reserves. "I'm not going to flame out." He was, however, teetering on the edge and needed rest. Else he'd fall, his mind exposed and without shields.

"Then we'll talk later—we know the location of your apartment." Lucas walked away, taking with him a cat who'd prowled so deep behind Ivan's defenses that she'd become embedded inside him.

As he rose to his feet, he looked for the small daypack Soleil had abandoned when she went to assist one of the injured. It lay ignored in the shadow of a closed doorway.

Once upright, he began a lazy and unremarkable walk toward the daypack, while never looking directly at it. The redheaded DarkRiver sentinel—Mercy Smith—spotted him, said, "You planning to collapse in the street? Be easier to give you a ride to your apartment than have to scoop you up later."

"No. I'll make it."

Eyebrows drawing together, she went to say something else when another member of DarkRiver came up to her. Ivan took that opportunity to grab the daypack and slide away. He knew the changeling facility for scents—Mercy would've tagged the bag as Soleil's if she'd gotten close enough.

Ivan didn't think anyone from the pack would steal her belongings. But they would go through the bag. That was simple security protocol. His hand tightened on the strap hung over his shoulder; no one had the right to take what Soleil wasn't ready to give.

Not even Ivan.

She'd made her choice about him, and he wouldn't manipulate her into another decision now that she no longer had all the facts . . . but he couldn't deny himself the pleasure of being around her in any capacity. The truth was, he hadn't even understood pleasure before her.

To Ivan Mercant, pleasure was Soleil Bijoux Garcia.

Despite his assurance to Mercy, he barely made it through the door of his apartment. After locking it, he stood and looked at the stairs that led up to his bedroom until he'd gathered a few more fragments of energy.

At which point, he literally pulled himself up using the banister.

Dropping Soleil's bag in the corner where it would be safe from prying eyes, he shut and bolted the door, set his security perimeter, then collapsed onto the bed, shoes and all. An image flashed against his closed eyelids in the moment between wakefulness and sleep—of a black spider, its carapace gleaming, that sat at the center of a web of shining jet, hundreds of cobwebbed black lines trailing out from its sleek body.

His vision telescoped into a pinprick of light . . . then was gone.

Chapter 17

Drug 7AX has passed all levels of testing and is now approved for usage. Dosage calibration needs to be exact to achieve intended "super soldier" effect.

Any deviation from the calibration guidelines will lead to severe side effects, including but not limited to mental decline, memory loss, erasure of personality, myocardial infarction, lung disease, and major neurological changes.

—Classified Report to the Psy Council by PsyMed: Pharmaceutical Development & Testing. Project Manager: Councilor Neiza Adelaja Defoe (circa 2017)

HE DREAMED THAT night. According to the Silence Protocol, Psy weren't meant to dream, but Ivan had always dreamed in vivid color. He'd wondered if his nocturnal stirrings were a remnant of his unusual childhood, but then one of his cousins had mentioned a dream—so it appeared the Psy Council had lied about dreams, too.

Or, he'd simply been raised with people whose Silence was as imperfect as his own. Most outsiders would see Grandmother as having the most perfect Silence of all, but Grandmother was also the head of a family that would coolly and calmly dissect any enemy who dared come for one of their own. Mercants took family with dead seriousness—and they didn't only see family in the perfect.

Ena Mercant's devotion was not a thing of Silence.

As for Ivan—his color-drenched dreams had been the only real freedom he'd had as a child. Things had changed, his life his own; perhaps that explained why the hues of his dreams had faded. Tonight, however, the dreamscape glittered, awash in the light of the woman formed of stars who stood in front of him under the canopy of a forest giant.

Lifting her hand, she laughed. "I'm made of stars!" Delight in every syllable. "Look!"

He took her hand, *felt it*, though he couldn't have explained the sensation. It wasn't of flesh on flesh. It was as delicate as starlight . . . and yet not. And though he wasn't a man to hold hands with anyone, he allowed her to wrap her starlight hand around his and tug at him.

Because he knew her, even if she was clothed in stars.

"Come on!" she said. "There's a lake over there—I can see the moon's reflection."

Releasing his hand halfway there, she ran to the water, her movements sinuous and graceful. "Cat." His whisper didn't reach her where she now knelt by the lake.

"What do you see?" he asked, coming down on his knees beside her.

She pointed down at the water, and when he looked, he saw their reflections. His hair dark and his face shadowed, except for the side illuminated by her light. She was stars on the water, a creature of such beauty that it seemed impossible she should exist.

Reaching out a finger, she dipped it mischievously in the lake, the motion reminiscent of a small cat playing with a bowl of water.

"Why did you do that?" he asked as their reflections rippled.

A shrug. "For fun," she said with a laugh. "Want to go swimming?"

"It's cold," he said. "You shouldn't get cold right now." She needed to conserve her energy.

Her smile faded, and she went down into a seated position with her feet in the water of the lake. "I'm hurt."

Echoing her, he dipped his own feet in the water. He could've sworn he'd been wearing boots just before, but his feet were now bare, his jeans rolled up. "No, it's just exhaustion. A little rest and fuel and you'll recover."

Head lowered, she leaned her body against his. "Inside," she whispered. "I'm hurt inside. I can feel it." She spread her hand over her heart. "They're all gone."

He understood loss, understood loneliness, and so he did the one thing he did with no one, not even Grandmother. He put his arm around her, holding her to his side, this fragile creature of starlight.

"I tried to save them." Her voice trembled, wet and broken. "I tried so hard."

"I know." That was why she'd been lying under all those bodies, with an ax in her back. "No one could've asked more of you."

Her shoulders jerking under his arm, her tears sparkles in the air. He didn't know how to deal with tears, but he knew what it was to lose the very foundation of your world, to become a planet with no sun, a place of ice and frost.

Shifting, he slid one arm under her legs while keeping his other around her back, and scooped her up into his lap. "You're not alone," he told her. "I'm here."

No answer, but she stayed against him, stars dazzling his vision.

Pressing her hand over his heart after her tears faded into a silence heavy with pain, she said, "Why is your heartbeat so strange?"

He looked down, saw the glow of arteries and veins shining through his T-shirt. They pulsed a vivid orange with an edge of scarlet. "That's the color of Jax when it's heated up. Some people like to drink it."

"Jax?"

"A drug." So strange, that it would be in his heart. No medic had ever warned him of deposits in that region of his body. "It opens the mind, intensifies the world, offers false freedom."

Sitting up without warning, her spine rigid, she took his face in her hands. "Don't put poison inside you." An order, the stars in her eyes shifting to a primal tawny gold. "Promise me."

"I've never taken Jax of my own free will," he told her, because this was a dream and he didn't have to fear that the truth would make her see him as defective. "My mother used it while I was in the womb— and she gave it to me when I was a child."

A haze of red in her gaze now, flames of anger licking at the gold and husky brown. "It harmed you?"

"My brain pathways are abnormal." There was no way to dress that up when the configuration of his brain was so bizarre that the neuro specialists his grandmother had hired didn't know what to make of it.

What *was* known was that of those adult Psy confirmed to have been exposed to Jax in utero, ninety-six percent experienced episodes of "serious mental instability" in their late twenties to midthirties. Ivan sat right in the center of that zone. "I thought I had it under control, thought my brain had figured its way around the toxic deposits. I was wrong."

She ran her fingers through his hair, and he thought she must be leaving behind a trail of starlight. "You're so afraid."

"Fear is useless. I'm pragmatic." He knew what awaited and he'd prepared for it, planned for it. But . . . he hadn't prepared for her, had never foreseen how desperately he'd want to fight the fate his mother had chosen for him.

"You're so sure the worst will happen."

"Ninety-six percent," he said, not quite ready to tell her that it was *already* happening; his short clock was now in its final countdown. "The remaining four percent had significant other abnormalities. I might have fooled myself for a time, but the fact is that no one escapes Jax when it's present during cell development and growth."

Hands fisting in his hair, she scowled. "I'm not done with this conversation, but I have to go." She looked over her shoulder, as if being tugged by unseen hands.

Desperation was a howl inside his skull. "Will you remember me when you wake?" he asked her. "Will you remember *us*?" As they'd been in the forest in Texas, a fragile bubble of happiness.

"I don't know. I'm so splintered inside I can barely see my way out." Starlight fingers brushing his cheek . . . and then she was gone, the stars falling until he held an overflowing handful that flickered and began to die, one by one.

Chapter 18

Gina: Hey, anyone heard from Soleil? She hasn't posted since before what happened and I can't see that Yariela has, either. I know it's only been three days, but I feel sick to the pit of my stomach. I just want to know they're okay.

Brett: Yeah, I'm the same. Best-case scenario is that they're just picking up the pieces and will respond to comms later.

Shamita: I hope so. I hate that no one from SkyElm has reached out to the rest of us for assistance. That alpha of theirs is a total ass according to my own alpha, but we would send help regardless. But we can't go in without an invitation.

Gina: Brett, you're a cat in the same general region. You heard anything on the feline network?

Brett: Nada. SkyElm's insular at the best of times, and right now, they seem to be ignoring all attempts at contact—my alpha tried to reach out directly, got nothing. The only thing I can confirm is that there *were* survivors—we were able to find that out via a human contact on the ground there.

—Chat log: Primal Care Forum (17 February 2082)

. . .

SOLEIL CAME AWAKE with no physical movement to betray her change in state. It was a skill she'd cultivated as a child, after being placed in temporary foster care with the kind of people who should've never been carers. But her cat wasn't having it today, too startled by the other scent in the room. Of a much bigger cat.

Her eyes flicked open.

To see a face of warm beauty leaning over her. The woman's eyes were the shade of rich caramel against skin kissed by the sun, the hair that tumbled over one of her shoulders an intense brown, and her presence a protective blanket.

Soleil knew her: Tamsyn Ryder, the senior DarkRiver healer.

Changeling healers had long had an informal alliance; they shared healing knowledge regardless of politics and other such vagaries. Back in 2080, however, Tamsyn had set up a forum to facilitate that sharing. Having the forum also allowed for information to be saved so it could be searched. Most of all, the forum was an open conversational space for healers across the world.

"Politics is for alphas and sentinels," Tamsyn had written in the introductory text. "Healers heal."

Before the massacre, the forum had been one of Soleil's favorite online places. She wasn't, however, worried that Tamsyn would recognize her. As SkyElm's junior healer, she'd never joined any of the visual communications.

"There you are." Tamsyn's voice was as warm as her presence. "How are you feeling?"

Soleil did an internal check. "Tired but okay." And with an echo of loss inside her that had nothing to do with SkyElm. It was colored in a strange glowing orange edged with scarlet . . . and in shards of blue, like the eyes of the man who'd saved her life . . . and now thought he owned it.

Hmph. Her cat tilted up its nose, tail flicking. But it wasn't angry. How could it be when it was convinced Ivan was *hers*?

Tamsyn helped her up. "Understandable given what you did during the incident." Her presence was deceptively gentle—because, if changeling gossip was true, Tamsyn was one of the most powerful people in DarkRiver. It was said that she'd dared override Lucas Hunter and come out of it not only alive but with Lucas's respect.

The thought of a healer being so treated caused a pang in Soleil's chest. Monroe had never harmed Yariela, had even taken her advice much of the time—but that was as far as it went.

"An energy drink," Tamsyn said, passing over a tall glass.

Since changelings weren't known to poison each other, far preferring more direct methods, Soleil took the glass and drank down half of it in one go. Tamsyn's approving look made her want to flush, her cat in awe of this woman who was all Soleil had once hoped to become: a strong healer who was an integral part of a pack . . . and a woman with her own small "pack"—a mate and children she adored.

A family. A sense of belonging. A home.

Energy fizzed in Soleil's veins. Startled, she looked at the drink. "What *is* this?"

Tamsyn's laugh was husky and warm. "Good, isn't it? It's a new formulation, based on Psy nutrient drinks. One of our young food scientists saw how the nutrients give Psy an almost immediate boost when they're stressed energy-wise, and wondered if she could formulate a mix for changeling bodies."

She nodded at the glass. "It's only half as effective as the Psy compound, but it packs a punch. Yuka is currently working on another iteration—and she's already drawn up a business plan where DarkRiver takes over the changeling energy drink market." Affectionate pride in Tamsyn's voice.

Soleil's cat curled up inside her, dejected and lonely and wanting. Yariela had done her best, as had other senior members of the pack, but SkyElm had never functioned in the way of a huge and supportive family. A studious packmate like Yuka would've been sniffed at and denigrated by Monroe and his cronies.

But it wasn't those cronies whom Lucas Hunter had executed. They'd all already been dead. The only ones left had been Monroe, Yariela, the two cubs, Salvador—a submissive packmate who wouldn't say boo to a goose—and two junior soldiers.

If the alpha of DarkRiver had stuck to killing Monroe and the latter two, Soleil would have been shocked but she'd have understood his reasoning; she wouldn't have agreed with it when it came to the soldiers—God no—but she'd have been able to see why he'd made that call. Lula and Duke had been baby dominants, but they *had* been dominants nonetheless. As such, they'd been bound to protect Monroe and could be seen as too loyal to him to set free.

The others . . . healer, cubs, a submissive. Dominants were meant to *protect* them. Yet he'd spilled their blood. It made no sense to her that the same man who'd given her a way out had also chosen an act so awful.

A knock on the door.

She watched as Tamsyn went to it, accepted something from the person on the other side before closing it again.

"Why am I alive?" Soleil blurted out.

. Tamsyn didn't startle at her blunt question. Instead, she passed over a small plate that held a helping of fresh rice and what looked to be chicken in a sesame sauce, with a side of steamed vegetables drizzled with what Soleil's nose told her was honey.

"You must be starving," the other woman said. "Eat first, then we'll talk. It's fresh—benefit of being in the heart of Chinatown."

Soleil's stomach rumbled right on cue. Her cheeks blazed. "Thank you." Food had so long been only fuel to her that she couldn't remember the last time she'd eaten a meal and enjoyed it—but that part of her had apparently awakened with her cat . . . and with Ivan. "How long have I been out?"

"Twenty-two hours, give or take. You went down late yesterday afternoon, and it's now midafternoon of the following day." The senior healer tapped the small screen on the bedside table to bring up the exact time and date. "You needed it. Especially since Lucas couldn't do anything to assist in your recovery."

A frown before Tamsyn said, "Why are you unlinked to an alpha? You're obviously an experienced healer and I've never known a single healer to choose the life of a loner. Most of us don't function well unless surrounded by pack."

Bleeding at the devastating blow her fellow healer had landed without intent, Soleil thrust the food into her mouth. It tasted of sawdust and tears, her throat threatening to tighten itself until she couldn't breathe.

Filaments of silver edged in orange-red in her mind, stars that wrapped around her. *Ivan.* She didn't know how or why, but she knew it was him. Her personal overprotective Psy. Looking after her as if he had every right to do so. She tugged the filaments and the stars around herself even as she indulged that grumpy thought. She'd rather be grumpy with Ivan than sad . . . just sad to the bone.

Tamsyn didn't push her to talk. Settling back in the armchair beside the bed, she looked at Soleil with the worried gaze of a changeling who'd been born to comfort and care. Soleil wanted to spill her guts, tell her all of it, but first she had to get her feet under her. She'd failed in her quest, but that didn't mean she couldn't confront Lucas Hunter and make him face the horror of his actions.

Never had Soleil been a coward, and she wasn't going to start now.

Not even if it meant her life.

. . .

THE DarkRiver healer didn't speak again until Soleil had cleared her plate. Then, taking it and putting it aside on the bedside table, Tamsyn said, "You carry so much pain in you, little sister."

Such a lack of judgment in her eyes that tears burned Soleil's irises.

"I wish I could take you home and care for you," Tamsyn continued, "but we must know who you are and why you're here. The times are too unsettled for us to simply accept an unknown into our midst."

Soleil couldn't process all of that. The idea of a pack ever just *accepting* anyone was alien to her. She'd always had to fight for her place by being so cheerful and friendly that people couldn't dislike her; even that might not have worked if she hadn't been born a healer.

You weren't cheerful with Ivan and he still likes you.

She squelched that annoying voice from the back of her brain. Ivan Mercant, she thought, wasn't the kind of man who went around "liking" people. He felt a responsibility toward her, that was all—and he struck her as someone who did not shirk his responsibilities.

An appealing trait in a man . . . if *she* wasn't the target.

Her cat rumbled its agreement.

But Ivan wasn't the problem right this minute. "Are you saying your alpha will execute me if I don't cooperate?" Soleil needed to know exactly how much rope she had before she hanged herself.

Tamsyn's eyebrows drew together in a deep frown. "Healers are not to be harmed," she said, as if that was an absolute truth. "And of all the people to *not* do such an act, Lucas sits at the very top of the list."

That was it. Soleil threw up her hands. "Why do people keep saying things like that as if I'm supposed to know something?!" Frustration burned away the calm with which she'd intended to approach this. "I don't know! Your alpha is a stranger to me!"

Tamsyn's lips tugged up at the edges. "There you are, little sister," she murmured, a feline gleam in her eyes. "I knew you were in there."

Shit. There went Soleil's intention of sliding under the radar until she wanted to act. But what was done was done. It looked like her temper had reappeared with her cat. She blamed Ivan. He was the one who'd poked her cat awake, hadn't he?

That cat prowled inside her mind, smug and happy because it had *found* him.

Meanwhile, the human side of her hadn't even known they'd been hunting a particular Psy.

"Lucas," Tamsyn said, her smile fading, "is the son of a healer." Gentle words. "She was murdered when he was a boy. Doesn't matter what you do or don't do, he will never touch you in violence."

Chapter 19

It's okay, mi ángel. Cry if you need to. Your Abuela Yari will hold you safe. Oh, my poor sweet Leilei.

—Yariela Castaneda to Soleil Bijoux Garcia (9 September 2067)

SOLEIL STARED AT the other woman, a brittle flame of hope fluttering to life inside her. Tamsyn was smart, well respected. Surely, *surely* she couldn't be so wrong about her alpha. But if she was right . . . What did that mean? Where was Yariela? Why had she vanished off the face of the Earth?

Soleil wasn't irrational. She'd done her research. After being told of Lucas Hunter's apparent actions, she'd looked for Yariela and the other survivors in every possible place they could be; she'd even used Yariela's passwords—which Yariela had never hidden from Soleil—to log on to the healer forum so she could see when Yariela had last accessed the site, even if she hadn't posted anything.

Nothing. No logged entries. Not since the massacre.

That, more than anything, had made Soleil believe Yariela must be dead. The forum had been the only online site her mentor used. She'd maintained no social media profile, but she'd loved hanging out with the older healers on the forum. They'd named themselves the Creaky Knees.

Soleil's own inbox had been full of worried messages, but despite how awful she felt about ignoring them, she hadn't replied. She'd believed that to do so would be to expose herself to DarkRiver and their murderous alpha before she could uncover what had happened to the rest of her pack. Because the fact that Yariela and six others had survived the initial massacre wasn't a mistake—three unaffiliated people had confirmed that piece of information for Soleil.

The first had been a neighbor of SkyElm's, the second a human priest who'd come by the pack's territory with a carload of food cooked by his parishioners and a willingness to listen and offer comfort.

"They weren't of my faith or my church," the dark-eyed man of some sixty years of age, his skin browned by the sun, had told Soleil. "SkyElm long preferred to mind its own business, so we had little contact with them. But at such a time, it's not about a particular creed, but about kindness, about compassion. I simply wished them to know they weren't alone."

He'd met Yariela face-to-face, and she'd thanked him, and spoken to him of the survivors, but she'd then hurried him off with the statement that her alpha was in no mood to have a stranger this close to their vulnerable.

The third confirmation had come from the hospital where Monroe had disavowed Soleil as a packmate. The orderly who'd dealt with him had remembered him. "He said his pack was only seven now," the slender human male had told Soleil when she began to hunt for the truth. "I remember because it was so sad. An entire pack decimated."

Throat thick, Soleil wanted to ask her questions aloud of Tamsyn, wanted to trust. Her cat strained toward this beautiful woman with her aura of maternal warmth. Stifling the urge because if she fell, she might break, might accept the unacceptable, she took the drink she'd set aside, finished it.

"I'm still really tired," she said afterward, the words tight. "Can I rest?"

Tamsyn rose to her feet. Bending down, she brushed her hand over Soleil's hair before pressing a kiss to her temple. Emotion clogging up her throat, Soleil couldn't speak until Tamsyn had left the room.

Even then, she sat there blinking for long moments until she could see again, her mind filled with memories of a small woman with delicate bones and skin of flawless ebony, her eyes a brown so dark they were endless.

Yariela was the only person who'd hugged and openly taken care of her after Soleil—quiet and withdrawn and crushed by grief—became part of SkyElm. Others had been nice to her in secret, but they'd been too weak to stand up to the dominants in public—and the dominants had all followed her grandfather's lead. He had been their alpha, after all.

A much younger Monroe had been his right hand back then.

Soleil had never blamed the ones whose care was given only in secret. Their pack had been broken long before the day their blood stained the snow. But they'd still been her pack, still been her family—and she would not rest until she knew what had happened to them.

She hadn't heard the click of a lock when Tamsyn left the room, but she knew there had to be a guard out there. As the healer had pointed out, Soleil was a dangerous unknown. Which left the window to the right. Before she explored that option, however, she got out of bed and checked out the other door in the room. As she'd expected, it went to the bathroom: the sink was to her left, the shower just beyond it, and the toilet in a private cubicle to the right.

A fluffy blue bathmat lay in front of the sparkling glass of the shower partition.

Someone had put a fresh set of clothing on the small vanity that held the sink. Fingering the material, she saw that it was stiff, new. She'd expected—and would've been happy—for it to have been used, from the stores the pack kept for members who found themselves coming out of a shift naked. Every pack kept such a stash of clothing in various places where packmates might gather.

Perhaps they hadn't wanted to risk her cat acting out. There was no way to completely wash out the scent threads of a pack from clothing that was worn by packmates on a regular basis. Those threads were often a thing of comfort. But Soleil wasn't pack. She was an intruder.

On top of the jeans, T-shirt, and sweatshirt were sealed packs of underwear.

There was no reason for her not to take a shower. Any escape attempt would have to be under the cover of darkness.

That in mind, she stripped and stepped under spray as hard as she could make it, so that it pummeled her skin. When she closed her eyes, she expected to see the dead, or the chaos from yesterday. What she saw were stars against velvet black. An endless sprawl, lovely and haunting and overlaid by a silvery web that emanated from a single dark star.

Wonder whispering through her veins, she found herself drawn to the dark star devoid of light. She should've been afraid. After all, what sat at the center of a web but a spider? Yet this dark star, it wasn't using the web to entrap people. It was doing something else to the stars hooked into the web. It was—

The water cut off.

Blinking it out of her eyes, she looked at the control panel and saw that it was set to eco-mode. She could've restarted it, but she was changeling, understood what it was to care for the land on which she stood. So she got out, clinging to the beautiful image that had bloomed in those moments where she'd expected only pain, only horror.

Suspicion had her scowling. It was Ivan. Of course it was. He was looking after her exactly as he'd threatened.

Cat and woman, both of them snorted . . . but she wasn't mad. Not when the result had been that haunting scene that had made her forget the blood and the grief for a pulse of time. She did wonder how he was doing it. Then again, the man had literally brought her back from the dead. What connection did that create? What bond did that build?

Her cat prowled inside her, missing him.

Mine, it thought again, and the human side of her unbent enough to admit that he was both wildly pretty and stubbornly courageous. He wasn't the kind of man who'd ever be comfortable with the label, but he'd been a hero on that street, holding the line under incredible pressure. And the intensity in those pale eyes . . .

A little shiver rippling over her skin, her body having woken from a long, numb sleep. It wasn't that she hadn't met other men over the past months. She had. Some of them had even hit on her. She'd had zero reaction to them; no desire and no anger. Just a physical and emotional blankness.

Neither had ever been an option with Ivan.

But she couldn't think about her fascination with the deadly Psy who'd found her broken body in the snow, didn't have time to figure out if her cat's reaction was some kind of strange imprinting.

The ocelot within snarled, insulted beyond measure.

The human half of her scowled, but both parts of her were in agreement on one point: she had to figure out how to get out of this place without being caught. According to Tamsyn, she was still in Chinatown, so DarkRiver hadn't taken her to the forested core of their territory.

Good.

The pack was incredibly security conscious when it came to the heart of their lands. The Chinatown HQ, by comparison, was relatively open. It had all the necessary security protocols, but as it was also set up to allow meetings with outside parties, it couldn't, by definition, be airtight.

She began to get dressed. Whoever had chosen the clothing had done a good job. Too good. The jeans fit snugly against her legs, and the T-shirt skimmed the lines of her body. While the sweatshirt—a dark gray—was loose, it was only fashionably so; Soleil felt exposed, all her weaknesses out in the open.

"Clothing is the least of my problems," she muttered, bringing herself back to harsh reality.

After finger-combing her hair, she walked out into the room—just as someone knocked on the door. Having caught Tamsyn's scent, she didn't hesitate to say, "Come in."

The healer poked her head just inside. "I wanted to let you know that I'm going to be here for a while, so just holler if you'd like to talk." A hesitation. "Are you sure you don't want to tell me why you're in the city?"

Tamsyn's gaze was patient, warm as she added, "Are you in trouble? Or scared of someone? We can help you if you are." The healer sighed when Soleil stayed silent. "I don't like leaving you closed up in this room, but we need to protect our vulnerable. Just . . . think about it, okay?"

A shift in the air currents as Tamsyn moved slightly and Soleil's entire world shifted on its axis, her heart kicking so hard it bruised. Either she was going truly insane, or she'd just caught a painfully familiar scent coming off Tamsyn. It belonged to a packmate. A Sky-Elm ocelot *cub*.

She tried to inhale deeper, confirm. But the scent vanished as quickly as it had appeared, a faint thread gone too soon. "I'm sorry," she said to the healer, her cat too confused to think straight. "I'm not ready to speak."

Eyes dark with worry, Tamsyn inclined her head. "I'll be here until about half past seven. My mate's taken our cubs and two of their friends to dinner at their favorite Chinatown restaurant—spic and span and in their best clothes." So much love in her voice. "I'm on tenterhooks to see the state of their clothing when they return."

Another tug on Soleil's changeling heart, another bite of hunger to join in, be part of a group, part of a pack.

Tamsyn left with one more encouraging smile.

Soleil waited only until the healer had closed the door behind herself before walking over to the window to check it out. It was one of those ones that slid up halfway, allowing her to look out into open air. Given her size in cat form, sliding out would be *just* doable.

The problem was that the window looked out into what appeared to be a side garden that belonged to DarkRiver. If she was right, this alley garden sat between two buildings owned by the pack.

While she couldn't see anyone watching her, she had no doubt that either the garden was under surveillance or there were guards posted at either end of the alleyway.

So she looked up.

Ocelots weren't arboreal by nature—but that didn't mean they couldn't climb with feline fluidity. From her vantage point, she saw that she was on the second floor, only one other floor above her. Easy enough to scale to get to the roof. Which was also no doubt under surveillance. Because DarkRiver was made up of cats, and they'd never forget that people could climb. But, she thought, what about the building to the back? That wasn't a DarkRiver property.

According to her research, that property was a private home. It didn't back directly onto the HQ, of course, a small buffer of land between, but it was close enough for a cat who didn't mind jumps. Soleil's cat had always liked those leaps, liked the sense of flying.

The jump was doable. But would DarkRiver have left that flank unprotected? Was that private home truly *private*? Or was it just held under a corporate identity that meant it didn't show up as pack property at first glance?

Since she no longer had her phone, she couldn't even look it up. The phone had been in a zippered pocket of her daypack. Gone. And with it, the last connection to her life.

The aeries had been stripped of personal items and closed up by the time she made it home, but she'd found a broken bracelet of Yariela's that had fallen into a gap in between empty drawers, as well as two painted stones the cubs had given her and she'd placed in her garden.

Mere fragments to remember an entire life. *Precious* fragments now lost.

Her lower lip trembled.

A flicker in her mind, the delicate spiderweb glittering to haunting life . . . this time in shades of silver shot with a striking pale blue. As she watched, the colors altered to a fiery orange edged with a red as dark as rage.

Wonder caught Soleil's breath all over again, the beauty of the construct no less beautiful for being edged in a tone so harsh. She clung to it as she considered her options.

"You know there's only one choice," Farah said from beside her, her chin propped up in her hands as she perched her elbows on the windowsill. "You need to find out the meaning of the scent on Tamsyn, confirm if it was real or . . . like me."

Eyes burning, Soleil didn't look directly at her friend; she never looked directly at Farah, not ready to face the awful forever truth. "How am I going to get to that other roof, though?"

This building hadn't been built as a prison, but it *had* been built with security in mind. There was no trellis that she could climb, no trees close enough for a cat to jump onto. Things a changeling mind had considered during the build.

Farah went as silent as the grave.

Agony tearing at her, Soleil slammed her hands against the window ledge.

That was when her eye fell on something she'd previously discarded: the fine decorative ledge that ran just below the window and seemed to go all the way around the building. It was a ledge far too slender for a leopard—or a human. Even a small human adult wouldn't be able to maintain their balance with nothing above them but air.

But she wasn't a leopard. Her changeling form was far smaller and more agile than theirs, her tail half the length of her body and built for balance. She might be too thin right now, in either form, but she wasn't weak, had made sure of that, her muscles in good working order.

She looked again at the ledge, narrowed her eyes.

Yes, her claws, sharp and curved, could grip it.

Crawling along the narrow space would take time. But it could be done. Especially under cover of darkness, when she could become a dappled shadow against the wall, a shadow that moved so very slowly that it caught no attention at all.

She visualized the climb in her mind, and as she did so, wondered if she'd be able to shift when the time came. Her cat hadn't emerged since the day everyone died. It had curled up into a ball deep inside her, and there it had stayed . . . until it saw Ivan.

It stretched luxuriantly inside her at the thought of him, and she felt its fur brush the inside of her skin, its claws prick the insides of her fingers. Oh yes, it was ready to come out again. And though it might be obsessed with Ivan, on one thing both parts of her were united: discovering the truth of what had happened to Yariela and the other survivors.

Chapter 20

Okay, y'all, we've discussed the whole wolf/bear food "situation." If one of those two changelings is your sweetie—or a possible sweetie—and they offer you food, consider it an engagement ring and start booking the mating ceremony venue.

Or, you know, run far, far away as fast as possible.

We jest, we jest! But while food *is* a powerful courtship ritual for many changelings, away from that context, it's also an act of pack love and care. The recipes in this edition of your *favorite* magazine celebrate those acts of love and comfort between packmates.

—From the July 2083 "Culinary Special" issue of *Wild Woman* magazine: "Skin Privileges, Style & Primal Sophistication"

IT COULDN'T HAVE been more than two hours from the time she decided to make the attempt to the point where she felt she had to risk it. The summer sun hadn't set yet, the world bathed in oranges and yellows.

Her preference would've been to wait till dark, but Tamsyn had mentioned staying around till half past seven and Soleil didn't want to risk missing her departure. She had no idea where the healer lived, or where she planned to go after leaving the HQ. And the only way to solve the mystery of the phantom scent thread that threatened to break Soleil's heart with hope was to track her, see where it led.

Another thing that had thrown a wrench in the works was that she hadn't simply been left alone in her room. First, a short and curvy brunette with subtly uptilted eyes and an open smile had knocked a couple of times, to check that she was all right and didn't need anything.

It had been strange and wonderful, her cat wanting to make friends with the other woman even though it knew it couldn't.

Not yet. Not before digging out the truth.

Monroe had always ranted and raved that DarkRiver thought it was too good for everyone else. Though Soleil knew her former alpha had been full of shit, she'd expected far different treatment for the simple reason that DarkRiver was a hugely powerful pack—and she was no one and nothing.

As it was, an older male juvenile with incredible bone structure, his hair light brown under his ball cap, and his eyes hazel with an unusual—she wanted to say almost *purplish*—tint to them had just dropped off a tray that held a mug of hot cocoa and a huge slice of cake.

"Tamsyn said you need to eat more—your body is close to breaking down muscle in order to fuel itself," he'd told her in a firm tone that she wasn't expecting from someone this young—especially when his voice was so clear and pure it threatened to distract her cat with its sheer aural beauty.

With a voice that hypnotic and a face that good-looking, this kid could grow up to be a rock star—or a cult leader.

"I'm no healer, man," he'd added with a shrug, his expression dubious, "but that doesn't sound good to me."

Since Soleil respected Tamsyn *and* had a weakness for cake, she'd taken the tray and done her best to get through the cake. It had proved unexpectedly heavy, and she'd quickly realized it was made with crushed nuts. Almond or pistachio, perhaps. A good way to pack in a significant hit of energy.

Soleil's stomach, however, could only hold so much, and she ended up leaving half the slice uneaten. It made her sad that she couldn't take it with her. Wasting cake was sacrilege—but she couldn't carry anything in her feline form.

A burp spilled out of her, an odd little rumble of a sound that made her cat rear back and pretend it didn't know her. Nope, not this creature that made such inelegant sounds.

She could almost hear Farah's giggle as she rubbed at her stomach. It remained concave, even though it felt as if she was full to her throat.

Stomach heavy or not, this was the best opportunity she'd get—DarkRiver usually gave her a half hour to forty-five minutes between checks. She'd have written it off as a security measure except they kept giving her things!

Cake, an extra blanket, a hot drink.

It bewildered her, how worried they seemed about her. She was, after all, an intruder.

Lucas is the son of a healer. . . . Doesn't matter what you do or don't do, he will never touch you in violence.

Heart aching for the boy the alpha had once been and confused by what to think of the man she'd considered a certain murderer only a day earlier, she walked to the window. Despite the lingering summer light, the world outside was quiet, haunted by all that had taken place so recently. No one was in the mood to be out and about.

The only other thing that might work in her favor was her cat's coloring and the pattern of her ocelot coat—this close to sunset, she should be able to become just another part of it against the pale tan of the external wall.

After stripping with quick efficiency, she made sure to put her clothing items in the laundry basket placed in one corner of the bathroom. Her parents might have been loners who embraced freedom above all else, but they'd also often packed up and left at a moment's notice.

As their child, Soleil had learned to be neat and tidy so as not to accidentally have her possessions left behind. And it would be rude to leave a mess, especially when everyone had gone out of their way to be kind to her.

"Ready?" she murmured to the other half of herself, still a little afraid the cat would balk. But it stretched, flexed its claws . . . and the world shimmered with light as her body broke into a million particles before re-forming into her other skin: a small cat of gold and orange with dark black patterns on its fur.

Her markings were distinctive, the black dots so close together they turned into lines in places. Twin black stripes ran down to the inner edges of large eyes designed to see the smallest movement, her ears erect and cupped. She was much smaller than a leopard or a jaguar, but that just meant she could slide through gaps that, to them, were impassable.

She had her scar in this form, too, a jagged line that bisected the fur of her face.

The cat shook itself to settle its fur into place, flicked the tail ringed by bands of black, then sniffed the air—and got a heavy wave of leopard scents in return. It reared back but didn't retreat.

Her cat had never been a coward.

Scared and sad, but not a coward.

Jumping easily onto the window ledge, she poked out her small and elegant head, then reached out to test the ledge with a single paw. Satisfied it was wide enough, the cat eased itself out onto that narrow strip. Part of its paws edged over the very side, but it ignored that. This was instinct, its focus on getting out of here—and to Ivan.

The human part no longer ascendant, Soleil rolled her eyes inside her furred skin. *He's not our priority*, she said.

The cat took a moment to yawn. But despite its desire to go to Ivan, it was the cubs that were at the forefront of its mind. Two tiny babies it had protected and shepherded around the forest more than once, amused by their antics even as it tried to be stern and teach them the proper way to do things.

Soleil padded slowly, oh so slowly, along the edge. And when she heard movement below, she froze. More leopard scents, heavy and strong. Would they smell her? In her favor was that she'd been around leopards the entire time since she was brought into the HQ.

She'd also slept for hours in a space thick with their scent.

It *might* give her just enough of a shadow scent that the people below would shrug off the part that didn't belong. Regardless, she didn't take the risk of moving.

Her ears pricked as voices began to drift up. She didn't dare alter her balance by attempting to look down, see them.

"No hits on her fingerprints or DNA," a male voice was saying. "Lucas says she's a cat, he's sure beyond any doubt. He just can't pin down the species."

"What about facial recognition?" Another unfamiliar voice, this one a woman.

"Still running," the first speaker said. "I'm hitting every database I can. Even managed to hack into the DMV."

"You're going to get arrested someday." A dry comment.

"Please, I'm too good to get caught. But even if she is in there, it's going to take some time. Facial rec takes a ton of computronic power."

"She still not talking?"

A grumble. "Healers. Obstinate as all hell and twice as bossy."

Laughter. "You're just grumpy Tammy put you on bed rest after that injury."

The grumble and the affection both startled Soleil. Those two were dominants, a wave of primal power in the air that made her cat's nostrils flare, but she could swear they considered Tamsyn their equal or maybe even more senior than them—and that they loved her.

Her cat wanted to whimper, need clawing at her. It *hated* being alone. Dreamed of a family like this one.

The voices faded as the cat fought its need to give voice to its pain, the two dominants wandering down toward the front of the building.

Soleil didn't worry about their hunt for her identity. They wouldn't find her in the DMV database. She'd never learned to drive—a lack that she'd cursed herself for many times over since she began her grief-maddened quest, but she still hadn't been able to make herself take that step. She didn't mind riding in cars, but to drive, to take control of a vehicle . . . No, she couldn't do it.

Her heart began to beat too fast, echoes in her mind of a ruined voice telling her she was sorry.

Baby, I'm . . . so . . . sorry. Get . . . out. Out, my . . . Leilei. Out . . . baby . . . the fuel . . .

The smell of burnt flesh, the tattoo of melted tires on asphalt, the pounding thunder of the rain, it came back in a crashing roar, like it had happened yesterday.

The animal opened its mouth, wanting to yowl in pain. She should've expected this. The human part had been ascendant for so long that the cat'd had no outlet for all the layers of its grief, and it was now getting shaky.

Stars in her mind, connected by that silvery-red spiderweb so lovely and delicate that the cat lifted a paw to bat against it. A mere touch of play, but it was enough to recenter her most primal half.

It began to pad its way along the ledge once more, using its claws and its tail to maintain its balance. It had to pass by one window on its way to the far edge. The cat stilled before nudging its head forward so it could sneak a look inside.

Not a bedroom, but a storage space set up with neat rows of shelving . . . through which Tamsyn moved with a small datapad in hand. The cat ducked back its head, fighting its natural tendency toward friendliness. Tamsyn was the most dangerous changeling to it now—she'd been close to Soleil, would recognize her scent if she caught a hint of it.

The only slice of good luck was that the window was fully shut. And when she dared another glance, it was to find that Tamsyn had her back to the window.

Heart thudding, her cat managed to get safely to the other side of the window.

It wasn't too difficult to reach the far edge, from where she gauged the distance to the rooftop on the other side. And realized she'd miscalculated. It was too far for even her cat to jump. Not wasting time, she turned right instead and kept on going along the ledge across the back of the building, looking for a tree, something that she could jump on to climb down to the ground.

Nothing and more nothing—until the large drainpipe that funneled water away from the roof and into what was most likely an underground water tank. Changelings didn't waste water when they could collect and recycle it. No leopard could've climbed down that drainpipe, their body weight far too heavy. It would've collapsed. But she had a feeling it would hold her far slighter weight.

She had nothing to lose.

The drainpipe gave a small groan when she jumped onto it, but it held. Deciding not to push her luck, she went down as fast as she could, parts of the pipe digging into her stomach as she slid down. The cat flattened its ears but kept going, leaving deep scratch marks on the plas.

The leopards would see that, of course, but she'd be long gone by then.

All at once, she was thumping onto the ground on her butt. *Ugh.* Her cat looked around to make sure no one had spotted that hideously embarrassing descent. No other ocelot would ever let her live it down.

But there were no ocelots here. Not unless that scent on Tamsyn had been true.

Driven by a sense of pounding urgency, she shook off her sore butt and ran around the side—and though she should've gone to the very front of the building and found a hiding spot from where she could watch for Tamsyn's exit, she went to a gate in the fence directly opposite where she'd come down.

The gate was closed but not locked.

Not worrying about who might see her, she shifted and unlatched it, then shifted back again. A naked woman would attract far more attention than a small cat that stuck to the shadows. Most people wouldn't see her in that form—and the ones who did would probably mistake her for a freakishly large housecat. Not a mistake that would hold on a closer look, but she didn't intend to let anyone get that close.

Sliding through the gate, she looked left then right, saw that the sidewalk was empty. Again, she should've gone right and made her way to the front of the building . . . but she went directly across the sidewalk and to a black car shaped as sleek as a bullet.

The passenger-side door slid back.

Her cat wasn't the least surprised to look up and see a Psy with eyes of piercing blue waiting for her. Bunching on her haunches, she launched herself into the passenger seat.

Chapter 21

Ivan Mercant: Telepath, 6.2, black hair, killer blue eyes, and ice-cold sexiness. Here's the tea, wild women. This fine specimen of manhood has long floated under our radar. How, we do not know. The man is so hot that certain bear ladies were willing to risk freezer burn to get close to him.

And it is thanks to our lovely bear readers in StoneWater that we now have knowledge of Mr. Ivan Mercant. They tell us he attended their alpha's mating ceremony to another Mercant (covered in our special mating issue!), slayed many a heart, and left without a backward look. Oh, ouch.

We know you're all wondering about the scary part of this description. Word is he's a security specialist—and that the bear dominants confirm they wouldn't pick a fight with him unless they meant it. Because the man doesn't play if you come for him or his.

Can we say *swooooooooon*?!

—From the "Scary but Sexy" column in the March 2083 issue of *Wild Woman* magazine: "Skin Privileges, Style & Primal Sophistication"

UNTIL THE MOMENT that a small cat of gold and black jumped into the passenger seat of his vehicle, Ivan hadn't known what he was doing here. Hadn't known why he'd canceled a comm meeting with his grandmother and left his apartment by stealth—because a Mercant always had a secret way out.

He'd just known he had to get here in time, and he had to do it without alerting the leopards. Now he stared at the stunningly gorgeous cat that sat there staring back at him with eyes so huge and wild that they held him captive. He had the most intense urge to stroke her fur but was rational enough to know she was a wild creature who hadn't given him the permission.

Somehow finding his footing, he said, "Your daypack is in the back seat," and pulled away from the curb.

But she hissed and clawed at his arm when he indicated that he was going to turn left. He looked down, changed the indicator to the right. "You want to be in front of the DarkRiver building?"

A nod from the cat who walked in his dreams.

"I'll find us a space where we won't be noticed straight off the bat," he said, "but we won't be able to hang around there for long. Cats see everything." The leopards might as well be part of his own family, they were so conscious of intruders and those who might present a risk to their pack.

The bears back in Moscow were security conscious, too, but they were more in-your-face about it. The cats had stealth down to an art. Or as Valentin would put it, they knew how to be sneaky.

Exactly like Mercants.

The ocelot who was Soleil slipped in between the seats to the back—flicking its tail across Ivan's chest as it did so, the pressure light but conscious. Ivan saw a shimmer of light in his peripheral vision, kept that vision directed resolutely forward as things rustled in back. He hadn't looked inside her bag—every part of his training said he should have—yet he hadn't.

Because that was Soleil's bag.

However, there'd clearly been a change of clothing in there, because when Soleil slipped back through the gap between the seats in her human form, she was wearing a large gray sweatshirt over thick black tights. She even had shoes—thin trainers, but better than bare feet if she had to get out on the city streets.

Ivan liked clothes—they allowed him to present himself to the world exactly as he wished. He also knew how Soleil had liked to present herself. Full of color and shine, sparkle and joy. But that had been before the massacre, before an ax in the back and a living burial in the snow.

His hands tightened on the steering wheel.

"I need to follow the healer." Her voice was husky, her body straining forward.

"Tamsyn Ryder." All part of his research into the pack. "Why?"

When she didn't answer, he glanced at her, at this woman who'd hooked herself inside his soul. "You need me and I don't work without full information. That's how people get dead." And he'd do nothing to bring her to harm.

A narrow-eyed glance. "Why are you even here?"

He thought of the sensation he'd felt against his face in the apartment, of fur and the slightest touch of claws. Softness and hardness. Strange and inexplicable. "Because you called me."

Feline eyes in a human face. "I'm not Psy—I don't have that power," she said, but there was something in her voice that said she wasn't quite certain. And the way she looked at him, as if seeing straight through him . . . no, it wasn't comfortable.

He didn't want her to see, didn't want her to know. Because then, she'd walk away again, and he'd lose even this fragile moment of time where she didn't see him as a monster.

Thief.

A low whisper from his conscience, a quiet reminder that he was using her lack of memory against her, that he was stealing this time.

It's only for a drop in the timeline of her life, he argued back. *I'll be removing myself from the situation soon enough. The truth would only make her wary when she has no reason to be wary. My sole purpose is to keep her safe.*

Gut tight because he *knew* that lying by omission was still lying, he said, "I'm very good at what I do," his voice ice tipped in frost as he fought the warring forces within. "I can help you, but only if I have all the data."

"She has a scent on her." Soleil's voice was rough. "I need to know the origin."

Ivan was a Mercant; it took him a split second to make the connection. "You're looking for someone." Someone important enough to her that she'd risked execution by coming uninvited into the territory of another predator.

The fact that Soleil Bijoux Garcia was a woman who'd fight for the people who mattered to her, it fit absolutely with all he knew of her. And if the spider's mind flared a touch red at the edges in a biting jealousy, Ivan was in control enough to shut that down right then and there.

It was far better for her that she'd decided Ivan wasn't one of her people. Because the woman beside him? She wouldn't let go once she committed. And in so doing, she'd have gone down with him.

Not acceptable.

An answer from every part of his psyche.

Soleil didn't respond to his supposition, her attention on the black SUV that had pulled to a stop in front of DarkRiver HQ. A tall dark-haired man with wide shoulders and the build of a changeling soldier got out of the driver's seat, just as Tamsyn Ryder exited the front door of the HQ in the fiery light of sunset.

"Nathan Ryder," Ivan murmured to Soleil. "Tamsyn's mate."

Nathan kissed Tamsyn, was kissed in turn, Tamsyn's palm gentle against his cheek. The slightest movement, Nathan leaning into her touch as he closed his fingers over her wrist, two people in such perfect harmony that even Ivan, with his stunted emotional growth, couldn't miss it.

He'd seen the beginning of such a bond with his cousins and their mates, but those ties were yet new. This was a bond matured by time and season after season of life . . . of love.

It struck him then, the depth of what he would never know, never so much as touch. All he'd ever have were memories of what could've been a beginning. It was more than he'd ever expected before Soleil, but an angry part of him that he could never allow freedom raged against the unfairness of that.

Ivan wasn't the one who'd chosen to inject himself with a toxic drug.

Yet he was the one who had to pay the price.

When the Ryders broke apart, Tamsyn opened the back passenger door and seemed to be speaking to someone in the back. Her mate held the front passenger-side door open for her when she closed the back door and turned to get in the car. Then she was inside, and Nathan Ryder went round to get into the driver's seat.

He was the oldest of the DarkRiver sentinels, but the added experience just made him more dangerous: the muscle on him was fluid, his movements of a changeling in the prime of his life.

"Tamsyn said her mate had taken their cubs and their friends to dinner," Soleil said, a haunted kind of need in her tone.

Ivan couldn't stand it, her aloneness. But he also knew that he wasn't what she needed—or wanted—to assuage it. So he gave her what he could: "The Ryders have twin boys."

DarkRiver was protective about information when it came to their cubs, so Ivan had only picked up this piece of it by watching. He'd seen the two boys with their mother, the three sometimes accompanied by other children, including a much smaller girl with eyes of panther green: Nadiya "Naya" Hunter.

Lucas Hunter and Sascha Duncan's child.

"That's what healers are built for." Soleil's voice was an ache of deso-lation. "For family. For pack." She spoke again before he could respond. "Can you follow them? I need to know." Anguish in every word.

"Yes." Ivan waited until the SUV was almost out of sight before pulling into the flow of traffic.

Soleil's body all but vibrated with emotion. "You're falling too far behind," she said at one point, her hands braced on the dash in the quickly falling darkness. "You're going to lose him."

Ivan maintained his pace. "The easiest way to get caught tracking is to be obvious about it. Nathan also currently has his mate and chil-dren in the vehicle." Predatory changelings were never more a threat than when they were in protective mode. "Any closer and he'll tag us."

Soleil's claws—small, perfectly formed blades—sliced into the leather-synth of the passenger seat. Jerking, she looked down, retracted her claws at once. "I'm so sorry." Hot blooms of color on her cheeks.

"It's nothing, a simple repair."

"I still shouldn't have done it." Soleil folded her arms across her chest, to make sure it didn't happen again. "I just—" A harsh exhale, then in a quiet, quiet voice she admitted the fear that haunted her. "I'm so scared I'm imagining it, imagining what I want to be true."

The man in the driver's seat, so icy and controlled, said, "We'll find you some answers today." And though his voice betrayed nothing, her cat snarled and swiped a claw through the air.

Glad to have something else on which to focus, she looked at him, *really* looked at him . . . and saw the tension in the line of his jaw, the vein that throbbed down the side of his neck. His shoulder muscles were tight, the hands he had on the steering wheel locked around the hard plas.

Her fingers flexed against her as she fought the urge to reach out, stroke back his hair, rub the tension from his nape. Strange, but she didn't think this lethal man would reject the touch.

Her cat rubbed against her skin, aching to reach out. Hating that he was hurting.

Things inside her clenched in pain that felt too intimate between two near strangers.

"Can I touch you?" It felt as if she didn't need to ask, her cat sure he'd given her permission already, would welcome the contact, but skin privileges weren't a thing to be taken. She had to be certain.

His spine went even stiffer, but he gave a curt nod.

She put her fingers on his nape without further discussion, her need to soothe him a raw compulsion. The contact burned. She jerked away her hand, stared at her fingertips.

Nothing.

Wary, she tried again. His skin was cooler than her own, and the burn, she understood at last, had been pure primal sensation. Her heart thudded, her skin hot and her breasts suddenly feeling fuller.

Oh yeah, her body *liked* him, wanted to melt him—and melt *for* him.

But this wasn't about her. Focusing on him, she used gentle and careful strokes on his nape and the sides of his neck to ease the tension that had turned him to all but rock. As a healer, she was used to having patience, but this . . . it wasn't about patience. She liked doing this. Liked touching him. Liked knowing it was helping.

Increment by increment perhaps, but it *was* working.

Her toes curling, she leaned a little more toward him, distracted by the spice that underlay the cool breeze of his scent. A warning that this man would bite. That was fine. She was a cat. She had claws.

The truck in front of them turned off—and Ivan turned off with it.

Soleil hissed, breaking contact with his skin, all thoughts of hazy pleasure overridden by panic. "What are you doing? They're going straight."

"They're headed home." A cool response.

"You can't know that!" She twisted in her seat in a vain attempt to keep the main highway in sight. "They could be going—"

"Nathan Ryder has his family with him and he's on the road directly to DarkRiver territory. I know where they live."

Perspiration breaking out over her skin, Soleil rubbed her hands on the thighs of her tights. "What? How?" DarkRiver was notoriously protective of its people.

"Because she's a healer." Just like the stressed and panicked cat in the seat next to Ivan—the same cat who'd just touched him with an infinite tenderness that threatened to drive him mad with thoughts of what could've been.

He might live for decades yet in the cage for which he was destined, and he knew he'd rerun her touch over and over again in his mind each and every day. Just as he'd rerun their time in the forest.

Fragments of another life to last him through an eternity of lonely madness.

It took everything he had to stay on the topic. This was important to her, and he would finish it before the spider took control. "The Ryder home is on the edge of the territory, and while access to it isn't open, it's far easier to get to than any other part of the territory."

He was in no doubt that DarkRiver had guards everywhere, however. Leopards were masters of stealth.

Again—exactly like Mercants.

"DarkRiver allows anyone to seek Tamsyn's help?" Disbelief in every syllable.

"Word on the street is that while she doesn't run an open practice, she'll stitch you up or treat you if you turn up on her doorstep—doesn't matter if you're Psy, human, or changeling."

Ivan had been as surprised as Soleil when he'd unearthed that fact. Changelings had a reputation for being closed units; they were so powerful *because* they were so untrusting of outsiders and so protective of their own. In many ways, the Mercant family functioned exactly the same. No one got into their family without significant background checks and extreme vetting.

No one but the people with whom Ena Mercant's grandchildren kept falling in love.

Ivan wondered what she'd think of his cat, then immediately squelched the possessive thought. Soleil wasn't his, could never be his. Not if he wanted her to have any kind of a life. There could be no cubs for Ivan, no colorful sparkling existence in the outside world.

Monsters lived in the dark.

"DarkRiver," he said past the crushing truth of that thought, "is seen as the protector of this entire city. Any local-body politicians have far less sway than the pack, though the pack doesn't appear to wield that power for political gain. It's a complicated situation."

"You're sure you can get us to their home?" Soleil rubbed her palms on her tights again, then lifted her hands to the soft beauty of her hair and began to braid it. "You can drop me off close by, and I'll sneak up in my ocelot form."

He stored away another memory, of her fingers so nimble in her hair. It was the kind of thing a woman might do in front of her mate. He'd never hold that position, but no one could begrudge him such a small theft. Of but a moment.

"Leopard guards will eat you before you see them coming."

A rumble from Soleil's throat, a reminder that she was far from helpless. "I've been keeping myself alive on my own for a long time."

Ivan went to reply, was cut short by a sudden wave of memory in his mind. But . . . they weren't his memories. A tall and thin body wove through a large crowd, contained and alone and *hurting*.

Alone. Alone. Alone.

It was a pounding internal beat alongside the noise of the crowd, the brush of arms and shoulders as people moved past, the high shrieks of a little girl who rode on her father's shoulders.

Not his memories. Hers.

Chapter 22

Access to the severed section of the PsyNet has so far proved impossible to gain. Multiple attempts have been made by various parties across the Psy spectrum, including from Designation A and Designations Tk-V and E. All have failed.

—Message to the rest of the Ruling Coalition from Kaleb Krychek

THE QUEEN OF the Scarabs took in her domain.

The barriers she'd designed were holding, the ring of dead space around the island a total psychic emptiness.

Excellent.

No one that she didn't bring in would be able to set foot on this island. It was now the perfect space for her to test her long-term plans. Because she did not intend to reign only over a single small island.

This was just the beginning of her conquest of the PsyNet and her attendant subjugation of its populace. "Step by step," she murmured as endless power rippled through her web, her Scarabs small infernos of energy. "Piece by piece. It will all fall. *They* will all fall."

Chapter 23

Your pack is the heart. The alphas who fuck up are the ones who start to
think they're the most important element of a pack.

—Lucas Hunter, alpha of DarkRiver, to
Remington "Remi" Denier, alpha of RainFire

"I'LL BITE YOU if you keep ignoring me." A threat made in a sharp
tone of voice that cut through the sudden vision that had hit Ivan—of
moving through a crowd wrapped in a cloak of aloneness.

Shaking it off, he said, "Unless you're hiding something, you don't
have the skills to bypass trained DarkRiver soldiers."

"Hmph." She held on to the end of her braid.

Lifting his hand toward her, he said, "Here. On my wrist." He'd
slipped a black elastic band over it this morning . . . for no reason.
He'd just done it.

A cat prowled in his mind, an edge of smugness to it.

And Soleil's fingers touched him again as she rolled the band gently off over his hand. He knew at that moment that he'd never again
be without a band for her hair. Even in his cage, he'd wear one, and
he'd dream of the day he could offer it to her again.

Foolish, stupid dreams.

Didn't matter. They were his.

Another unexpected image in his mind, of a small cat creeping through the grass toward him, a cat with markings similar to Soleil's but its body much smaller. Then it was bunching that tiny body and launching itself at him.

He jolted within, but only so he could catch the cub. But they were gone, mist through his hands. And he knew right then. She was looking for a child. "I'll get you in. But we'll have a very short window of time to get in and out—if you intend to do violence, however, we won't make it out alive."

DarkRiver soldiers were some of the most highly skilled he'd ever seen; not only did they have the advantage of natural feline skills, it was obvious they'd trained those skills to a knife-sharp edge. They had to have been ruthlessly strong in the first place to hold their territory against the SnowDancer wolves—and now that the two packs were allied, it was highly probable that leopard and wolf trained together.

Underestimating them would be a serious—and probably fatal—mistake.

Even his cousin's brash alpha bear mate, Valentin, had been known to slam down a tankard of beer and say, "Lucas's cats are lethal. No one sees them coming when they don't want to be seen." A grin that creased his cheeks as he shot his mate a private look. "Good thing I know how to get along with sneaky cats."

The only reason Ivan knew he could get Soleil through to the Ryder home tonight was that—if the schedule held to what he'd previously observed—the soldier on patrol duty near their entry point would be a junior in training. As to why he'd observed the security protocols—because all information was power.

The choice of guard was likely because Nathan Ryder was at home during those days and well able to protect his mate and cubs. A good opportunity to give a younger member of the pack live training. Any mistakes wouldn't be terminal.

"If you're thinking about entering their home, forget it." He had to set the right expectations or she'd hurt herself through lack of knowledge. "Nathan is deadly, and while I can hold my own against him, it'll leave me with no ability to protect you. And Tamsyn can take you out."

He felt more than saw her head snap toward him, her scowl black. "I'm not a weakling."

He thought of her broken body in the snow, and of the courage it must've taken to go out there in the midst of such brutal carnage. "I know. But DarkRiver trains *all* its people—even submissives and healers. She's also a mother with cubs to protect. She'll rip off your head before you see her coming."

Ivan had needed no one to tell him that the maternal drive to protect would eclipse even the healer tendency toward gentleness. Not every mother was protective—he knew that all too well—and, from what he'd observed, Tamsyn Ryder allowed her boys a lot of freedom. But she also always put herself on the street side when they walked on the sidewalk, and even at her most relaxed, it was clear that she knew where her children—and any other cubs in her care—were at all times.

She reminded Ivan strongly of Ena. No harsh orders, no screaming or yelling, no rules so tough they stifled growth. But all the cubs listened when Tamsyn told them to do something. And they looked at her with the absolute and pure trust of children who knew she was the adult; they didn't have to worry—because she'd handle anything that came at them.

Ivan had never known that kind of childish freedom until he came face-to-face with Grandmother. And then, he'd understood it down to the bone. As he understood that Soleil would one day grow to have that same calm presence, that same warm steel to her. He'd caught glimpses of it already in her determination to find the person she sought . . . and in her tenderness with him, a man who was nothing to her.

Now she folded her arms. "You're right," she admitted in a grudging tone. "But I don't know if I'll be able to find the scent outside." She
went to thread her hand through her hair, pulled back when she remembered the braid. "Whatever happens, I'll get an answer tonight."
Fierce, implacable will. "Even if that means I go up to their door and
knock."

"What's your plan B?" Ivan always had a plan B, and he'd come up
with one for her if needed. "If you don't find what you're looking for?"

"My original aim was to kill Lucas Hunter."

Soleil didn't know why she'd blurted that out. She kept on crossing
lines with Ivan, but it didn't feel like crossing lines. It felt natural, as
if they'd known each other in another lifetime.

A deep pang, skirts whipping around her legs as she ran through
a forest while laughing and looking back at someone who was chasing
her. She wasn't scared. She was exhilarated, playful.

Ivan's voice snapped the gauzy thread, the images fading into gray.
"Your original aim? Has it changed?"

She squeezed her eyes shut, rubbed a fist over her heart. "It was a
ridiculous aim from the start. Grief-crazy thinking. I could never take
him out."

"If you could, would you?"

Soleil shook her head, accepting the truth that Farah had been
urging her toward from day one. "I saw who he is to so many people
on that street yesterday. I felt the connections that bind him to countless others." A burn in her eyes. "How could I, as a healer, end his life
knowing that the flow-on effect would be catastrophic?"

Opening her eyes, she dashed away tears. "This city is stable.
DarkRiver is stable. If I hurt him, I betray all it means to be a healer—
but if I do nothing, I can't live with myself. So I've decided."

She stared straight ahead. "If I don't get the answer I want tonight,
if it's all a dream created by grief, I'll confront him. Ask him why."

She could feel Ivan's attention as he waited for her to tell him the rest, but Soleil couldn't speak. She hadn't spoken to anyone about the loss of her pack, about all the dead, all the blood. And now, today, when she parted her lips, all that came out was silence. While inside her head played two cubs in the grass. They'd been so mischievous, so intent on creeping up on her and pouncing.

She'd always known they were there, of course, their small bodies making the grass rustle as they crept along on their stomachs. But she'd pretended to be startled, pretended to fall back onto the grass as they "attacked" her. Such small, warm bodies wriggling on top of her in excitement at having made a successful hunt.

She'd growled and grabbed them close to her chest, and they'd nuzzled at her.

Her hand lifted to her cheek, the echo of their small furry faces against her an almost tactile sensation. Her throat closed, the knot of grief in her chest expanding until it filled every part of her.

She could barely breathe, each inhale jagged shards in her lungs. So when that silvery web shimmered into her mind, stronger, thicker, even more dazzling, she grabbed hold of it, wrapped it around her like a glittering blanket, and used it as a shield against the grief.

It tasted of Ivan. Of course it did.

And somehow, in the strange comfort offered by the beautiful stone frost of the man who'd saved her life and now thought he had rights to it, she found her voice. "My pack is dead. SkyElm is dead."

"There were survivors."

"Yes, seven survivors—and me."

Ivan didn't question the way she voiced that, simply listened.

"A human neighbor told me after I finally remembered myself and came home." She'd learned of Monroe's rejection by then, but she hadn't come back for her erstwhile alpha. "The neighbor had lived next to the pack a long time." So long that even Monroe had accepted him.

"Only seven," she murmured, her heart breaking all over again. "But it was more than none. It was enough for us to start again.

Then . . ." She exhaled on a full-body shudder. "Then they all vanished one night, and when the neighbor went looking, he found blood in the aerie that belonged to my former alpha."

Still, she had hoped. Knowing who Monroe had been, she hadn't been surprised that he'd ended in blood. "After seeing the blood, our neighbor got in touch with a nonpredatory changeling he knew from his work. That person picked up the scent of a leopard."

Their reaction had been stark terror.

"It took me a long time to track down who the leopard might've been. A lot of rumors, a lot of whispers, but in the end it came down to this: my alpha, Monroe, did something to bring DarkRiver's wrath down on him. Lucas Hunter executed him."

"A rumor?"

"No, that last part isn't rumor." Black-and-white images in her mind, the text of the message crisp and clear. "Such executions are listed in a master document that was set up as an adjunct of the Peace Accord that ended the Territorial Wars. It's to stop revenge attacks when the execution was warranted.

"I'm not senior enough to have access to the document, so I don't know why Monroe was executed. But I have a friend in another pack—a librarian—whose alpha has openly said that no one has any argument with Lucas Hunter's actions."

"Your alpha broke a changeling law that couldn't be forgiven."

"It's the only thing that makes sense. And Monroe . . . he wasn't a good person." She felt no loyalty to the man who'd made her feel unwanted since childhood, then flat-out disowned her. "He was a bully and I think he picked the wrong target."

"Yet you wanted to kill Lucas Hunter."

"Because there were *seven* survivors." She tugged the silver web tighter around herself in an attempt to ward off the chill that was the incipient death of hope. "Monroe and six others: our senior healer, Yariela; a submissive packmate; two young soldiers—and two cubs.

"All gone without a trace. My librarian friend was also able to confirm that SkyElm is now a dead pack. Our line no longer exists in any of the records kept among changelings, and our territorial lands have been forfeited back into the trust that holds open territories."

She strangled the sob that wanted to escape; tonight wasn't about tears but about answers. But she couldn't stifle the pain that bled into her words. "I need them to be alive, Ivan. If they're not . . ."

"Is there any other reason your pack would be listed as dead?"

"No. It's tradition for a pack name to be put into a holding pattern even when they have no alpha and so need to join another pack. It leaves room for a child of the original pack to one day pick up the mantle. A pack is never listed as dead unless there are no surviving members."

She'd made very certain of her understanding of that point. "But my pack stops at the moment of Monroe's death. There is no continuity, no future possibility. And my friend confirmed that no one has had any contact with the survivors."

Ivan could see why Soleil believed what she did, but he was a hundred percent certain that she was wrong. Everything he knew of Lucas Hunter told him the man was a protector. He might be aggressive in his defense of his pack, but that didn't extend to harming innocents caught in the crossfire. Ena, too, had been known to get those innocents out of the way, even when she was on a quest for vengeance.

True alphas didn't need to subjugate the vulnerable to be powerful.

But Soleil needed to know the truth without question—so he would help her find out. With that in mind, he got them back on the road toward leopard territory—but he pulled off onto a dirt track before reaching the official start of the highly secure zone. After driving for about ten minutes, he brought the car to a stop in the shadow of multiple forest giants.

This area was just far enough out from the pack's core Yosemite territory that it wasn't as heavily patrolled. He'd spotted a number of sensors, but two individuals shouldn't set off any alerts. It could easily be members of the pack out for a stroll. Because, as far as he could tell, there were no cameras.

It made sense given the precautions that kicked in beyond this point.

Stepping out into the soft dark of a night lit only by a half moon, he led Soleil along the path he'd already mapped out in his head. They walked in silence until he said, "Will you tell me why Monroe refused to claim you?" If the alpha hadn't already been dead, Ivan would've done the task.

That's what healers are built for. For family. For pack.

The devastation in her voice was not a thing Ivan would ever forgive. And Monroe had sentenced her to that agonizing aloneness with the full knowledge of what he was doing.

"I failed to protect the pack," Soleil said flatly. "Monroe told me so when we met in the midst of the massacre, both of us covered in blood and close to exhaustion. He screamed at me that I'd failed, that I was pathetic, that I had no right to call myself a packmate."

"Healers heal. It's an alpha's job to ensure that the pack is protected." Ivan's voice was a stone honed to a killing blade. "I know a bear alpha. He would've eaten your alpha alive for speaking such an ugly and dishonorable lie."

She swallowed hard. "Monroe's mate and child died in the massacre. I couldn't do anything to help them." Their blood had flowed like water, drenching the soil to a viscous darkness. "I think he must've gone a little mad from the loss."

"A healer's heart is a too-kind thing at times, Lei." He lifted a finger to his lips on the last word and she realized they'd reached the boundary from where they'd have to move in absolute silence.

"Be sneaky like a cat," Ivan murmured.

She stared at him. That hadn't sounded like a Psy thing to say. But she'd ask him about that later. For now . . . she'd be sneaky like a cat.

Chapter 24

Loving
Extraordinary
Ocelots *(*Teacher's note: interesting choice, K. Tell me why it fits.)*
Playful
Aleine!
Roaming
DarkRiver
Stealthy

—Completed school word challenge on subject of
the student's choice by Keenan Aleine (age 7.5)

SOLEIL'S OCELOT ROSE to the surface of her mind, taking over her movements. Her feet were light on the fallen leaf debris, her body sliding through the forest with the comfort of a creature at home. Because though this wasn't her territory, it felt more hers than any city ever would.

Beside her, Ivan was a ghost. If she hadn't known he walked right beside her, she'd have doubted he was even there, the cloak of stealth he'd wrapped around himself impenetrable.

It annoyed her. She wanted to poke at him to get a response, barely restrained the very catlike urge.

Ivan held up a hand, the movement sharp.

She curled fingers into her palms, her heart squeezing, an image of the cubs in her mind. *Please, please be alive.*

That was when she caught a faint scent on the air currents. The hairs on her nape bristled, ice in her veins. Touching Ivan's arm to catch his attention, she mouthed *leopard.* The half moon lit up the night enough that he saw her.

A quick nod, after which he tested the direction of the wind, and indicated that the two of them should stand exactly where they were, in the shadow of a tree with enormous roots so tangled it was a piece of art. She did so in silence, her ears pricked for any hint of sound, of a presence . . . but her pulse still kicked like a horse at the gleam of black on gold that passed in the distance.

Biting down hard on her lower lip, she tried to control the beating of her heart, though she knew even the leopard's sharp hearing wouldn't be able to discern that from such a distance. Far more likely that he'd catch her scent, but the leopard moved on, unaware of the two watchers who stood frozen in the night.

Her ocelot allowed its muscles to soften.

Ivan turned toward her right then, a cobweb of stars in his eyes. It was gone the next second, that silvery network that both haunted and protected her, and he was nudging her to move on. They didn't talk, but she never lost her awareness of Ivan, the lethal stealth of him a love song to her cat.

A glimpse of light through the trees.

Her pulse was a racehorse by the time they hit the final edge of trees, beyond which lay a large yard. On the left was a garden lovingly tended that held thriving vegetables with large leaves and rounded fruits, while to the right sat a wooden climbing frame full of ladders and ropes and all kinds of other things that rambunctious cubs would appreciate as they learned their bodies and their skills.

When she went to go that way, Ivan snapped out a hand, clasped her forearm. "They'll have cameras watching the back of the property." Not an ounce of emotion in his tone, but his grip on her told a different story. "Motion-activated lights are a guarantee."

"I need to see if there's a scent on the play equipment," she whispered. "It's the best possible spot." She tried to think, but her mind was in chaos, because tonight, she would know. Good or bad or crushing, she would know.

"You're much smaller in your ocelot form."

The haze cleared. "Yes. I'll shift." God, she could kiss him right now. "I may not set off the sensors and even if I do, all they'll see is a small feline shadow they might dismiss as a large housecat."

"If an alarm does go off, you'll have a very short window of time." He paused. "We may be able to slip out if you run back to me the *instant* the lights come on or you hear an audible alarm. Nathan Ryder won't leave his family and cubs unprotected to chase after us, and the young soldier on duty is someone I can handle."

Soleil hesitated, looked at him. "You won't hurt him?" He was just a boy, one who'd been given a duty to perform and who was probably incredibly proud of it.

Ivan gave a curt nod. "I can take him out without doing any permanent harm. That won't be the case with Nathan. If I come up against him, it'll be a battle to the death."

So make sure it doesn't come down to that, was the unspoken warning.

Gut clenched, she went to drop her hands to the bottom of her sweatshirt and peel it off over her head when she caught a movement in an upstairs window at the back of the house.

She halted, frowned. "Do you see that?"

Ivan followed her gaze. "My night vision isn't as acute as yours, but yes, I can see movement."

"It's a child." Her eyes widened. "Good grief, he seems to be dropping a rope of knotted sheets out the window." Mouth falling open, she watched as a small and nimble body scrambled carefully down the rope before jumping to the ground and waving to the other face that had appeared at the window.

That body came down far more slowly and with care, nowhere near as confident as the first. But they weren't done yet. Number three followed, this child even more hesitant, but they were encouraged on by big gestures from the two below and by whoever it was that remained at the top.

When the third child finally made it to the ground, they were caught by small helping hands. The most confident one patted the child on the back, clearly telling them they'd done a good job.

Her heart *melted*. Naughty cubs were a sight she'd missed so much.

Then came another sleek, fast little body scrambling down the rope.

She watched in silence as the four small bodies streaked toward the climbing frame. And she saw that they were all in pajamas, their feet bare and their hair tousled.

Giggling softly, the four began to clamber up onto the frame.

Right as a much smaller feline raced unexpectedly from around the side of the house to join in the fun. A housecat, she realized, even more astonished. It appeared the housecat was a pet, because it was stroked and petted, and welcomed. A housecat kept by leopards, she thought with a shake of her head, wondering if she wasn't in some childhood storybook.

"The sensor lights should've come on," Ivan murmured, his eyes on the children. "The Ryders would never permit the twins and their friends to be so unsupervised." He looked toward the back window from which poured golden light, said, "The parents are watching." It wasn't a question, but a statement. "That's why the external lights haven't come on."

Her heart twisted again at the idea of two indulgent leopards letting the cubs believe they were getting away with such innocent mischief. The children just playing long past their bedtime. But . . . it was more than that, she realized slowly.

The two confident ones—little boys with dark hair—were encouraging and helping the other two, even though at least one of the other two looked to be a fraction older. The boys were whispering that the other children could do it when they tried something, and they were cheering them on when they succeeded.

The night was still, quiet, and she was so overwhelmed by the mischievous beauty of the moment that it took her a long time to understand what she was seeing. It had been eighteen months. Children grew an enormous amount in eighteen months. Their hair grew longer or was cut in different ways, and their bodies changed from pudgy and baby soft to longer and more angular.

She still couldn't believe it, her blood a roar in her ears . . . until the night wind shifted and blew across multiple scent threads. Leopards, small and tangled in the same web of scents that surrounded Tamsyn, but below that and not as dominant were scents that sang to every part of her ocelot's heart.

"Razi and Natal." The names whispered out of her, so quiet that she wasn't certain how Ivan heard her.

But he did, and he said, "They're yours?"

She nodded in a jagged burst. "The tallest boy, and the girl." Happy and healthy and alive, and playing with their two impish leopard cub friends.

She knew she should stay in place, knew she should think this through, but her cat had been patient far too long. And it had been alone far too long. Shoving up to the surface of her skin with no argument from the human side of her, it took over in a shower of light. Her clothes disintegrated off her. A matter of moments and she'd shed her human skin, and now stood there in her ocelot form.

She looked up, met the frost and stone of Ivan's gaze.

She half expected him to try to stop her, but he just melted back into the dark. She knew that he would watch and if she was under threat, he would intercede. Ivan would always protect her. It was in her bones, that knowledge.

Young as they were, none of the children had spotted the shift happening on the far edge of the yard, but the two leopard cubs' heads snapped up the instant she stepped out of the shadows. They yelled out, "Dad! Mom!" without hesitation, giving up their surreptitious play in the face of danger.

Natal and Razi turned toward her, and for a moment she thought they'd forgotten her. It wouldn't have surprised her. They were so young. But even as the back door slammed open and lights flooded the yard, both children ran toward her with yips of excitement, their bodies shifting midrun in a shower of sparks so that when their small bodies hit her own, they were in the forms of ocelot cubs.

TAMSYN grabbed Nathan's arm and though he was a DarkRiver sentinel, aggressive protectiveness built into him, he didn't shrug her off. "Boys."

The twins ran back at their father's single command, positioning themselves beside their parents. Tamsyn had known they wouldn't run into the house, not when their friends were still out here. She was fairly certain Jules was going to grow up to be a dominant who'd head into soldier work, Rome a healer, both of them with protective streaks a mile wide.

Meanwhile, their adored pet, Ferocious, perched on top of the climbing frame, hissing at the intruder.

The intruder didn't care, wasn't watching. She was . . . crying.

Tamsyn's eyes burned; she hadn't known a big cat could cry like that. But this cat did as it nuzzled and licked the fur of the two children who were cuddling against her as if they'd found their mother. "I don't think we have anything to worry about," she murmured quietly to her mate.

But Nathan wasn't looking at the poignant reunion taking place in the searing brightness of their backyard. His eyes were aimed at the darkness, their color leopard green. This time when he moved, she let him go. Skirting around the adult ocelot and the two cubs, he made for the edge of the yard.

Well aware he could handle himself, Tamsyn turned to ensure that her boys were behaving. As she did so, she caught sight of the rope created out of sheets being pulled back inside the house.

Roman, who'd stayed behind to distract her, while his partner in crime went to hide the evidence of their escape, said, "I thought you said their mama was in heaven?" And though he was doing it to distract her, she could tell the question was real. Slipping a small hand into hers, he looked over at his friends as they climbed all over the adult ocelot.

"Yes, their parents are in heaven," she murmured. "But this is obviously someone they love." Her scent was familiar, of the thin healer who'd refused to give DarkRiver her name.

The back door opened behind her, an older female voice saying, "Tamsyn, I heard—" Words cut off on a startled burst of air that turned into a cry of piercing joy. Even as Tamsyn was turning to greet the healer of some eight decades of age who'd gone to bed at the same time as the children, saying her old bones needed time to relax, Yariela shifted in a fragmentation of light.

The shift took as long as it took. Age didn't change the speed of it. But the ocelot that came out of it moved slower and it had white in its coat. Such a symptom of age was rare in felines, but changelings tended to show it more often. Tamsyn had found the odd thread of silver in her mate's pelt when she looked close, an echo of the silver threads that had appeared in the dark of his hair. Her Nathan was aging like a fine wine: the man just got better-looking.

But though this older ocelot moved more slowly, she did so with clear intent, and was soon standing face-to-face with the intruder, while the two children bounced up and down next to them.

Then the younger adult ocelot was bowing her head and the older one was rubbing the side of its own head against hers, before she went down onto the ground, her body a curve of welcome into which the intruder curled their own body, and the children curled their bodies in turn inside her curve.

Tamsyn didn't realize she was crying until Roman looked up and said, "Mama? What's wrong?" His own eyes were big and full of emotion, her sweet boy with a healer's heart.

Crouching down just as a whirlwind emerged from the house to snuggle under her other arm, she said, "I'm happy."

Roman patted away her tears with one small hand. "Happy tears," he said, parroting something she'd said to her boys more than once. He kissed her on one cheek, while Julian echoed the move in perfect synchrony on the other side.

Oh, how she loved these two, and how she loved the man who'd disappeared into the night-cloaked forest. The mating bond pulsed strong and fierce inside her chest, and she knew he was fine. He was a sentinel. One of the deadliest men in the pack, for all that he now had silver in his hair. There were very few people in this world who could take down Nathan Ryder.

But there were also very few people who could get through DarkRiver's defenses, and she didn't think the ocelot healer had done it on her own. Who had she brought with her? If it was an enemy, that would complicate matters considerably. For now, she hugged her boys and said, "Come on, let's go inside and give our friends some time to be together."

She'd make food, because food was comfort. And she'd give up on the idea of getting these two tiny felons and their friends back into bed anytime soon. Some nights called for special measures. As for school—well, she knew their teacher, and she'd make sure the children did at-home learning when they woke up the next day.

Tonight was about love, about family, about pack.

Chapter 25

PRIORITY NOTICE
Attention: Ena Mercant

Please be advised that we are currently holding a child who claims to be
of the Mercant line. Unless you respond prior, he will be held in our
custody for the next thirty-six hours before being sent to child
resettlement services.
Child's DNA scan attached for familial DNA matching purposes.

—Bureau of Death and Family Notification Services (9 May 2059)

IVAN UNDERSTOOD FAMILY. Every Mercant understood family.

Cor meum familia est.

My heart is family.

It was the founding tenet of their clan.

So he understood that Soleil had found hers. The way the children
had jumped on her with such unfettered and innocent joy had been
confirmation enough—and he'd known he should get out of there.

But should he do that, Soleil would feel the need to hide his identity. She might not remember the Ivan he'd been once, the one with
whom she'd played in the forest, but she was a woman of courage and

honor. He'd helped her. She wouldn't give him up—and in so doing would strike a blow against her own deepest need: to be accepted into this pack that held the last remnants of her family.

Family was precious. Especially when you didn't have any.

So he didn't run, didn't slide away into the dark. Even a leopard of Nathan Ryder's caliber would've never found Ivan if he'd used the minute's head start he could've had. He was very good at being a ghost, had been born a ghost.

And though his family would remember him, he would also die a ghost, the man he'd become in the more than two decades since Grandmother first took his hand erased by the spider's voracious hunger. No hint of the Ivan who talked high fashion with Arwen, or the one who'd gone to a bear party because that mattered to Silver, and not even a glimmer of the Ivan who sometimes walked on the cliffs of the Sea House with Grandmother.

Today, however, he was still himself, could still make choices that were all his own. So, positioning himself in a beam of moonlight, he put up his hands to show that he held no weapons.

Nathan found him unerringly in the dark, his eyes aglow with the leopard's night vision. A rumble from his chest, the warning of a predator who'd located an intruder close to home—close to his mate and cubs.

Ivan knew that he was in a perilous situation. Nathan was considered one of the calmest heads in DarkRiver, but Ivan was in a place that he should not be; he'd aroused Nathan's most primal protective instincts. Right now, the leopard was closer to the sentinel's skin than the human side.

What Ivan said now could be the difference between a bloody fight to the death and the resulting ripple effect it would have on Soleil—or peace. Parting his lips, he said, "I had to help her find her family. Family is everything."

A frown on the leopard sentinel's face, the easing of the rumble in his chest.

"Ivan Mercant." Nathan's voice wasn't quite human. "How do you know the ocelot?"

"Soleil," he said. "Her name is Soleil Bijoux Garcia. I was the one who found her badly injured body after the SkyElm massacre."

"There were meant to be no other survivors."

"She was misidentified as human—and by the time she was aware enough to seek out her pack, they were all gone." He said nothing about her alpha's rejection, would not make her vulnerable in that way. "She believed them to have been murdered by your alpha."

Exhaling, Nathan thrust his fingers through his hair, glanced back toward where an older ocelot had joined the other three. "Shit," he said. "No wonder she refused to tell Tammy and Luc anything." He nudged his head. "Come on, you're in this now."

They walked out of the trees just as Tamsyn Ryder was ushering her boys inside, but Ivan saw her head lift, her gaze meeting Nathan's. Her eyes then skated over to Ivan, lingered as she frowned. A second later, she walked inside—leaving the door open for him and Nathan.

When Nathan gave the group of ocelots a wide berth, Ivan followed suit to ensure he didn't inadvertently trigger the sentinel's barely leashed protective instincts. But he couldn't help looking back. Soleil lifted her head, her eyes wet. When she began to get up, he shook his head, trying to show her that everything was under control.

She finally settled back down, but he felt those big wild eyes on him all the way to the door. Could all but hear her grumbling at him. Strange, that she'd worry about him when his use to her was over. She was with her family and he was just a stranger she couldn't remember.

Honor, he reminded himself. She was a woman of honor.

Nathan and Tamsyn's kitchen was large and warm, a place built for gatherings. He was surprised they were permitting him to see it—he could take a photo, give it to a teleporter, opening their home to a silent invasion. Then again, this was a pack used to Psy—no doubt, they were expert at methods to quickly alter a physical location so it couldn't be used for a teleport lock.

Two identical little boys of around six or seven years of age sat swinging their feet on high stools at the breakfast counter, one in blue pajamas with the stars and the moon on them, the other in pajamas featuring a fantastical creature. A dragon, Ivan thought, that's what it was.

They gave him suspicious looks out of dark blue eyes identical to their father's. Then the one wearing dragon pajamas smiled, the sun coming out from behind a cloud. "Hi, we're going to have cookies even though it's bedtime! Want one?"

His twin scowled. "You're not supposed to talk to strangers, Rome."

"He's with Dad. He's not a stranger."

On the other side of the counter, Tamsyn said, "Welcome to our home." The healer's eyes were assessing. "Friend or foe?"

"Friend. My grandmother usually prefers her grandchildren not make enemies unless the people concerned are out to harm our family." In which case, all bets were off and you *would* go down.

Tamsyn's lips curved. "Alpha Nikolaev speaks highly of Ena Mercant."

Connections, threads, points of contact. "Valentin is of the opinion that he is my grandmother's favorite changeling."

Tamsyn laughed, but Ivan didn't take that as a sign that he'd been designated a non-threat. He was also conscious that Nathan had stepped away—still close enough to eviscerate Ivan with his claws should Ivan make a move to hurt his mate or cubs, but far enough away that Ivan couldn't hear the low-voiced conversation he was having on the phone. No doubt a call to his alpha.

What had happened here today, it would require Lucas Hunter.

So when Tamsyn invited Ivan to take a seat, he did so at a round table at the other end of the space from her cubs. Nathan shot him an approving look and joined him at the table after finishing his call. All the while, part of Ivan was straining at the bit to go outside, find out what was happening with Soleil.

Flashes of warmth, of gold and black fur spotted with threads of silver, of small claws patting at her in excitement, of tiny teeth nipping at her.

The visual was so vivid that he found himself curling his fingers into his palm, as if he had claws of his own. Should anyone have asked, he could've described the different scents of the other three ocelots, and that was an impossibility. He simply didn't have those olfactory glands.

Yet his mind continued to manufacture scents, manufacture sensations, until he knew what it was to be surrounded by pack, the children's small bodies wriggling against her, while the body of her elder held her warm and welcome. The knot in her chest, the heaviness that had crushed her since she knew herself once more, it began to unravel, until she could breathe again, could *feel* again.

Soleil was home. At last. She was home.

"Hmm." Tamsyn was staring at him. "It's not a mating bond, but it's something."

Ivan stared back at the healer.

She tilted her head at an angle that punched memory through him, of another cat in human form who'd done exactly the same action. "You carry her scent too deep for casual contact. Deep enough that it could be mistaken for a mating."

Nathan stirred. "*That's* what's been bugging me," he muttered. "You want to explain, Mercant?"

The idea of having Soleil for a mate, of having a bond as Nathan did with Tamsyn, as Silver did with her bear, he *wanted* it. More than he'd allowed himself to want anything for a long time.

"I don't know what it is," he said. "I've tried to set her free, but I can't." No matter how many times he'd searched, he hadn't been able to find the strand of his web that connected him to her, her to him. It might feel like it was coming from her, her cat prowling through his mind, but logic said it *had* to be him.

He was the Psy, the telepath.

His was the web, so sticky and impossible to escape.

Warm laughter from Tamsyn, her eyes sparkling. "Oh, what I scent isn't a Psy thing, Ivan. She's marked you, and we cats tend to be possessive."

Ivan wanted to believe that until it was a compulsion. "She doesn't know me."

"Are you sure?" Tamsyn stirred something on the stove. "I think her ocelot knows exactly who you are."

Nathan coughed into his hand, his expression amused when Ivan glanced over. "Guess you better figure out how to tangle with a cat."

SOLEIL was so full of emotion that she couldn't separate one from the other. Joy, sheer joy, confusion, love, worry, so much more. She wanted to hold the cubs close, wanted to press herself tight against Yariela, wanted to rub their scents all over her and hers all over them.

She was home. Home at last.

But she was worried about Ivan. The leopards would consider him a threat. She had to make sure they knew that the only reason he was here was because he'd wanted to bring her home.

Panic fluttered in her at him being alone with unfriendly predators.

Stirring from the cuddle pile of her pack, she rose to her feet. The others stood with her. When Yariela went to lead them inside, she followed along on quick feet. In front of them, the two cubs ran to the door and back again, too excited to stay still.

Open wounds inside her began to scab over. The cubs were alive. So was Yariela. Which likely meant gentle and kind Salvador was also alive. She wouldn't know about the soldiers until she asked. But this changed everything.

Lucas Hunter hadn't murdered her pack. He'd *saved* them.

Emotion choking her but not enough to overwhelm her worry for Ivan, she followed Yariela through the doorway—and found herself looking immediately to the right. Right into the eyes of *her* Psy. He was uninjured . . . and sitting in front of a plate of cookies.

She blinked, shook her head. Nope, still cookies there.

Ivan wasn't eating the cookies, however, quite unlike the boys who sat on the breakfast stools to her left. One of them dropped a cookie toward an ocelot cub; it was snatched out of the air by sharp little teeth.

"Boys," Tamsyn said in a firm maternal tone that had all involved parties attempting to imitate angels complete with shining halos. "As for you two on the floor. You know we eat off proper dishes in this house."

Razi and Natal ran around the counter to nuzzle at Tamsyn's legs, their bodies fluid and their markings an echo of their parents'. Smiling fondly, the healer bent down and scooped them up in her arms to nip at their noses. Unrepentant, the cubs pretended to bite her ear while only licking at her earlobes. Laughing, she put them on the counter near the twins, where they both sat up neatly, ready for cookies.

Every so often, they'd look back, as if checking to see that Soleil was still there.

Soleil's cells burst with purest happiness. The children were happy, healthy. DarkRiver had given them not just a home, but love. Soleil would do everything in her power to pay back that gift. Now, however, she needed her human voice. But though she was changeling and used to shifting into her skin, she felt shy doing it in front of strangers.

Even as she went to nudge Yariela, ask the question with her eyes, Tamsyn said, "Spare clothes are in a trunk by the front door. Yariela, will you show her the way?"

Of course a healer's home would be stocked with clothing for those who might drop by. People always dropped by the homes of healers. That was just how it was. Even Soleil, young healer though she'd been, had been used to visitors—there to chat, to grab a bite, or to get looked over for small wounds.

She'd had a special stash of colorful bandages that she'd put on the cubs when they came to her with scrapes and scratches. The little ones had loved them so much that they quite often wouldn't shift for a day or two, just so the bandages would stay on their skin.

Now she followed Yariela's slower form to the trunk. Leaving Soleil there, the senior healer disappeared down another hallway, no doubt going to her room to get her own clothes. After shifting, Soleil changed into a pair of sweatpants that were far too large in the waist but were the right length for her height. They had a string tie at the top, so she used that to cinch it tight.

On top, she threw on a T-shirt of soft pink that actually fit pretty well, along with a hoodie of multihued shades that zipped up the front and seemed like something a juvenile might've helped purchase. She liked it. It was bright, open, more Soleil than anything she'd worn since the massacre.

She *felt* more real, more herself.

There was a mirror not far from the front door and when she glanced into it, she saw that she looked good. It had little to do with the clothes, however. It was the brightness in her eyes, the shine in her face. Happiness, she realized. She was glowing with happiness.

And though her heart tugged her toward Ivan, this Psy her cat had claimed, she followed the deep familiarity of Yariela's scent to her room. She needed answers to her questions before Lucas Hunter got here. Because he would be coming.

Chapter 26

Not every changeling with the dominance to be alpha has the heart for it.

—Lucas Hunter, alpha of DarkRiver, to Remington "Remi" Denier,
alpha of RainFire

"OH, MY LEILEI, come, come," Yariela said with a teary smile when Soleil hesitated on her doorstep. "My sweet girl." She closed her arms around Soleil when she sat down on the bed next to her.

Her eyes caught on a couple of colorful little cat planters on the bedside table, each holding a tiny succulent, and she had the oddest feeling that there should be three, but then Yariela was enfolding her in her arms and her entire world reduced to the care of this woman who'd taken a brokenhearted little girl and lavished her in such love that she'd healed, had flown.

The healer who was her grandmother in every way but blood felt so very fragile, far from the strong woman Soleil had known, but her hug was just as all-encompassing, her love a storm.

"I'm so happy to see you, Abuela," Soleil managed to choke out, breathing in the scent of the ocelot who'd mothered her since she came into SkyElm. "I thought you were all dead." Sobs overtook her. "The pack was erased in the records."

Yariela kissed the top of her hair, squeezed her tight. "After all that happened, after the lack of honor displayed by Monroe, we as adults— all of us who survived—made the decision not to saddle the cubs with that history.

"Our babies will be told of it when they come of age, but as far as the records are concerned, they will be of DarkRiver. SkyElm's terrible history won't shadow their lives." Dark, dark eyes held Soleil's. "I'm so sorry, my Leilei, we didn't think anyone else had survived. I would've *never* left you if I'd known."

Soleil wiped the elder's tears. "It's not your fault. Monroe knew." She had to say that, had to make sure Yariela never blamed herself for it. "He chose to reject me."

Eyes burning, she admitted to the truth she'd already shared with Ivan. "I tried so hard to save Em and Robbie, but I couldn't." The alpha's mate and their treasured cub had died in her arms. "I really tried, Abuela. I gave it all I had." Her heart had shredded itself into a million pieces as she felt Robbie slip away, such a small and bright light, one she'd helped birth into the world at Yariela's side.

"I know, my Leilei. I know." Her mentor kissed Soleil's hair again, her voice unsteady. "I saw their bodies in the aftermath. Those injuries . . . not even the most senior healer could've saved them, even had they been rushed into the infirmary right away."

A sob caught in Soleil's throat at Yariela's confirmation that it had been too late long before she got to mother and child; the senior healer's words could never erase the guilt that haunted Soleil, never silence all the hollow-eyed ghosts that followed her, but they softened the serrated edges of that guilt.

"I'm sorry I couldn't be with you at that time," Yariela said, her voice quiet with pain. "You should've never had to face such a terrible thing alone."

It was Soleil's turn to comfort. "No, Abuela, you burned yourself out with helping our packmates." Echoing with the horror she'd felt at the sight, this memory was as sharp and bloody as a razor. "I saw you collapse, saw Duke drag you to safety." The young dominant's eyes had been shocky, but he hadn't bowed under the weight of the deaths all around them.

Yariela's sigh told Soleil that the elder healer continued to tangle with her own demons, her own guilt. "So," she said, weaving her fingers through Soleil's, "that's why Monroe denied you your rightful place in SkyElm? Because of Em and Robbie?"

Soleil nodded. "I'll never know for sure, but it's the only reason that makes sense." Because while Monroe had never liked her, he'd accepted her usefulness as a healer.

Gritted teeth from Yariela, her eyes suddenly a pale ocelot gold. "Then his reasoning held no reason at all. Or it was that of an egoist who refused to face the consequences of his own actions. Monroe made the mistakes and blamed you for them. Em and Robbie and the others were left unprotected because *he* decided that flank was safe enough not to need any guards."

Yariela's hand clenched on Soleil's. "I can feel an unending sorrow for the loss of that sweet babe and his gentle mother, and I can hurt for Monroe's pain without losing the clarity of my sight. And what I see is that that decision was but one in a line of bad ones.

"Long before that dark day, Monroe decided our pack would accept only ocelots rather than any strong feline changeling that wished to join us. It left us weak, with too many vulnerable and not enough dominants, not enough soldiers. We became prey because he allowed it to be so."

Dropping her gaze, she released a tired exhale. "He was a good man once." A shake of her head on the heels of her words. "But he wasn't, was he? He followed your grandfather's example and never treated you well, though you were the very heart of our pack, the sunshine around which we warmed ourselves."

Shaky with emotion at the force of Yariela's denouncement of

Monroe and what he'd done to her, Soleil said, "What happened when Lucas Hunter came to SkyElm?"

"Monroe tried to have Lucas's child kidnapped."

Soleil sucked in a breath. This, she hadn't known.

"Lucas executed him," Yariela said. "The rest of us were welcomed into DarkRiver should we wish it. We were only six. Seven now." A tremulous smile, Yariela lifting up her soft cotton tunic to wipe Soleil's face.

Memories of childhood, of Yariela rocking her as Soleil cried for her parents. They might've been feckless loners who'd never made any plans for the future, but they'd *loved* her.

"The leopards are good people," Yariela murmured. "We've been welcomed and treated as packmates. Even that dangerous mate of Tammy's treats me with the respect due an elder."

"Duke and Lula?"

"Sí, sí, they're well. But you won't see them for a few weeks—they've been taken up into SnowDancer territory to do high-altitude training." A grin that was the clouds parting after the blackest storm. "Oh, what a surprise they'll get when they come down the mountain!" Though Yariela's eyes were yet raw from her tears, her laughter was as familiar as the sky, a balm to Soleil's soul.

"Salvador has bloomed here," Yariela continued. "The cubs usually stay with him, consider him their adopted papa, but we decided to give him the weekend off because he has gone courting."

This time her smile was that of a gleeful cat. "A human who builds ships. Can you imagine our Sal on a boat? She is as sweet as him, though—and the cubs already adore her. They'll make such a happy family. You'll be the indulgent tía that spoils Razi and Natal, I think."

Overwhelmed in the best way, Soleil lifted her hands to her mouth, dropped them on a crash of startled joy. "Oh, yes! I'll be the one who takes them on wild little adventures and lets them eat junk food."

"Yes, this is just as it should be."

"Abuela?" Soleil took Yariela's soft wrinkled hand. "You vanished from the forum."

"I have been sad for a long time, my Leilei." The older healer rubbed at her breastbone. "Sick to the heart. You see how I am." She waved a hand over her body. "So old and faded, though in years I should yet have a third of my life left to live—others of my years are active and lively. But my soul sickness . . . it bled into my bones."

She patted Soleil's hand. "I never had cubs of my own, but my bonds to the pack kept me happy. But even those bonds wouldn't have held me to the world much longer after the passing of my mate. I was fractured in the very soul.

"Then your grandfather walked into my home with a silent niña at his side, and I knew why I must live." Running her palm over Soleil's head, she beamed though her eyes were wet again. "You became a piece of my heart, my Leilei. I could barely go on when I thought you dead, even your body lost to us, so that I could not say good-bye to mi niña preciosa."

Tears rolled down her face. "I no longer had interest in much. I had to use what little energy I had left wisely—making sure the cubs settled well into DarkRiver, and learning to feel something akin to happiness, because Razi and Natal would be sad if I didn't."

Soleil hugged the woman who had loved her until she stopped hurting, and she cursed Monroe for his cruelty in what he'd done to her. He'd known he would shatter Yariela's heart when he disowned Soleil, yet he'd done it all the same. And he hadn't even had the guts to tell Yariela of his actions.

Soleil would hate him to the end of time for that cruelty, and she wouldn't feel bad about it.

But as of this moment, she was out of time.

She'd sensed the faint hum of a car coming closer half a minute ago, now heard the engine shut off.

The alpha of DarkRiver was here.

Chapter 27

I don't know how Lucas Hunter does it. Then again, he's a cat. They find the strangest things funny.

—Valentin Nikolaev, alpha of StoneWater, to Silver Mercant, director of EmNet

IVAN HAD KEPT his breathing even by sheer force of will until Soleil reappeared in the doorway through which she'd exited the kitchen. He'd known she was safe, was still inside the house, but he wanted her close to him when she spoke to Lucas Hunter.

Then there she was, dressed once again in borrowed clothing, her hair tumbling over her shoulders and her eyes coming directly to him. Ocelot eyes, her humanity still only a surface skin, the cat at the forefront.

Rising to his feet, he said, "Are you all right?" It was an inane question and Ivan didn't ask such questions. Except he just had, his need to look after her a burn in his blood.

"I'm perfect." Her gaze went to the four children at the counter, her face soft.

The twins had remained in their human forms, while the two ocelot cubs had stayed in cub form. All, however, were gathered together, huddled around a plate of cookies as well as two glasses of water—and two shallow bowls of the same.

Scratching one cub's head, Tamsyn had said, "Your tummies won't have room for milk *and* cookies since I happen to know that some small people in this kitchen already had dessert tonight."

The twins had grinned, while the ocelot cubs had butted Tamsyn's hand for more scratches and pets.

Ivan had watched the scene with a quiet fascination; he'd never thought about the small things that would be different in a changeling household. Never thought that when a child was in animal form, they'd prefer to drink from a bowl instead of a glass. Of course a loving home would have accommodations for either form.

To a changeling, they were both parts of the whole. It was only the Psy who so often thought in strictly limited terms, as if the world could be squared off into neat boxes. But that structured world was also the one in which Ivan knew how to exist, how to function—rules had been a necessary lifeline for a boy who'd been half-feral by the time he came to Ena Mercant's attention.

"I don't know what to do," he'd said to her as she walked him to his first lesson with a tutor, the corridor around them bright and clean in the sunshine pouring through the large windows to one side. "Mama's man said I was stupid."

Ena's silvery blue eyes on him. "Yet he is the one who ended up dead in the morgue from a drug overdose." She'd paused, held his gaze. "You are a very clever child, Ivan. Never allow the words of others to steal your worth—always remember that it is the weak and cowardly who attempt to devalue others. The strong uplift without fear, share their knowledge to help others grow."

Ivan had thought then of how Grandmother had taught him to use a knife and fork, how she'd told him that he didn't have to hoard food, that he could always get more from the kitchen, and how she'd instructed him to put his dirty clothes in the laundry chute.

It had been so hard for him to let go of those precious possessions. He'd only really believed they'd come back to him when he found them ironed and placed on his bed for him to put away. The same day, he'd gone back for a second serving of breakfast and no one had ordered him to stop. Cousin Canto, who'd told Ivan he'd just "escaped" the infirmary after an operation, had even winked and put extra dried fruits on top for him—because he knew they were Ivan's favorite.

Ivan had realized he could trust Grandmother to tell the truth. "I can't be clever if I don't know what to do," he'd pointed out, trying to make her see. "I only know how to be the *other* Ivan." The one from his life before Grandmother, before a kitchen stocked with food, and a bedroom full of sunlight where no one touched his things.

A long pause before Grandmother's face became hard in a way that he'd already learned wasn't about him. "Of course," she'd murmured that day. "Very well. I shall teach you how to behave in specific situations, give you the tools to handle them as they arise—they will give you structure as you adapt to your new life."

Ivan had long ago adapted—but he still preferred structure. It was why he'd never quite fit into Silver's pack, though the bears had welcomed him as a relative of their beloved Silver Mercant. He saw the bears' generosity and warmth of heart, understood the incalculable value of such beings—but he'd rather shoot himself in both feet than live in the midst of that joyous chaos.

Soleil was a changeling, too, her world as primal.

Ivan would've never fit into her world, either.

Hand fisting on his thigh and a film of ice over his chest, he watched Soleil with quiet focus as she went to stroke the cubs' fur and steal a cookie from the plate, the children giggling at her attempts at stealth.

Just when he thought she'd forgotten him, she glanced over, a look in her eye that he couldn't read . . . but then he felt the swipe of a cat's claws in his mind. Not painful. Just a . . . flexing.

A reminder that he was marked.

Ivan stared at her, wondering if he'd tipped over the edge without noticing and was now living in a delusion. Even if he was, he didn't care. So long as she saw him, saw the ghost who was Ivan Mercant.

Everything Ivan had done since Grandmother brought him home, everything he'd become, he'd done within the boundaries of his family. Not because they'd asked him to—but because those ties were the only solid things in his life. If he wasn't a Mercant, he was nothing.

Until Soleil, he'd never wanted *anything* for himself.

He knew that the visceral depth of his need was a sign of increasing volatility. It was hot, unstable. And when Soleil walked toward him, it got hotter, even less stable.

Dangerous, so dangerous.

He was conscious of Nathan moving away to talk to Tamsyn, could still hear the children's chatter, but it was all background noise. He should've stepped back, created space between them. Yet when she lifted a hand, he lowered his head a fraction . . . and she pushed his hair back from his forehead.

Thief. Thief. Thief.

Ivan ignored the whispers of his conscience. He wanted to close his eyes, wanted to savor what might be the last physical contact he ever had with her . . . but there was no more time. Moving with an assassin's grace as the alpha of DarkRiver entered the room, Ivan tried to put Soleil behind him. A small growl before she poked him in the side with her claws, then shifted to stand at his side.

"Luc." Tamsyn Ryder kissed Lucas on the cheek as she passed him with all four children. "Quick, my cublets. It's cartoon time." Her twins scampered on ahead with whoops of joy, one ocelot cub right on their heels, while she carried the smaller cub in her arms. Taking the children out of what might become a danger zone.

An older woman followed Lucas into the room. Her skin was the dark of night and her body small with fine bones, her face a symphony of lines that told the story of a life lived.

A deep tug inside Ivan, a wild sense of knowing. Family, she was family, though he'd never before met her in all his life. She turned at the same moment, saw him, and a look, bright and dazzling, lit up her eyes, her hand rising to her mouth.

Fighting his protective compulsion toward her because it was clear she was safe here, he turned his attention to the biggest predator in the room.

Lucas, however, had another target. Moving to Soleil, he gripped her chin between thumb and forefinger, the contact gentle but firm. "So," the alpha said, "you came looking for your own."

"Actually," Soleil said with a wild courage that made Ivan ready himself to defend her. "I came to kill you. Vengeance for having destroyed the innocent survivors of my pack." She made a face. "Quite ignoring the fact that I'm a healer and don't kill people. Idiot."

Lucas's grin was unexpected, his cat prowling in his eyes. "You'll be a welcome part of my pack."

Soleil's cat bared its teeth in suspicion. "Just like that?"

"Oh, we'll run background on you, make sure you're not some kind of shadow operative, but I gave my word to the survivors of SkyElm that they were welcome in DarkRiver—and I don't go back on my word." When his fingers tightened slightly on her jaw, she had to fight from shooting a glare at Ivan.

She could all but feel the tension in his skin, his need to protect her. But breaking eye contact with Lucas Hunter at this moment would be a very, *very* bad idea. The predator looking out of his eyes would view it as a weakness, or an indication that she was lying.

"The choice is yours," Lucas said, a growl in his voice that wasn't a warning but a simple sign of his nature. "But if you stay, you do so under my authority, as a member of my pack. You want to take another path, you need to do it away from this territory—I'll give you safe passage out of it, and if you want to come back to visit, you'll have to follow the same rules as any other predatory changeling."

He was being kind. It might not seem that way to a person who wasn't changeling, but Soleil was and she understood. Lucas didn't have to give her a choice at all—with how she'd sneaked into his territory, he would've been well within his rights to simply kick her out and tell her to stay out.

But to sign her life away under the control of another alpha? It made her freeze, shudder. She knew alphas weren't all cut from the same cloth, but the only alphas she'd ever known had rejected her at every turn. Even to the extent of leaving her in a hospital not knowing herself, her body and mind in pieces.

When it came down to it, however, there was no choice here. The way the cubs had run to her, the way they'd *remembered* her . . . Someone did want her here, did need her here. And though she was sure now that the leopards would do everything in their power to give these babies a good home, they'd need to learn things that only another ocelot could teach them. And there were so few ocelots in the country, even fewer whom the cubs knew and trusted.

"I'll stay," she murmured, somehow managing to hold Lucas's gaze through teeth-gritted will; she wasn't the senior healer, wasn't yet even part of the pack. "I acknowledge you as alpha."

A sudden sense of peace within her. Because her cat was a creature of pack. It could be afraid and want this at the same time. The same way it had hated but needed Monroe.

"You're a healer," Lucas said. "I'll have to blood-bond you into the pack."

She knew that, had expected it, but appreciated the warning. A second later, she realized the explanation hadn't been for her—Lucas was very aware of Ivan standing ice quiet and predator-still, ready to intervene.

Scowling, she shot him a glance that told him to stay put—the last thing she needed was for her Psy to end up shredded to pieces by Lucas's claws. His expression didn't change, those eyes of his still and pristine and as apparently uninvolved. But in her mind shimmered his web, silvery and with an edge of orange and red.

Giving up on nonverbal communication, she scowled. "There's gonna be blood. Don't freak out."

Ivan stared at her. She had the feeling that no one had ever told him not to freak out before. But his body eased a fraction and he leaned back against the wall, arms folded. She didn't take that as a sign that he was calm. His web continued to hover, cold as a burn.

When she glanced back at Lucas, she was *almost* certain he was fighting a laugh. But, not making a comment on the interaction, he slashed a line on his palm using a claw, then slashed a fine line down her cheek.

Having expected the cut to be on her throat or perhaps on her arm, she flinched. The web went hard inside her, lines of razored steel. This time, the look she shot Ivan was very much *I* will *handle this.*

He narrowed his eyes but stayed in position.

Lucas placed his hand against her cheek at the same time. A jolt ran through her entire body as his blood mingled with her own, the impact sucking all the air out of her lungs. She inhaled jaggedly in the aftermath, staring at the leopard who was now her alpha.

"Hold on," he murmured, the power of him a thing of teeth and claws—a power that was a shield under which she now stood. "It's not done yet."

A thunder of sound through her entire body, a wild pulse made up of hundreds of hearts, a roar for a single breathtaking beat of time followed by pure silence . . . but she knew all those hearts still sang for her. The pack welcoming a new member, welcoming *her.*

For this was a bond of pack, not a bond between two people as such.

Tears burned her eyes.

She hadn't known, hadn't understood that the alpha-healer connection was a true bond, a primal thing that now lived beneath her
skin, connecting her cat to Lucas's leopard. It was this bond that
would allow him to feed her energy should she need it—and it was
this bond that would allow her to heal members of the pack, whether
ocelot or leopard.

It was a thing beyond flesh and blood, a wild changeling synergy.
But it wasn't intimate—not like her strange bond with Ivan. She could
sense Lucas's presence through the bond, could reach to him for help,
but that was it. He remained opaque to her as a person.

Leaning in, Lucas pressed his lips to hers. A tear rolled down her
cheek. Because that gentle kiss, it was alive with the energy of the
pack, an energy that spread through her like a fire that healed. The cut
on her cheek began to seal up—almost but not all the way. The scar,
though it would last only a few days, was a public statement that she
was now DarkRiver.

One of Lucas Hunter's cats.

Chapter 28

A Mercant's fidelity, once given, is a thing of stone. It cannot be cracked or warped except by an act of conscious malice from the other party. There are some who call us foolish for risking it all for those to whom we are loyal—but we are incapable of half measures. That is why we give our loyalty so rarely.

—Lord Deryn Mercant (circa 1510)

IVAN'S HANDS FISTED where he had his arms crossed over his chest, a hollow ache inside him. He didn't know the mechanics of what had just happened, but he'd felt a psychic bond shimmer into place when blood met blood.

Alpha to healer. Healer to alpha.

Grandmother would be very interested in this . . . but he wasn't going to tell her. This belonged to Soleil, a private and personal moment that he'd been permitted to witness because she trusted him.

He swallowed hard, hoarding yet another treasure in the box of memories he'd take with him into the cage that was his destiny. Jealousy ran hot red through his veins, warring with his relief that she'd be safe now, even when he couldn't watch over her. He should be more evolved, a better man, but part of him was still that little boy who'd never had anything of his own.

Yet even that little boy would choose safety for Soleil over his own need.

As he watched, Lucas took a soft disposable towel that the older woman in the room had dampened with water and used it to wipe Soleil's cheek clean. Ivan noticed that whereas Soleil's scar had begun to seal over, the one on Lucas's hand stayed fresh.

After getting rid of the biodegradable towel in the trash receptable meant for such items, and washing the blood off his own hand, Lucas turned, hands on his hips, and Ivan got the full attention of his eyes. But instead of speaking to him, the alpha frowned and glanced at Soleil. "You've marked him. There's a bond there."

Soleil shrugged, a comfort to her that spoke of a new trust. "My cat wanted to keep him." Shifting to stand next to Ivan, she said, "He's mine and he only breached your border to help me. Don't hurt him."

Ivan wanted to throw up his hands, the action one he'd seen from a bear and never understood the purpose of until today. *"Lei."*

"What?" She glared at him, while Nathan coughed once more into his hand. "It's the truth."

"Trust a healer to make things complicated." Lucas growled before Ivan could make his mind understand that *she* was trying to protect *him.* "He's not your mate, but he's something."

Soleil took Ivan's hand, the act making him freeze. He wanted to tell her to stop, that it wasn't the right decision if she wished to be accepted into her new pack. But when he tried to break the handclasp, she dug her claws into him, her expression a fierce warning. And he remembered . . . Soleil Bijoux Garcia fought for her people.

Things inside him broke, a glacier crashing into an icy ocean and causing a tidal wave. He could barely breathe, the greedy need in him wanting to steal this, steal her. It would be so easy. Such an awful, soul-destroying lie.

"I have no ill intent," he said to Lucas, because those words were far simpler, required nothing of his emotions. "My family simply wished to know more about DarkRiver."

Lucas gave a curt nod. "Tell the head of your family that we don't appreciate sneaking around—if she wants to know us, she can come talk to me face-to-face."

Ivan wasn't sure which element of that to address first. Nobody ordered Grandmother to do anything, and as for the other—"According to the bears, no one is as sneaky as a cat."

Nathan gave up and started laughing in truth, his hands braced on the kitchen counter while the older woman snorted with amusement.

Lucas's eyes gleamed. "Just pass on the message," the alpha said, then turned to Soleil. "He needs to leave tonight while I decide what to do about your odd not-mating bond. I can't have an unknown dominant near our cubs—especially when I have no understanding of mutual safety from his alpha."

This time, Ivan spoke before Soleil could part her lips. "I'll go." He squeezed Soleil's hand in silent repudiation when she stirred. "And I'll speak to my grandmother, tell her of your invitation to meet."

Claws raked at the mark inside his head that was Soleil's. His cat was annoyed with him—but she walked with him to the back door, not saying anything until they were in the center of the yard. Far enough away from sharp changeling ears that they could be private.

Someone inside was thoughtful enough to turn off the sensor lights, too.

That was when Soleil broke their handclasp. "So you're going." Eyebrows lowered, she folded her arms across her chest. "Just like that?"

Ivan decided he didn't understand cats. "It's the only viable option."

She sniffed, tapped her foot. "I need to be with the cubs and Yariela tonight, but this conversation isn't over. I'll find you tomorrow."

Ivan wasn't a good man. He knew that about himself. For one, he had no trouble putting a bullet into the head of those who took advantage of the weak, then dumping their bodies where no one would ever find them.

But he had never been a liar. "We met before I found you in the snow," he said coldly, knowing he had to snap the thread between them while he still could. "You saw the monster in me and chose to walk away."

Instead of flinching at the bomb he'd dropped without warning, Soleil cupped one side of his face, tilting her head in a quintessentially feline way. "I figured that out already, beautiful." A slow smile. "My cat isn't in the habit of marking strangers—and as for the walking-away part, no."

"No?"

"I don't need my memories to tell me that I would've never just walked away from you. You're too important to me, Ivan Mercant."

Ivan was lost. That was when Soleil wrapped her arms around him, her cheek pressed to his chest.

Ivan didn't know what to do, where to put his hands.

"Hold me back," she ordered.

No more walls left, he enclosed her body in the circle of his arms. For a long, silent moment filled with the scent of her, the warmth of her, he could almost pretend that he was normal, that he could be like Silver, like Canto, even like Arwen. That he could love, and be loved in turn, and have a person who was his own.

Then crystalline sparks flared against his irises, and he knew his thoughts for a delusion. He'd been damaged long before he could protect himself. And the damage would hurt everyone with whom he came into contact. Sooner or later, he'd self-destruct—but before he did, he would steal pieces of anyone close to him.

It was wired into his brain.

Breaking away from Soleil, he took a jagged step back. "I can't find the psychic thread that connects us. When I do, I'll cut it."

Soleil folded her arms again, raised an eyebrow. "Did you feel my blood bond with Lucas?"

Ivan thought of the jolt of primal energy that had prickled over his skin, raised the tiny hairs on his nape. "Yes."

"That's a changeling thing, not Psy. You won't find a link to cut." Leaning in, she put a hand on his shoulder, her lips close to his ear. "And my cat is supremely possessive of you." A pause. "Do you *want* out of this?"

He wanted to lie, wanted to tell her to set him free. "I'm not normal, Soleil. Not any kind of normal. Even among Psy, I'm *not normal*. And you have other priorities. Focus on them." Turning before she could respond, he walked away.

SOLEIL stood there for the longest time, staring after the beautiful, deadly man who'd vanished into the dark, her soul stretched in two. Her cat wanted to chase him until he told her what haunted him. It was convinced that he needed her—and the human side of her agreed.

His loneliness and hurt was a knot in her heart, a thing old and scarred.

Yet she also needed as much to be with Yariela and the cubs, their need as potent.

"Soleil, sweetheart." Tamsyn's voice. "Come inside. I've made up a room for you."

The cubs' warily hopeful faces in her mind, Soleil made herself move her feet and walk into the house, where Lucas now lounged on the cozy kitchen sofa, under "attack" by four cubs. Two ocelots and two leopards. Growling, he gripped Natal by the ruff of his neck, only to let go when Razi and one of the twins pounced to rescue their friend. It was obvious all five were having a grand old time.

Had Ivan ever played this way, so young and carefree?

A whisper of skirts against her legs, her laughter floating in the air as she turned to look back at the man who chased her. Fleeting glimpses of a face in shadow, of eyes of striking predator blue.

Oh. Oh. We played.

She clutched at the memory, fought desperately to unravel all the pieces of it, but it floated away, lost in the mists inside her mind—just as Yariela tucked her arm through Soleil's, the scent of her a piercing symbol of hope.

"It's something, isn't it?" her mentor murmured. "To see an alpha be so with the smallest of hearts?"

Chest tight, Soleil nodded. "Where's Nathan?"

"Tracking your Ivan out of the territory." She patted Soleil's arm when Soleil jerked toward the door. "Don't worry, Leilei, they know he's yours. I think they're tracking him more to make sure he's safe than because they're worried about trusting him." Soft eyes. "The way that man looks at you, mi ángel. He'd cut off his arm if you asked."

Who, Soleil thought, was that person for Ivan?

Me, said her cat, and daintily licked a paw.

He's ours.

Yes.

Chapter 29

Drug 7AX has leaked into the general population and is being sold under the street name Jax. Investigations are currently underway to identify the source of the leak, but in the interim, street users are being monitored to build a database of reactions on uncalibrated usage.

—Classified Report to the Psy Council by PsyMed: Pharmaceutical Development & Testing. Project Manager: Councilor Neiza Adelaja Defoe (circa 2022)

IVAN WENT HOME.

He didn't attempt any detours, didn't try any tricks, he just drove straight to a parking garage close to the apartment he'd rented for the duration of his stay. The apartment hadn't come with a garage of its own, but he didn't mind the easy ten-minute walk—he'd covered the same distance in less than half the time mere hours ago, driven by the compulsion that had led him to Soleil. The walk usually allowed him to clear out his mind, find balance again.

Balance was everything; balance kept him sane.

Today, however, he kept tripping over images of huge ocelot eyes, a hand gripping his own, and the passionate strength of Soleil's arms as she hugged him. As if he was the vulnerable one.

I would've never just walked away from you. You're too important to me, Ivan Mercant.

His shoulders began to tighten, his pulse to race . . . and the spider flexed.

Gritting his teeth, he wrenched it back and attempted to rebuild the walls that had fragmented tonight. Control, creating boundaries around his noxious psychic power, that was all that kept the ugliness at bay. Without it . . . without it, he would've been a cold, dark nightmare, a bloated spider that violated and swallowed everyone in its path, a monstrous *thing* far beyond a psychopath.

"I don't believe that of you, Ivan," Grandmother had said to him when he'd told her that as a child. "You came to me the instant you realized what you might be doing, and you weren't in any way reveling in your ability."

"That's because I didn't want to disappoint you, Grandmother," Ivan had said with deep honesty, because he never lied to the woman who'd given him a life worth living. "If I was still on the streets, I'd have used it to survive."

A long look before his grandmother inclined her head. "You're old enough to know yourself. Do you think you could've lived with your actions?"

A snapshot of memory, his mother's cold body, blankness where her mind should've been. The idea of that multiplied over and over . . . "Maybe not at the start," he'd said, his hair flying back in the sea winds. "But the street, it has a way of eating away pieces of you. It would've eaten the good part of me one day."

Ivan respected his grandmother above anyone else in the entire world, but Ena had been born a Mercant, had grown up a Mercant. She'd never been wholly alone—as Ivan had been even when his mother was alive. Jax had owned his mother, until she was barely conscious of the son she professed to love.

"Love you, my boy," she'd say with a hazy smile, and he'd wonder if she even saw him.

Ivan knew the truth: that hunger, cold, violence, pain, loneliness, it eroded who the person had once been.

And created a monster.

He'd already been riddled with spots of emptiness by the time he became a Mercant. Those spots had scarred over in the years since, the blank spaces filled by the loyalty and fidelity of his family, but the damage done was permanent.

Once inside his apartment, he shrugged out of his jacket, put it aside, then walked into the kitchenette area to mix himself a nutrient drink. Tamsyn Ryder had offered him food, but he'd declined, not wanting to divert his attention in even so small a way. She'd still put a plate of cookies in front of him.

The cubs had been vocal in their enjoyment of the cookies, but Ivan didn't enjoy food. Perhaps he could have once. With Soleil.

I packed a whole bunch of things for our picnic, not just the tart.

For her, this cat who'd emerged out of the forest and walked right inside him, he'd have tried dish after dish. Just because she'd asked. But that time was gone, his personal clock almost to midnight. There would be no more evolution for Ivan Mercant. His future path held only a dark and crumbling devolution.

He knew his inability to embrace the sensation of taste drove his eldest cousin crazy. Canto appreciated food, as did Arwen. Silver had always been more like Ivan, but she'd changed since her mating. Or perhaps it was more correct to say that she'd shrugged off the weight of Silence to accept her true nature.

Ivan's true nature was a horror born of a drug that promised ecstasy, but that eventually stripped Psy of their inborn abilities. He often wondered how long his family would continue to see him as one of them when it was so clear that he didn't have within him the potential they all did—to leave all vestiges of Silence in the past and live a life beyond what had been mandated for them by the now-defunct Psy Council.

Ivan could only go so far, and no further. Not because he cared about Silence. But because he had to maintain the cage in which lived the devouring spider of his true psychic ability. A man who had to do that couldn't break his shackles.

Ever.

"Grandmother's like me," he reminded himself, because Ena Mercant had been too long in Silence to drop it. But even Ena had learned to live among a pack of bears . . . and the cubs followed her for a reason; she might be firm and strict but below that sat a cool, dark well of ferocious love.

She'd held her entire clan together with that same unspoken love. As a child, Ivan had known that no matter what, no matter when, if he needed help, Grandmother would come for him. *Always.*

Ivan was too scarred up for such a well, a hollow man who could never give Soleil what she needed.

A musical sound.

The doorbell.

Figuring it had to be one of the cats checking to ensure that he was in his apartment, he brought up the door feed on his phone. And sat up ramrod straight. "What the hell?"

He left his half-finished drink on the bedside table and jogged down the stairs—to open the door to a slender man with eyes of an unusual silver-blue against olive skin, his hair as straight as a ruler and cut with sophisticated ruthlessness, and his cheekbones a thing of catwalks. He wore crisp jeans of darkest blue and a fine black sweater that was probably cashmere, and held a small tote bag.

Arwen grinned. "Hello, cousin!"

"What. Are. You. Doing. Here?"

A shrug. "Genara was visiting an associate in San Francisco and I hitched a ride. Haven't seen you for a while."

"Why is Genara visiting her associate at midnight?"

"She's a woman of intrigue and mystery," Arwen said with zero concern in his tone for those mysteries and intrigues.

Ivan should've seen this coming. Genara, a deadly teleport-capable telekinetic with a murky past, and Arwen the empath who worried about everyone, were fast friends. A more dangerous combination Ivan couldn't imagine.

"So, you going to invite me in?"

Ivan stepped aside. He was in no mood for company, least of all of the one family member who might see right through him. "Come up." No point taking him to the empty box of the downstairs lounge; Ivan had seen no reason to get furniture for it when he didn't ever use the space.

His cousin sprawled easily onto his bed, palms braced behind him. "Well," Arwen said after a look around, "it's an upgrade from the last place. Hideous wallpaper—I'd be embarrassed to claim that if I was the designer—but at least there are no stuffed creatures." A shudder, followed by a startled, "I like the cat statue. Whimsical."

Ivan didn't correct him about the little multicolored cat that sat on the bedside table. "You want nutrients?"

"No. I ate." Then he *stared* at Ivan.

"Have I turned green?" Leaning against a wall facing Arwen, Ivan folded his arms over his T-shirt and stared back; he was fully confident of his ability to withstand the worst torture—and then there was Arwen.

"Noooo." Arwen frowned as he stretched out that one-syllable word to an improbable length. "Except for the whole whimsical-statue thing. I suppose it came with the place?" More staring. Followed by a gasp as he sat up straight in a rapid snap of movement. "What's her name? Is it the same woman as before? The one you've been missing all this time?"

Ivan barely held back his jolt, his gut clenching and arm muscles rigid. "What?"

"The changeling who's in you like Valentin is in Silver." Arwen's handsome face scrunched up into a frown, his gaze suddenly far more intense. The gaze of an empath. "It's not the same as those two, but I can definitely feel a bond."

"She's just someone I helped once," Ivan forced himself to say. "It's a temporary bond, will fade with distance."

Piercing gaze and soft voice, Arwen said, "Changelings are possessive, Ivan. And if she's marked you deep enough that it speaks to an empath, there's nothing temporary about it."

Need clawed at Ivan, ripping open the scars. "Arwen." A tight word. "I can't talk about this."

The gentlest of his cousins just nodded. "Okay. Want to walk to the halfway house instead?"

It was Ivan's turn to stare. "How do you know that?" That was his secret, his obsession.

"Family of spies, hello." Arwen pretended to shrug on an invisible suit jacket. "I do have some spy skills, you know. Infected with them by osmosis."

"Why are you spying on me?"

"Because I worry about you." Guileless, sincere words that laid Arwen's heart right there in the open and made Ivan wonder all over again how Arwen managed to exist in this world without being smashed into a million pieces.

Good thing he was surrounded by a family of sharks. As Ivan's healer was now surrounded by a family of ruthless leopards.

Safe, they'd keep her safe.

"Oh, before I forget," Arwen said. "I got you a present." He shook the tote. "Brand-new blazer from your favorite designer."

"Thanks." Arwen had impeccable taste, so Ivan knew the piece would be one he'd have chosen himself; his cousin understood the power conveyed by clothes, understood the mask Ivan preferred to present to the world.

As for the unexpected gift, that was par for the course for Arwen.

Arwen had been a boy of only five when eight-year-old Ivan joined the family, and he'd soon started to bring Ivan things: a plant he'd grown from seed, a perfect spiral shell he'd found on the beach, his favorite study tablet, even the raggedy old scarf that he had a habit of wearing everywhere, rain or shine, sun or hail.

Ivan hadn't understood what Arwen wanted from him until a teenaged Canto had looked at him with cardinal eyes full of stars and said, "He just wants you to be happy." Quiet words that held a deep power. "He's small, so he thinks if he gives you things that make him happy, you'll be happy, too."

If Ena had saved Ivan, Arwen had taught him what it was to be generous, to live in a world without a constant mental balance sheet, to give for no reason but that it might bring joy to the receiver. What ability Ivan had to love, the small thimbleful of softness that had allowed Soleil to sneak into his heart? It had been born courtesy of Arwen Mercant.

Ivan would never do anything to hurt his cousin. And if that meant visiting with Arwen at a time when Ivan's soul was draped in midnight, the spider stirring, so be it. "Come on," he said, pulling on his jacket. "Let's go on that walk."

After they left the apartment, he made no attempt to hide where he was going. It was no secret, after all. He'd walked there countless nights by now.

"How did you find the halfway house in the first place?" Arwen asked, shoving his hands into the pockets of his jeans.

"After I first landed and saw there were no Jax junkies hanging around, I figured the cats had rounded up the addicts and thrown them out." DarkRiver hadn't held on to power here by being soft.

"Still, I couldn't let it go—how could a city this big have *no* users? Didn't make sense." Not when Jax was a plague that had infected the Psy since the first generation born into Silence. "So I dug. Family of spies."

Arwen laughed, the warmth of the sound an echo of another laugh, one that had dug its way into Ivan's soul. "Spies R Us—Pasha says we should use that as our corporate name," he said, referencing the bear with whom he was entangled. "Think Grandmother would go for it?"

"You tell her while I watch."

"Hah." A grin. "I'll send Pasha in as the ritual sacrifice."

After that, they walked on in silence. Arwen could be a very comfortable companion. Back when Ivan had been in his early teens, Arwen would sometimes come into Ivan's room and just sit there reading his book while Ivan studied. It hadn't been until much later that Ivan realized he'd always felt more centered afterward.

Empaths. Just couldn't help taking care of their people.

Same as healers.

Chest tight with all the emotions he had no right to feel, he turned left, leading Arwen to the halfway house. The large residence was a place where users could choose to get clean at no financial cost—but someone with a more pragmatic mindset had also arranged for a significant open area right up against the home.

Because sometimes, junkies didn't want to be inside, screamed at the walls, thinking that they'd lost themselves in the phantasmagoric world that existed for some long-term users.

Ivan's mother hadn't lived long enough to reach that stage.

It was to this open "backyard" protected by regular DarkRiver patrols that he took Arwen. A user had lit a fire in the large metal barrel that sat in one corner, and several people stood or sat around it, their faces shrunken and sallow and their eyes bright. Others sat wrapped up in blankets that looked relatively new and rocked back and forth. Still others slept under the stars, uncaring of the cold night wind.

None of them bore open wounds, or had broken bones, or showed any other signs of ill treatment or a rough life—other than, that is, the marks left by long-term drug abuse. Somebody was looking after these people.

His investigations told him that it was DarkRiver's charitable arm in conjunction with the Psy Empathic Collective. Because none of these junkies were changeling or human. They were *all* Psy, Jax a drug designed for them. It collapsed Silence and opened up the mind, at least for short bursts of time. In the end, however, it not only burned out the users' ability to speak and think, it stole the very thing that made them Psy, but by then, the junkies were too far gone to care.

Ivan's mother had still been able to telepath when she died, but barely. Her voice had gone from a firm, clear sound in his head to a rasping whisper he could barely hear. He'd have wondered if she'd called out to him at the end, panicked and helpless, but he knew she wouldn't have; she'd died lost in the petals of the crystalline flower, her son far from her thoughts.

Jax wasn't needed now, of course. Silence had fallen, emotion no longer a crime. Most of the users here would've begun to inject or inhale it before the fall, perhaps in a hopeless quest for freedom—or perhaps just because they'd wanted to run from their lives. There were, however, a startling number of fresh young faces.

He'd spoken to some of them.

"Too hard, too hard, too hard."

A refrain he'd heard from more than one mouth. They'd turned to Jax because they were scared of who they were outside the Protocol.

"I'm nothing and no one, a null value," one youth had whispered to him, as if imparting a great truth. "Just a drone. No personality. No self."

Caged mice who no longer knew how to live in the wild, she and

others like her sought only to numb the world, forget their pain—
because there were plenty of psychic scars beneath the drugged-out
stares, plenty of stories of traumatized children and crushed souls.

"The sadness here," Arwen said, his eyes pools of silvery darkness,
"it hangs like a cloud."

Though Ivan had never been a toucher, he'd made an exception for
Arwen after realizing how much physical contact meant to his cousin.
Arwen was too generous, too much the empath, to ask for anything
that would make another person uncomfortable, but Ivan had eyes
and a brain, had figured it out.

It turned out that he didn't mind touch if it was about taking care
of another person. Except for Soleil. With her, for her, he'd been a
different man—for a fragment of a moment in time.

*I don't need my memories to tell me that I would've never just walked
away from you. You're too important to me, Ivan Mercant.*

It didn't matter how much he wanted to believe Soleil's statement,
didn't even matter if her words were the purest truth. He'd been another Ivan then, had touched the shooting star of her and believed he
had a chance at some kind of normality.

He'd been wrong.

Chapter 30

I'm getting reports from hospital empaths that they haven't been able to successfully communicate with the still-conscious Psy who appear to be on the island. All attempts—including by my most senior people—have failed.

Of significant concern is that a number have slid from incoherence to catatonia, while those who fell into comas during the incident remain in that state, their brain waves erratic.

My Es are picking up constant pulses of panic and terror, and the medical teams are worried about the patients' hearts. They're beating at a rate that's not sustainable.

—Message from Ivy Jane Zen, president of the Empathic Collective,
to fellow members of the Ruling Coalition

THE COLD REALITY of his future a vise around his mind, Ivan put his hand on Arwen's shoulder, squeezed.

Reaching up, Arwen touched his fingers to Ivan's in a silent thank-you. Then he took a quiet breath and went to take a seat next to a young woman with a vacant stare. Sophisticated haircut, cashmere sweater, and shoes handmade by an Italian cobbler—yet Arwen didn't hesitate so much as a second before he came down on the dirty lawn chair.

Because Arwen was an E first. The rest was pretty window dressing.

Soleil would like him. And Arwen would like her.

He wanted to tell Arwen about her, even though he had no right to her. If she'd marked him as the cats and Arwen both claimed, then he had to convince her to remove that mark. He *would not* drag her into the cage with him.

And though the spider was the ugliest of his scars, the rest of him wasn't exactly pretty. There was a reason he walked to the halfway house almost every night. As a reminder—of what he could've been, what he could *still* become.

Even now, a hidden part of him understood why these people took the drug. He'd experienced the lying beauty of it far too young, his mind opening up like a flower in bloom. A crystalline flower with a thousand petals, a thousand possibilities of life and existence.

He hadn't known what was happening. He'd been a child, a toddler really. He shouldn't even have those memories, but perhaps it was a side effect of the drug, the impossibility of forgetting. He'd wandered the crystalline pathways for hours, perhaps days. All he knew was that he'd woken on the floor of their grungy motel, thirsty and hungry and with the dirty carpet's rough weave an imprint on his cheek.

He hadn't cried. He'd already learned not to cry. His mother wouldn't hear him, and if one of her friends was in the room and conscious, it might result in a slap to the face and an order for him to shut up.

Not all his mother's friends took the "special medicine" she'd given him after he asked her for food. The medicine ones weren't so bad— they mostly just sat there with strange smiles on their faces, their eyes holes with nothing behind them. He didn't like the dead eyes, but those friends were better than the ones who were wide awake and full of meanness.

That day, however, he'd seen he was alone with his mother—but he still hadn't cried. Instead, he'd hungered for the crystalline flower, for the pretty and warm place without boundaries—unlike his real world, in which he was either trapped inside small filthy rooms or huddled under a blanket on a street corner, with a woman who had eyes of dazzling blue and hair of black.

"My baby boy," she'd say as they shivered under the blanket. "Tomorrow will be different, just you wait. I have a line on a great job." Red veins in her eyes, trembling hands. "We'll buy you all the eats you want, get you a nice fluffy bed. It'll be like a dream."

Swallowing hard, he thrust his hands into his pockets and told himself to call Arwen back, turn around. But he didn't. Because that was part of the test. To stand here in a place where he knew he could buy the drug with a single nod, a single moment of eye contact, and *not* do it.

The doctor who'd watched over him since Grandmother brought him home had told him to stop baiting himself this way, but Ivan had no intention of doing that. He understood what Dr. Raul didn't—Jax seduced with counterfeit beauty, forged happiness. Each time he stood in a place like this, with hollow-eyed people stripped of pride and sense of self, he understood the truth: that Jax was a leash, same as Silence.

There was no freedom or beauty in the crystalline flower.

A junkie was a junkie, regardless of whether their drug of choice was heroin or Jax. Once hooked, they'd do anything to feed their hunger . . . even sell their "precious baby boy." It had happened only once, that cold calculation on his mother's face, and though she hadn't gone through with it, Ivan would never forget.

Jax stole *everything*.

"Back again?" croaked a man of about five feet whose face had shriveled inward, his once-pale skin now mottled and discolored by dark marks—the remnants of old scabs he'd picked at until they bled.

He hugged a plush blanket around his shoulders, a battered paperback in one hand.

Ivan had bought him that blanket, after seeing him on the street one day looking into the window of a shop that sold them. It wasn't that Clarence didn't have access to a blanket, but he'd wanted that particular green one.

A small enough thing, but it had made him light up from within.

Ivan had the feeling the other man was actually much taller than five feet. But he'd been walking hunched over for so long that he'd forgotten how to straighten up. Regardless of his physical state, however, his small brown eyes were sharp, his mind present; Clarence had taken up the assistance of the halfway house, given up walking the crystalline flower.

"You better be careful," the older Psy man said, "or cats will start to think you're here jonesing for a fix." A hacking cough, followed by a jerk of his head. "And bringing soft creatures like that one around. What were you thinking? You throw deer to wolves, too?"

"He'll be fine." Arwen might be soft of heart, but he could be paradoxically tough when it came to helping wounded birds; the girl with the previously blank gaze was already whispering to him. "You're well."

Another rattling cough, but Clarence nodded. "Body is fucked up from all the poison I shoveled into it, but I do have better days—gives me hope." His eyes shone. "She still calls to me, that crystalline bitch. Still tells me of all the splendor I could experience, all the pathways I could dance."

Clarence had once been a scholar of mathematics, but literature had been his "one true love." A love he'd been forbidden from pursuing under Silence. Too much emotion in stories, too much passion, too much empathy.

These days, Clarence read story after story, novel after novel. The halfway house had given him a computronic reader, but he treasured paperbacks, hoarded any he was able to trade for or buy.

Tonight, Clarence looked Ivan in the face, a sense of weight to him. "You'll never understand, young man. You can't. You've never seen the searing wonder that exists when Jax lights up the neural pathways."

Ivan didn't correct him. The only people who knew the reality of his childhood and what it meant for him were Grandmother, Dr. Raul, Silver, and Canto. Canto because he'd been fourteen when Ivan came into the family—plenty old enough to know that something was wrong with his newest cousin. And Silver because she was Ena's successor.

Grandmother had asked Ivan's permission regardless before informing Silver. "I won't take the choice from you."

"Tell her," Ivan had said at once. "She needs to know of all possible weaknesses in the system."

"When it comes to sheer willpower, Ivan, you are the strongest of my grandchildren," Ena had said. "I have stubborn grandchildren as a rule, but you push it to the nth degree. I have every faith you'd rather cut your own throat than ever again taste Jax."

Silver had brought up the topic with Ivan only once—after Ena first told her of Ivan's history. "Ivan, Grandmother says you consider yourself a weakness in the Mercant armor. That's the most ridiculous thing I've ever heard—you and Canto *built* our current security armor.

"As for mental strength? It's not even a question. You stood up to Grandmother even as a child—if that's not a sign of implacable will, I don't know what is."

That was it. The end of the discussion as far as his cousin was concerned. Even when someone had tried to hurt Silver, no one had looked at Ivan with a jaundiced eye. He'd been investigated and cleared per the same checklist he'd have used himself against anyone else in the same position. Soon as he was cleared, he'd been fully briefed on the investigation with the—correct—assumption that he'd want to do everything in his power to eliminate the threat.

Silver *didn't*, however, know about Ivan's habit of eliminating hostile Mercant enemies who didn't play by the accepted rules—or his tendency to take out Jax dealers. He only targeted the utterly evil for the former, was far broader in his approach when it came to the latter.

"Plausible deniability," Grandmother had said, then given him a penetrating look. "I don't suppose you intend to stop anytime soon?"

"They're vermin." Ivan felt no guilt whatsoever for his actions. "I'll make sure it never touches Silver."

An arch look. "Dear boy, Silver would fillet us both if she knew we dared keep this from her."

"But we protect her," Ivan had murmured. "Her, and Arwen, and even Canto. They all have a shot in this new world. I'm not going to bring them down with me."

White lines around Ena's mouth, a rare sign of tension. "You are my grandchild. I did not raise you to be a shadow in bloody service, and none of your cousins would want that for you if they knew of it."

"I know." She'd given him every advantage, tried to channel him toward paths far less dark, but Ivan had never wavered. He knew who and what he was.

A prowling cat in his mind, the memory of fingers against his cheek.

What would Soleil think of his murderous little hobby?

"Is it worth it?" he said, asking Clarence the question he'd never been able to ask his mother. "All the destruction the drug's done to your body, and to your relationships with others?"

"What relationships?" Clarence snorted. "I have deeper relationships with the leopards and humans who run the halfway house than I ever did with my own family. Cold as ice they were, took Silence real seriously."

A sudden heaviness to his features, the folds of his face drooping. "If only I'd been born a few decades later . . ." Looking up, he pinned Ivan with a gaze far too powerful for a man this emaciated and tired.

"Don't waste this chance, young man. You have what I could've only imagined—the freedom to build bonds, to be more than a lone star in the dark."

With that, the old man—who wasn't so old after all—shuffled away, going to sit in a lounger next to someone who was clearly still addicted. With her layers of clothing and her treasured cart of belongings next to her, the woman looked like any of the homeless. What gave her away as Psy was the obsidian of her eyes.

Most Psy eyes only did that in the throes of a huge use of power—or under great emotion. But with the Jax-addicted, it could become a permanent state. It wasn't common, and it didn't appear to affect their vision, but it was a strange and eerie thing even for a man who'd seen his own eyes do that while looking into a mirror.

No light would ever again fill the addict's eyes, not even if the therapists managed to wean her off the drug. From what he'd learned since he'd found out about this place, that was unlikely to happen. Another resident had told him that ten people in the local population had eyes of permanent black. Only one had been open to rehabilitation—and though he'd gone through the full program and was holding on to his sobriety, his eyes remained obsidian.

Another shuffle, this one more stealthy, one of the users sidling up to him. "You looking for a hit?" It was a low murmur, the eyes that flicked up at him rimmed in red. "I got extra." Then he named a price that was double the street price.

Ivan could've ended this man then and there, but all that would've done was eliminate a user. This man was just trying to make a quick buck so he could then go and buy more of his poison of choice. Ivan's targets were those who produced the poison and spread it out.

"No," he murmured. "I'm looking for a lot more than that. Finder's fee involved."

The user's eyes grew bright. "I knew it," he hissed. "I knew that you shiny ones must be using. Life is nothing without the light it gives."

A shudder of purest pleasure, an awful, terrible thing to witness. "You just have the money to look better. Look like you're not inside the flower."

Ivan let the man have his delusions; it was all some of these people would ever have. "Do you know anyone who can hook me up or shall I talk to someone more connected?"

As expected, the junkie bristled. "Hey, I found you. This is my score." He leaned closer in a waft of odor—unwashed flesh and the miasma of the streets—that threatened to send Ivan back to his childhood. "What's the finder's fee?"

"Whatever I pay the dealer, I pay you ten percent of it."

He could see the man attempting to do the math, fail, his pathways too degraded. So he gave him an exorbitant number. When the time came—*if* the time came—he wouldn't give this junkie that money. Because to give him money would be as bad as feeding the poison into the junkie's veins himself. Instead, he'd transfer the money into the accounts of the halfway house, as he'd always intended.

The junkie's eyes were hot little spotlights in his shrunken face. "Deal," he said. "Deal." He scratched at his arms. "I'll speak to the one who can provide. I'll find out how much he can get you."

"Remember, you never saw me," Ivan ordered. "You don't know who I am. Just one of the shiny ones trying to get a big score for his friends."

A gleam of a feral kind of intelligence, that of an animal starving for food. "How much is that worth to you?"

This time, the stare Ivan gave him was the flat, dead one that so worried his grandmother. The junkie shriveled away. "Okay, okay." He threw up his hands, the palms pockmarked with scabs where he'd dug at his own skin. "Was just asking. Where do I find you?"

"You don't," Ivan said. "I'll find you."

Then he walked away and over to the shadows on the far side of the encampment, knowing the junkie would be anxious to track down the dealer, make his money. Ivan didn't particularly care about the dealer, either—oh, he *would* kill the man, take him out of circulation, and he'd feel no guilt about it. But first, he'd get from him the name of the one higher up the chain, and he would do that again and again until he got to the person at the very top.

"You've walked here nearly every night since you've been in the city," said a deep and smooth male voice at his side.

Chapter 31

"Do not steal from empaths. I find any of you doing that shit, we'll be having a long private conversation in the dark."

"But what do we do if they just *give* us stuff? My neighbor E actually full-on threw a sweater at me because it was cold!"

"Yah, man. The other day, this E just stopped me in the street and told me he was taking me out to eat because I needed some TLC. I couldn't even say no, he had such, like, soft eyes. It's like they're witches. Only the kind that isn't evil."

—Conversation between gang members caught on Enforcement surveillance (New York, April 2083)

IVAN DIDN'T STARTLE at Vaughn's comment; he'd sensed the DarkRiver sentinel prowl up to him, had known something was coming. "No crime in that."

Vaughn D'Angelo slid his hands into the pockets of the black cargo pants he was wearing today, his upper half clad in a simple olive green T-shirt that hugged his biceps. Lucas Hunter's right-hand man, Vaughn had hair of amber-gold that he tied back in a queue, and eyes so close to gold that Ivan wondered if they changed when Vaughn shifted form; the sentinel was as lethal a predator as the DarkRiver alpha. Only Vaughn wasn't a leopard.

That particular fact wasn't common knowledge, but neither was it a secret. So Ivan's family knew that Vaughn was a jaguar, one who'd been raised in DarkRiver. "What was it like," he found himself asking Vaughn, "being a jaguar in a pack of leopards?"

"Worried about our new healer, are you?" Vaughn's voice held no amusement or open interest, but Ivan didn't make the mistake of assuming that the man had no strong feelings on the point.

"News travels fast," he said.

"I'm a sentinel. And DarkRiver works as well as it does because we talk to each other." Folding his arms, he said, "Why do you come here?"

Ivan considered many answers, discarded all of them, settling for a bland, "I like to walk. It falls within my walking route."

Unexpectedly, Vaughn allowed his obvious lie to pass. Maybe because he didn't need to know Ivan's status as a drug user—or not—in order to keep track of him. Though Ivan was certain that Vaughn wasn't the one who'd been placed to watch him all this time. He was too senior, would handle matters far more important than keeping track of a lone Mercant who'd done nothing threatening to date.

"Growing up as a jaguar in a leopard pack," Vaughn said, "it was fine."

That told Ivan nothing. He didn't know why Vaughn had decided to speak to him, but it wasn't to share personal information. Then the jaguar surprised him. "Luc says you're linked to our new packmate. Not quite a mating bond. What's that all about?"

Ivan stopped himself from shifting on his feet by sheer force of will. "I saved her life once, that's all. It'll pass."

He could feel the jaguar staring at him. But again, Vaughn let it go. And Ivan remembered that cats were stealthy hunters, could wait for a long time in utter motionlessness before they struck.

Vaughn wasn't letting anything go; he was just biding his time.

Odd, how many similarities he was discovering between them and his own family. Never would he have predicted that he'd find such parallels with a clan of changelings.

"Make sure you don't forget that healer when you leave." The sentinel nodded toward Arwen. "They tend to give until there's nothing left—but you already know that."

"Why do you call him a healer?" Arwen's designation wasn't a public thing; to most of the world, he was a telepath who worked in marketing and communications for businesses connected to the family.

"I can smell it," was the deadpan response. "Or it might be that he just gave that addict his thousand-dollar sweater."

Ivan glanced over, swore under his breath. "I can't leave him alone for a single minute."

Vaughn slapped him on the back. "And you're all but mated to another healer." A glint in the near-gold of his eyes. "Welcome to the rest of your life."

As the sentinel melted away into the dark, Ivan went to rescue Arwen. "She'll just pawn it for money for drugs," he said to his cousin as the two of them walked away.

"At least she'll be warm until then."

Sighing, Ivan began to shrug off his jacket so Arwen could throw it on over his thin tee. But Arwen shook his head. "I'm heading home soon as we get to your place. Meeting with other Es." He turned those uptilted eyes on Ivan.

"What?" Ivan all but grunted.

"I just want to say something. Please listen." No lightness now, nothing but the power of an empath.

Ivan gave a curt nod.

"I never read people, not on purpose. I did as a kid, though, before I knew how to control my abilities."

"That's not a problem." Ivan knew too well what it was to have psychic abilities he couldn't control or didn't understand.

"Please, Ivan. *Listen.*" Arwen halted on the street.

Echoing him, Ivan turned to face his cousin.

"I don't know if it's because of the accidental reads when I was a child," Arwen said, "or just because I've grown up with you, but I've always believed you don't think you deserve to be happy."

He continued when Ivan didn't answer. "I know there are things I don't know about you." A wry smile. "You're all so protective, it would be infuriating if I didn't love you so much. I'm not a glass vase, you know—I won't break under hard pressure."

Shaking his head, he waved away the exasperated complaint. "But no matter what I do or don't know, I'm very certain of what I feel from you now—an ember of happiness." Open, unshielded eyes that shone with love unhidden and offered without expectation. "Don't throw that away." A whispered plea. "You deserve joy, Ivan. Hold on to her, on to the spark of joy inside your heart."

IVAN still hadn't processed Arwen's words by the time he walked into his apartment alone, Genara having been waiting for Arwen when they arrived. It was just as well that—her friendship with Arwen aside, the telekinetic was about as sociable as Ivan—she'd made no effort to prolong the evening.

Arwen, meanwhile, had simply looked at Ivan, his hope a silent but potent thing.

Strange, how such a gentle being could have so much steel to him when it came to the people he cared about. Then again, he *was* Ena Mercant's grandson.

Ivan closed the apartment door behind himself on that thought.

He was used to aloneness, even sought it, but Arwen's statement had inadvertently torn open a yawning emptiness within. In seeking to help him, his cousin had shown him exactly what he could've had if the spider didn't live in his head, born of toxins so complex that no medic had ever been able to explain the process that had created him.

A mutation.

That was how his DNA had been described in one dry medical report. And that was what he was: a mutated version of normal, one so far off the curve that the curve no longer existed.

Perhaps he'd have risked a relationship with Soleil if the problem had been mere genetics. He'd have explained why they couldn't procreate together, and asked if she'd be all right with adoption. He knew the answer to his question already; she was a healer, wasn't she? Big open heart and an inability to do anything other than embrace wounded or lost creatures.

She'd have enfolded those children's tiny souls in love.

But the problem wasn't only genetics. The problem was what the genetics had birthed: a bloated and monstrous thing that would swallow everything in its path. Including the obstinate cat who refused to let go of him.

A flexing of claws in his mind, the prowling brush of fur.

Gut tight, he fought against the wonder of that, of a bond primal and raw. The first thing he did when he walked into his bedroom was strip and walk into the shower. He always felt coated in filth after a visit to the halfway house area. He knew the reaction was a psychosomatic one, that there was nothing the users could do that would cling to him—but still, he stood under blazing-hot water with his eyes closed until he felt clean at last.

Not clean enough to touch Soleil, but enough to pass in the outside world.

Then, after rubbing his hair and body dry with a rough towel, he headed to bed. He was tired, needed to recharge. He was on the edge of sleep when he found himself confronted by a cat with eyes of tawny gold. She prowled inside his mind, her fur sliding against his skin, and her claws running lightly over his body.

Ivan didn't attempt to push out the intruder. His shields down, he admitted that he wanted her here with him. A deadly confession, a deadly need.

SOLEIL kissed Razi's furry little head and stroked her hand down Natal's back while the moon and the stars rotated slowly around the room from the night light plugged into a wall socket. It was Razi's favorite, Yariela had told her, given to her by Lucas when their alpha discovered she wasn't sleeping, her world full of nightmares.

"He slept in his panther form beside her and Natal for a whole week after we came here," Soleil's mentor had said, her eyes drenched with devotion for her new alpha. "He didn't leave until she was able to sleep the night through two nights in a row.

"I worried his mate would be angry with us for stealing so much of his time, but oh, Leilei, she's a healer, too. One of the Psy empaths with the stars in her eyes. Their niñita is much younger than Razi, but she's a fierce little panther, protective of Razi in a way you'll have to see to believe."

Laughter. "The twins are insistent that little Naya is their baby. And she's insistent that she isn't a baby!" Cheeks creasing, she'd said, "I would pity those boys in the years to come, for she's not built to accept their protective tendencies, but I have a feeling all three will be quite the hellions together—and they're teaching our cubs how to be ferocious and naughty, too."

Only those who'd lived under the subtle suffocation of SkyElm's negligent alpha could understand the value of that gift. The rot had begun with Soleil's alpha grandfather, but Monroe had taken it to the next level, until it poisoned their pack. But these two babies would grow up wild and free, sneaking out of windows and, as they grew older, probably sneaking *into* windows.

The thought made her smile as she petted each cub once more.

Razi and Natal had insisted that she put them to bed, giving her heart another boost of sheer joy. Though the Ryders had another spare room the cubs could've used, Tamsyn had told her that the two always preferred to bunk with the twins.

"We weren't ready for them the first time they stayed over," the healer had said, "and threw together a big fluffy futon for them in between the boys' beds. Next thing you know, it's morning and all four of them are on that futon."

Feline delight in her eyes, the healer had leaned in close, her inner warmth a kiss of love that surrounded Soleil. "I should've known. The cat in me still wants to jump onto the futon with them, and the boys are waging a campaign to get futons for their beds when they outgrow their current ones."

Tonight, the twins had gone to sleep in their own beds . . . or she thought they had. Until she glanced over to her right and saw dark blue eyes looking at her. She knew this cub's name now, though she could only distinguish him from his brother by his pajamas. "Why aren't you asleep, Roman?" she whispered.

A sweet, sweet smile, and then he held out his arms for a hug. Heart so melted by now it was just goo, she moved to sit on his bed so she could cuddle him, too. His hair was silky soft and still smelled of the shampoo from that night's bath, his arms warm and unexpectedly strong.

When he let go, he snuggled back down into bed, blinked sleepily for a couple of seconds . . . and was asleep with cub rapidity. An adorable little snore escaped him a moment later, had her pressing a hand to her heart. She made sure his blanket was tucked snugly around him, checked one last time on the other three cubs, then made herself leave the room.

A hallway light glowed softly to light her way, but the rest of the house was quiet. Tamsyn had given her the room directly opposite the children's, so she was soon changing into a sleep tee she'd borrowed from Tamsyn. The rest of her nighttime routine didn't take long, and her body sighed when she hit the bed.

The bedding was plush and soft, and below the fresh scent of washing powder, it held the scent of the Ryder family. Impossible for it not to, when it was in their home that she slept.

Pack. They were her pack.

Their scent was comfort.

As was his.

The sophisticated, beautiful, dangerous Psy who'd saved her life, then brought her home. Cool and deadly though his scent might be, it didn't scare her in the least. How could it when she knew beyond any doubt that he would never hurt her? She might not remember their first meeting, but the knowledge of who he was to her was there in their every interaction—and even in the infuriating way he kept on trying to warn her off.

Soleil scowled and turned onto her back to stare up at the ceiling.

Her cat prowled inside her skin, not happy at being so far from him, even unhappier about the fact that he'd walked into the dark alone.

She might've lain awake for hours had her body and mind not been shattered after the events of the day; the deluge of joy after the pain she'd carried for so long, it had smashed every one of her foundations.

Sleep crashed over her in a silent black wave.

She bit back the whimper that wanted to escape as her heavy eyelids closed despite her attempts to keep them open. With sleep came the ghosts of all those she hadn't been able to save. They stared at her with dark, accusing eyes, their faces pale in death and their bodies bloodied and broken.

"I'm sorry." A faint whisper before her exhausted body and mind shut down, dropping her deep into the abyss.

Chapter 32

Re: *Query about the remains of Norah Mercant*

As per standard operating procedure for deceased found in such circumstances, she was cremated within two hours of discovery. Her cremains are due for final destruction tomorrow. Please advise if you wish to collect and make your own arrangements for disposal.

> —Bureau of Death and Family Notification Services
> (10 May 2059, 11:02 a.m.)

Re: *Query about the remains of Norah Mercant*

Yes, we will collect the cremains. A teleport-capable Tk will be arriving at 11:15 a.m.

> —Ena Mercant (10 May 2059, 11:04 a.m.)

"Ivan, we have your mother. Would you like to bury her in our private cemetery? The authorities are unaware of it and she won't be disturbed there."
"Is she ash, Grandmother? She told me the death guard makes people like us into ash."
"Yes, I'm afraid it was done before I was ever notified. You won't be able to see her again. I'm sorry for that."
"She wasn't inside there anymore. She was hollow."

"The respect we give to the dead is not to the hollow shells left behind, but to the people they were in life. And she was your mother. I know you're angry with her, but that is also why such ceremonies are important: they allow us to create a line between what has been and what is to come."

"She always wanted to see the sea. She heard about it, but she never saw it. Can we take her there?"

—Conversation between Ena Mercant and
Ivan Mercant (10 May 2059, 12 noon)

SOLEIL KNEW SHE was sleeping, but she still couldn't stop the dreams from unfurling. They always began the same way, with bloody claws ripping away the soothing nothingness of rest, to expose faces and bodies and a world that shimmered gray with fog.

It had been foggy that morning when it all went so terribly wrong.

She'd been frowning as she walked through the trees, the cool brush of the fog against her skin and her cat alert inside her. Her head had been full of worry about the man with pale eyes who she'd had to leave with no warning. He was so *important* to her, and he'd think she'd left because she didn't want him. She had to fix that, had to—

Her chest clutched, her breathing speeding up.

The fog was whispering away, the dead ready to confront and accuse her.

"I'm sorry, I'm sorry," she whimpered in her dreams. "I'm so sorry."

But the boy who stood in front of her wasn't bloody or broken or gray. He was warm with life, his eyes a piercing pale hue and his hair wind-tousled black. "Why are you sorry?" he asked. "You didn't kill her. She killed herself."

Trembling, she went to go to her knees so they'd be at the same height . . . but they already were, her body as small as his, and her hands delicate and childish. "What's happening?"

A frown marring that smooth brow, he looked down at the hands she'd spread out in front of herself, then lifted his own hands. "Regression?" he muttered. "Dream mechanics." He didn't sound like a child.

Soleil couldn't help it. She poked him with a finger . . . and jerked it back as fast when she felt flesh and bone. Looking down at the spot on his shoulder that she'd touched, he frowned again, then looked back at her, so solemn and serious that it made her sad.

"Why do you have green hair?"

Her hand jerked up, touched the strands. "I got paint in it today." No, not today. A long time ago, when she'd still had a family of her own, including a mother who'd delighted in allowing her to play wild. "My mother let me do anything I wanted."

"So did mine."

Cracks of silver across his face, across the world, across the dream, until the entire thing was a fractured pane of mirrored glass, and she was falling, falling . . .

Soleil jerked awake on a gasp, her heart thunder and her mouth dry. Looking around with wild eyes, she half expected that very lifelike dream boy to be standing next to her. But he wasn't. Of course he wasn't. He was a man now. A very dangerous man who her cat had claimed. "Mine," she murmured. "Mine."

Pushing her braid over her shoulder, she reached for the glass of water she'd put on the bedside table. It was only after she'd gulped it down that her eyes registered the time on the vintage bedside clock.

It was six in the morning. She'd fallen asleep at midnight.

Six hours of uninterrupted sleep. Well, but for the dream—but that had been more unsettling than terrifying. And there was something . . .

Narrowing her eyes, she rolled the dream backward, and there it was, the most important fragment of memory from what she thought of as her lost month. Heart thudding, she pushed off the blanket and got out of bed.

She didn't know what she was expecting when she looked in the mirror in the attached bathroom, but her hair was still black and she was still an adult of twenty-seven years of age, and she still had a face that was too thin. She used to have rounded cheeks and generous curves. These days, she was just bones held together by skin, and it wasn't a good look on her. Her Psy could pull off razor cheekbones, but Soleil's body was made for softness.

Her Psy.

Yes.

Determined to figure things out between them today, she got naked and walked into the shower. Afterward, she released her hair from the braid, brushed it out, then dressed in the same pants as last night. She paired them with a fine wool sweater in bright fuchsia.

"One of the juveniles left it behind the last time she visited and I washed it for her and set it aside," Tamsyn had told her. "I know she won't mind if you borrow it."

It was the brightest color Soleil had worn in the time since the massacre. Making a note to give some kind of gift to the juvenile in thanks when she had the means to do so, she opened her bedroom door; instinct and need had her padding across to the cubs' room. All four lay on the futon in a happy pile, the twins on either side of Razi's and Natal's curled-up bodies. They were still in the forms in which they'd gone to bed, and appeared in a deep sleep, but Natal stirred a mere second after she touched his fur, his sleepy eyes blinking open.

"Hello, Nattie." Stroking his head, she kissed his nose, keeping her voice to a low whisper. "I'm going out but I'll be back later." She hadn't wanted to wake either cub but knew she couldn't simply vanish, not after all that had gone before. "You'll tell Razi?"

A firm nod before he butted her hand in a silent demand. Laughing softly, she scratched and petted him until he fell back into sleep. He was young, but she thought he'd remember—she also intended to give the cubs a call once they were up, reassure them that nothing was wrong and she was fine.

Heart tight with love, she left the sleeping cubs and padded down the stairs and into the kitchen, where she saw that the coffeemaker had already turned itself on via the timer function.

Inhaling the scent, she set out three mugs, figuring it had to be either Tamsyn or Nathan—or both—who'd be rising soon. That done, she picked up the pretty pink tote-style handbag Tamsyn had given her when she'd asked if she could borrow a bag, and stocked it with the small travel medical kit that Tamsyn had put together for her at her request.

Then she added energy bars, a packet of mixed nuts, a few water-soluble sachets that would get extra calories into her, and a bottle of water—all from the pantry cupboard Tamsyn kept stocked for pack-mates.

"Grab whatever you need," she'd told Soleil. "It gets restocked as it's used up. And feel free to help yourself to any baking I do. Plus, the fruit bowl is a free-for-all. To be honest, my whole kitchen is"—a grin—"*except* for my special cookies." A bump of her shoulder against Soleil's. "Don't tell anyone but I'll share with you."

Smiling at the memory, she added an apple to her impromptu lunch.

Not long afterward, she felt a stirring of power in the air, her cat on alert even before Nathan walked into the room.

"You're up early," he said with the slightest brush of his knuckles against her cheek, the touch of a senior member of the pack a thing of welcome to her cat. "Couldn't sleep?"

"Had an odd dream and woke up," she said past the knot in her chest, taking in his freshly washed hair, jeans, and long-sleeved blue shirt that he'd folded up to the elbows to reveal muscled forearms. "Are you on duty?"

A small nod. "Tammy insists on getting up with me, so she'll be down soon. Save some room for her pancakes." The way he spoke of his mate, the quiet love entwined in every word, it made her heart ache with memories poignant and old: her parents had spoken of each other that way, too.

"How else could I snag you for skin privileges without our lovely but incorrigibly curious children poking their noses in?" Tamsyn said as she walked in, her eyes sparkling.

Soleil was sure Nathan blushed before he turned to nip Tamsyn lightly on the ear. The other woman laughed and patted his chest, before kissing his jaw. And Soleil felt the bond between them, strong and enduring and encompassing anyone that came near in its warm radius.

"Good morning, sweetheart." Tamsyn walked over to give Soleil a gentle hug. "Blueberry pancakes?"

Overwhelmed by the protectiveness she felt from them both, Soleil just nodded.

Then she sat in the kitchen and watched the dance of two people who'd been in each other's lives so long that they spoke without speaking. While Tamsyn cooked, Nathan used a datapad to clear up work that must fall on him as a senior sentinel. Every so often, however, they'd look up and exchange the odd word, or just a smile.

At one point, Tamsyn waved the spatula in her hand. "Since you saw Rome and Jules mastermind the great escape last night, I'm sure you don't need the warning, but just in case—they *will* attempt to use their wiles to make you an accomplice to their crimes. Be on guard."

Thinking of the two adorable boys who'd taken Razi and Natal under their wing, Soleil twisted her lips to one side in a thoughtful pose. "I'm only a junior healer," she said at last, her cat glorying in being part of a bigger whole once again. "I'm allowed to be a criminal."

Nathan groaned. "Great. All they need. Another adult enabler." But he had laughter in his eyes as he said it. "All these gray hairs?" He pointed at his full head of black hair threaded with strands of silver. "Each and every one due to our two demons. And now they have two more accomplices in training."

Soleil heard in his tone the affection and love of a father who enjoyed his children and their friends. "Natal and Razi, they seem happy."

Recognizing it for a question, Tamsyn told her about the ocelot cubs, about how sad and withdrawn they'd been at the start, how much healing and therapy it had taken for them to step out of their shells. She also spoke about sweet and kind Salvador, with Nathan picking up the thread to update her on Duke and Lula.

"Two were green as grass," he said, the steel in him suddenly obvious. "Should've never had the responsibilities they did in SkyElm. They're now junior soldiers in training and having a far better time of it—they get to be young, to party with their friends in their off time, figure out who they are in the knowledge that there are stronger and more mature people holding the reins of the pack."

No matter how many questions Soleil asked, the couple didn't tire of answering them. "Have you met our boys?" Tamsyn said with a laugh when Soleil mentioned her insatiable need to fill in the gaps. "At one point, I swear Jules was asking a question every ten seconds."

The breakfast passed quickly.

When Nathan rose to grab his jacket, she said, "Are you going into the city? Can I catch a ride?" Her need to see Ivan hadn't abated at all in the time she'd spent in this kitchen, her soul torn in two. She hated that he was so far from her, and from the rest of her pack.

He should be *here*, should be part of all this, not cold and alone.

"Sure, you can ride with me." The sentinel kissed his mate goodbye. "Tell the boys to behave," he said to Tamsyn, "and I'll take them mud sliding later."

Tamsyn murmured something that made Nathan grin and kiss her deeper, before stepping back. But when Soleil would've followed him to the garage, Tamsyn stopped her. "Just a moment, honey. I have something for you."

Opening a drawer, she pulled out a card. When Soleil saw that it held an embedded credit chip, she blushed. "I was planning to pick up a job as a waitress—I saw some *help wanted* signs yesterday." It was how she'd supported herself after leaving the hospital.

"There's no need for that." Tamsyn touched her shoulder. "You're part of DarkRiver now, officially a junior healer under my command. You'll be paid according to your experience. Consider this an advance against your income."

Soleil didn't know how to process that. "In SkyElm . . . It didn't work like that." Monroe had controlled all the money, with everyone having to apply to him when they needed something.

Soleil had set up a small business as a teen after figuring out that there was a market for rare dried culinary herbs; she'd felt *so* guilty for fudging the books so she could tuck away a small percentage of the profits, but she'd hated begging Monroe for money even more. She'd bought her clothes at thrift stores to make her funds stretch out, crafted her jewelry out of pieces others had discarded—and discovered she had a skill there, too. People had loved her colorful jewelry, paid her to make them bespoke pieces.

Together, those things had given her the bare basics of an income.

Of course, she'd still had to bow and scrape to Monroe now and then so he wouldn't get suspicious. "There was food," she clarified, feeling awful and disloyal to her old pack for her thoughts. "Anyone could grab a meal in the pack kitchen, and Monroe paid all the utilities." He hadn't kept up with repairs to the aeries, or maintained the private road to their settlement, but they'd all had places to live. "It wasn't that bad."

Tamsyn's mouth tightened. "This might be a hard thing to hear, sweetheart, but your old pack was based on a seriously unhealthy foundation. Each member of a pack is meant to contribute to *and* gain from the strength of the pack—and as a DarkRiver healer, you'll be working damn hard, trust me. I have no doubts that you worked exactly as hard for SkyElm."

Shaking her head when Soleil would've interrupted, she said, "Food and utilities are the bare basics; those things alone are definitely not equal to a professional salary. Especially when SkyElm was an extremely financially healthy pack. Your alpha had the means to properly pay you and so does DarkRiver."

The senior healer pressed the card into Soleil's hand. "Use it or you'll be answering to me." A smile to take the sting out of the order. "I can sense your strong healing abilities, but do you also have medical training?"

"A little." Still feeling awkward, but not wanting to insult her new pack, Soleil put the card into her pocket. "Yariela talked Monroe into allowing me to attend a paramedic course."

"Think about whether you'd like to study further," Tamsyn said. "We have non-changeling packmates who bank on us—I've actually begun to have some success using my healing ability on them, but it's nowhere near as smooth as with other changelings. I'm guessing you worked mostly on ocelots?"

When Soleil nodded, Tamsyn said, "Even within changelings, healing can be unpredictable with those outside the healer's own species—but I haven't had any issues with our non-leopard feline packmates, so I'm guessing you'll be fine healing up injured cats who aren't ocelots." She rubbed Soleil's shoulder in gentle encouragement. "It's the blood bond with Lucas, I think. Gives us the 'in' we need. Still, having medical training as backup means we don't always have to rely only on our healing energy.

"But"—a smile—"that's a discussion for later. Today is for you—

and for that cool-eyed Psy you've claimed." An intent look. "Go find out why your mating bond is incomplete . . . unless . . . do you want it? The bond?"

"Yes. He's mine." No hesitation, the truth a song inside her.

"Then go, find the answer so you can both settle into the pack." A pause. "Though I have a feeling your Psy would do anything for you even without a bond. Be careful with him, little sister. He might look tough, but when strong men fall, they fall all the way. You're his weakness."

Throat thick and the need to go to Ivan a pulse inside her, Soleil nodded before she joined Nathan. She'd expected the ride to be a touch awkward, since even in a high-speed vehicle, it was a long drive. But Nathan had a warm and easy presence, and he didn't feel the need to fill the air with chatter, so she could just look out the window and think about the man she'd never expected but who she refused to give back.

Soon enough, Nathan was pulling up at DarkRiver HQ. "When you're ready to go home, just come back here," he said. "You'll be able to catch a ride with whoever is heading toward the territory next." Familiar dark blue eyes on her, this pair tempered by age and experience. "Do you drive? We can assign you a vehicle."

She shook her head, made herself say it. "My parents died in a crash. I was trapped with them."

Expression gentling, Nathan brushed a hand over her hair. "Then don't worry about it. You'll never have a problem hitching a ride with a packmate. Now go drum some sense into your Psy, and if he annoys you, you come to me."

Soleil suddenly understood what it must feel like to have a big brother. "Thanks, Nathan," she said, already a little in love with this man who'd been a stranger yesterday.

It was only after leaving his vehicle that she realized she didn't have Ivan's address. Her cat rolled its eyes and told her to go left.

Farah appeared beside her as she walked. "So," her friend said, "you don't need me anymore, do you?"

Soleil's eyes burned. "I'll always need you," she whispered, knowing that the Farah-shaped hole in her heart would never fill. "No one will ever take your place."

"I know. I'm the best." Hooking her arm through Soleil's, she laid her head down on her shoulder, her curls tickling the side of Soleil's face. "But you're not fractured anymore. You'll make new friends—you've already begun."

Soleil couldn't speak, but she reached up to touch that ghostly face.

A lopsided smile as her friend came to stand in front of her, Farah's big brown eyes full of mischief. "Love you, Leilei. Go wrangle that sexy man of yours." She winked. "Do everything I would do."

She was gone a heartbeat later, her voice held like a precious jewel in Soleil's heart, and the sadness of losing her settling like a thing old and weathered inside her. No longer was it a loss sharp and stabbing, and she even found herself laughing softly as she thought of the trouble Farah had gotten her into over the years.

God, she'd miss her best friend.

It was about ten minutes later that she found herself walking up the steps of an unfamiliar home bracketed between other narrow, old-fashioned homes of the same period. She didn't know which period, architecture far from her strong suit, but she thought it might be well over two hundred years ago.

The security system at the door, however, was top-notch and required a voice and retinal print for access. So she pressed the doorbell. When Ivan didn't answer the buzzer, she went to the security panel and scanned her palm. As expected, it was rejected—but it brought up the menu she wanted, which listed other ways access could be gained, should the scanners be down.

Please enter numerical code.

She began to type in a code below the flashing red instruction. She wasn't even thinking about it . . . until the instruction turned green to signify she'd passed that stage of entry.

Security Question #1: First name of eldest cousin.

Her fingers flew over the touchpad, typing out Canto, a name she'd never before heard in her life.

Security Question #2: Grandmother's home.

Soleil typed in: The Sea House.

Security Question #3: Where is she buried?

Soleil hesitated, a dark—and heavily masculine—wave of sorrow sweeping over her, then typed in: Nowhere.

Access granted.

A click, as the door lock disengaged. All the hairs on her arms standing up, she stepped through, then pushed it shut behind her. She should've been afraid of what was going on, the depth of their half-functioning bond, but all she felt was a certainty that this was where she was meant to be, urgency pounding at her.

She'd come into a small entryway, a narrow corridor to her right and a set of steep steps directly in front of her. "Ivan!"

Silence.

Her heart thunder, she began to climb.

Chapter 33

Ivan, call your grandmother.

—Ena to Ivan (20 July 2083)

IVAN KNEW HE was in trouble. He'd woken early, right after a hazy dream about a girl who'd looked a whole lot like Soleil, then decided to check out the situation in the Net.

That was where he'd made his mistake.

He'd emerged into the Net across from the psychic island that had broken off during the major PsyNet incident. Though he could "see" it, the dark mass was utterly blank to his psychic vision, as it was to everyone else. He'd caught the news reports yesterday, learned of a number of people whose minds had vanished from the PsyNet, but who were alive.

It should've been a simple matter for those people to tell others of what was going on in that fragment of the PsyNet, but every single individual found to date was either unable to communicate in a lucid fashion, in a coma, or catatonic on both the psychic and physical levels. Whatever was happening on the island had crashed all their brains.

Communication had proved impossible, though hospital empaths had reported erratic bursts of fear and confusion from their patients. That last piece of data wasn't public knowledge, but of course Grandmother knew of it without having put any of her children, her grandchildren, or their partners in a compromising situation.

The latter had never before been an issue, with their entire family below the radar. But now Silver was the director of the biggest emergency response organization in the world, Canto was bonded to a member of the Psy Ruling Coalition, and Arwen was an official member of the Empathic Collective and had taken the Collective's oath to protect the privacy of those he treated.

"Really, Ivan," Ena had murmured on a recent call, "soon, we shall be far too visible to run an information network."

"Maybe, Grandmother," Ivan had replied, "it's time to return to our roots. Back when Mercants were the knights to a king, walking right in the open rather than being the shadows behind the crown."

Onscreen, Ena had raised both eyebrows, the sky a turbulent gray behind her and her upper body clad in a shift of delicate bronze silk. "Once again, you surprise me. Perhaps you're right. Perhaps we come to a moment of change—after all, the world is in flux."

Her words had played in Ivan's mind as he wandered closer to the island. As he did so, he became aware that, in the aftermath of the incident, he'd forgotten to sever the fine threads that connected him to the people he'd saved. Links that had formed at the moment he grabbed hold of them and threw them to safety. Those threads had become stronger in the interim, turned silver with the barest touch of flame.

His abdomen went rigid in the physical world, but he was unable to sense any power flowing his way. He hadn't turned them into a spider's prey. For now, at least. Because the fact the threads had gained in strength was a warning that the spider wasn't only stirring, it was wide awake and looking to feed.

A moment of sheer panic before he remembered that his bond with

Soleil was a changeling thing. Nothing he could even see. No way for the spider to devour her. Not that he could trust it would remain that way as the spider gained in strength, the psychic mutation of Ivan stretching out its limbs in endless greed.

He went to sever his connections to the survivors from yesterday, hesitated . . . because some of those threads led to the island. He'd thrown people to the closest safe area. For many, that had meant the island. Which also meant they were probably now in a coma or locked inside their minds.

In trying to save them, he might have doomed them.

Jaw set, he used the threads to try to tug himself onto the island. Per the family-wide alert he'd received before he left the apartment yesterday evening, no one had been able to access the island to date. Psy minds literally could not cross empty psychic space.

It was akin to asking someone to walk over to the next neighborhood by crossing an expanse of outer space. It was neurologically and physically impossible. Psy minds couldn't survive in that dead space.

Except . . . Ivan was now standing on the island, his hands glinting with the flame-kissed silver of the threads he'd used to travel here. As if they'd acted like a spacesuit, keeping him alive for the journey. Which meant he *was* taking energy that wasn't his to take; he might not feel bloated with it, but that he was alive was an answer in itself.

Ivan had become the monster he'd spent a lifetime fighting.

He turned to look back the way he'd come, his gorge rising . . . and saw nothing but a wall of obsidian. His mind was anchored on the other side, this part of him a roaming echo—but he could no longer see his mind, far less the silvery bonds he'd used to reach this strange place. Neither could he make telepathic contact with any of his family.

A definite problem.

A roaming mind couldn't survive separated from the main part of the mind, and vice versa. At a certain point in time, the two parts would both begin to fragment, with the roaming part absorbed into the PsyNet. Giving him, in effect, a psychic lobotomy. At which point, his physical body would die.

Great.

However, since he'd learned young that to rail against that which couldn't be altered was a waste of time, he didn't try to throw himself against that infinite wall of black. Rather, he focused on the psychic structure of the barrier. The ones behind this island had been clever. Instead of trying to control each individual mind on the island, they'd simply isolated the entire island.

That had to be burning massive amounts of power.

Power such as that generated by Scarabs before they imploded.

Because Scarabs were inherently unstable. That was the problem, had always *been* the problem. Silence had been designed as a solution partially to deal with this exact scenario: to assist Psy who burned so hot, so out of control that they went insane or died in childhood, their brains unable to cope with the psychic overload.

That amount of power required very specific neural machinery. Machinery such as that in a dual cardinal's brain. And dual cardinals were the rarest of the rare, genetic anomalies so unusual that there was no statistical model for their occurrence in the PsyNet.

Had the Scarabs not been unstable—both psychically and mentally—no one would've worried about them. Rather, they'd have been studied for the potential for untrammeled psychic power. Because while not every Psy wanted to be a brutal power, it was a safe bet that most at the lower end of the Gradient wouldn't turn down an opportunity to safely supercharge their psychic abilities.

But, as with Ivan's own ability, it turned out that becoming a Scarab wasn't a choice—and it wasn't safe. Thanks to Grandmother's standing in the PsyNet, a standing that meant she'd been briefed fully on the entire situation, Ivan knew that Scarabs *had* been studied once—a generation into Silence.

Project Scarab had initially been lauded a great success. Removing the psychic rules mandated by Silence had removed the "dimmer switch" on the abilities of affected Psy.

It had also destroyed them.

"They all died," Grandmother had told him, her tone solemn as she stared out at the roiling waves of the ocean. "Either by their own hand, or at the hands of Council executioners. They were too unstable, fractured at the very core—and that instability, that psychic chaos, threatened to destabilize the Net."

Yet the separation of this island from the Net *hadn't* been chaotic.

No, it had been very well planned, and it had succeeded in its goal. Which meant that the Scarab power was being somehow stabilized. A task so difficult that, per information supplied by Grandmother's byzantine maze of personal contacts, only a rare few empaths had succeeded in doing it, and even then, the stability of their subjects was precarious at best.

He added it to the list of questions for which he needed to unearth answers. The priority was to find out the reason for the comas, catatonia, and disordered states. Especially as it appeared that, as of now, he was the only person outside the island who could access it.

With that in mind, he began to move away from the edge of the broken-off segment. It might be that the solution to his problem of being stuck here, cut off from his mind, might also lie deeper within the island.

If it didn't . . .

Death had never worried Ivan. He'd been up close and personal with it at too young an age. He'd always figured that when it was his time, it was his time. But to die because he hadn't set up a fail-safe—a stupid basic error?

He'd have to haunt his own dead body.

That this was an unknown situation that had thrown everyone wasn't an excuse. He was a security specialist, his job to consider how things could go pear-shaped. Yet he'd assumed he could get himself out of this—because he'd been getting himself out of various situations all his life.

"You, Ivan, take independence a touch too far at times," Grandmother had once said to him. "You don't always have to rely only on yourself. Such violent independence can become a weakness."

He'd been sixteen then, had politely listened to her words—then ignored them. Canto, Silver, Arwen, they'd worn off some of his edges with their unrelenting support, so that these days he *did*, at times, reach out to them for an assist.

At the core of it, however, he hadn't changed. And he'd proved Grandmother right. "You can say 'I told you so' if I make it out of here," he muttered in the strange psychic space he now inhabited.

Since he couldn't extricate himself, he'd have to hope that one of his family would give in to their nosy instincts and come looking for him before it was too late. Even then, they were unlikely to be able to wake him since he'd separated his mind into two parts. What they *could* do was ensure that his body stayed alive, while he fought to find a way out before it was too late and his mind simply stopped.

Because Ivan wasn't done with life. Not yet. Not while he was still himself enough to watch over Soleil, ensure that her new pack would treat her well, and that she'd live a life of happiness.

A small cat prowled inside him, swiping at him with an annoyed paw for what he'd done, the mess he'd gotten himself into. Mad, he had to be going mad to believe that their wild bond had followed him here, but he carried that annoyed cat with him as he walked in this psychic space unlike any he'd ever explored.

It was nothing akin to the PsyNet, with minds neatly grouped or laid out in various patterns, each with a small section of the Net to themselves. Here the minds sat jumbled up against each other, or hung twisted in streams of violent psychic energy that crackled with random bolts of lightning.

Driven by instinct, he'd avoided the bolts but now deliberately took a glancing hit—he needed the data. It felt like being sucked into a cyclonic vortex that didn't know whether it was twisting clockwise or anti-clockwise, creating brutal opposing forces that threatened to rip him apart.

Shaking it off with effort, he looked once again at all the minds being buffeted, felt a cold chill run through his veins. If the lightning continued . . . People were going to start dying. Soon. Those bolts held far too much unrestrained power, enough to crash and crush.

This explained the comas, the catatonia, the mental chaos.

He was no expert in psychic mechanics, but it was obvious that there were no safe zones. The power was too erratic. The only way for those caught in this zone to protect themselves would be to hunker down behind shields so heavy they could no longer interact in the physical world—but those would only last so long, and anyone not in on the plan for separation would've been taken by surprise, with no time to realize what was happening before they were hit by a bolt.

These people were in a critical countdown.

A tug on the part of him that held all those silver threads.

It led to a mind under considerable pressure from the bolts. He recognized that mind, though that should've been impossible. It was of a person he'd thrown onto the island, away from the abyss. In the same way he recognized this mind, he knew that it was on the brink of total catastrophic failure, far too weak to survive much more.

The cat nudged at him, told him to *remember*.

The memory came in a rush: Of the healer with big brown eyes who owned Ivan, and an alpha changeling with claw marks on one side of his face. A primal bond sealed in blood. A bond that would permit a transfer of power.

Ivan was no alpha. He was a monster, a spider that sucked others dry. He could kill this person if he opened up that part of his mind, the very part that had shoved a tendril outside a once-solid cage and formed the link between them. Yet if he didn't, they'd die regardless.

Thoughts grim, he consciously opened the door of the psychic prison for the first time in nearly two decades, releasing the spider but using all his adult knowledge in an attempt to reverse the polarity—his aim to pulse energy from himself *down* that silvery thread. Giving rather than devouring.

The mind flared with light, became stronger.

It had worked.

Shocked, he stood there for a second, staring. Why had he never considered this before? It was a *good* skill. He received his answer a heartbeat later. Because now that the spider was free, it was bunching in readiness to shoot out more lines of its web, hook in others, begin to *feed*.

Ivan slammed it back into its prison, feeling the pushback as it fought him. He'd have to be extremely careful with any future assists, act at rapid speed. To allow the spider to linger was to expose everyone in the vicinity to the mutation in him that just wanted to feed and feed and *feed*.

As if his mother's craving for the crystalline petals had burned itself into the cells of her son, creating a monstrous creature that was never satisfied, no matter how much power it had at its disposal. He'd always seen his mutated ability as a spider because of the web, the connections, but it could as well be termed a locust.

One that fed and fed, leaving nothing but a lifeless desert in its wake.

Moving on, searching for others to whom he was connected and could help, he saw that some minds in the ChaosNet were different. They glowed not with the dull starlight of the minds under assault, but with a dazzling kaleidoscopic energy that reminded him of the crystalline flowers . . . and they absorbed the lightning strikes rather than being damaged by them.

"Scarabs," he said, realizing he was seeing them in their purest form.

Not stable, not with the way those minds twisted and turned, the energies coming off them chaotic fuel for the lightning. Full of an enraged power. There were also a hell of a lot of Scarab minds. Nothing that could be explained by random chance. This, he understood at last, was the Island of the Scarabs, with the other minds caught in the slipstream, nothing but helpless fodder.

Yet, chaotic energy or not, the island held steady.

There had to be a controller behind it all, a mastermind . . . an architect.

Another tug on his mind, another desperate person struggling to survive. He offered an assist, even though it was dangerous. He still did it. Over and over again, until he couldn't avoid a lightning strike.

It blanked his mind, shot pain down his psychic pathways.

He barely held on to consciousness—he was critically low on psychic energy *and* he almost hadn't won against the spider. A lethal combination. Because the spider's goal was survival above all else. Set free, it would take and take and take, until there was nothing left on this island but empty husks.

Chapter 34

Power
Corrupts
So say they
I say
Power
Is a tool innocent
The corruption
An inner rot

—"Power" by Adina Mercant, poet (b. 1832, d. 1901)

A SHIVER IN her web, an unexpected shift . . . and an odd resonance.

Almost a sense of recognition.

She perceived it through all the points of contact in her new network, all the points of power.

Pausing in her current structural stabilization of the island network, she attempted to pinpoint the reason for the blip and found no evidence of an anomaly. After a moment, she shook it off. It was nothing, could be nothing. She knew everything that happened on the island.

It was her domain and hers alone.

"Soon, my children," she murmured. "Soon we will reign, for we are evolution." Stronger, faster, powerful enough to tear the PsyNet itself into pieces.

This was but the first piece.

A piece full of beauty, so much power arcing through it that the network burned. And if it burned out a few weak minds, so be it. Only the strong deserved to survive, *could* survive.

The Scarab Queen leaned back in her chair and closed her eyes, the better to see the new world she'd seeded into creation.

Chapter 35

SOLEIL DIDN'T HESITATE when she reached the top of the stairs. She turned straight into the room on the left. Where Ivan lay silent and still on the bed, dressed in nothing but a pair of thin black sweatpants.

Her eyes went to the extremely shallow rise and fall of his chest, his breaths coming too far apart for it to be healthy for a Psy male of his size and age. The fine black tattoos that marked his skin were a shock—Psy just didn't go for body ink. Except for her Psy, it seemed.

What she caught of the imagery that played over his chest was beautiful but haunting, glimpses of ghosts seen out of the corner of the eye and visions of worlds unknown, but she had other priorities at that moment, her heart racing as she took stock of his physical situation.

She'd learned basic Psy biology and health indicators in the paramedic course but upgraded her knowledge through self-study when things first began to go wrong with the Psy population next to Sky-Elm. She'd wanted to be ready to render first aid.

So she reacted quickly to take Ivan's vitals.

His pulse was too slow, his skin cooling further by the second. "Ivan," she said, using a sharp tone she'd found very effective on patients.

No reaction.

She put her hands on his shoulders, shook. "Ivan!"

The barest flutter of his lashes.

Her mind made the connection at once: it was the increased physical contact that had gotten through to him. Tactile contact was often a strong part of changeling healing, so it made sense to her. And Psy *did* have a primal core to their nature; she'd seen the dark side of that on the bloody field of the massacre. This, too, was a matter of life or death, albeit one devoid of violence.

She made the call. She didn't have any more time. Already, he was missing a breath for each one he took. Stripping off her sweater to reveal the simple white bra she wore underneath, she lay down beside him with her head on his shoulder and wrapped her arms around him, making as much skin-to-skin contact as possible.

She also kept saying his name, calling him back to her as she would a traumatized or emotionally wounded changeling. Inside her, her cat swiped out with its paw and she swore she saw streams of shattered starlight.

"Ivan! Wake up!" Then she *reached* for him in a way she couldn't explain. It felt like she was punching her hand right into the core of his soul, gripping tight, then dragging him out from the suction of a malevolent force.

Ivan's body went rigid before he took a huge gasp of air, both his arms snapping up to lock around her with such force that she should've been afraid. But she wasn't. Not with him. Never with him.

She continued to hold on as he gulped in air, his body still too cool, but his heartbeat now rapid. "You're safe." Her cat butted up against the silver starlight of him in her mind. "I'm here." She stroked her hand down his side, not the least surprised by the muscle of him. He moved with warrior grace, his body a fluid machine.

"Lei?" A rough sound, his arms yet locked around her.

But when she pushed up, he eased his hold so she could sit up and look down on him. His eyes were open but they were muddy, hazy— and she didn't like that at all. Her cat was furious that he'd allowed himself to walk this close to the edge, but this wasn't the time for temper so she throttled it back.

"Psychic burn?" she asked, once again taking his pulse.

He managed to give a nod.

"You need to replace that energy." When she went to move away, however, his arm tightened a fraction around her waist. She could've broken his hold—he had no real leverage given his position—but she noted that his breathing had also speeded up, his pupils expanding.

Soleil understood fear better than most. She had a feeling her Psy had very little experience of it. Whatever had happened had shaken him. "Just need to grab something from my bag," she said, and managed to reach out from the bed to drag it close.

Shifting so she had her feet on the floor without breaking the contact between their bodies, she dug inside the bag until she found the calorie-boosting sachets she'd thrown in there. Not as good for him as the nutrient packets designed for Psy, but energy was energy. His body would divert it to where it was most needed.

Having spotted a glass of water on the table, she poured two sachets in there and gently shook the glass to try to mix it in. He sat up, was ready to take the glass from her when she passed it across.

His throat muscles moved hard as he gulped it down in the way of young adults playing drinking games. Opening her bottle of water, she refilled his glass as soon as he was done, adding two more sachets to it. He finished that as quickly, then took the nut bar she handed him.

After finishing it, he took the other one she held out. "How did you know I needed an assist?" he asked after eating half that second one.

Soleil threw up her hands. "Of course I knew!" And, now that she could see he was safe, she gave in to the squeaking, excited bouncing in her heart and picked up the small cat planter she'd seen on the table when she'd picked up the glass of water. "I gave you this."

He'd frozen when she touched it, now nodded. "Have you remembered?" Rough words.

"Pieces." Pieces that made her ache with the hunger to know more. "Will you tell me what I've forgotten?"

Swallowing down the bite he'd taken, he gave a curt nod. "You walked out of the forest after I'd injured my leg, sewed me up, and told me not to be an idiot and rip it open again. Unable to forget you, I returned to the same spot until you came back. I showed you a cave. We had a picnic and played in the trees."

Soleil's mouth had fallen open partway through that military recitation, and the strange thing was, as flat and emotionless as it was, it made her cat run in excited circles, her heart sighing. Because all she really heard was "unable to forget you"—and that was all she needed to hear.

"You made a mushroom tart," he added. "It's not my preferred mode of ingesting nutrients."

A smile in her very bones. Oh, he was adorable in how he was trying not to hurt her feelings by telling her he'd hated it. And she knew then exactly why she'd fallen for him—because the man behind the mask of cool steel? He was kinder than he would ever acknowledge or even truly understand, loyal, and wonderful.

Putting the cat planter carefully on the table, she pounced on him.

He dropped the energy bar to the bed, his hands coming to her hips as she straddled him.

"Hello," she whispered, looking into those pretty, pretty eyes that fascinated her cat. "I can't forget you, either."

"I see you in my dreams." His voice was like cool water, sliding into her veins. "Once, you were made of starlight."

Flickers in her mind, half-forgotten ghosts of things past. "You were a boy last night in my dream." She ran her fingers over the intricate lines and patterns on his chest. "This art is beautiful but it makes my heart hurt."

"I'm afraid I'll forget my life one day," he said, grit in his tone. "So I carve memories into my skin." Closing his fingers over her wrist, he moved her hand to a spot right above his heart.

When he released her and she lifted her palm, she sucked in her breath. Because there she was, a laughing woman almost hidden in the trees as she ran, her hair flying behind her and her face half-turned to look back, her long skirts tangled around her legs. All this time, he'd carried her in his skin. Over his heart.

Throat closing, she bent to press her lips to that spot.

The shudder that rocked him was a hard thing, but he didn't try to stop her, and when she rose back up to look at him, his eyes were infinite black, a pool of endless darkness. There was so much she wanted to ask him, her desperation to know him a biting need.

But she was a healer first and foremost, so her first question was, "What happened today?" Terror crept a blanket of ice over her body. "You were so far away that I almost couldn't find you."

Ivan didn't know how to handle the worry Soleil made no effort to hide, so he fell back on the technicalities of his inadvertent stay on the island, broke it all down for her. "I need to think about what to do next, before I contact anyone else. Right now—"

"Right now you're close to a psychic flatline." A glare. "You are not going to do anything. And if I understand it right, burning yourself out won't exactly help those trapped minds."

Ivan knew she was right . . . and he also knew he didn't want to move from here, the weight of her on him a pleasure he'd never expected and now couldn't surrender. "After you vanished, I thought I'd imagined you." He rubbed his fist over the tattoo. "I half believed I was drawing a phantom."

"I never vanished. Yariela had a heart attack the day I left. She's as close to a grandmother as I have—the *only* family I have. I was like a child, unable to focus, unable to function." Rapid-fire words, one tumbling out over the other. "My mind kept running a horrible loop of the day my parents died, ending my whole world, and now my Abuela Yari was sick.

"I ran home in a panic." Her eyes shimmered wet. "I wanted to message you en route. I didn't have your direct contact code, but I thought I might be able to find a number for the wolves online—and that was when I realized that in my rush to leave, I'd somehow forgotten my phone at my friend's.

"It just made everything worse, because I couldn't even get updates about Yariela. Then, after I got home, all my energy went into watching over her." Her hands cupped his face as a tear rolled down her cheek. "The idea of losing her . . . my chest was so tight it felt as if I couldn't take in air."

Her breath hitched on the heels of those words as she relived the memory. "I don't remember all of it, but I remember the morning of the massacre. Yariela was out of the woods—though nowhere near healthy. She should've stayed in bed, but you know what she did when all hell broke loose?"

Ivan didn't have to pause to think of the answer. "She dragged herself out of bed and went to assist." Because she was a healer.

Eyes wet, Soleil nodded. "But that morning, before the horror, it was the first time I'd taken a true breath. My plan was to contact the wolves and have them pass on a message to you. I knew you wouldn't be angry with me. Not my Ivan. You'd understand. Because you knew I was yours."

If she'd broken him by disappearing, she'd just shattered him into innumerable pieces with those words. "No, Lei," he said roughly. "Don't claim me. I'm not who you think I am."

"It's too late." She ran her hands up into his hair. "I've never had many people who were mine, Ivan. I don't let go of those who are. And you're mine. You know it and I know it. It's a wild song between us."

He wanted to argue with her, but lying to her had never been an option. "What happened to your people?" he asked, drinking her in with a thirst that might never be satisfied. "To your pack?" He knew the final outcome, but not the road that had led to the devastation.

Dropping her hands to her lap, Soleil flexed then fisted them. "My mother was human, lost her parents as an adult, had no ties to any other living family and often told me she liked it that way. Said she'd been a loner even before her parents passed away, that it was just her nature and that we—my father and I—were the sole exceptions to her need for solitude. My father was a loner, too—but he was also the son of the alpha of SkyElm. My grandfather."

As with the initial time she'd mentioned the man, back when Ivan had first fallen for her, he heard no respect or joy when she spoke of her father's father, just pain and a kind of tiredness that was of the heart. He understood the latter not with his own empathy, but with hers. Her healer's soft heart, so full of compassion—and yet even it didn't have any softness for this man. "Tell me."

A twist of her lips. "It's nothing startling. He blamed my mother for 'stealing' my father away from his rightful place in the pack, because my father left with her after they met. And even though I was an ocelot, my grandfather saw my mother in me rather than his son, and he only took me in because I'd otherwise have been adopted into another ocelot pack—he couldn't stand the public dishonor."

A shrug. "Then he washed his hands of me, and the majority of his dominants took their cue from him and treated me like an intruder. Without Abuela Yari . . ."

He understood now, that Yariela was to her what Ena was to him: the foundation. "I will treat your abuela with all honor and respect."

A sudden, dazzling smile. "I know." Fingers brushing his lips. "As for SkyElm's problems as a whole, it was long-term bad management. A kind of inward-looking xenophobia that led to too many elders and young, not enough trained dominants.

"We just didn't have the strength to hold back the Psy." She thrust a hand through her hair . . . and in his mind flickered the image of a stern older man with a white beard against brown skin.

"Who's the man with the beard?"

Soleil didn't look surprised at the question that should've made no sense. "My grandfather," she said. "I don't know if the rot started with him, but it was well set in before I came into the pack. It was just a damaged and toxic place."

"An alpha can change the whole shape of a family."

Soleil held his eyes. "Who's yours?"

"My grandmother."

"Will you tell me about her?"

"Yes. But before I do, you need to know who I am." He squeezed her hips when she would've spoken. "You need to know who you're claiming."

Narrowed eyes, her gaze feline, but she didn't swipe at him. Instead, she kneaded at his shoulders with the delicate little claws that had emerged from her hands. "Tell me then," she ordered. "Tell me the truth of Ivan Mercant."

Chapter 36

"He's sad, Canto. I want to make him happy."
"Sometimes, you have to let people be sad. At least until they're ready to come out of that sadness."
"His heart is all hurt."
"I know, Arwen. I know."

—Conversation between Canto Mercant and Arwen Mercant (circa 2060)

IVAN STOOD BESIDE the dead body of his mother. He knew she was dead because though he was only eight years of age, this wasn't the first time he'd seen a dead person. His mother's friends had a way of dying. And now she was dead, too.

He knew he should be sad or angry or worried, but even though he could only *just* fake Silence so they wouldn't get caught, he found at that moment that he felt nothing. It was as if his brain had gone white, a buzz filling his head. He stood there and stared at his mother where she lay crumpled on the floor of the motel room.

All he could think was that she wasn't even on the bed. She'd been on the bed when he went to sleep last night. She must've gotten out and maybe had wanted to sit on the brown sofa that had a big dent in the middle. Like a giant had sat on it. But she'd never made it there.

Clutched in her hand was a half-empty injector.

He knew from the human family dramas he watched while she slept that he shouldn't know about injectors, but he'd seen them all his life. He knew how to prime an old one so it would work, and sometimes he did that for his mother when she cried for her medicine. Part of him felt bad letting her take her medicine. He wasn't sure it was good for her.

"You're only a baby," she'd say. "Listen to your mama. She needs her medicine. Now be a sweetheart and fix this for me. Your little hands are so clever."

As he stared at her, he wondered when they would come.

The people who checked on the dead always came. Only for the dead though, never for the live people like Ivan and his mother.

"We're rejects from Psy society, my sweet boy," she'd slurred one night. "They ignore us as long as we don't make too many disruptions in the PsyNet. Quiet minds is all the fucking Council wants. We aren't worth the bother to chase down for their precious Silence Protocol."

She'd lifted a finger to her lips, made a shushing sound. "That's why you have to be quiet, quiet on the Net. Got to have a good shield. Don't let emotions drip out. They don't know I have you." A huge grin. "I hid you so good. You don't exist."

Ivan wasn't sure he liked not existing. But he also knew he couldn't believe everything his mother had told him. She used to tell him all the time that she was going to get a proper job so they could have a home all their own. Once, she'd even walked him past an apartment with pretty flowers in the window and said that would be their home soon.

Mind still a blank, he sat down next to her and waited for the people to come.

"Why do they come?" he'd asked once.

It had been one of his mother's friends who'd answered him, a thin man with dark skin and lots of marks on his face. "No one's allowed to just disappear from the PsyNet. The death guard come to make sure no one murdered us. Not that the Council cares about us riffraff, but it's about power, see?" The man had tapped his temple. "Can't let the humans or changelings think they're stronger than Psy."

Ivan hadn't understood most of that, but it didn't matter. Nothing mattered.

Hours passed, and no one came. He wasn't surprised. He wondered if they had his mother's name on a list somewhere, of people who weren't important at all. Even when they were dead.

He was still wide-awake and staring at the door when the handle turned. If it was the death people, the manager would probably have given them a key. It was the first time in a long while that he and his mother'd had a room with a door that wasn't broken.

When Mama dressed up and played her instrument, no one knew she was Psy. The humans and changelings thought she was human, and they gave her money as they did to other humans. Ivan thought it would be nice to be human. They were allowed to love music and to dance.

Two men walked into the room, both of them dressed in black.

". . . a Jax user," one of them was saying as he entered. "Shouldn't—" He cut himself off when he realized it wasn't only a woman's body on the floor.

Turning to the man who'd entered behind him, he said, "Did she have a child listed on her record?"

His partner pulled up the information on a small datapad, said, "Yes, but the child was meant to have died at birth. Her record is sketchy at best, but it does say she worked in computronic security once—must've had the skills to hide him. No one's going to notice one extra mind in the Net if they don't know he exists."

They were talking about his mother as if she were a thing, not a person. But Ivan still wasn't angry or sad or anything. His mind remained white. He just stared at these men, wondering if he would be killed. His mother had always been afraid that they would come for her.

"I'm a rebel, sweetie," she'd say. "I don't follow their stupid Silence rules."

Maybe, a long time ago, he'd thought that was interesting and exciting. That was before he saw his first dead body, before he began to understand that what she was doing to herself wasn't rebellion but the opposite: even at eight years of age, he understood that his mother had given up. She'd chosen her medicine over fighting. And now she'd chosen to leave Ivan.

"The child is listed as being born in an approved birthing facility," the second man said, "and as dying at home. No investigation listed. Then she drops off the grid."

"At least he's still young enough to be molded into a useful citizen." Striding toward him, the man looked down on him from his tall height. "What is your name, child?"

He thought about what to say, and something in the whiteness of his mind, the blankness of it, gave him a razor-sharp focus. And even though his mother had only said the name of her family once or twice, he remembered it. "Ivan Mercant," he said.

The man stared at him. "That's a very unusual family name."

Ivan stayed silent, not sure what the man wanted him to say.

"Where did you hear it?" the man demanded, then waved it off. "Ridiculous, to think that a Mercant child would be in a place like this. That family looks after its own." He bent to run a scanner over Ivan's mother's body. "Dead," he pronounced. "Has been for quite some time."

"DNA matches profile on record. No Mercant link," his partner said.

"That answers that question."

"Are you sure we should dismiss the child's claim?"

"Are you seriously suggesting that he might be a Mercant?"

"I'm just saying that I wouldn't want to be in the shoes of the person who found a lost Mercant child and didn't inform that family. It's a simple administrative act to send through a data packet with the details of the child and a sample of his DNA."

The man kept on talking, while the other, older one stared at Ivan with cold eyes. "As I said, the female's record is thin at best—it could be total fiction, but we have no Mercant DNA on file, so we can't do the comparison ourselves."

The man with the cold eyes hesitated, then gave a short nod.

Living on the street, Ivan had long ago learned to understand power. Today he understood that the Mercants had power. They had made this man do something, change his decision, without ever being in the room.

Ivan hoped his mother hadn't lied about being a Mercant. But he wasn't afraid. The white blank remained. Until the man told him to get up onto his feet, that the body disposal team was on its way. That was when the white began to crack, cold blue flames burning their way to the center.

Ivan knew that if he allowed it to burn all the way through, he might go mad, might rage. So he fought the crumbling edges—but he didn't fight his urge to reach for his mother's hand and remove the ring she wore on her right ring finger.

"What are you doing?" the older man snapped.

Ivan put the ring into his pocket. "It's mine." His mother had told him it was his, that it was a family ring and it would pass on to him.

A piece of me to carry with you, baby boy. So you'll know that I'm always with you.

"Leave it, Jin," the other man said while Ivan listened to the memory of his mother's voice. "It's just cheap rubbish."

Ignoring them, Ivan turned, looked at his mother, and said, "Good-bye, Mama."

If she'd been alive, she'd have hugged him close, pressed kisses over his face. That was what she'd done in the good times between doses of her medicine. That was when he'd seen the sparkle in her eyes and the light in her face that made her so beautiful. Now and then, she'd be in such a good mood that she'd sing the spider song.

Spider, spider, my beautiful spider.

He'd asked her why she sang it and she'd said that sometimes, when she took her medicine, she saw an "astonishing" web glittering with fire. Ivan hadn't liked the spider song, but he'd liked how happy she'd looked when she sang it. But those times had come less and less and less, until he couldn't remember the last time his mother had been his mother.

He didn't want his last memory of her to be of cold skin against his lips, against his body. So he didn't kiss her good-bye, and he didn't hug her good-bye. But he couldn't leave her like that, on the floor, without care. Still ignoring the man who clearly wanted him gone, he went to the bed and got a pillow, then dragged off the thin blanket.

Jin made as if to grab Ivan by the shoulder, but the other man stopped him with a shake of his head. He must've telepathed Jin. Whatever he said, it made Jin walk out of the room and stand outside the door. The one who'd stayed behind watched as Ivan put a pillow under his mother's head, then covered her up with the blanket.

"What will they do to my mama?" he asked.

"The Bureau will decide, but given that you're claiming to be a Mercant—was your mother the Mercant or your father?"

"My mother." Ivan didn't know his father.

"In that case, it's possible her body might be held in cold storage until the Mercant family either verifies your claim or repudiates it."

He didn't like to think of his mother in cold storage, and it made the blue fire burn the white even hotter. So before it could burn away altogether, before he could become like the man on the street corner who held his head and screamed at nothing, he took one last look at his mother, at how peaceful she seemed now, asleep on a pillow, and then he walked out of the motel room.

Chapter 37

Luc, the comm conference is up and running. Full encryption and authentication enabled. Ena Mercant will be dialing in in the next two minutes.

—Dorian Christensen, sentinel, to Lucas Hunter, alpha (8:30 a.m.)

TEARS ROLLED DOWN Soleil's face, the image of a small boy standing up to those two heartless men over the body of his mother burned into her memories. "I'm so sorry," she whispered, touching her fingers to his jaw.

"It was a long time ago," he said, and she saw in his eyes the same sepia distance she had from the memories of the deaths of her own parents.

But where she acknowledged that the loss still hurt, she knew he never would. "I'm glad you found your family. They obviously came for you."

A slow lowering of his lashes, and when he raised them back up, his eyes were obsidian, eerie and lovely. "I was fourteen when I started to question the improbability of my grandmother losing one of her children, much less one of her grandchildren.

"If you knew her, Lei, you'd know that Ena Mercant *never* loses track of one of her own. The one time anything like that happened, she wasn't responsible for the child, and she *still* had that child under her care in a matter of months."

A frown. "But you said your mother was a security specialist, good with computronics."

"Not good enough to escape the reach of my grandmother—the Mercant network would've been scanning constantly for her DNA, would've tagged her one of the many times she ended up in jail for low-level possession. They always take DNA during booking, add it to the main system."

"Wait, wait." Soleil held up a hand. "Where were you while she served her jail terms?"

"The terms were short and she wasn't so deep into her addiction to the crystal flower by then—she managed to make arrangements with some trustworthy street people."

Soleil covered her mouth with her hand but didn't interrupt. He understood her shock. Now that he was an adult, he could hardly imagine the scenario in which a mother would leave a vulnerable child with other junkies. He had to have been younger than three the first time around.

"No Mercant would ever make that choice," he said. "It's just not in their bloodline. I knew that, like I knew they'd never have lost track of me. So I went looking for the truth even though I didn't want to find it. I *wanted* to be a Mercant more than anything, part of a family that is as much a pack as DarkRiver or StoneWater."

He could still remember that day, every cold second of it. "I broke into closed medical records, confirmed that I have no Mercant DNA. None. It was another one of my mother's grandiose lies."

Soleil searched his face. "What happened?"

"I was so angry. My Silence has always been less than perfect due to my mother's drug habit and how it impacted me in the womb. She also gave me small doses when I was a boy."

"A heart full of fire," Soleil whispered, spreading her fingers over that heart. "You told me in a dream. I saw it."

He nodded, left it at that for now. He'd save the worst of it for last. "I confronted Grandmother and asked her why she'd lied."

"What did she say?"

"That day," he said, "for the first time, I came face-to-face not with my grandmother, but with Ena Mercant, the woman who scares powerful people in the PsyNet." Her focus had been pure, her will granite.

"She told me that a small boy looked her in the eye and told her he was a Mercant. That boy, she said, had more courage in his bones than the grown men more than twice his size who'd escorted him to the meeting with her—and who couldn't meet her gaze."

A memory of a slender hand gripping the back of his neck, the hold not the least painful—but unbreakable in its sheer intensity. "Blood, she said, wasn't the only way to be a Mercant."

Then he spoke the rest of the words she'd said to him, the words carved on another part of his skin. "'We are who we are because we treasure courage, treasure strength. Many of our best and brightest have come from outside the bloodline. You *are* a Mercant, Ivan. Never again say that you're not—not unless you wish to deal with me.'"

He could hear each word in her voice, steely and cool and resolute. "Then she pulled me to her in an embrace I could've never expected— Grandmother doesn't do physical contact. But that day, she held me above the crashing waves of the sea and she said, 'You are one of mine, Ivan Mercant. Now and always.'"

Soleil's eyes were no longer human. "I love her already."

"I think the feeling will be mutual." Soleil might be a healer, but she had within her the same fierce steel when it came to protecting her people.

"When can I meet her?" Soleil raised an eyebrow. "And yes, I'm asking to be introduced to your family."

His gut clenched at the idea of a thing he'd never expected, never thought he'd deserve.

You deserve joy, Ivan. Hold on to her, on to the spark of joy inside your heart.

His desire to believe Arwen, to give Soleil what she wanted, was a violence inside him. But he hadn't told her the whole truth yet, had saved the worst horror for last. And that horror didn't permit happiness. Not now that it was awake.

So, for the second time, he told her about the spider that lived in his mind, formed of the poisonous deposits of Jax in his neural cells. Her answer was the same as in the forest, the cat inside him as determined to stay. But things had changed.

"I can't control it anymore." His voice was rough, raw. "Grandmother's shield, the one she helped me create when I was nine and the power first activated, it's fragmenting and I can't put it back together. It crumbles every single time."

Soleil narrowed those wild ocelot eyes. "What are you trying to tell me, Ivan Mercant?"

"Without that shield, I suck people dry—I take their psychic energy and then I take the physical energy that powers the mind. I take and take until there's nothing left, until they're husks devoid of mind or life." While he didn't gain access to his victims' psychic abilities, his theft of their energies supercharged his own nasty ability. "I become a murderous monster. And my control is all but gone."

Claws dug into his skin. "So, what's the solution? Because I know you have a solution—and I'm certain I won't like it."

"The only way to handle it once it breaks out is for me to create a cage so powerful that it'll effectively crush my mind." The man Soleil knew as Ivan Mercant would be gone, buried as deep as if he lay in a grave.

"It'll put me in a coma, where I've informed my neurologist that he is to organize experiments and observation. There's no point in erasing myself when my brain could offer a way forward for another child born with the same neural defect, the same twisted ability. I'll never come out of that coma and will eventually expire."

Instead of crying or berating him, Soleil folded her arms across her chest. "And your grandmother has agreed to this ridiculous plan?"

"She doesn't know."

"Ha!" Soleil pointed at him. "Because you know she'd stop you. Well, same here."

"Soleil, this isn't something you can fix by willpower or medical techniques. The known children of Jax addicts all experience serious neurological issues that can't be fixed."

"Known children? What's the sample size of the studies you're referencing?"

"Eleven," he said. "Not many Jax addicts manage to procreate."

"*Eleven?*" She threw up her hands. "Maybe there's a reason those eleven were chosen for the study. Maybe the others found ways to escape their pasts and are living big beautiful lives! Maybe their parent or parents gave them up for adoption and no one ever had reason to test them for Jax because they showed no ill effects!" Her chest heaved. "You ever think of that?"

"It's not realistic." Too hopeful, too much a thing of raw want.

Soleil's lips twitched, and then she was laughing—but it held a dangerous edge. Claws digging into his shoulders, she leaned in close. "You currently have a cat in residence in your head. I'll eat that spider alive if I have to. Don't you talk to me about realistic."

That was when he saw the predator in her, the ocelot that could be a stealthy hunter, primal and deadly. She wasn't rational right now, wouldn't listen to reason. Aware he had very little time left, he didn't push it. She'd be forced to face the truth when the time came—and by then, he'd find a way to make her promise to snap their bond.

His entire body went cold at the idea of her being linked to him when he shut down. If she'd been with him on the island, then the bond was deep enough to wrench her into the abyss with him. She'd fall where she stood, her mind locked in the cold dark with his own.

No. He would not allow that. "We'll talk about this later," he said, swallowing his dread at the thought of her light just blinking out from the world.

Still glaring at him, arms folded mutinously, she said, "I want your grandmother's number."

"No."

"Scared that we'll rip off your head together?"

Ivan might not have any knowledge of relationships, but he knew when he was being hunted, being driven into a corner where his stalker would pounce. "We'll discuss this later," he repeated. "Right now, I need to share what I learned on the island, see if there's anything that can be done for those trapped minds."

Soleil frowned, the black cloud of her hair sliding over her shoulder as she bent her head in thought. "You're right, but you're also being squirrelly. Never mind. I can be patient."

Ivan had never in his life been described as "squirrelly." Arwen would collapse in laughter if he heard. But Ivan would take it for now if it would get Soleil's mind off the perilous track of getting in touch with his grandmother. Because he knew Ena; she'd agree with Soleil, would want to save him.

"You contact who you need to contact," Soleil said right then, leaving the bed—and her position straddling him.

He immediately missed the warmth of her, the feel of her, her touch.

A glance at him, anger still sparking in those wild eyes, but she leaned in, cupped his cheek . . . and kissed him with ferocious possessiveness. "I'm still mad," she said after she broke the kiss that had downed him more effectively than any punch. "You also need more food, more fuel—I love those cheekbones but they're about to cut your skin." She looked around his room. "Is there more food in the kitchenette?"

When he shook his head, she said, "Then I guess we're going out to a restaurant." The words were more a command than a suggestion. "I'll give you a few minutes to get dressed, use that time to call the cubs and Abuela Yari. Meet you downstairs." An instant later, she'd picked up her pink bag and was gone, this woman whose shattered body he'd picked up and carried in his arms once upon a time.

The roles had very definitely been reversed.

Rising, he had a one-minute shower because he'd sweated during that nightmare walk on the island. He also used the time to think about who he should contact about the situation on the island—this wasn't a case of passing on intel to the family, who'd then share it. As the only one who'd stepped on the island, he'd need to handle this himself.

He was still thinking on the situation after he got out and changed into a pair of jeans and a black button-down shirt, over which he threw on the black blazer Arwen had gifted him. He wanted Soleil to see him how he could be, civilized and sophisticated. He wasn't only the rough assassin who she'd always met.

Only when he was walking down the stairs after sending a quick message did he realize that he was severely overdressed. In his desire to impress her, he'd gotten it all wrong.

Chapter 38

Kaleb, I have information you need to know: in summary, I can get on that new PsyNet island. Are you aware of the current situation on the ground there?

—Message from Ivan Mercant to Kaleb Krychek (9:00 a.m.)

SOLEIL LOOKED UP, able to sense Ivan walking down the steps even though he was preternaturally silent for a Psy. You'd have thought he was a cat if you didn't know better.

All the air punched out of her chest at first sight of him. His hair was damp and finger-combed, his body clad in jeans and a black shirt over which he'd thrown on a blazer. He wore the same boots as yesterday. Overall, he looked like he'd walked out of a fashion magazine.

And the way he looked at her . . .

She glanced away, then back. Furious though her cat was with him, she adored him, too, and that was never going to change. He was in her, Ivan Mercant, and she'd have it no other way.

And now she knew what he looked like *under* the clothes, too. She'd do anything to have a chance to kiss each and every tattoo, explore every single inch of that honed body.

Her thighs clenched.

Cheeks hot all over again, she went to open the door. And heard a slight rustle at her back. When she glanced over, she saw that he'd taken off his blazer and hung it over the newel post at the end of the staircase. Odd, but she could've almost said that there was a sense of discomfort about him.

"I liked the blazer," she found herself saying.

He hesitated, looked at her as if trying to read the truth of her statement. But then he put it back on. Her heart thudded, something small and soft inside her getting stronger, more intense.

Be careful with him, little sister. He might look tough, but when strong men fall, they fall all the way. You're his weakness.

A wave of tenderness stole her breath. He might be stubborn and arrogant in his belief that he knew the right answer to what he'd decided was an insurmountable problem, but he was also more vulnerable to her than she'd understood until this moment.

"I bought you a dress," he said without warning. "When I came to find you at the hospital. Because your other dress had been so badly damaged. I could only find an automated shop, so it's not the best quality."

With any other man, she'd have thought he was trying to insult her current choice of clothing, but Ivan, she already understood, didn't think that way. So it was disappointment that bit at her. "Oh." She fiddled with the strap of her bag. "What happened to it?"

"I have it upstairs."

This time she did stare at him—and yes, that was very definitely discomfort on his face. "What?"

"I've carried it around with me since the day I bought it." He glanced away, as if unable to hold her gaze.

She was already his, but she kept on falling faster and deeper. And he thought she was going to just let him lock himself up and throw away the key? Oh *hell* no. "Can I see it?"

A nod, and he headed back upstairs. She followed him, putting her handbag on the floor of the bedroom as he went to the closet. He opened it to reveal neat rows of clothes, including three suits. Her stomach pitched at the thought of what Ivan would look like in a suit.

"Smoking" was the word that came to mind.

He bent down to grab something as she was waving a hand in front of her face to cool herself down, said, "I have your daypack. You left it in the car."

Soleil put it beside her handbag when he passed it over. "I knew you'd keep it safe."

Reaching up to the shelf above the hanging rail without responding to that, he picked up a sealed bag like she'd seen come out of the one automated store she'd ever experienced. "I'll go outside if you want to try it on," he said after giving it to her.

When she nodded, he left, closing the door behind himself.

Her fingers trembled a little as she opened the sealed package. To reveal fabric of a joyous lemon yellow. She gasped and picked it up by the shoulders. It fell in a sweep of the softest linen imaginable. It was sleeveless, the straps made up of tiny white embroidered flowers.

The same flowers appeared as a splash on the hem of the dress, which would hit her just above the ankles. There, the white blooms were joined by pinks, darker purples, myriad other shades, until it was a wildflower meadow.

Giving a little skip of joy, she stripped out of her borrowed clothes and pulled on the dress, not looking in the mirror until she'd zipped it up. All the air rushed out of her. The color made her skin glow, and the little flower details just made her happy.

She immediately felt prettier, more real, more herself.

Turning, she put her other clothes in her daypack, then chewed on her lower lip. The dress didn't fit quite right because of her weight loss, and she didn't want to advertise that. But she didn't want to put her sweater back on, either.

Her eyes went to the leather-synth jacket hanging in the closet.

Flushing but determined, she took it out of the closet, shrugged into it, then rolled up the sleeves of the well-worn leather-synth. It was butter soft. Far too big on her but in a fashionable way. She looked like a woman wearing her boyfriend's jacket.

Her cheeks pinked.

Twirling a little and feeling happy, just happy, she slung her pretty pink bag back over her shoulder and opened the door.

Ivan was waiting at the bottom of the stairs, watched her with unwavering intensity as she walked down.

"I borrowed your jacket," she murmured. "Sorry." But she wasn't sorry, not when the scent of him surrounded her—and not when he was looking at her in a way that said she was the total center of his attention.

He didn't respond verbally, just held the door open for her so she could slip out. "I sent a message to Kaleb Krychek," he said as they walked down the street, then told her the content of that message.

Soleil raised her eyebrows. "You have his direct number?" The entire world knew that Kaleb Krychek was a *power*. The one time she'd been anywhere near his vicinity—far on the other side of a public square—he'd made the hairs rise on the back of her neck, her cat sensing a mortal threat.

"Only my grandmother and my cousin Silver—she used to be his senior aide—have his personal line," Ivan told her. "But I have access to another priority line. Family connections."

"Some family." She laughed and when Ivan glanced at her, she said, "I've gone from being a lone ocelot who knew no one and nobody important to being a member of one of the most powerful packs in the country—and my sweetheart is part of a family that sounds like it might be the mafia, but I'm okay with that."

Ivan didn't seem to know how to respond to being called her sweetheart.

Grinning, she tucked her arm through his and leaned up to press a kiss to his jaw. He'd given her skin privileges and he'd never withdrawn them and she intended to take full advantage of them to strengthen their bond. She was a cat, wasn't she? Sneaky was in her DNA.

His skin was smooth and unbristled under her lips. He must've run a shaver over it in the shower. "You smell so delicious, mi cariño," she murmured, giving him a little nuzzle.

"Lei." A rough sound, but it wasn't one that told her to back off.

She looked up, heart sparkling, to see tension in the lines of his face, color on his cheekbones. Her tough, dangerous man didn't know how to handle her. It was adorable. "This place looks good," she said, nodding at the small Chinese restaurant to their right. "What do you think?"

"Food is fuel" was the cool response that betrayed nothing of the tension yet in his body. "Taste doesn't matter."

"So I should find you a place that does mushroom tarts, then?" Laughing at his icy look, she tugged him toward the restaurant, her cat rubbing up against her skin, playful and delighted by him.

It was busy inside, but not jam-packed. "Too many people?"

"No. I grew up in a city."

Her heart hitched. Because he hadn't only grown up in a city, he'd literally lived on the streets, a boy with no real identity. A boy whose mother had erased him so he'd fit into her chosen life. Overwhelmed by a surge of protectiveness, she took them to a table at the back where he'd have the most personal space.

After they were seated, with Ivan choosing the seat that put his back to a wall, she took charge of ordering, sticking to simple items with the highest energy values. The staff member who took her order was a polite and efficient woman; she also couldn't stop sneaking glances at Ivan.

Soleil even caught her biting down on her lower lip.

Her cat smirked. Yes, he was delicious. He was also *hers*. The other woman could look all she liked, but try to touch and she'd be dealing with a shredded hand.

"That's it," she said after completing the large order, because though she'd had a good breakfast, she was hungry, too. Which told her that she'd spent more energy pulling him back from the island than she'd realized. "Thank you."

The waitress left with one last quick glance at Ivan.

He didn't reciprocate. When his eyes fixed on a point just beyond her left shoulder, she said, "What is it?" Her cat hissed at the same instant.

"Krychek," he said. "He decided to respond to my message in person."

Chapter 39

It's rumored that Krychek is a dual cardinal. Anyone have any actual intel on that? It would definitely explain the level of his power. I'm fairly certain the man could flatten a city without breaking a sweat.

—Anonymous poster on an online bulletin board

A COLD WIND at Soleil's back, the force of Kaleb Krychek's power a dark wave akin to a storm. The entire restaurant had fallen silent at his entry, stayed that way as he walked toward them. It was as if the diners were all holding their breath—but it wasn't only the silence of prey.

There were changelings in this restaurant—leopards and wolves who'd clocked the mark on Soleil's cheek the instant she entered, and inclined their heads in quiet welcome. All of those changelings watched him with the eyes of fellow predators. They knew he was dangerous, and though he might be permitted in the territory, they never forgot the threat of him.

"I apologize for interrupting," he said on reaching them, his voice midnight that sank into your bones and his flawlessly fitted suit black on black. "But I must speak to you, Ivan."

In front of her, Ivan had become a blank wall. If he saw Krychek as a threat, it was invisible to the room. No trace remained of the man who'd been so awkward about the blazer, or the one who hadn't known how to deal with her calling him her sweetheart.

It hurt her to know that he was so used to shutting himself off that he could do it at will.

"Join us," Ivan said, his tone flat, giving nothing away. "Soleil is an important part of this conversation."

Krychek glanced at her with those eyes of starlight obsidian before taking a seat—on a chair that was suddenly there where it hadn't been before. He was a teleport-capable telekinetic, that much was public knowledge. But she'd never seen such a seamless exhibition of telekinetic strength.

Wild Woman magazine was right in calling him "as hot as lava"— he was one of the best-looking men she'd ever seen. But like lava, he was better viewed from a safe distance. Which made her intrigued about the woman who was his mate. She'd picked up the news of his mating at some point, been befuddled by it. Who would want to sleep with a man who was the living embodiment of a cold and icy death?

Ahem, Soleil, whispered the part of Farah that would always live within her, *your sweetheart is currently doing an excellent impression of a gorgeous statue carved out of black ice himself. Other women might possibly find him intimidating.*

The echo of Farah had a point.

"To answer the question in your message," Krychek said to Ivan, "no one knows what's taking place on that island. No one, except, it appears, you."

The silence that fell this time was between the three of them, as Soleil and Ivan processed the meaning of his statement.

Ivan spoke at last. "I realize that's the Ruling Coalition's public stance, but I find it hard to believe given the extent of your power."

"It's the truth. Even I can't bridge a psychic cavity that large." No annoyance or frustration or anger in his tone, nothing at all to give away his emotions.

"The anchors, too, have been thwarted," Krychek continued. "Though the island remains linked to the main anchor network, it's precarious. They tell me the connection through which anchor energy should flow—the veins and arteries of the system—are viscous and close to impenetrable."

Most people didn't know much about anchors or how they worked. But Ivan had grown up with Canto in his life, and Canto was a cardinal anchor. "That's a bad move on the part of those behind the island," he said. "Even multiple anchors can't maintain the island without the shared energy of the others."

"They don't seem to be worried about that for the present." Krychek shifted those pitiless cardinal eyes to Soleil. "You're not Psy. How can you impact the situation?"

It was a perfectly rational question, but the spider stirred; it wanted Krychek's attention off Soleil, the protective urge as deadly as the weapon in his boot. "She can pull me off the island. All other connections are severed or blocked the instant I set foot on it."

Krychek didn't ask him to explain the nature of his bond with Soleil, just gave a short nod. Soleil, meanwhile, was staring at Krychek out of the corner of her eye—and he might've thought it the stare of prey waiting for a predator to strike, except that her claws were out, and very visible against the wood of the table.

A silent warning that she had teeth.

And she would use those teeth to protect Ivan.

He still hadn't worked out how to process her protectiveness. But it would have to wait, because he couldn't afford to be distracted with Krychek only inches from him. "I'm happy to feed you information from the island," he said. "The people on it will all die if we don't get them out."

"Four already have," Krychek said, his tone unchanging. "All four were elderly. They succumbed in the hour directly after the separation. Scarabs also took an anchor who falls into that demographic: Ager Lii is currently in a coma, their vital signs weakening and their anchor region being stabilized by others around them."

Ivan didn't need the cardinal to spell it out. He'd heard Canto say more than once that there weren't enough anchors to go around. They couldn't afford to lose any of them. "Any chance Ager Lii went with the Scarabs by choice?"

Kaleb shook his head. "According to Payal, Ager was too content with their life to risk it. The anchors don't have enough data on the other four As on the island to make a call about whether any of them did it by choice."

Ivan didn't like to think of the elder A locked inside their mind and body when Ager had only just found freedom. Ivan didn't understand all of what had occurred with the anchors recently, but he'd picked up enough from Canto to know that Ager, in the twilight of their life, deserved a chance to enjoy those years after a lifetime of selfless service.

A tap on his foot, a whisper of fur against his skin.

Flicking up his gaze, he met Soleil's . . . but she was still watching Krychek, her eyes slightly narrowed. Yet the glide of fur against his skin, it continued on, a phantom caress. Because his Lei was always with him and he was becoming possessive of that gift. Possessive enough to make a very bad decision if he wasn't careful.

"How can I assist you?" Ivan did well with defined goals, because a goal allowed him to create a plan of attack. "What do you need to know?"

"The only way to get those people out is to collapse the island," Krychek said. "All our models state that their minds will immediately reconnect to the largest available psychic network."

Ivan could see the logic in that—Psy minds needed biofeedback to survive; their brains would begin the search for a new network the instant their current one shut down. "So you want me to either find a way to collapse it myself—or get you data that allows you to collapse it."

"Concisely put." Krychek rose, buttoning up his suit jacket as he did so. "When can you next enter the island?"

"Not today, that's for sure." Soleil's voice was harder than he'd ever heard it—and she didn't lower her gaze even when Krychek pinned her with his. "He almost fried himself the first time around. He goes in now and he'll be dead."

Krychek stared at Soleil for a long moment, then said, "Healer."

Soleil smiled—and it was full of teeth, her eyes no longer human.

"I'll leave you two to work out the logistics," Krychek said, "but there is a time limit on this. Ager Lii is apt to last two days at most, the others in comas an additional forty-eight hours beyond that if we're lucky."

Krychek teleported out on that chilling statement.

Soleil, her fur yet ruffled, snarled. "It's like talking to a shark. No, strike that. I met a changeling shark once—she was ruthless, but she was also passionate about her clan. Krychek, on the other hand . . ." She shivered.

"He has what changelings would call a mate," Ivan said after a pause to allow the waitress to deliver their food; it was obvious no one had wanted to approach their table while Krychek was present.

"I know." The ocelot retreated from her gaze. "So does Hawke of the SnowDancer wolves. Some women must like to flirt with death while they're naked."

Ivan stared at her.

She looked back, blinked. "Oh." A grin. "Oops. I keep forgetting I'm one of them." A fading of her smile, her eyes sliding from human to ocelot again as she said, "I've been alone so very long, Ivan. I have such an ache within. But only for you."

Inside Soleil, her cat curled up into a tight ball. Its pain was intense. The lack of intimate touch in her life . . . of any affectionate touch over the time since she'd woken in her hospital bed, it had hurt, and it still hurt.

Skin privileges were an integral part of an adult changeling's life. Changelings weren't human or Psy, needed the physical contact to thrive. Soleil had been lucky enough to have had affection and friendship in her life, but she'd never found a true lover. Any intimate skin privileges she'd exchanged had been with generous and kind friends who'd sensed her touch hunger and offered to assuage it.

A thing of comfort rather than carnal pleasure.

Soleil treasured their gift of touch, but she'd always wondered if there was something wrong with her that she'd never experienced the carnal heat that so many of her kind talked about, the storm of the blood that made a cat want to scratch and bite and mark her lover.

Her eyes flicked up to meet those of searing iceblue, the banked heat in them scalding. And her panties went damp, her cat arching its back inside her. Nope, there was absolutely nothing wrong with her. She'd just had to find the right man. "I want to bite you," she said, the words falling out of her mouth before she was aware of thinking them.

He said, "I've never been naked with anyone." Words potent with tension, that dangerous gaze never moving off her. "Sex was verboten under Silence."

The entire world retreated, the silence a paradoxical roar in her ears. Breath coming faster, she just stared at him, unable to imagine that this lethal, beautiful man had never shared his body with a lover. But then . . . he didn't share much of himself at all, did he? Shields and walls, those were the things that composed Ivan.

"What?" It came out a strangled sort of word, her voice rough. "Not even after the fall?" Her cat snarled in jealousy at the idea of anyone else touching him, but it was also mad that he'd denied himself the comfort of such intensive physical contact.

As a healer, she knew just how much touch meant, not only to changelings but to humans. Humans didn't need it to the same extent as a changeling, but they withered without it all the same.

Psy couldn't be so very different.

And fact was fact: the man was gorgeous and sexy and even if he'd never dropped his mask of frigid ice, a lot of women liked dancing with danger. He would've had no problem filling his bed every night had he wished it.

As if summoned up by her thoughts, their waitress returned to the table. "Is everything all right?" she asked brightly, subtly angling her body toward Ivan. "Do you need anything else? Anything at all?"

"Everything is fine," Ivan said, his tone polite but empty of any ounce of emotion. It was as if he hadn't even noticed that the woman was all but salivating over him. "Thank you for your assistance."

"Of course." The waitress gave a tight smile and walked away.

Soleil almost felt sorry for her. Ivan Mercant packed a serious punch.

"To answer your question," Ivan said after the waitress was out of earshot. "The only woman I've ever considered in that context is sitting across from me. You walked out of the forest and something inside me hungered. For your smile, for your words, and for your touch."

Her cheeks went hot at what was outwardly a cool and curt recitation, her breasts heavy and taut. "Eat," she rasped. "You're going to need your energy." Because her cat was through with waiting—and so, it seemed, was the man with eyes as cold as frost.

She couldn't take her gaze from him as he began to fuel his body with focused attention. A beautiful, honed knife of a body. Her hands itched to trace the lines of his muscles, learn the places where he was hard and where he was soft, nuzzle her nose into the curve of his neck, kiss and lick every inch of ink on his skin.

Snapping up his head without warning, Ivan pulled back the sleeve of his blazer to reveal a communications device as small as a watch. When he swiped it over the reader on the table, she realized it must hold a credit chip, too. The screen glowed blue to show that they'd cleared their bill, complete with suggested tip.

"Ivan—"

A single glance that made it clear he was in no mood to wait. And she remembered . . . they were bonded. In a way that sent erratic bursts of information across from one to the other.

And she'd just been indulging in fantasies erotic and wild.

As she watched with her heart in her throat, he caught the attention of a busboy and asked the lanky youth—who Soleil's nose told her was a leopard juvenile—to package up their mostly uneaten food to go. "Fast as you can." He slid a physical credit token onto the table, the amount it represented equal to half their bill.

Eyes going wide, the juvenile *moved*, and had the food back to them in a matter of minutes. The boy pocketed the tip after Ivan thanked him for his quick work, then grinned and went to hug Soleil before hesitating. Smiling, she wrapped her arms around him and squeezed tight. He was one of hers now, a cub to protect.

Wrapping his arms around her in turn, he squeezed her back as hard. "Welcome to the pack," he said, the scent of him sharp and young and wild.

"Thank you, baby." It just came out, that gently affectionate word.

He blushed and ducked his head but took it with a smiling roll of his eyes. Because she was a healer, and this was a pack in which healers were cherished and respected.

As she was heading to the door, she realized she didn't know the boy's name. But that was okay. Because she had his scent and he already felt safe enough with her to have hugged her. Even with her deadly Psy right next to her the entire time. Because the boy had sensed that Ivan was no threat to him—children knew, they always knew. "Thank you for indulging the cub."

A curt nod. "He was excited to see you."

She went to reply but Ivan put his hand on her lower back as she walked out the front door and her mind short-circuited, her cat remembering exactly where they'd been before the small interruption. Her body snapped right back to taut, exquisite readiness. She wanted to arch her back and moan, the slight contact a tease she could hardly bear.

The sun out on the street was a burn on her overheated, oversensitized flesh, her clothing suddenly too heavy, too rough against skin that wanted only to touch skin. "Ivan." A husky plea.

He took her hand, the bag of food in his other. "We're going home." Cool, controlled words that crept over her skin like a caress from an assassin's blade. "You can eat after."

After.

She almost orgasmed then and there.

Chapter 40

Lover, lover
Die for me
In this sweet kiss
This carnal b—

—"Unfinished work 7" by Adina Mercant, poet (b. 1832, d. 1901)

IVAN DID HIS research before every operation. He liked plans, liked having worked out every possible scenario.

He'd have researched sexual contact with the same single-minded determination had he ever believed Soleil would come back into his life and want to interact that way with him. But he hadn't, and so he had no plans, nothing but an urgent physical drive that threatened to wipe his mind of all rational thought.

He fought it long enough to say, "You're sure? Even knowing—"

"I'm sure." Her voice was breathless from the speed of their walk, her eyes no longer human . . . and the erotic images that kept flashing into his brain without warning an education.

He could do that. And that.

He hesitated. So many of the images were of her touching *him*, caressing him. As if she found him as much a compulsion as he found her. His penis threatened to go fully erect; the only reason it hadn't already done so was that he'd thrown literally all his years of control into suffocating the reaction until they were in the apartment.

He still barely made it.

Slamming the door behind them with a force he'd never before shown, he used his palmprint to activate full security, then ran a telepathic scan as Soleil raced up the stairs ahead of him. He followed, his heart pounding and his skin so hot that he half expected to see steam coming off it.

No intruders detected in his telepathic scan.

He set it to run automatically in the background as he entered the bedroom behind Soleil and shut the door. First, he put the food carefully aside. She hadn't eaten; he'd seen that. He'd feed her after, his need to look after her a driving force. But first, he had to touch her, the hunger inside him a new thing he didn't have the language to describe.

As he pulled off his blazer, she threw off his jacket.

He was only three buttons into unbuttoning his shirt when she kicked off her trainers and tore her dress off over her head. Her bra joined the pile of clothing a heartbeat later. His brain just . . . shut down.

She was . . .

Mouth dry, he swallowed, unable to take his eyes off her as she walked toward him, her breasts bouncing a little with each step. She stopped when almost to him and raised her hands to squeeze her own breasts, her lips plump and her pupils dilated. "Ivan, I need your touch."

Ivan needed no further instructions.

Snapping out of his frozen state, he covered the distance between them in a single stride and hauled her against him, one hand on the back of her neck, the other splayed on her lower back.

When she gasped, he fought to think. "Was I too rough?"

A small growl in answer, before his changeling lover hooked her legs around his waist with a single jump, her claws kneading lightly at his shoulders as she nipped at his throat. Ivan's erection was a thing of stone by now, rigid almost beyond bearing, but her lips, her teeth, her mouth as she explored his throat threatened to push him over the edge.

"I don't have control," he gritted out.

Wild eyes holding his. "Neither do I." A tearing sound, his shirt in shreds around them.

Ivan protected his clothes. They were important. Except now. Now, he just wanted to be naked. Groaning as Soleil pasted herself against his bare chest and claimed his lips for a kiss, he palmed her buttocks with one hand and walked them toward the bed while they kissed.

A rational part of his mind knew that he was probably technically very bad at the skill, but Soleil didn't seem to care. She devoured him, and he devoured her in turn, and all the while, her thighs gripped his hips, as if she'd climb him. Ride him.

Soleil ripped away her mouth, her lips wet in the aftermath. "God, yes. I want to ride you into oblivion."

Another transfer through their bond.

Pulling her head back to his with a hand fisted in the softness of her hair, he kissed her hard and deep, using all the things he'd learned in the first round. When she bit lightly at his lip and pushed at his shoulders, he released her directly onto the bed. He knew what she wanted, could see it in his mind. Flashes of his body, of his skin, of his erect penis.

His hands shook as he tried to undo his belt. "Fuck." Ivan rarely swore; it was about control, about maintaining discipline—but he didn't have any today.

When Soleil got up on her hands and knees and crawled across the bed to kneel in front of him, her face at eye level with his abdomen, he forgot to breathe. *"Lei."* Fisting his hand in her hair again, he let her take over, let her undo his belt, lower his zipper with care over the steely outline of his erection.

Black, his mind went black.

When he stumbled back from her, she made a rumbling sound in her throat that was very much a growl. But he couldn't be close to her and not break. And he didn't want this over. Kicking off his shoes and socks, he tore off what remained of his clothing.

His erection jutted out, wet at the tip.

Soleil was off the bed and on him before he saw her move.

Changeling.

Cat.

Taking him to the ground in a tumble he controlled so she wouldn't hit the floor first, she rubbed her body against his, his erection captured between her thighs, sliding between her slick folds. And he realized she must've torn off her own panties.

His back arched, his eyes threatening to roll back in his head. Gripping her hips, he shifted her so that she was astride him. Then he said, "Take me." Because he was hers, had been hers from the moment she walked out of the forest.

Primal eyes but tender fingers brushing over his lips, she didn't draw it out. Neither one of them was in any mood for slow. Slow would hurt today. Moving into position, she pressed a kiss to his throat . . . and then she took him. With a wild possessiveness that left him with fine claw marks on his chest and a passionate tenderness that had her hair cocooning them in softness as she kissed him even as her body moved with erotic abandon.

His brain had no pathways to process this experience, so he just gave in and surrendered to her. To his cat who owned him, body and soul. And when his spine locked, his entire body turning to stone before it broke into a million splintered stars, she fell over the edge with him, her cry high and her head thrown back to reveal the line of her neck.

It bore the mark of his lips.

SOLEIL wasn't sure she was still alive. She could hear someone's pulse. Maybe it was hers. Or maybe it was that of the man on whom she lay, his inked skin her pillow and her hands spread out over him. They were all but pasted together with sweat, and his hand was fisted in her hair, his other one on her butt.

He liked doing both, she realized hazily. That was fine with her. She liked it. She'd have made it clear if she didn't. And he didn't seem to mind the light scratches she'd given him. She stroked her fingers over them now, smiling in satisfaction, the cat inside her smug. "I've marked you."

A rumble under her was the only response.

She smiled again, kneading lightly at his chest with her claws while she just enjoyed the full-body contact with the man who was her mate. Of course he was; there was no question on that point. She'd also figured out why the bond hadn't completed itself—because her Psy was trying to protect her.

Honestly, she'd be irritated with him if she didn't adore him. Also right now, she was pleasure drunk. Her toes couldn't even curl, they were so lazily sated.

She kissed his chest again.

He flexed his fingers in her hair, curled them back in.

As he lazily stroked her bottom, her eye fell on a shred of white not far away. "Damn," she muttered. "That was my last pair of panties."

"We'll go shopping." His voice was husky and languid in a way she'd never before heard from Ivan Mercant.

Curious about what he looked like in the aftermath of what had been an unashamedly carnal bout, she made herself rise up into a seated position, her bottom half against his abdomen. Then she took in her lover.

His perfect hair was deliciously mussed, the ice blue of his eyes foggy, and his lips delicately bruised. Kiss-bruised. Touching her fingers to her own lips, she smiled. "We're a pair." And that was before she took in the scratches on his neck. Oh, her cat was sneaky, all right. It had marked him where no one could miss it.

His eyes shifted from her face to her throat.

"What?" she said.

"I marked you, too."

Delighted by the idea, she wanted to find a mirror, see, but she wanted to be with him more, so she prowled up so they were nose to nose, her hair thrown over one shoulder to pool against one side of his body. "Hi."

He ran a hand over her spine. "Hi."

They just looked at each other and oh, they were kissing. Slowly, and with intense focus, as if nothing else existed in the entire world. And it didn't, not for these moments in time caught between pieces of chaos. This time was theirs, and Soleil intended to enjoy them to the hilt, well aware that Ivan's priorities would have to shift the instant he was back up to full psychic strength.

She was a healer, had no argument with his priorities. Those people needed him.

But that time hadn't yet come, so she could monopolize him without guilt. Kiss him with lush eroticism while he touched her as if he'd never touched anything so beautiful, even though she was too thin, her ribs and hip bones sticking out, barely any curves to her.

Then there were the scars. So many scars quite aside from the familiar ones from the childhood accident. Changelings had good healing capabilities but she'd been badly wounded, and her body had directed its energy into keeping her alive. The scars would fade over time, but they were yet rigid and obvious.

The one where the ax had thunked into her back was the deepest, but there were myriad others, all of which Ivan touched and stroked the same as he did the unmarked parts of her body. As if learning her piece by piece.

And the way he'd looked at her when she'd first stripped for him? Oh, the man had been fixated on her breasts, hadn't given a fig about any scars. He'd just wanted to put his hands on her. It made her lips curve as she made her way down his body.

Because her Ivan had loved her body before, and he loved her body now. She could imagine him touching her just the same when she was an elder of a hundred and twenty with skin seamed by life and bones that no longer worked quite the same. And oh how she hoped they'd get that moment—and all the ones that came before it.

Kissing the image of her he had written on his skin, she found herself being tugged up by a gentle pull on her hair when she would've wriggled her way farther down.

Lifting her head, she said, "I'm not done."

"I want to taste you as you imagined."

Soleil parted her lips to ask what he was talking about, but then he squeezed her hips in a nudge to move up and she got it. Her entire body went hot. She blushed at the sheer brazenness of her thoughts, but fantasizing about naughty things with her man wasn't a crime.

"We need to get a control on this bond," she muttered, her cheeks hot.

Ivan shaped her buttocks with his hands. "No. I like instructions and suggestions in this area." Then he urged her higher.

And because she had about as much willpower as a noodle when it came to resisting him, she went. Up, and up. Until he was gripping her hips to hold her in position, and tasting her exactly as she'd fantasized.

He drove her insane.

It wasn't about technique or sophistication. No, it was about Ivan Mercant's sheer enthusiasm for the task. He explored her with his tongue and his lips as if he couldn't get enough of her, his attention to detail on luscious display. Soleil whimpered and came.

He licked her through it.

Then started all over again—after pressing a tender kiss to the inside of her thigh.

God, the man was lethal.

Chapter 41

Dear Aunt Rita,

I've been dating my Psy neighbor for a month and things are getting physical. Only the thing is, he's a virgin. I'm *fine* with that, but I think he feels a little lost so he stops things anytime the flames start to burn.

What do you think I could do to put him at ease, because I really, really want to jump his hottie bones. (I did ask him if he wanted to exchange skin privileges and got a definite yes.)

~Mare who wants to be Bare

Dear Mare who wants to be Bare,

First thing—you may need to slow this express train to Orgasmsville to allow your lover to catch up. Remember, Psy have only just begun to embrace touch.

Secondly, I suggest leaving the current issue of *Wild Woman* just lying around when he's in the vicinity—opened to page 27. You're welcome.

~Aunt Rita

—From the August 2083 issue of *Wild Woman* magazine: "Skin Privileges, Style & Primal Sophistication"

. . .

SOLEIL WAS SUNK. Because if this was the sexual education of Ivan Mercant, she definitely didn't feel like the teacher. "No more." She tugged at his hair after a second orgasm racked her, her internal muscles clenching over and over.

Another kiss to her thigh before he released her so she could wriggle her way down to collapse over his body. His cock, hard and ready, burned a line of heat against her thigh.

"I'm up for it," she managed to gasp, "but my muscles seem to have melted."

A big hand in her hair, a kiss pressed to the side of her face, the scent of Ivan in her every breath as he shifted to a seated position, taking her with him. Then he was somehow on his feet with her in his arms. She kept forgetting how highly trained he was, his muscles honed to an edge.

Placing her on the bed, he came down over her, and *mmm*, she liked this position, too. His weight on her felt so good, and his eyes were right there for her to look into—and see just how far he was gone. Heavy-lidded, pupils dilated, this was not the Ivan Mercant who kept the world at bay.

This was her Ivan.

Palming her breast, he said, "I need to be inside you first." And then he was using that hand to nudge her thighs apart so he could explore her with his fingers. He dipped one finger inside her, caught his breath, before pulling out his finger in readiness to slide his cock into her.

He took his time, careful with how much of his weight was on her. She could've hurried him, but she was too lazy . . . and she liked how he looked after her. It made her feel cherished and wanted and adored. She stroked and petted his shoulders, dropping kisses where she could reach because she wanted him to feel the same way.

The blunt head of his cock pushed into her.

She sighed, her pleasured flesh quivering around him. She got her lazy body moving enough to take him deeper, her legs spread wide and her knees raised and it was a gorgeous slide of flesh on flesh, heat on heat, their bodies all sweat and pleasure. Once seated inside her to the hilt, the pressure deliciously intense, he shuddered, then palmed her breast again.

It felt like sweet, hot honey in her veins this time around, a slower and deeper ride, the intimacy all the more for how slow they took it. All the kisses, all the touches. All the whispers against each other's lips as they learned what brought the other pleasure.

Afterward, they lay tangled together, face-to-face, and talked.

When she said, "Tell me about your family," he spoke about Canto, the anchor who was everyone's big brother; about Arwen, the empath who couldn't help looking after every member of his personal tribe; about Silver, the cool-eyed negotiator who was "Ena in training"; about the younger members the family kept protected from the world—and of course, about his powerhouse of a grandmother.

And she thought: *He loves them even if he won't acknowledge it.* It made her happy, that he'd had love in his life, whether overt or covert. Love was love and it altered the pathways of the mind and the heart, taught a person that life wasn't only pain. Even his mother, she thought, had loved him in her own broken way.

As if he'd heard her thoughts, he said, "It wasn't only darkness with my mother. One of my earliest memories is of the two of us sneaking into a playground after nightfall, both of us giggling as we crawled under the chain link. She must've been taking Jax for her Silence to be so bad, but she wasn't showing any external effects at that time.

"That night, she pushed me on the swing and we spun together on a merry-go-round. Later, she spotted me while I climbed from one side of the jungle gym to the other. And afterward, I remember that she had food, that we sat at a picnic table and ate and drank and I went to sleep in a warm bed."

Soleil's heart ached for that young woman and her son. "Do you know how she fell into Jax?"

"It was hard to get any real information out of her, and I was so young. I don't even remember if she ever told me any other last name but Mercant—the only clue I have is a ring she said was a reminder of where she came from, but even Grandmother wasn't able to trace it to a family in the Net.

"It doesn't have a real emblem on it, just a kind of a swaying line that doesn't match up with anything in the Net's archives. I looked, too, once I was older. My mother wore it always, so I'm certain she didn't lie about its origins, but I also think she took it for exactly that reason—because it couldn't be traced back."

"You don't wear it?"

"I keep it with me, but it's—" When he hesitated, as if searching for the right words, she said, "I get it. It's complicated." The ring was a symbol of pain as much as it was a piece of memory.

Ivan let her weave her fingers through his hair, let her nuzzle at him.

It was several minutes later that he said, "I remember her saying once that she was born into a family of vipers. Jax was an escape to her. She saw it as rebellion. I saw it as giving up." No anger in his tone, nothing but old memories.

He traced her facial scar with one gentle finger, the same way she might trace one of his tattoos. Because it was part of the story of her life. "What was it like," he asked, "having a human mother and a changeling father?"

"My normal," she whispered. "I used to pounce on her in my ocelot form and she'd squeak, then rub my belly and kiss my face and tell me I was the cutest little kitten ever." The memory hurt but it was beautiful, too.

"Sometimes, she'd catch me when I was being a really naughty cub and tickle my stomach until I couldn't stop laughing—I liked the tickling, because she never did it when I wasn't in the mood and because she'd always be laughing, too, both of us in hysterics when my father found us.

"I can still remember him standing there, looking down at the two of us and shaking his head." Those had been the best days, days saturated in a kind of forever sunshine in her memories.

"My father sometimes slept in ocelot form, other times in human. I could find either when I woke early and went to jump on them to wake them up." She smiled at the memory of her mischievous childhood antics. "One thing I remember is that they were always touching when I found them asleep, her hand fisted on his fur or his arms wrapped around her."

She told him of their road trips and she told him of their final ride together. The car skidding off the road, killing her father on impact, leaving her mother badly injured and bleeding while the pungent smell of fuel filled the air and the storm winds howled outside.

How her mother had told her to get out in case of an explosion, and how she'd tried to help her mother only to feel the loving quicksilver and shining talent of Hinemoa Bijoux's life slip away. How a passing motorist had found her sitting mute and bloodied and rain-drenched beside the car a long time later.

Ivan stroked her back and held her and she could bear to speak the words.

Another question, another answer. Another glimpse into one another.

So many things she and Ivan talked about as they lay together, DarkRiver and Mercant, Psy and changeling, Lei and her Ivan, and the whole world was perfect for a single fragment of time.

Chapter 42

They told me I was broken. They told me I was flawed.

—Sascha Duncan, cardinal E & defector (2079)

SOLEIL COULD FEEL the tension in Ivan as he walked her back to DarkRiver HQ after she finally ran her errands—which had included some clothes shopping, underwear included. Which of course, she didn't have on now, since she wasn't about to slip on intimate clothing without washing it first.

Which meant lots of airflow right up through her dress, to the tender place between her thighs. So tender. She wasn't the least bit sorry. She'd adored every single instant of what had led to that tenderness. But now their time was over—Ivan wasn't back to full psychic strength, but she needed to get back to the cubs; it was too soon after her return for her to disappear for an entire day.

Her cat missed them desperately.

She'd made Ivan promise that he wouldn't set foot on the island without giving her enough time to get back to him, so she could haul him out well before it became dangerous. Never again did she want to see him so motionless and cold, his mind and body in danger of a permanent separation.

It terrified her that he was even going to try again, but as a healer, she understood the drive to help. And she understood that Ivan Mercant was a hero, even though he'd never put it that way; this man wouldn't ever choose to protect himself at the cost of the lives of others.

She glanced at him on a crashing wave of protective possessiveness. He looked frostily urbane and aloof, her Psy, when she knew he was anything but that with the people he let in. He'd paired the blazer she liked with another black shirt from his wardrobe since she'd shredded his previous one, wore jeans and boots, his hair neatly combed and mirrored sunglasses over his eyes.

He'd hitched her daypack over one shoulder.

Half of her wanted to jump his bones again, while the other half was as tense as a piece of guitar wire. It wasn't that Ivan had issue with her need to go see the cubs, or even the promise she'd extracted from him. No, what he had an issue with was the fact that he couldn't drive her back to her territory, his welcome there in serious doubt since their mating bond remained a strange halfway thing. He'd have risked it, but Soleil wasn't about to—he meant far too much to her.

But when, after another ravenous kiss, she made a move to step inside the HQ, her cat fought her. *Hard.* Hard enough that she snarled, rebellion and need sparking in every vein and artery.

Cool male fingers closed over her wrist at the same time, and when she whipped back her head to look at him, she saw that Ivan had pulled off his sunglasses to reveal eyes gone a flat black. His fingers tightened, his jaw working, the fabric of his blazer taut across his shoulders. "I'm fighting to release you." It came out as sharp as a blade.

Her claws already out, she could've struck at him, but there would be no point. This wasn't a one-sided thing. Her cat wasn't ready to release him, either, the need to hold him a violent compulsion.

A shimmering silver web in her mind, the threads hard and cutting today, ready to form into a cell. The future that Ivan foresaw for himself, his mind encased behind shields so brutal they would savage this man who put his life on the line to save strangers, whose loyalty to his family was absolute . . . and who would do anything for Soleil.

Ivan Mercant, she understood deep within, had no limits when he loved.

Her cat swiped at the horrific image of the proto-cage, ripping it to shreds as she tugged him closer, until he was close enough that he was able to release her hand. "It's time to talk to Lucas."

Eyes yet inky black, Ivan said, "This isn't normal." His jaw worked. "My ability . . . I think it's wrapped you up in its threads."

"The holding on is mutual," she said. "Let's figure out how to deal with it. Because I refuse to be separated from the cubs *or* from you."

They entered the HQ.

The receptionist was a slender young Asian man with a huge smile that faded after he spotted Ivan. "I'll need to call up." He'd risen to his feet at their entry, now reached for the comm.

Before he could activate it, however, a familiar figure came down the hallway. The redheaded dominant Soleil had seen on the street— this time with a child in her arms, an auburn-haired toddler in tan shorts and a navy polo-neck tee who was fast asleep on her shoulder, his head turned into her neck and one tiny hand curled up against her chest.

She wore fitted jeans of well-washed blue, with a white tee belted in at the waist, her ankle boots a pop of red, and her hair pulled back into a smooth ponytail. The lithe muscle on her flowed over curves and valleys, her status as a predator obvious to anyone with eyes.

Equally obvious was that she was stunning—the kind of stunning that was a knock to the head that left a man seeing stars. "I'll handle it, Aaron," she said with the firm warmth of a dominant who was confident in her power, didn't need to posture and flex.

The young receptionist stood down—and it was only then that Soleil realized he'd been on alert. Slender he might be, but he was a dominant, probably a fully trained soldier. Of course DarkRiver wouldn't have someone who could be easily overwhelmed at the front desk.

"Name's Mercy," the redhead said. "Sentinel. Aaron here is a junior soldier in charge of a small security team—they're going to miss him when he moves into the senior ranks next year, but Aaron's too brilliant to be held back just because of his age. Aaron, you know Ivan Mercant." Amusement in her eyes. "Soleil is our new healer—she studied under Yariela."

Flushing at the praise from the sentinel, Aaron raised a hand. "Hi. I'm friends with Duke. He talks all the time about how you were right there on the front lines, how you fought and fought to help people. Said he never knew how much courage a healer could have until he saw you take blow after blow and keep going."

Soleil had never had much to do with the young soldier, so the knowledge that Duke had remembered her with such honor . . . it mattered. Swallowing the lump in her throat, she said, "It's lovely to meet you, Aaron. I'll have to squeeze Duke extra tight when I see him."

Aaron smiled, then nodded a hello at Ivan. "I tracked you all over the city. Feel weird about it now. Sorry, man."

"It was the job," Ivan said. "No offense taken."

As Aaron retook his seat, Mercy brushed her fingers over Soleil's cheek in an unexpectedly gentle welcome. "Here to see Luc?"

When Soleil nodded, Mercy began to lead them upstairs. Despite Mercy's outward friendliness, Ivan kept up his guard, well aware he was in the presence of one of the deadliest members of DarkRiver. Dominants with cubs to protect were lethal, and per his research, Mercy Smith had already been lethal to begin with.

"I'd introduce you to my little hooligan," she said, patting the boy's back, "but he finally zonked out after arguing with me that he didn't need a nap. You wouldn't think a baby barely past a year of age could argue, but Ace clearly got his demon genes from me and my brothers."

A kiss pressed to the top of her son's head that held unhidden tenderness. The sight made Ivan's gut clench on memories far less bucolic. His mother had kissed him that way at times, but she'd be slurring her words at the same time, her mind already walking the petals of the crystalline flower.

"He's adorable," Soleil whispered from beside him, his healer with her heart made of softness and empathy.

"You offering to babysit?" Wicked feline amusement. "Word of warning—he comes as part of a pack of three. Two boys and one girl. All with a full share of the aforementioned demon genes. Their poor papa had no idea what was coming."

"Triplets?" The single word from Soleil was a gasp. Then, tilting her head a fraction, she said, "I swear I can smell wolf on both of you. It's so deep . . . *Oh*. The poor papa is a wolf."

Ivan wasn't as startled by the news. He knew Mercy Smith was mated to one of the SnowDancer wolves. It was another thread that tied the two packs together. The child in her arms was yet one more link in what was effectively the most powerful alliance of packs in the country.

It was no wonder his grandmother was intrigued by them.

When Ivan leaned forward to open the door to the upstairs area, he got a smiling "Thanks" from Mercy. He didn't take that as an indication that he'd been accepted by the pack.

The immediate area beyond the door was an open-plan space with a number of workstations. Several were empty at that moment, but a man with hair of shocking white-blond worked at a drafting table, two women stood in front of a whiteboard figuring out what looked to be a complex residential plan, while a couple of other packmates sat at computer stations.

Ivan recognized a number of them from his research.

Each and every one shot Soleil a salute or a smile of welcome.

Her cat's happiness echoed down their bond. Because she was with her pack. With her family. He waited for a stab of envy or jealousy, for the spider to flex inside its monstrous carapace, but it didn't come. Because he knew what it was to be alone; not even the darkest part of him begrudged Soleil the bonds of pack.

But where Soleil had received friendly smiles, Ivan got narrow-eyed looks. They weren't hostile. More confused. Because the cats were sensing a bond that shouldn't exist, a bond that he had to break if he wanted to keep Soleil safe . . . except he didn't think he could let her go. Never again could he let her go.

Fuck.

"Introductions later!" Mercy called out to the room, then turned to Soleil. "Luc has to leave for a site visit in a half hour, so we need to catch him before then."

Ducking her head inside the open office door at the other end of the room, Mercy said, "Luc, our new healer needs your attention. Oh, and his lordship here has informed me that he, Belle, and Micah want to come over to play with Naya. Doable tomorrow?"

Soleil's hand clenched on Ivan's. When he glanced at her, he saw a bewildered kind of wonder in her expression. "What is it?" he murmured under his breath, while Mercy laughed at something Lucas had said, his voice inaudible to Ivan except as a low rumble.

"Not once in all my years," Soleil whispered, "did I ever see a Sky-Elm dominant speak so casually to our alpha. As a friend and an equal." Huge eyes, a shaky smile. "There's so much I have to learn about my new pack, Ivan."

Mercy turned back to them before he could respond. "Go on in. I'm heading to the nursery to return the escapee and look in on the other pupcubs."

"Pupcubs?" Soleil pressed her hands to her cheeks, her shaky smile switching to one of pure delight. "You call the triplets pupcubs? I can't handle it."

Chuckling, Mercy stroked her sleeping son's back. "Come over sometime after you're settled in. I can't promise peace, but I can promise that the tiny hooligans will be charming as they lure you into their schemes."

Then she was gone and they were in Lucas's office, Ivan closing the door behind them to ensure privacy.

The alpha's office featured a desk, a large window that could be opened, and shelving that held various items—including framed handprints made in colorful paint. The size of those handprints told her they were from a child. His daughter, the Naya that Mercy had just mentioned.

Lucas himself had moved around to stand in front of his desk. Folding his arms over his T-shirt-clad chest, he leaned back against his desk. Look at him in his black T-shirt and faded blue jeans, and you'd never know that he was the effective CEO of a major construction powerhouse.

"So," he murmured, panther green eyes going from one to the other, "you two have completed the mating . . . Or something like it. It's still off in a way I can't work out, but the scent bonds are embedded so deep now that no shower will ever wash them off."

The dark heart of Ivan roared in a silent and feral triumph. She was *his*. Fighting that triumph, he forced himself to lay it out. "I have a defective brain structure," he said, earning himself a low growl from Soleil. "It may be affecting how such a bond would normally function."

Lucas's eyes didn't go cold, his expression difficult to read. "You know," he murmured, "another Psy once told me that they were flawed, imperfect. Turned out they were wrong."

"I'm not wrong." Ivan could wish he was until he was blue in the face, but he had the brain scans to prove it. "Damage from my mother's use of Jax while she was carrying me."

Lucas's pupils flared. "Understood," he said before shifting his attention to Soleil. "You're the healer. What do you feel?"

"He's mine." Blunt, argumentative, not at all in any way submissive. "He's just being stubborn and self-sacrificing."

"*Lei.*" Knowing she'd never bend on this point, he turned to her alpha. "It's not safe for her to be linked to me. I'd release her"—the words were torn out of him—"but the bond isn't one I can see."

Lucas rubbed his jaw. "My mate tells me that changeling healers have psychic abilities, but it's a kind of psychic ability that can't be measured on the Psy Gradient, and isn't visible to the usual Psy senses."

That fit with everything Ivan had learned during his time with Soleil.

"Our bond is real." Soleil held her alpha's gaze, her courage unflinching. "I need to be with Nattie and Razi, but I also need to be with Ivan. I want him to have permission to come into pack territory."

Straightening to his full height, Lucas unfolded his arms to place his hands on his hips. "Mates don't betray one another," he said.

It wasn't a question, but Ivan responded regardless. "I would cut my own throat before I'd betray Soleil—and she's loyal to DarkRiver. You have my word I'll do nothing to put the pack in harm's way."

"I know. Soleil's a healer. Their mates are inevitably protectors."

Soleil bristled beside Ivan. "Ahem."

Her alpha shook his head. "Doesn't mean you can't protect yourself—but that you won't if in a situation where people are wounded. Your first instinct will be to assist. Ivan's will be to blow off the heads of anyone who tries to hurt you."

Ivan decided he liked Lucas Hunter; the man understood him.

Inside his mind, Soleil's cat sat grumpily because she knew damn well that the alpha wasn't wrong.

"You've been assigned an aerie close to Yariela, as well as Salvador and the two cubs," Lucas told Soleil, "and they have to be my priority." A glance at Ivan. "Are you safe around children?"

Ivan thought of the spider that sat in hunched readiness inside his head. "At present, I have full control over my actions and I've never harmed a child. But I may destabilize without warning."

"Bullshit," Soleil said, so angry at him for how he saw himself that she forgot herself in front of her alpha.

Lucas didn't react except to raise an eyebrow. He might be far more dangerous than Monroe, but his presence was a thousand times more stable. Soleil had the feeling this man never just flew off the handle—he was the calm heart of the pack, the one who steadied everyone else.

His scent alone was enough to comfort her cat, and she'd never before had that experience. For the first time in her life, she understood what it meant when changelings said they had a good alpha. Despite what she'd just thought, she realized then that it wasn't about personality, about whether an alpha was gregarious or quiet, full of laughter or more inclined to just smile now and then. It was about their ability to be the center that held, no matter what.

And it was about heart.

Monroe's heart had been a small, jealous thing.

Lucas's was wide enough to embrace each and every member of his pack—and that included strays like her who'd been enfolded into the pack. She was one of his now, was a cat of DarkRiver.

"For the safety of the vulnerable," he said right then, "I'm going to have you shifted to an aerie on the very edge of our forest territory. It'll mean a thirty-minute run to visit the cubs."

Soleil wanted to hug him. So she did. "Thank you."

Warm arms around her, affection given freely by this man who had no need to be cruel to hold on to power.

"I'll give you the location now," he said after they drew apart. "You two can drive there yourself. No restrictions on seeing anyone in the pack, but only you, Soleil, can go deeper into the territory until Ivan's certain of his control. Otherwise, they have to come to you."

"Of course." Soleil didn't believe Ivan was in any way a threat, but she wasn't about to break Lucas's faith in her—especially when Ivan was determined to think the worst of himself. Even now, she felt the grim shadows threatening to swamp the shimmering flame-kissed silver of him. "Thank you for your trust."

A slow smile. "I feel you inside me, healer of DarkRiver," he murmured. "I know who you are down to your core."

Lucas directed his next words to Ivan. "I've spoken to your grandmother. She's an alpha, too, and she's raised a powerful pride of children and grandchildren. Ena has given me her word that your family wishes to be an ally and not an enemy."

"My grandmother doesn't lie, not when she says things so bluntly," Ivan said, and Soleil found herself startled by his phrasing.

To Soleil's surprise, Lucas chuckled. "I'm a cat, Ivan. I understand all about sliding through small openings and taking out prey without warning. But face-to-face, predator to predator, there is no sophistry. We wear only our true skins." He straightened. "I see why your grandmother has such a fan in Valentin."

His gaze went once more to Soleil, those green eyes taking her in. And she had the thought that he was judging her status, her wellness. When he said nothing, just went to get them the location of the aerie, she knew he'd decided she could handle the situation.

Her alpha's confidence in her meant so much it threatened to close up her throat, her cat overwhelmed in the best way.

The Psy who'd just infuriated her squeezed her hand in silent comfort.

Chapter 43

While the latest scans show no changes in your brain, I am concerned about the increased levels of neural activity centered in the affected region.

—Dr. Jamal Raul to Ivan Mercant (18 June 2083)

SOLEIL WHIRLED ON Ivan the instant they were alone in the car he'd driven over from the parking garage while she made a quick visit to the nursery. "Your brain is not defective!" she said. "A difference doesn't equal a defect."

He pulled away from the HQ in a smooth move. "A part of my brain is literally misshapen." An ice-coated tone that wasn't the same as that he used with strangers—this one, she was sure, was a shield against red-hot anger. "There's no way to sugarcoat that, or erase it, or change it. It's an indelible part of who and what I am."

"So are my scars," Soleil said, touching the one on her face. "Does this make me defective?"

He shifted the car into manual drive mode, and wrenched one of the controls back hard. "It's nothing the same." No snapping, his voice even . . . and his jaw as hard as titanium, while inside her mind shimmered a web of silver flame gone rigid.

The man was in no mood to listen.

Well, she wasn't a cat for nothing, she thought as he parked at a loading zone near his apartment and jumped out to quickly grab a few of his things. As Lucas had said, cats knew all about sneaking through small gaps, and finding new ways to get into locked places. She'd find her way through this locked gate, too.

God, he was gorgeous and infuriating, she thought as he emerged from the apartment with a duffel bag in hand. She wasn't the least surprised when a woman across the street literally stopped walking to just *look* at him. He, of course, was oblivious to the carnage he left in his frosty wake.

Dropping his bag in the back with her stuff, he then returned to his position in the driver's seat. He pulled away from the curb in silence. Oh, this definitely wasn't his usual control. This was tightly contained fury.

A growl rumbling in her chest, she settled back in her seat. Then she poked at the bond between them. Ivan hissed out a breath, his hands tightening on the steering wheel as he pulled out onto the main highway.

As they shot down it at high speed, he gritted out, "What are you doing?"

"Testing our bond. Need to see where the issue is." She knew *exactly* where the issue was; the problem was in getting him to not only accept it, but accept that this bond was going nowhere and he might as well surrender to it.

Until then, she was happy to aggravate him so he couldn't ignore it. Yes, she was a cat.

A quick glance from Ivan before he put his eyes back on the road. "No, you need to find a way to cut it." A stony order. "My mind is built to suck the minds of others dry. Do you have any idea what that means? I could take everything you are, everything you have the potential to be."

His breathing was just slightly uneven. "That little boy you saw today? Mercy's pupcub? One of the younger cohort of my cousins, someone I was meant to protect, was that small when I took control of his mind without warning. He wouldn't wake up one day, no matter what anyone tried. He couldn't. Because the spider had him in its grip and it knows only to feed!"

She snarled at him, really snarled, in a way she'd never before done at anyone in her whole life. "You were a child at the time, too! One who had no idea what was going on!" A pointed finger. "And as far as I can tell, you're not the one sucking anyone dry in this relationship. *I'm* the one who took your energy to keep me alive."

He didn't answer for long minutes. When he did, it was with a grudging acceptance in his tone that was the first crack in the wall of frost. "Our bond does seem to function in an unexpected way." Stiff words. "That doesn't mean the spider can't grab hold of you—it did that outside the HQ. Threads of power, of control. Never forget that."

"You're fooling yourself if you think you had me under any sort of control," she said with a laugh that held only anger. "And, sweetheart, if you were in control of yourself, I'll eat my shoe!" Soleil was in no mood to be gentle with him when he kept on treating himself in a way that aggravated every ounce of her nature.

She'd never known a man who needed tenderness, affection, love more. All things of which she had an endless amount to give. Yet instead of letting her love him, he kept asking her to break their bond, kept rejecting her at every turn. It hurt her as much as it angered her. She'd had enough! Her cat raised its nose in the air, both parts of her looking stiffly in the other direction.

Two minutes of silence, and then Ivan said, "I thought I was content with aloneness, with quiet, but I don't like your silence." Reaching out, he closed his hand over her own.

Uncurling her fingers, she wove them through his. Rebuffing his olive branch was beyond her, no matter how infuriated she might be. Not only because that was just how she was built—to love with every cell in her body and for always, but because she could sense the need inside him.

Ivan loved his family and from what she'd learned of them from him, they loved him back, though only one of them—the empath—would likely put it in those terms. But people could only love a person as much as they allowed themself to be loved.

And Ivan, she thought, had only allowed them to love him so much and no more. Well, too bad for him—if he was with her, he'd have to get used to being looked after, being adored, being hers.

"My silence would only ever last a minute or two," she muttered, giving him a weapon he could use to hurt her—except that she was certain he wouldn't. Not her Ivan. "Even at my angriest, if you reach out to me, I'll be there. And if you don't reach out to me when you're in pain and need comfort, I *will* bite you."

A pause, followed by, "You sound very sure of that."

"I am. So if you were intending to ever shut me out, get rid of that thought right now."

"I could never ignore you, Lei," he said with that intense Ivan Mercant focus. "When I'm around you, you're all I see. You're like a star, you shine so bright. If I had my way, I'd keep you forever." He flexed his hand on the steering wheel to bone white tightness. "Now you know. I'm a monster who'd keep you tied to me even though nothing good lies at the end of that road."

Her skin hot and her cat at the surface, Soleil said, "It's not up to you. It's up to me. In a mating dance between a man and a woman, it's the woman who makes the decision."

A sharp glance from Ivan. He hadn't known that, she realized, hadn't understood how this primal dance worked.

"People," she continued, "have been making decisions for me my whole life. My parents decided to roam and take me with them, never once asking me if I maybe wanted to spend summers or the school terms in a pack."

Soleil had loved her mama and papa to her very bones, but she'd been born a healer, had craved the arms of pack until it was a constant pulse of hunger inside her, a gnawing she hadn't realized wasn't normal. She would've *never* left them on a permanent basis, but even short stints in a pack would've healed her in ways she hadn't understood as a child.

She and her parents could've approached a friendly pack, asked for that accommodation. Having seen how DarkRiver was run, she knew that a large number of packs—maybe even most of them—would've been open to hosting the baby healer daughter of two inveterate loners.

"Then, after my parents were gone," she said, "the authorities decided that I should be placed with my grandfather, this man who was a total stranger to me and who hated my lovely, artistic mother with every fiber of his being. That same man decided that I should grow up an outcast within SkyElm."

Soleil believed in an afterlife, and she hoped that her mother'd had a chance to ream out her grandfather in that afterlife. Hinemoa Bijoux would've destroyed him for how he'd treated her cherished baby girl. A grieving young Soleil had often imagined such a confrontation and found great delight in it.

"I'm through with all that," she said now, her eyes on the flawless profile of this man with so much courage and heart if only he'd see it. "The only person who gets to decide my future is me. And I've decided that I'm going to be yours."

IVAN couldn't speak.

The last time he'd been claimed with such unyielding intensity, it had been by his grandmother—and that had been a welcome into the family. This was the first and only time in his life that he'd been claimed on a personal level. Claimed with such obdurate possessiveness that he could feel the cat's claws in his mind, holding on to him, daring him to try to break away.

"*Lei.*" It came out as cracked as his failing shields, rough and full of broken edges.

"No buts." A hint of the ocelot in her tone, a rumbling bass to it. "You want to snap our bond, end us before we begin on the basis of something that *might* happen."

His jaw worked. "My shields are failing. That's not conjecture but truth. The spider has already captured multiple minds in the Chaos-Net. Because of where they are, how they're trapped, I can't let go of them without consigning them to death, but the longer the connections hold, the stronger the spider becomes."

He could feel his twisted power growing, stretching, readying itself to strike. "It's not a case of if but when it'll take over—and I refuse to become that creature, but more, I *refuse* to take you with me."

"Okay, let's forget about whether you've thought of all possible options to deal with your ability if it does break out, and look at the situation through a different lens," Soleil said in a reasonable tone of voice that immediately made him wary. "What if there's a massive earthquake tomorrow and I fall into a crevasse and break my neck? Boom. The end of Soleil Bijoux Garcia."

He'd have braked to a screeching stop if he hadn't been so experienced a driver, his motions almost automatic. "What are you talking about?" he managed to get out past his thumping heart.

Instead of answering his question, Soleil said, "My parents died without warning, after twelve years with each other, years drenched in love." Her voice trembled. "We don't have the choice of knowing what the future holds—but we have a choice in how we live our present.

"I choose to live mine with you, regardless of what may come." No hesitation in her, nothing but a depth of commitment that sang in their bond. "I don't want to be *safe*, Ivan. I want to be with the man who is my mate because you are the greatest gift of my life, the one gift I never ever thought I'd find."

A shaking breath. "The thing is, I've just realized I can't steal your choice from you. That would make me as bad as the people who did it to me. So if you truly don't want me, I'll do what I can to break the bond—I don't know if it's possible, but I'll try.

"But Ivan?" The barest touch of fur brushing *inside* him. "Don't you dare do it with the idea that you're saving me. Because you won't be. It's too late for that. It was too late the day we met." No tremor now, nothing but passionate conviction.

"You're my mate. Losing you would destroy me. I would rather have a single perfect day with you than a lifetime without you." Emotion turned her voice rough, but she kept going. "Only ask me to break the bond if you don't want me."

He heard her swallow before she said, "Choose to live with me, Ivan. Choose to love with me without boundaries and shields, whether that's for a single day, a year, or decades."

For the second time, she'd stolen his words from him. Overwhelmed by the enormity of what she'd said, the choice she'd made, he just kept on driving—but because he understood her now, he made sure to keep his hand in hers, and to squeeze it to tell her that he was still there, still with her, just needed time to process.

Lifting their clasped hands, she kissed his knuckles, and they drove on in a silence heavy with the choice she'd asked *him* to make. The hardest thing anyone had ever asked of him . . . because it meant that when the abyss beckoned, he'd fall with her in his arms, taking her into the nightmare with him.

Chapter 44

Nzxt: On the scale from one to ten, what species of changeling is the most aggravating?

CC2: Oh, you trying to start a ruckus, Nzxt. I'm not getting involved.

Vixen79: That's because you're a panda, CC. Way more zen than the rest of us. I vote for wolves.

Nzxt: Disqualified. You're just pissed at that last wolf boyfriend of yours. I say it's cats. Ever tried to ignore a cat? They (a) either don't care, or (b) refuse to be ignored. You can never win.

CC2: Aren't you dating a cat? Tiger, right?

Vixen79: Ooooh, *BUSTED*! Disqualified for being a cheater pants! I think that means *your* species is the most aggravating!

—Forum of *Wild Woman* magazine

SOLEIL DIDN'T PRESSURE Ivan. She loved his stubborn head and she was beginning to learn that her mate was a man who needed to work things through on his own timeline. So she'd give him that. And she'd keep on loving him.

Of course, if he tried to reject her, she damn well wouldn't let him get away with lying to either one of them. Didn't he realize she could feel his devotion to her through their bond? It was a thing of steel and ice and flame-kissed silver. If he tried to tell her he didn't love her, she'd call him a liar to his face.

Would she keep her word if he pushed it?

Yes.

It would splinter her into so many pieces that she'd never quite be right again, but she'd honor his choice as no one had honored hers. Even the thought hurt, but she took her own advice and didn't borrow trouble, instead choosing to live in this beautiful today where she had her mate beside her and they walked in a lush forest on the way to their new home.

Her feet crunched on the leaf litter as she followed the tracking on her phone to the exact GPS coordinates Lucas had given them . . . to find herself under the shadow of the spreading branches of a massive sequoia.

She gasped at the sheer beauty of the tree's arms, the way it allowed the sun to peek through in glorious filaments while providing an umbrella of shade and protection at the same time. Its trunk was a thing of age and time, so wide around that it would take ten or more people to encircle it.

It took her a minute to spot the aerie. It was perched far higher than anything in SkyElm. Ocelots were, by nature, terrestrial, but aeries off the ground made sense for security reasons. SkyElm had, however, kept those heights down to a level where someone in an aerie could easily talk to a packmate on the ground.

That wouldn't work here. A person would have to shout and hope for the best. God, it was beautiful, set solidly on one of the higher branches, and clearly designed to be reached by a cat. Though it did have what must be a hastily arranged rope ladder that had been unfurled so that it hung near to ground level.

A gift from her pack to her, she thought, her heart full. Because she had a mate who wasn't a cat. "Do you like heights?" she asked the Psy at her side, a Psy who was looking around with an expression that said he wasn't quite sure what to make of his new living situation.

"How am I going to climb that when I wear a suit?" was the cool question.

She laughed, delighted with him. "It won't be that bad," she said after leaning up to kiss his jaw. "Things only come out to eat you at night."

No laughter, his attention on the space all around them. "I like it." Quiet words, his hand sliding to stroke her lower back as if he couldn't be with her and not touch her.

Her cat got all bashful while wanting to snuggle into him. When she gave in to the urge, he just curled his arm around her as if it was perfectly natural for her to nuzzle at him under a forest sky.

"I never thought about how cats like space, too," Ivan murmured. "I would fit in a pack like this. I wouldn't feel like an outsider."

Soleil wanted to do a little jump at this sign that he was thinking about a future in which he walked beside her as her mate. "Come on, let's go look inside."

"I think it must be an old security aerie, from a time before Dark-River extended its security perimeter," Ivan pointed out as they neared the rope ladder. "Explains why it's so high."

"That's why you're the security genius and I'm a cat. Race you up!"

As a child, she would've shifted right then and there, not bothering about her clothes, but she loved her dress—the dress that Ivan had gifted her—too much to ruin it. So she stripped out of it as well as her shoes and bra. Convenient not to have to worry about panties, she thought with a grin.

It was only when Ivan sucked in a breath that she realized he was standing there watching her—and his eyes were flames of ice. Smiling, delighted, she padded over to him on bare feet, her skin touched by sunshine and shadow as her unbound hair brushed her back. Bracing herself up against him, she nibbled at his throat, pressed a kiss there.

His hands slid down to squeeze her buttocks with the same frank pleasure he'd shown before. It shocked her a little all over again—in the best way. She loved that her outwardly sophisticated Psy was so bluntly carnal in his sexual tastes.

Soleil shivered at the contact but drew away before they got distracted. "I want to see the aerie!" She shifted in a shower of light, her cat soon shaking its fur into place.

He'd seen her before, of course, but she still preened for him, showing off the arch of her ears, the strength of her tail, the way her markings looked in a beam of sunlight.

His expression was one of wonder as he crouched down to run his hand over her back. She flowed like liquid under him, showing him exactly where she wanted to be petted and adored, and knew that there'd be nights when she'd curl up beside him in this form and let him just stroke her. Because she was changeling, the cat as much a part of her as the human.

When her eyes threatened to go heavy-lidded, however, she pulled away and bounded over to the tree. At the bottom, she glanced back and waited. Getting the message, he jogged over to the rope ladder and put his hand on the step above his head.

Then he looked at her and raised an eyebrow.

Laughing within, both parts of her so pleased with him, she jumped up onto the tree and they raced their way to the very top. Though ocelots prefered the ground, they could climb with the best of them.

She beat him, of course, but he was very fast, this man who held her heart. He pulled himself up onto the verandah high above the ground with liquid ease—where she'd waited so they could explore their home as a couple.

Then together, cat and man walked into the aerie.

The human part of her mind stirred to the surface, the cat not as interested in internal things. A number of large and colorful cushions sat on the floor, while pretty curtains of scalloped white fabric hung at the windows. When she poked her head into the small bedroom, she saw a large futon-style bed with a simple bedspread of white with tiny green leaves on the edges.

A hand-knitted blanket, the color a soft mint green, lay folded at the bottom and when she sniffed at it, she whimpered. It carried Yariela's scent. Her mentor had knitted this, and someone in DarkRiver had made the effort to move it here so it would welcome Soleil home.

"What's the matter?" Ivan crouching beside her, his hand on her back.

She used one paw to pat at the blanket, an image of Yariela at the forefront of her mind, and love spilling over into her blood.

"She loves you." Ivan had picked up the image, she realized, understood the depth of her emotions.

He petted her until she found her feet again, could keep on exploring.

Noting the blank walls and bookshelves empty of anything but a single potted plant, she realized the aerie had only been furnished up to a point. There was enough here to make her and Ivan comfortable—but not enough that it was as if someone else had decorated the space for them.

The most personal thing in the aerie was Yariela's housewarming gift.

A stir in the air, Ivan moving to the bookshelf. Sliding a hand into his pants pocket, he took something out and put it on the shelf. Curious, she bounded over the bed to land beside him . . . and looked up to see the cat planter she'd given him sitting beside the potted plant.

Oh, he was wonderful. And sneaky. He hadn't had it on him while driving, so he must've grabbed it from his duffel while she stretched out the kinks after getting out of the car.

Home, he was saying he was home.

Soleil's feline heart ached. She'd pounce on him but a little later. For now, she rubbed her body against his legs as she went to nose around the rest of the place.

She discovered a kitchen area that flowed off the living room, sanitation facilities placed right in back of the aerie, and when she jumped up onto a desk by the window in the bedroom, she saw a quickly sketched plan laid on it that would add another room to the place.

A second sketch sat beside it: a small cabin at the foot of the same tree, with a notation that it would be wired for full comms and have a touch-activated door and floor that would send an alert to the aerie at the slightest sign of a visitor.

Tilting her head to the side, she considered the oddity . . . then understood on a tide of emotion. Her pack was telling her that if she liked this aerie, she could make it her own. She could have a home, a true home, where she was welcome and where the cubs and Yariela and all her packmates could visit her, stay overnight if they wanted.

The cabin would be for the babies who couldn't yet climb so high, and elder cats who didn't want to bound up to this perch . . . and because she was a healer, her home needing to be accessible to all. Especially wounded packmates who might not be able to use the comms.

That was why Tamsyn and Nathan didn't live in an aerie, she realized. Maybe Soleil would one day make the same choice, but for now, she loved the option she'd been offered—to have the aerie above and the specially configured cabin below. But most of all, she loved that she had a place that she could make into a haven for her mate, a man who wanted to protect her so much that he might forever break her heart.

IVAN was a creature of cities. Yes, he liked his own space, but he liked that in the midst of cities, with the constant buzz of life outside. He'd been born in a city, had been raised in one, and though he'd spent time in more isolated situations—such as when he'd stayed with his grandmother at the Sea House—that wasn't his natural milieu.

So this treehouse in the sky should've made him uncomfortable, should've felt like a scratchy coat on his skin. It didn't. As he walked around the living room, bending down to check out the large cushions meant to function as seating, then going over to the verandah that had railings on only three sides, he found the tension just melting out of him.

The way the tree leaves rustled, the way the wind blew softly, the way the sunshine speared through the clouds, it was all an extraordinary beauty. But he knew his contentment had nothing to do with that. It had to do with the sleek cat who was currently exploring the bedroom area.

He could hear her because she was making no effort to be quiet—and he knew she'd shifted out of her feline form even before she appeared in the doorway, a goddess naked to the skin with a smile in her eyes.

In a heartbeat, contentment roared into a feral kind of hunger. He'd already taken off his blazer inside, didn't have that hurdle. Partially unbuttoning his shirt as he strode to her, he pulled it off over his head and dropped it on the verandah, kicked off his shoes, then took her face in his hands.

Kissing, the raw intimacy of it, was still so new and yet so vital to his existence. He wrapped her up in his arms, this woman of heart and steel, and he kissed her long and deep, drinking her in until she moaned, small claws pricking into his back.

He stroked his hand down the sweeping line of her back to the curves below. She was still too thin, but she wasn't fragile in the least, her strength a thing of courage and grit. So he held nothing back. Could hold nothing back. He kissed her with the fury of the turbulent storm inside him.

Nimble hands at his waist, her fingers slipping his belt buckle free, undoing his jeans, unzipping him. His entire chest clenched when she closed her fingers around him. He still wasn't used to anyone else's hands on his body, far less on that most intimate part of him. She squeezed gently, then slid her hand down before sliding it back up.

Ivan's control shattered like a glass wall that had been hit at the bottom, the cracks spreading outward at a velocity nothing could stop. His mind hazed by need, by greed, by hunger, he didn't want to stop it. Closing one hand around her throat, he rubbed the pad of his thumb possessively over her plump lower lip. "Bedroom."

As she shivered, he took his hands off her only long enough to strip off what clothing remained on him. She returned to his arms the instant he was done, small claws stroking up and down his spine and a purr rumbling in her chest when he bent to suck at her throat.

Because his lover wasn't human or Psy, was changeling.

He nudged her backward, leading her to the bedroom even as he licked and tasted and kissed. He'd never get enough of her, of his healer with the spark in her eyes and the heart so soft it saw goodness even in him. Who had chosen him over life itself.

I would rather have a single perfect day with you than a lifetime without you.

The words reverberated around and around in his mind even as he picked her up, then put her with care onto the low bed. Her eyes were of the ocelot, tawny and gold and wild. Lips curved, she rose up onto all fours, then onto her knees to stroke her palms over his thighs.

He went to nudge her back so he could join her on the bed, but that wasn't what she had in mind. He bit off a single harsh word, not ready for her mouth closing over the head of his erection, the hot wetness, the suction. It went straight to his brain, the sensations exploding inside him in violent bursts that threatened to melt his neural tissue.

He valued control above all things, but this was Soleil. His mate.

Fisting handfuls of her hair, he held his body in place as she drove him to the edge of sanity, and demanded more, still more. When he felt the release begin to build in him, a tight knot at the base of his spine that was shoving outward with inexorable force, he managed to grind out a wordless warning.

His mate kneaded his buttocks with her claws, and sucked hard one last time.

Chapter 45

Je t'aime . . . mi corazón. I was . . . so lucky . . . to get to love you and
our . . . petite Leilei. See you . . . in . . . in—

—Hinemoa Bijoux

IVAN LAY ON his back, his chest heaving and the tiny hairs at his
forehead damp. He was fairly certain his heart was racing at Mach
speed.

Soleil lay on her stomach next to him, kicking up her legs while
giving him the most satisfied smile he'd ever seen. As if she was delighted with herself. It was a quintessentially feline expression and he
adored it. He wasn't a man used to thinking in such terms, but it was
the only one that fit.

She was so smug and happy with herself. He loved seeing her
this way.

When she pressed a kiss to his chest, then rose, he grabbed at her
hand. Looking over her shoulder, she said, "I'm just getting a glass of
water." A wicked grin. "Got something a little salty in my mouth."

A touch of heat on his cheeks, he released her hand. He wanted to
smile at her because what he felt inside, this deep warmth, it was a

thing of smiles and laughter. But he didn't know how to smile, had never done it in his life.

His Lei could teach him, he thought. As long as they were together, anything was possible. Ask him only a month earlier and he could've never imagined this day where he lay sexually sated in bed while a beautiful naked woman padded around their residence.

Pushing up into a seated position as he waited for her to return, he found his mind ricocheting back to their conversation in the car, a conversation that had turned his world on its axis.

People have been making decisions for me my whole life.

Don't you dare do it with the idea that you're saving me.

I would rather have a single perfect day with you than a lifetime without you.

"One perfect day," he whispered, and thought that he wouldn't trade this day he'd had with Soleil for anything, not even a lifetime.

That was when she walked back into the room, a glass of water for him in hand. Tilting her head to the side in that way she had of doing, she said, "What is it?"

He took the glass she held out but put it beside the bed rather than drinking it. "I understand."

"What, mi vida?" Seated on her knees beside him, her hair a dark rain over her shoulders, she ran her fingers through his own with an affection he'd never known he needed and now craved.

"That if I balanced this day with you against a lifetime without you, this day would win by such a large margin that it's not a competition at all." The man he was with her, it was an Ivan that was the very best of him. He'd be hollow without her. As she'd be without him.

It was a cataclysmic thing to accept, that he was so very important to her. But it was the truth. He felt it in her every touch, every look, in how her cat prowled inside his skin, and in her sheer delight at being with him. It was a thing as bright as the stars, as full of sunshine as his Lei.

Pupils huge and dark against the wild tawny-gold of her irises, Soleil lifted trembling fingers to his cheek. "Yes?" she whispered.

Turning his head, he kissed her palm. "Yes."

And his entire world . . . shivered, things that had been subtly out of alignment falling into perfect lines.

"Oh," Soleil whispered, her eyes wet. "Oh, there you are."

He enfolded her into his arms. "For always." For however long that always was for the two of them. Because they would fall together now, the mating bond complete in every way.

SOLEIL was still a touch shaky from the impact of knowing Ivan was now hers without conditions, without shields of any kind, but it was a happy kind of shaky—that was about to get even happier.

Salvador was bringing the cubs over to her. When she'd called Tamsyn to ask where Natal and Razi were so she could visit, she'd learned that they'd gone home with Salvador—and that they were awfully excited to see her new aerie after Tamsyn had mentioned it.

So Soleil invited Salvador to bring them over. After she and Sal cried on the phone at being reunited, she said, "Some kind packmate stocked up the pantry with supplies—I have countless people I need to find and thank—so I have everything I need to make cookies. They should be ready by the time you arrive."

After she and Ivan'd had a quick shower together, full of tender touches and wonder at the bond that sang through them both, she'd retrieved her clothing and got to baking, while Ivan made a trip to the car to get their gear.

To protect the native vegetation, the pack had rules about where vehicles were permitted, so it was a twenty-minute round trip for him. Or it should've been—he'd apparently decided to run part of it, because he was back in under fifteen, hitting the verandah with the bags just as she popped the cookies in the solar-powered eco-oven set into the wall.

"You sure you're not a cat?" she said with a laugh when he prowled back in, her shopping bag in one hand and his duffel in the other, with her daypack slung easily over one shoulder.

"Cat or Mercant, not much difference that I can see. Sneaky runs in the bloodline." No smile on his face, but she could feel it in the mating bond and it was a little bubble of happiness inside her. Happiness she clung to, refusing to look at the grim cloud that hovered on the horizon.

Last time she'd asked, Ivan had said he'd hit full psychic strength early morning the next day. At which point, he'd walk back into the ChaosNet and be forced to use his ability, further eroding his control on it.

"Ivan?" she said when he emerged from the bedroom after dropping off the bags.

He looked up from his phone. "Sorry, message from Canto with an update on an ongoing security issue we're looking into. It's not urgent." Slipping the phone away, he came to lean his shoulder on the wall at the end of the counter where she was preparing the second sheet of cookies. "What is it?"

"Your grandmother helped you create your shields against what you call the spider, right?"

"Yes, but they no longer work—or only to a limited capacity."

Soleil used a fork to flatten the balls of cookie dough. "It's been two decades, give or take. Why don't you talk to her again? Could be she has some new ideas."

When he stayed silent, she looked up. "I know you don't want to do it because she's never going to accept your cage plan—but that ship has sailed all the way to outer space. Your mate isn't about to accept that, either." She shook the fork at him. "No point being a chicken about your grandmother's fury."

A narrowing of his eyes before he walked over . . . and nipped sharply at her ear, exactly as she might do to a misbehaving cub.

Squealing, she threatened to poke him with the fork. He managed to stay out of reach as he got behind her and wrapped her up in his arms, pinning her own gently to her sides.

"Take that back," he murmured in her ear, the rumble of sound making her toes curl onto the wood of the floor.

"No."

He tickled her.

"Hey!" That wasn't fair! He wasn't supposed to know how to tickle! But he'd somehow learned, and she couldn't take it. Giggling so hard she dropped the fork on the counter, she said, "I surrender!"

"And?"

"And you're no chicken." Turning her head, she nuzzled his jaw, her cat so utterly delighted with him for playing with her that she'd let him get away with anything right now. "Where did you learn the tickling?"

"I caught a glimpse of the memory when you told me about how your mother used to tickle you."

Of course he'd remembered that, because he remembered everything about her. Now, holding her from behind, he rubbed his face against the side of hers. "You're right about one thing—the situation has changed. I'll talk to Grandmother. You can meet her, too."

A fleet of butterflies in her stomach. "I'm ready." No, she wasn't, but she'd fake it until she made it.

Five minutes later, Ivan told her he'd set the meeting for six thirty that evening, on the heels of when Salvador would be heading home with the cubs. Sal had told her in advance that they'd promised to have dinner with Yariela, so they wouldn't be staying to eat.

"Yariela said she'd have invited you," he'd said, a smile in his tone, "but then she heard that it'll be your first night in your new aerie with your mate and told me to make sure the cubs and I didn't hang around too long." The affectionately teasing tone of a packmate.

Oh, how she'd missed these small interactions, all of them part of the larger tapestry of being a member of a pack. "Talking of hearing things," she'd said in turn, "how was your date, hmm?"

Salvador's blush had been apparent in his voice. "I'll tell you all about it when I come over."

That time arrived all too soon, and Soleil yelped at the realization that she still had no panties. Ripping open the relevant package, she picked the thinnest pair, then ran into the bathroom to handwash them. At some point, Ivan, who'd been on a call, came over to see what she was doing. "Why," he said, "are you using a hair dryer to dry those?"

She ran the long flat stick over the lacy panties she was holding in one hand. "Because I don't want to wear wet panties!"

"I thought changelings weren't troubled by nudity."

"I'm not worried about Sal and the cubs, but we're heading to see your grandmother straight after and I am *not* meeting her without panties!"

Arms folded over the casual short-sleeved black shirt he'd changed into, he leaned against the doorjamb. "Grandmother is a woman of many talents, but she doesn't have x-ray vision."

"Doesn't matter." She willed the stupid thing to dry; it was a damn itsy bit of lace she'd bought in an Ivan-induced sensual fugue. "*I'll* know."

"I'll just tell her you had a wardrobe malfunction."

Her head all but swiveled on her neck. *"What!"* Then she felt it, the ripple along the mating bond that was Ivan Mercant teasing her.

She pointed the dryer at him. "I will get you. Later. After I dry these damn panties."

Someone, somewhere had mercy on her and the lace was dry enough to wear comfortably by the time she had to scramble down the tree to meet the cubs. Ivan was already there, having carried down the cookies for her, as well as a closed bottle of chilled milk. He'd then done a second run to grab the glasses and a picnic blanket that he'd already spread out by the time she—and her panties—made it down.

His eyes went straight to the spot between her thighs.

Heat blazed on her cheekbones. *"Behave."*

No smile, but his eyes warmed, and she felt it again, that ripple in the mating bond that told her Ivan Mercant would one day laugh. He had wickedness in him, her mate, just didn't know how to show it on the outside yet.

All they needed was time.

Swallowing hard, she looked to the right. "I can hear them." Small excited rustles as the cubs ran toward her, Salvador's stride more measured and calm.

Then there they were, two tiny ocelots so excited to see her again that they pounced right into her arms. Laughing, she kissed and snuggled their small, warm bodies, meeting Salvador's gaze over their heads. Her packmate had come in human form, a bag slung over his shoulder.

Dark-skinned and of medium height, his build stocky, he had the softest brown eyes in the universe—and they were wet at that instant. "Leilei, it really is you," he whispered, dropping the bag to the side to hug her, the cubs happily squished in between them.

Her cat keened inside her, so happy to see him, scent him, that it was overwhelmed. She wanted to shift but didn't want to drop the cubs to do so, and she was wearing a pretty new dress that Ivan had chosen when she'd asked his opinion while deciding between two options.

It was all wonderfully too much.

When they broke apart at last, Salvador's eyes went immediately to Ivan, who'd been standing quietly by the tree. "I'm sorry. That was rude." He wiped away his tears, his eyes sliding shyly away from Ivan's in the way of a submissive who'd come face-to-face with an unfamiliar dominant. "I should've said hello."

"I would be the same with a lost member of my family," Ivan said, her mate who understood how much such bonds could mean. "I'm Ivan. You must be Salvador."

And though Soleil knew Ivan wasn't a toucher, he held out his hand so Salvador could shake it, a gentle introduction designed to put a tactile-natured changeling at ease. She knew without asking that he would've tempered the strength of his handshake to echo Sal's.

Some people would see that as manipulation, but Soleil knew her mate. He'd done it so that Salvador—a member of her family—would feel comfortable around Ivan. Because that mattered to Soleil . . . and because Ivan Mercant was a protector at heart, a hero who'd never apply the label to himself.

The contact made Salvador smile, his body immediately more at ease.

The cubs jumped down from her arms at the same instant and ran around the tree before trying to climb it. They were too little, of course, but their antics made her and Salvador laugh.

Sal had so many questions for her, and she for him. When she glanced at Ivan, he gave a slight nod, telling her without words that he'd keep an eye on the cubs. Sending him a wave of love through the mating bond, she let herself focus on the kind and brave member of her pack who'd put his life on the line to protect the cubs during the darkest time in SkyElm's history.

She and Sal had been chatting for several minutes when she became aware of the silence from the cubs; she glanced over to see Ivan crouched down, both cubs in front of him. They were staring up at him and he was returning the scrutiny with as much interest. When Razi hesitantly put a paw on his knee and rose up on her hind legs, he scooped her up against his chest with one hand.

Nattie, not to be left out, jumped up on Ivan's knee, then climbed up onto his shoulder with the liquid fluidity of an ocelot cub. Where he settled in, his tail flicking against Ivan's chest. Razi, meanwhile, was licking his jaw and play-biting at his throat. He tugged her back with utmost care, then met her gaze and shook his head before pretending to nip her on the nose.

Razi made a happy sound and so did Nattie—right before the two swarmed him in an effort to "win" the battle. Ivan handled their wriggly, playful bodies with ease while giving them the freedom to play.

"He's a good man." Salvador's words were quiet but potent. "When I heard that you, of all people, had mated a Psy, I couldn't imagine it. But now I see . . ." He leaned against Soleil. "They went to him because he carries your scent, but they're playing with him because of who he is."

Soleil's heart, it could barely withstand the beauty of the moment. She'd remember it always, this instant when her frosty-eyed Psy allowed two ocelot cubs to climb all over him without ever losing control of the situation. "He'll make an amazing father." It was a bone-deep knowledge, a thing primal.

That certainty only grew over the joyous time that followed. The cubs shifted into their human forms when they sat down to eat the cookies, and Salvador got them both into little overalls of olive green that he'd brought in the bag.

"Otherwise," he said, "they'll run off into the woods and come back with cuts and bites." He waved a finger under Razi's button nose, her skin a shock of cream and her silky dark hair cut in a style that reached her shoulders and was fringed over her brown eyes. "*Certain* cubs seem to forget their human skin isn't as tough as their cub pelt."

Giggling, Razi threw her arms around him, while Nattie, his eyes a greenish hazel he'd inherited from his mother, and his hair all black curls against rich brown skin, grinned around the cookie he'd already half eaten. He sat leaning against Ivan's side, one of Ivan's arms braced behind him.

When she met her mate's eyes, she caught a painfully vulnerable expression in that gaze of striking ice—but alongside it was a violent protectiveness.

Ivan Mercant wouldn't only make a wonderful father, he'd be a dominant the cubs in the pack adored. Because he had in him both the gentleness needed to not hurt their small hearts and the strength to maintain discipline, giving cubs the boundaries that made them feel safe.

Soleil couldn't believe he was hers.

Her cat preened, delighted with itself for having grabbed hold of him before it was too late. And for this time under the late-afternoon sunlight, Soleil allowed herself to simply bask in that happiness. The darkness could wait.

Chapter 46

My grandmother is many things. First and foremost, she is a warrior for our family.

—Canto Mercant to Payal Rao

ENA WAS USED to being on top of situations, but this one she'd never seen coming. "He is as Ivan as always," she said to the sleek black cat who sat by her side looking out into the stormy seas beyond.

His message to her had been simple: *Grandmother, I would like to introduce you to my mate. I also need to speak to you about my ability.*

"His mate." She took one final sip of her tea, then set the delicate teacup aside. "And I have heard nothing of this even though Arwen and Genara were both in San Francisco of late." As the cat twitched its tail, she sighed. "Yes, Arwen is a vault on such things, and Genara had other business. So, let me go and see this woman who has managed to make Ivan lower his shields."

Mating was for life, so there wasn't anything Ena could do about it if Ivan's mate was someone not worthy of him. Then again, there was a lot Ena could do about many things. Her moral lines were gray at best when it came to actions to protect her family. And Ivan . . .

she'd always felt she needed to protect him even more than the others. So of course he turned out to be the one who wouldn't accept protection at all.

A stir in the air at her back.

Turning, she saw a woman of about five-two with hourglass curves—curves that had been denigrated under Silence, yet this woman had carried them with cool will and an equally steely refusal to bow down to the surgeon's scalpel. She was dressed in tailored and wide-legged pants of gray into which she'd tucked a cream-colored blouse that buttoned up to the neck and at the cuffs. The woman's dark hair was pulled back into a neat twist, her makeup flawless against the warm brown of her skin.

"Payal. Thank you for taking the time." Payal Rao, anchor, member of the Ruling Coalition, and CEO of a major business empire, was a powerful and busy woman. Normally, Ena would've rescheduled this meeting until one of the other family teleporters was available—but Ivan asked for her so rarely and she'd made a promise to herself that she'd always respond when he did.

"It isn't a problem, Grandmother." Payal's eyes held a brightness that had grown in the time since their first meeting—a brightness Ena saw echoed in her eldest grandson, Canto. He and Payal had bonded to the core.

"Canto has told me to spy for him," Payal said in her clipped way that betrayed nothing. "He has no idea why you need a teleport into DarkRiver territory, and it's annoying him so much that he's currently baking croissants from scratch."

Ena had come to view Canto's fiancée as another grandchild, liked her a great deal; she understood better than most what it was to hold a shield against the outside world for so long that it became all but automatic. Looking at Payal just now, no one would guess that she'd die for Canto—and kill for him.

"We are in the same boat," she told Payal. "It appears Ivan has mated."

Payal blinked once. "In DarkRiver territory?"

"Exactly so." Ena slipped on a light evening coat of a soft camel hue over her tunic of rich brown and simple flowing pants of the same, the heirloom ruby pendant she always wore a familiar weight against her upper abdomen. "Lucas Hunter's pack is known to have Psy and human members, so it may not be a changeling."

She slipped her hands into the pockets of her coat. "If it is . . . Well, I didn't expect Valentin, either"—a truly vast understatement—"and next month I am to stay in the bear den for a weekend." Ena often wondered if her grandchildren had conspired to unsettle her in her later years.

"Talking of unexpected things," she said, "how are the wedding plans progressing? Canto mentioned musicians."

Payal's smile was a stunning dawn. "Traditional tabla players," she said, motioning with her hands to indicate flat drums. "They'll announce Canto's entrance into the wedding venue."

Yes, Ena's grandchildren were making her later years interesting to say the least.

"Are you and Magdalene still available for wedding lehenga shopping?" Payal asked, her tone even.

But Ena sensed the need within this woman who'd grown up in a pit of vipers. Unlike with Ena's clan, family had never been a safe place for Payal. She hadn't yet internalized what it meant to be embraced as an honorary Mercant—including the loyalty that came by default.

"I wouldn't miss it," Ena said. "Has Magdalene shared her portfolio of color scheme combinations for your wedding décor?"

Payal's eyes widened. "No."

"Ah, I may have jumped the gun. Do act surprised when she presents her gift. And know that it is given without any expectation that you will utilize one of her schemes. She just wishes to be involved."

Though Canto had long forgiven his mother for the inadvertent part she'd played in his ugly childhood, Ena knew that Magdalene continued to carry a knot of guilt deep within. It was Ena's hope that seeing Canto so happy with Payal would soften that terrible knot in her daughter.

"Do you believe she'd wish to take over the general planning?" Payal asked with a gentleness not many people ever saw in the tough CEO. "Canto and I would remain involved, but it'd take the heavy administration off our shoulders."

"I think she would find it an honor to be asked," Ena said to this woman with a capacity for empathy so strong that it had survived the evil toxicity of her childhood.

"I will reach out to her." Payal glanced at her timepiece. "It's time."

When Ena indicated she was ready for the teleport, Payal put a hand on her shoulder. A moment of spatial disorientation before Ena found herself standing under the spreading branches of a huge tree, the sky streaked with the golds and oranges of early evening in this part of the world, and the ground littered with leaf debris.

More trees surrounded them on every side, though there was plenty of space between their aged trunks, the entire area warm with the diffuse light that rained down through the canopy.

Ivan had told her the provided teleport lock would bring her to a spot on the very edge of DarkRiver's forested territory—it was a complicated emblem that hung from the branch of the nearest tree that created the teleport point. Take that away and this was just another patch of forest indistinguishable from thousands of others.

Ena took no insult in not being invited into the inner sanctum. This was a new mating, Ivan's welcome in the pack currently an unknown to Ena. The bears had "stolen" Silver with joyful glee, then opened their entire pack to the Mercants, calling them family.

Leopards were not bears, however, Lucas Hunter a very different alpha from Valentin Nikolaev. The leopard alpha reminded her an unusual amount of members of her own family. It was the glint in the eye, the sense of things prowling beneath the surface.

A stir in the trees, Ivan striding out hand in hand with a tall woman with dark hair that was pulled off her face by two simple combs, her lovely oval face marked by a scar on one side. She carried the scar with comfort, the warmth of her eyes and the depth of her smile the most striking things about her.

Ena was struck by a perplexing moment of familiarity.

"Grandmother, thank you for coming," Ivan said. "Payal, it's good to see you again."

"I look forward to many such meetings," Payal said, then nodded a greeting to the woman at Ivan's side. "With both of you. I'll leave you now so you can converse privately with Grandmother." She teleported out, having already telepathed Ena that she'd return as soon as Ena wished to go back home.

Ivan met Ena's gaze with the impenetrable paleness of his own before turning to his mate. "Soleil, this is my grandmother."

"I've been waiting for this moment since Ivan first told me about you," Soleil said. "I'm so happy to meet you, Grandmother." Open admiration and warmth in her expression, not a single shield or self-protective instinct in sight.

Ena sighed internally. "I, too, am pleased to meet you, Soleil," she said to the healer whom Ivan had mated.

You do realize, she telepathed her grandson, *she and Arwen will become firm friends and hound us all to take better care of ourselves?*

A quiet joy in Ivan's eyes, a subtle gentling of the soul that she hoped would bring him the peace she'd never been able to foster in him.

"You're a healer?" she said to Soleil, to confirm her guess.

Soleil's laughter was sunshine, wrapping around Ena the same way Arwen wrapped her up in his arms from behind when he thought he could get away with it. Her empath grandson had altered Ena, altered all of them, and she had the thought that Soleil would do the same. Healers had a way of loving until it became a fact of life, a simple acceptance that settled on the skin and the soul.

"Is it that obvious?" Soleil said with a look up at Ivan that held the same primal possessiveness Ena had seen when Valentin looked at Silver.

Healer she might be, but she was also a predatory changeling with her mate.

When she turned back to Ena, her eyes were no longer human. "Ivan is beyond lucky to have you in his life, Grandmother. Thank you for loving him as a boy so he had the heart to love me as a man."

Only a healer would say such a thing to Ena Mercant, a ruthless matriarch whose Silence was meant to be flawless. Truly. How did her grandchildren keep doing this to her?

"Come," she said, "let us walk and get to know one another."

Ivan stayed quiet as the two of them spoke, and the more Ena learned of Soleil, the more she began to realize that this woman had a spine of steel. Of course she did; no weak-willed creature would've broken through Ivan's refusal to admit that he was worth more than a life in the shadows.

And it was those shadows about which Ivan told her when they began to talk of his ability. He'd already mentioned to her that his shields were fragmenting, but she hadn't realized the situation was this bad. "Excuse me?" she said, her tone frigid, when he told her his plans for the psychic cage.

"Don't worry, Grandmother," Soleil muttered, her arms folded and feline eyes narrowed. "I already told him that's not an option."

If Ena had not already approved of Soleil, she'd have passed the mark at that instant. The thin woman across from her was not playing when it came to Ivan's safety. "Show me the shields," Ena said.

They spent the next twenty minutes going over every technical detail. The problem was that Ivan appeared to have thought of all possible options, tested them, and confirmed that they wouldn't work.

Ena's heart thudded in her mouth, her mind filled with the memory of his small and cold hand in hers as she walked him out of the sterile room where he'd been taken after his mother's death. That too-quiet, damaged boy had become a man of courage and loyalty who'd found happiness at long last.

Ena refused to let him down now.

But even Ena Mercant, she realized in the darkest part of night, many hours after she'd left Ivan and Soleil in the forest, couldn't magic an answer where none existed. No one in the world had a brain like Ivan's, and the problem wasn't in the structure of his shields or their complexity. It was in the fact that his ability was morphing at a rate far beyond the capacity of *any* shield to contain.

It was as if the power he'd named the spider had been *designed* to penetrate shields—Ivan's and everyone else's. But such a neural design made no sense in the Psy world. It might have if Ivan could control it from his end, the power a dark one but a power nonetheless. But Ivan had never been able to control it . . . so when it broke free, it would enmesh him as much as any one of his targets.

The sea crashed below her home, smashing at the rocks, while Ena ran headlong into the realization that this time, she might not be able to solve the problem, might not be able to save a member of her family.

Chapter 47

There's a minute possibility that the DNA trace is failing because the DNA involved is classified. I would put the chances of this at under 0.1%—because we'd be talking about such highly classified DNA files that it's getting into the Council superstructure.

Those individuals keep a steely grip on their familial connections. No one vanishes unless the family wants them to vanish—and in those cases, the vanishing is final. I'm not giving up, but even we don't have the connections to get to a small number of those classified files, so let us hope that 0.1% chance is so unlikely as to be negligible.

—Rufus Mercant (2071)

IVAN WOKE WITH the birds, while the world outside was yet dark. Soleil was curled into him, her hand on his heart and her body warm with life. But inside him spread a growing chill.

A secret part of him had hoped his grandmother would have an answer he hadn't considered, but he'd seen the truth in her gaze before she left yesterday. He knew she'd have stayed up through the night, would've tapped all her contacts in the hunt for a solution, but even his grandmother couldn't fix the unfixable.

A stirring beside him, Soleil yawning and rubbing her face against his chest. "It's early." It was a very feline complaint, the cat that lived inside his mind grumpy with it.

He massaged the back of her neck, her hair silky and thick under his fingers. "It's time, my Lei." His psychic reservoir had reached full charge. "I need to return to the ChaosNet."

Soleil went motionless for a long moment before she rose up onto her elbow to look down at him. "Eat first," she murmured, her eyes dark with the knowledge of what he risked today. "Go in as strong as possible."

He nodded, tugged her down for a kiss. They'd loved again with their bodies in the night, and he hoped that there would come another dawn where he could lie with her in their home and kiss and caress and pet her. But today, they both rose after that kiss, to ready him for the task to come.

They ate breakfast on the verandah, by the light that poured out from their living room. Because while the birds were awake, the sun was far from rising. Afterward, Soleil laid her head on his shoulder, her hand locked in his, and said, "Remember, I'll be here to pull you out at any stage. Just call me through the mating bond. I'll hear now that our bond is complete, I'm certain of it."

Ivan had thought to go inside their aerie, lie on their bed, but now made a different choice. "I'll go in from here, surrounded by the trees and the birds." He turned to look at her. "You like it here."

She shifted to meet his gaze, her own fierce and wild. "I love you, Ivan Mercant. You'll kick those Scarabs' butts." A hard kiss. "I'll get you a cushion for your back, and if I feel anything going wrong, I'm going to haul you out."

"I know." He felt her love for him, her fear for him, in every cell of his being. She didn't seem the least afraid for herself, even though whatever happened, it would impact them both. "Te amo, ma chérie, today and tomorrow and always."

She swallowed hard at his use of the lovingly mixed-up language of her childhood. "Come back, Ivan. But if you can't, I'll walk with you wherever you go."

He carried her words with him into the ChaosNet. She was a tug inside him that was invisible, but that he knew led the way home. So it was that he stepped into the chaotic lightning-shot island with one goal in mind: to find some way to collapse it so that the minds within would reintegrate into the PsyNet.

Already, he could see the difference from the last time he'd visited: a number of minds had gone dull, and he knew that those were the people who were declining, not just comatose but in a critical state where their brains flickered between life and death.

It was, he found, difficult to ignore pain in front of him—he was pragmatic, had long ago learned to see death as an inevitability—but these people hadn't chosen to play on this field, had been hauled onto it without permission. They'd been made pawns in someone else's game, their choices ripped from them as Soleil's had been ripped from her.

Regardless of his response, however, he couldn't divert his attention to help them; such an action would deplete his psychic reserves, put him back right where he'd been after his first visit. He'd do far more good if he could complete his assigned mission and bring down the island.

He'd told Krychek before he went in, so the other man could put all the various hospitals on alert, as their patients might go into cardiac arrest or show other signs of catastrophic failure at the moment of disconnection. The medics needed to be warned *not to interfere* with lifegiving measures unless the patient didn't stabilize within five seconds.

A healthy Psy mind should only need half that long to reconnect to the massive sprawl of the PsyNet. Any interference in between could cause neural disruption that critically disturbed the process.

Krychek had confirmed that the hospitals were already on standby for such instructions, and that he'd blasted out a telepathic alert that

it was happening today. Now all Ivan had to do was deliberately splinter the ChaosNet.

He'd have attempted to collapse the foundation by somehow taking out the anchors without killing them, but there was no way to
identify an anchor on the PsyNet. Canto had confirmed that for him
last night when he'd called and spoken to his cousin.

Ivan always had plans for an operation, but today, there could be
no plan. This place was too chaotic, too much an unknown. He'd have
to act in the heat of the moment the instant he found a fatal vulnerability in the system.

That in mind, he began to move quickly through the psychic space,
gathering as much data as possible. He couldn't avoid all the lightning
strikes—not when the psychic space was full of them—but he didn't
take any major hits. Around him, the landscape was warped and sluggish, the data in the network so fragmented that it was of no use.

Which was why it took him a long time to pick up the echo that
ran through every inch of the ChaosNet: *Scarab. Queen. Scarab. Queen.
Scarab. Queen.*

Over and over and over in an endless loop. Obsessive and compulsive and not rational. Even if they managed to pass themselves off as
rational on the physical plane, their minds were lost in a fog of compulsion.

Compulsion toward their Queen.

Despite his earlier suspicions, Ivan had no proof that this was the
Architect. To date, the Architect's actions had all been very rational—
they had played the long game. And they'd played it well enough that
even his family hadn't managed to unmask them.

A mind up ahead that had been shooting out lightning bolts suddenly burst outward in a supernova of light and energy that buffeted
Ivan's mind with brutal force. He was only able to survive because his
shields were titanium. But when the dust cleared, nothing remained
of the Scarab who had once existed.

That echo again: *Scarab. Queen. Scarab. Queen. Scarab. Queen.*

That was who'd done this, broken the PsyNet by using the Scarabs. Because the world wasn't an even playing field. Some people had more power, more charisma. If Grandmother, for example, had wished to turn Ivan evil, she could have: he'd been a badly damaged child when he came into the family, Ena his savior. She could've molded him into nothing but her obedient shadow with very little effort.

These Scarabs, too, would've been damaged when the Queen captured them in her web. But it couldn't only be charisma and timing. Scarabs were too powerful when their brains broke the chain that Silence had imposed on them—they would've long ago subjugated anyone less powerful.

Ivan hissed out a breath on the physical plane: a Scarab powerful enough to control other Scarabs would be a nightmare. This individual might be even more powerful than Kaleb Krychek—and that could lead to hell on Earth.

He took a significant blow from a black lightning bolt right then, shuddered, but shrugged it off. His internal power meter, however, dipped once again. The longer he stayed here, the more hits he'd take, and the less power he'd have if he did work out how to collapse the island.

The only mercy was that the spider inside him sat silent, unmoving. He'd have hoped the mating bond had made it go quiescent, but he knew better. His power could coil and strike at any moment. As Soleil's cat could pounce; that cat, too, sat unmoving, watchful.

Making a call on gut instinct, he began to arrow in toward the center. This island was a new construct, with nothing akin to the PsyNet's psychic weight to it. Whatever stability it had, it had to come from the core, else it'd be folding in on itself, the weight on one end more than the other.

The PsyNet, in contrast, was so big that it had no true center. It was different depending on each individual's location. The island was minuscule in comparison. It made sense that it would have a central point from where everything else flowed.

He expected to find a mind brighter than the others, the Queen to whom they paid homage, but when he reached the place that he was certain had to be the center, his internal compass telling him that he was now equidistant from most of the coast on any side, he saw nothing.

There was literally *nothing* there.

Not a single mind, only endless darkness. Since Ivan took nothing at face value, he went closer, still closer. That was when he realized that no lightning bolts passed through this area, either, the region as eerily still as the eye of a hurricane.

A shield?

But he had zero issues moving through the dead zone . . . and that was when he felt it—a subtle draw that tried to suck him downward. In truth, there was no up or down in the psychic space, but that was how his brain made sense of it: that something was pulling at him, trying to siphon his energy.

It wasn't a sinkhole. No, it was something much more subtle. He knew all at once that the dead psychic zone around it was formed of all the minds it had already sucked dry of energy.

A cold realization in the center of his brain, a creeping sense of the familiar. Had he been a cat like his mate, he'd have put it in scent terms: it was as if he'd scented something he knew, a psychic presence that was no stranger, was rather so akin to him that it . . . felt like family.

His stomach roiled.

Sensing the spider inside him beginning to stir, he pulsed the psychic space with his own brand of energy. It was a silvery wave brushed with flame, glittering and powerful to his gaze but invisible to everyone else.

The cat inside his mind pawed at the threads of shimmering silver.

A reminder from his mate that this power wasn't invisible to *everyone*.

It lit up the entire area before it was sucked down by the darkness—but he'd taken a snapshot right before the moment when everything went black. And what he saw was a sprawling black spiderweb, at the center of which sat a bloated monster.

A hard tug on the bond inside him. A literal bite that he felt through the psychic space—just as a cold black spidery hand scraped over his mind. He snapped his eyes open to find Soleil looking down at him with eyes gone ocelot.

"Did you bite me?"

"You wouldn't wake up," she said, her fingers on the side of his neck. "And your pulse was starting to weaken. It was just a nip—didn't break the skin."

He raised his fingers to the other side of his neck, still able to feel the echo of that bite, that wildness. "I have to go back."

"You're weak," Soleil argued. "Your hands are trembling. Look!" She lifted one of his hands.

"Get me all the nutrient sachets you have," Ivan said, gripping at her wrists. "There's another spider in there, Lei, and it's killing those people. I don't think they have much longer. I have to go back."

Fear a hot beat in her eyes, she nonetheless rose and raced inside to gather what he needed. Ivan, meanwhile, put together a plan of attack. He'd have only one shot at this. That fucking spider was bloated with a vast amount of power, which meant its black web must have captured a massive number of minds on that island.

"She calls herself the Scarab Queen," he told Soleil when she returned with a glass, a pitcher of water, and the pockets of her dress filled with nutrient sachets their packmates had stocked in the pantry.

Rebooting energy by overdosing on nutrients wasn't ever a good idea. The resulting crash could stop his heart, but all those people would die if Ivan waited another day. Not only that, but the bloated spider would then have even *more* power—power enough to capture another piece of the PsyNet and suck it dry.

And with each dead piece of the Net it left in its wake, it'd become more capable of "eating" bigger and bigger pieces. Left alone, it was conceivable that it could annihilate the entire PsyNet, piece by desiccated piece.

He dumped five sachets into one glass, drank it down, then asked Soleil to mix another. "She's the monster I'll become if I don't stop myself." He had a vision of himself as a bloated spider just like her, hunched over the defenseless minds of all those he'd captured.

All those who he was murdering.

Soleil's hand on his cheek. "I'm with you," she whispered. "No matter what. Always and forever and back again."

He gave himself a single moment of peace and turned his lips into her palm.

Chapter 48

Ager's vitals are beginning to deteriorate even faster than predicted. I'm sorry to report that they are on the brink of a total neural shutdown. You must prepare for the worst.

—Dr. Lee Luang to Payal Rao, bearer of Ager Lii's medical
Power of Attorney

THE SCARAB QUEEN stirred out of her torpor and reached out a slow psychic hand to capture the beautifully strong power she'd sensed the second prior. Most of the power coming to her was dull, even her Scarabs failing her. She'd chosen the wrong ones for this experiment, chosen the weak ones.

It was no huge problem. She'd simply make better choices next time around. But there was someone in this network whose power was a breathtaking punch. Not only that, it resonated along the same frequency as hers—she knew that if she took it, she'd amplify her own power by an order of magnitude.

Her lethargic pulse accelerated the instant she made contact . . . but then the power was gone, blinking out of existence without a trace. Had it been a Scarab that had imploded? She saw no debris, no psychic dust. But that had to be it, because she'd made certain no one could leave this island of their own will.

She sighed. What a great pity to lose all that pure power. Power that felt so similar to hers that it would've melded with hers without issue.

A moment of clarity in the power haze.

Could it be that one of her children was becoming like her? A burgeoning threat to her reign?

Yet when she searched her domain using the receptors in her web, she found no one akin to herself. She remained one of a kind, the blip she'd felt nothing but an anomaly.

Satisfied that all was well, she began to settle back down. Another part of her blared a warning that she'd become too heavy with power, could no longer strike with the rapidity of a cobra, but she switched off the warning. She had no need to be fast, not here. This place was her training ground—and her psychic depository.

Here, she would feed. Feed until nothing was left.

And when she emerged, she'd be a power unlike any the world had ever seen.

Chapter 49

Spider, spider, my beautiful spider.
With your web so bright, and your silk so strong.
Spider, spider, I see you.

—Norah Mercant (b. unknown, d. 2059)

IVAN MADE SURE to stay on the verge of the Scarab Queen's field of death. From what he'd experienced the last time around, he had to get close to stir her out of her stupor—and he needed her to remain inert, half-asleep.

She was too powerful for him to take her on one-to-one. With the amount of energy she'd stolen from her victims and hoarded, she'd break his mind with a single action, then swallow him whole.

One strike.

That was all he'd have. A single attempt to cut the threads of her control. He knew from his own experience that a sudden severing of a thread of his web equaled a wound. Grandmother had been aghast when she'd accidentally injured him the time he'd webbed himself to other children—he'd come to her, dropped all his shields so she could see the nightmare web.

It had still been invisible to her. Today's experience with the Scarab

Queen told him that only another spider could naturally see a fellow spider's web. With his grandmother, it had taken a visceral link, core-mind-to-core-mind. He'd then asked her to cut the threads. After checking to see what the repercussions might be and finding no obvious issues, she'd carefully severed a single one.

It had made Ivan seize, his body racked with pain.

When he was conscious and stable again, he'd asked her to do the rest. She'd refused. "I will *not* hurt you. We'll find another way."

That other way had been for Ivan to learn to do it himself. If *he* severed the thread, it didn't cause him any harm. That made sense. The spider wouldn't want to be attached to anyone it considered dead weight, its primary and only goal to feed. The dead were no use to it.

His theory was that if he severed a large number of the Scarab Queen's threads, it would send her into convulsions on the physical plane. The best-case scenario would be that she'd drop out of this network and it would collapse by default—since she seemed to be the center, the core holding it together.

Worst-case would be if she was wounded and in pain but still able to cling to the ChaosNet. In which case, Ivan would have to find a way to kill her. The simplest answer was also the deadliest—he'd attach her to *his* web, suck her dry. The amount of power she was holding, however, would overload his mind and kill him.

Kill Soleil.

Rage burned through him in a cold fire, but the cat inside him stood unbowed, his mate's courage endless. They would do this, because to do nothing would be to sentence all the people in this web to death. And the spider wouldn't be satisfied with that. It would feed and feed and feed until it had absorbed the entire PsyNet.

Inside his mind, Ivan's own spider stretched, avaricious and hungry. It wanted all those minds, wanted all that power. And for the first time in his adult life, Ivan was going to set it free and hope he could contain it once it was over.

A jagged inhale, a quiet exhale.

It was time.

He'd thought of how best to achieve his aims, had settled on spreading his web over and around the Scarab Queen. He'd always visualized his web as hard and cutting, so it took him very little effort to envisage each thread as razor-sharp.

Holding his breath in the physical world, aware of Soleil's hand locked tight with his, he spread his web over the dead zone.

Softly, softly, Ivan.

He pushed the edges of the web outward to the point that he began to sense minds, then halted, because his aim wasn't to damage any of those minds, not even those that belonged to Scarabs. They might be out of control, but cut off from their Queen, they might not be evil.

Then, his mate beside him, inside him, he dropped his razored web directly over the Scarab Queen's web.

Her psychic scream was so piercing that it made his ears bleed.

Gritting his teeth through the agony, he did a rapid check to ensure he'd cut as many lines as possible . . . and saw that he'd severed every single one. The Queen was marooned in the dead zone, bleeding out from countless wounds, all her threads hanging limply around her.

They began to curl up and die even as he watched under the light of his silvery web . . . and she was gone. Disengaging completely from the web to save herself. Ivan could only hope that she was dead, but he couldn't follow her—in fleeing the murderous tangle of her web and his, she'd detached herself from the island she'd created, had probably already linked up with another part of the PsyNet.

The center gone, the island began to implode.

That should've been the end of this, Ivan's plan an unparalleled success—he'd even managed to keep his ability under control—but horror crawled through him as he saw minds sliding into the maw of the implosion. They should've all been dropping out like flies, their minds' self-protective mechanisms in effect now that the spider was no longer keeping them captive.

This destroyed psychic island existed in the *center* of a much larger and comparatively stable psychic network. It shouldn't even have required conscious thought for them to drop out of danger and hook back into the PsyNet.

Yet none of them were doing it.

"Too weak," he said on the physical plane. "They're too weak to cut themselves free." He couldn't do it for them either, not when he wasn't linked to any but a rare few. Even those ones, he saw, he couldn't release—they wouldn't survive. Their minds were almost at flatline, with no capacity to re-engage with a psychic network if he dropped them from this one.

They'd just fall.

"Hold them, Ivan." A soft murmur against his ear, a sense in his mind of arms opening wide to hold the broken.

Because his mate was a healer.

He wasn't. He was a spider. "I'll kill them." It came out twisted with pain.

"You haven't yet. And they'll die without you."

Knowing he was consigning Soleil to the abyss with him, he released the last leash he had on the spider. Threads of his web shot out in all directions, a shimmering thing that wasn't hard and cutting now but soft and delicate. The better to grab hold of the minds in freefall. Mind after mind after mind after mind . . . until the ChaosNet shimmered with a silver web kissed by flame, and Ivan was the spider at the center.

Agony wrenched at him for what he'd become after all, but he wasn't done yet. The Scarab minds still in the system continued to cause chaos. So he threw more and more of his web around them, until their chaotic energy was contained in spidersilk . . . and the slipstreams of this network finally went quiet, peaceful.

Not knowing how long he'd have control over the spider, he released his psychic energy through the lines of the web, in the hope that it would help strengthen the trapped minds. The web burned silver fire. And Ivan's power ran out, his Psy senses going blank as his body and Soleil's both slumped toward one another.

Chapter 50

Red! Red! Red!

—Priority medical alarm: patient—Ager Lii

THE SCARAB QUEEN fell to the Earth with a scream still emerging from her physical mouth. Her mind, a thing of vast power, reconnected to the PsyNet without effort, but her body was out of her control.

Falling out of her office chair, she convulsed violently on the floor, her arms and legs flailing against the side of the heavy desk and chair. One wrist broke from the force of the impact. Blood dripped from her mouth, her ears, her nose.

Any other being would've died then, the electrical signals in their brain haywire. But the Scarab Queen planned for contingencies. Through all this, she'd always kept a small part of her mind separate and protected, a part that was her fail-safe. Now that fail-safe took control and took stock.

The damage to her body and mind was severe, the sudden severing of her web having caused a massive shock to her system. No one else should've been able to even *see* her web, much less impact it. But they had. And she had to deal with the consequences.

Her body was shutting down, organ by organ, but her brain, while bruised, could be saved if she rerouted all her energy into protecting it while keeping alive only what was necessary for the survival of her brain.

"Sir!" A door banging open, footsteps racing to her.

The man who knelt next to her was young, strong, handsome. Gender didn't matter, not to her. She was beyond that. And he was one of hers, a Scarab who'd given himself fully to her. She could take him, lay her consciousness over his.

No, said the most stable part of her. *We need* this *brain structure to do what we do. His brain is not designed to create a web, and we can't manifest those pathways into existence, can't make him more powerful. We will be limited by his limits.*

She understood.

In so doing, she sacrificed first her upper limbs, then her lower extremities, then her stomach and digestive organs, and more, until all that was left was her brain, her heart to pump the blood around her system, and her lungs and autonomic system. She could breathe, her heart beat, and her brain was alive, but she'd never walk again.

The muscles and cells in the shut-down parts of her body were already atrophying and dying under the strength of the energy draw. There would be no coming back from that. But not even such drastic measures would've worked had she not hoarded so much power.

"Full . . . medical . . . emergency," she gasped to this child of hers.

"I've alerted the team," he said. "They'll be here in thirty seconds. Just hold on, sir." He turned her over onto her side so she wouldn't choke on her own blood. A smart decision; she would utilize him often in the times to come.

"Twenty seconds! Sir!" His voice was fuzzy, difficult to hear. "Sir!"

No more extraneous energy left. Heart or lungs? Partial shutdown of both, so that enough remained for oxygen to get to her brain. If her brain was starved of oxygen, it would cause catastrophic damage.

"Just ten more seconds, sir! They're coming!"

Her heart stopped, her lungs following.

Her brain began final shutdown procedures.

Chapter 51

Mercy, you're the closest. *Go.*

—Lucas to Mercy

SHE WAS MADE of stars again, his Lei. His mate. And she stood in the center of his web, this web that had collected so many minds. He didn't want her to see him, the bloated spider at the core, but she took his hand, and she led him to the very nucleus of the nightmare.

"Look, Ivan," she said, and pointed.

He didn't want to see, didn't want to look. But she leaned up to press her lips to his cheek and whispered, "Please, for me."

There was nothing he wouldn't do for her. So he looked.

No spider hunched below, but the space wasn't empty. At the center of the network was . . . "It's a heart." A huge silver heart that burned with flame-kissed silver fire and pumped in time with Ivan's heartbeat.

He opened his eyes to find Soleil's open, too, her cat looking at him through irises tawny gold and wild. Content in a way he'd never before been, he just looked back at her, the two of them face-to-face on their bed.

The security specialist part of his brain activated. "How are we in bed? We were outside."

Even as Soleil's gaze flared, he twisted to get out of bed . . . and groaned, his entire body feeling as if he'd been stomped on by a horse. An angry one. That was when he remembered all the nutrients he'd taken to artificially boost his psychic strength.

He should feel worse. It was a miracle he was awake and functional.

No, not a miracle, he realized looking back at Soleil. He wasn't in worse shape because his mate had taken some of the backlash. She sat up slowly, sleep lines on one cheek and a wince in her expression. "Ouch," she said, "everything aches. And I need to go be unladylike right *now*."

She was in the sanitary facility part of the aerie before his brain computed what she'd meant. That alerted him to the realization he, too, needed to use those facilities. But it took him so long to get his creaky body upright that Soleil was out by then. Deciding that if they were under threat, those threats would've had plenty of time to stroll in while he was moving about as fast as a hundred-year-old tortoise, he went in to do what needed to be done.

Afterward, he washed his hands, then threw cold water on his face. He was moving a little better and feeling more awake by the time he wiped off the wet and walked back out. Soleil was standing in front of the mirror that hung on one wall of their bedroom, fixing her hair with slow hands. As he watched her, he did a telepathic scan.

That he hadn't done that straight off the bat told him exactly how bad a hit the two of them had taken. The first mind he touched was changeling and opaque to him . . . except he identified it at once as belonging to Lucas Hunter. Because Soleil knew her alpha, the knowledge shared with him through their bond.

The next mind was Psy and "felt" like Arwen's, but it wasn't Arwen. After that, he found Grandmother, the resonance of her permanently embedded in his brain. That mind was followed by . . . Arwen's. Yes, that was definitely his cousin. And neither his cousin nor his grandmother was far away. In point of fact, he thought they were right below the aerie.

Inside DarkRiver territory.

That was when he hit a mind so opaque that he could have no hope of guessing its identity—so he simply walked outside and looked over the verandah railing. "Lei," he murmured, knowing her sharp hearing would pick it up, "Kaleb Krychek is down there with Lucas, a woman I recognize as Lucas's mate, Sascha Duncan, my grandmother, and Arwen. I think that's everyone."

Soft footsteps before she peered over the railing, too. "Guess what?" she said. "I looked at my phone. It's tomorrow. I mean, it's tomorrow from when we collapsed."

Ivan double-checked her statement against the PsyNet. "We've been out for thirty-two hours."

They stared at one another before Soleil yawned. "No wonder I'm starving." Reaching into a pocket as she leaned against him, she pulled out an energy bar. "Here, I grabbed a few of these from the kitchen."

One arm hooked loosely around her waist, he all but inhaled one, then another as she finished one and said, "I scented Lucas, Mercy, and Tammy in the aerie, as well as two unknowns. At least one didn't smell of leopard but had a scent you and your grandmother both carry. I'm guessing maybe your cousin?"

Ivan nodded. "I can't see Grandmother climbing up here."

"I wouldn't count on that, vida mía." A kiss to his cheek, the way she had of just touching him in affection already something he craved. "Your abuela is a force where the people she loves are concerned."

Ivan couldn't argue with that. "Shall we go down?"

Soleil nodded. "But first—" Grabbing his face in her hands, she kissed him until his world spun. "We're alive."

The wave of black dread he'd been holding back crashed down on him. "I don't want to look in the ChaosNet. I have to have murdered countless people by now."

Sliding a hand down his arm, Soleil linked her fingers with his. "It's not a spider, remember? It's a heart, the center that holds. Just like an alpha. You haven't hurt anyone."

The confidence in her voice was a kiss.

"I'm a healer," she whispered. "I'd know if you were killing anyone. Look, Ivan."

Gut clenched, he opened his eyes in the ChaosNet. Except . . . there was no chaos anymore. All the minds he'd wrapped in spidersilk remained wrapped up. Alive, functional, but unable to spread chaotic energy. As for the other minds . . .

He sucked in a breath, looked into Soleil's eyes. "Everyone's alive. Stronger. Not at full strength, but stronger." No longer in danger of flickering out. "I'm the same. Not anywhere near full strength, but neither wiped nor bloated with power."

Pressing her forehead to his, Soleil repeated the words she'd spoken to him before. "You're the center that holds. The energy feeds into you, then feeds back out into the network as needed. It's a perfect closed system, exactly like a pack. Once you all heal, it will be an amazingly healthy system."

"I can't . . ." He exhaled, their foreheads yet touching and breaths mingling. "I'll need time to figure all this out." To accept that he hadn't become a devouring monster; it was too big a thing for him to comprehend. "Let's go talk to everyone."

This time, they went down together, Ivan climbing down first, with Soleil climbing down above him. "Don't look up my dress," she ordered him with a grin before they began the descent.

"I don't make promises I can't keep," he said, but when it came down to it, he was more worried about her safety. She displayed nowhere near her usual wild grace, her body yet shaky.

"You're in the network," he told her quietly as they climbed down. "Not visibly, but I know you're there."

"Of course. We're mated." A dazzling smile he felt through the mating bond as his feet touched the forest floor.

He grabbed her waist as she came down, made sure she was steady on her feet before he turned—to almost be bowled over by Arwen slamming into him. He locked his arms around his cousin, aware that Lucas had enfolded a smiling Soleil in his own arms.

"Hey," he said, running a hand down his cousin's back, this man who had always cared even when caring for Ivan was a rewardless exercise, "I'm good. Alive and undamaged."

Arwen was trembling when he drew back, his usually perfect hair a mess and his eyes red as if he'd been crying. "You vanished from the PsyNet, from our familial network. I thought you were dead."

Wrapping his arm around his cousin's neck, Ivan drew him close once again, held him tight. "I'm sorry about that. Things didn't go as I'd planned." This time when he let go, Arwen moved aside so Ena could walk up to Ivan.

"He wouldn't believe me when I told him you were alive. He insisted on putting his eyes on you." The slightest touch of her fingers to his jaw. "I must admit I had my doubts as well."

That was as close as Ena would ever come to admitting fear, but Ivan needed no grand actions or declarations from his grandmother. He knew exactly what he meant to her. "I'm not sure quite what happened," he said, holding out a hand instinctively as Soleil came to him.

Her fingers touched his, her cat in his mind.

"I made contact with Lucas the moment you vanished from the PsyNet," his grandmother told him. "He'd already felt a violent impact through his blood bond with you, Soleil, and had diverted one of his sentinels to your aerie. She was the closest person to you at the time."

Arwen pushed a trembling hand through his hair. "The sentinel confirmed you were both alive and breathing but otherwise unresponsive, got you inside with help from another packmate who was close by, and then Lucas said we should come." A wobbly grin. "I would've come anyway, even if I had to fight off leopards."

"Empaths." Lucas Hunter scowled. "You're a menace to yourselves. My leopards would've eaten you alive."

The cardinal-eyed woman next to him—quite famously the first Silent empath to wake to her powers—laughed. "Don't listen to a word he says, Arwen. He'd snap the neck of anyone who dared hurt an E."

Another voice broke into the conversation, a voice as black as the heart of midnight, a thing of power and cold. "A number of the people uplinked to the island have woken from their comas."

Ivan looked toward Kaleb Krychek, who'd joined the rough circle that had formed. Arwen still stood right next to him, his shoulder touching Ivan's, a touch with which Ivan was more than comfortable. He'd never wanted to hurt Arwen, and the sudden loss of Ivan from their network would've devastated him.

Ena stood beside Arwen, Krychek next to her, while Lucas Hunter stood beside Krychek, his mate between him and Soleil. Ivan had no idea how or why Krychek had access to DarkRiver territory, but he was comfortable here, that much was obvious in the way he stood at ease under the canopy even though he was in a formal black suit.

"Are any of them talking?" Ivan asked.

"Yes. According to them, they're in a stable psychic network with a unique biofeedback loop that seems to be flowing from a center they can't see." He raised an eyebrow. "I'm assuming that's you."

Ivan nodded. "The anchors? Ager Lii?" The foundation without which nothing could exist.

"Alive and aware—though it appears at least two of the other four As on the island have Scarab Syndrome."

It was the worst kind of news, Designation A already critical in terms of numbers.

"Ager Lii isn't suffering from the syndrome," Kaleb clarified. "They've confirmed that the new network is stable, and that its link to the main part of the Substrate appears to be opening up. So while the island remains separated from the rest of the PsyNet on the upper level, it stands atop the same foundations. It won't starve of anchor energy."

Ivan exhaled slowly at the realization that the island's psychic network was more than functioning. It was functioning *well*. "I can't explain the mechanics of it to you."

"It's simple," Soleil said from beside him. "You have the capacity to create and maintain pack bonds, just like Lucas. You can feel every packmate in the back of your mind, can't you, Luc?"

Lucas inclined his head. "Talking of which—there are a lot more heartbeats in my consciousness as of thirty-two hours ago. Nothing near as strong an awareness as I have of the members of the pack, but I know they're there. An entire network of people at the far periphery of my view."

Soleil's mouth made a rounded O, while Ivan just stared at the alpha.

"Looks like our blood bond has linked the two groups." Lucas folded his arms, legs spread.

"Psy, human, changeling," Sascha murmured. "That's what's always been needed in the PsyNet, a trinity of energy. Soleil, Yariela mentioned your mother was human?"

Soleil nodded.

"Pack energy, too, has to be feeding into the Psy network through Soleil. We have members from all three races." Sascha frowned. "But Lucas darling, you don't feel any drain?"

"No."

"Might be that all that's needed for the stabilization of a psychic network is the mere *presence* of changeling and human energies." Sascha's smile was a thing of warmth. "It's going to be a fascinating puzzle to work out. Later. Right now, you two must be starving— Tammy finally agreed to go rest an hour ago, when she felt you start to surface, but she left us with strict instructions to feed you."

"So." Ena's soft voice as Lucas shifted to reveal a large basket of food. "You've succeeded in creating an island that is perfectly balanced within the trinity." A tone in her voice that Ivan knew was pride.

Her next words were telepathic, only for him: *You were never the spider, Ivan. You were born to be the heart of a network. I regret that I didn't understand this at the very beginning.*

The words rang in Ivan's head as Krychek slid his hands into the pockets of his pants. "It's too bad your brain is one of a kind." His eyes gleamed black with stars. "This would be the perfect solution to our problem, erase all our issues with the prior plans to fragment the PsyNet."

"There's at least one more mind like mine," Ivan pointed out, an image of a bloated black carapace in mind. "The original spider who created the island."

"No," Kaleb said. "It's analogous but not the same—it siphoned power, correct? You, however, act as a redistribution center."

Ena stirred. "We can still learn from what Ivan has done. It's possible we could create a network based on the framework."

Kaleb murmured back a response, Ena replied, but Ivan was no longer listening.

All his life, Ivan had believed his ability a curse. To hear it being spoken of as an advantage . . . yes, it was going to take a lot of getting used to, but when he looked over to see Soleil grinning as Sascha handed her a huge chocolate chip muffin, he knew nothing was impossible.

He loved and was loved, words he'd never thought he'd ever think.

"The embers are so warm I can feel them," Arwen murmured from beside him. "She loves you with all her being."

"I know," Ivan said as Soleil turned and waved the muffin at him with a laugh. "I know."

Chapter 52

Ivan, I just got a hit on your DNA. Uncle Rufus and I maintained the automatic background search as you asked—this is the first time it's had a hit. I'm sending you the details, but it looks like a full match—this man is likely your father.

He's human, showed up in the system when he was processed as a suspect in a murder case in the vicinity of his residence. Enforcement tested all adult males within a certain radius. He was cleared straight-away and his DNA is already being wiped from the records, but the automation caught it before the wipe.

I've backed up the record and am attaching it here so you can run your own comparison search to confirm.

—Canto Mercant to Ivan Mercant (9 October 2083)

"HAPPY ENDINGS ARE for human and changeling fairy tales."

"I like that about you," Soleil said, "you're so positive." Ignoring her mate's dark look, she took his hand. "Whatever happens, whoever your papa turns out to be, it doesn't change you. You're my Ivan, courageous and loyal and with serious moves in bed."

Lips curving a fraction as she fanned her face, Ivan curled his fingers over hers. "Canto was able to track down his criminal record—he had multiple minor busts for drugs over the years. No sign the authorities took his DNA as required. Busy shift, sample lost before it was logged, could be any number of reasons why. But"—he paused for a second—"he hasn't been arrested or cited in the past decade."

Tucking her unbound hair behind her ear, Soleil took in the nursing home across the street, beyond a small patch of lush green lawn. "You think he got too sick to score drugs? Was just caught up in that DNA dragnet as a matter of form?"

"It's what makes sense." The structure in which the donor of Ivan's paternal DNA resided was old but tidily kept, and while it had no real grounds of its own, it was situated right across the road from a large park maintained by DarkRiver as part of the pack's commitment to the city.

A place of verdant growth and wild color.

"Odd, that I'd find him here, so close to the place I now call home."

"You say odd, I say fate." Soleil leaned up against him, the pretty fall of metal and jewels at her ears making a musical sound. "Just like it was fate that I packed up my bags on a whim and went to visit Melati while you were doing that lunatic course with your equally lunatic wolf friends. I was meant to find you."

Ivan wasn't sure he believed in fate, but he believed in his Lei. There was no one else he could imagine by his side as they navigated the surprises of life—because there'd been plenty of them in the two months since their mating. This was just the latest.

"If you have to be in a nursing home," Soleil murmured, the dark magenta of her dress vivid against the denim of her jacket, "this isn't too bad." Her tone, however, was dubious.

Because even the most luxurious such residence would crush a changeling's spirit—which was why packs had their own ways of looking after their elders and others who needed care. Soleil would never end up away from the forests that fed her soul.

"What do the Psy do with their elders?" she asked, the sparkling stones in the earrings he'd given her dancing in the sunlight.

"Under Silence, people who could no longer contribute to society just vanished." He squeezed her hand when she sucked in a breath. "Not in my family. Grandmother doesn't let go of her people, re-member?"

"If I wasn't mated to you, I'd proposition your abuela. I'm serious."

Amused at how much she adored his grandmother—and content to his core with how deeply Ena returned her regard, he said, "I forgot to tell you. Arwen's invited us to dinner tomorrow night. His bear is cooking."

"Bears," Soleil said with a mock frown. "Charming troublemak-ers one and all. You know Valentin keeps asking me to teach him how to be extra sneaky?" Laughter in her tone now. "Last time around, I told him he already has a degree in sneaky—he conned Silver into mating with him, didn't he? He laughed so hard he almost fell off his chair."

Ivan could imagine his cousin's big, brash mate doing exactly that. As he could imagine his feline mate making just such a quip. Strange as it was, it turned out that cats and bears liked one another—perhaps *because* they were so different. Each found the other a source of endless fascination.

As for Ivan's family, they'd been welcomed in DarkRiver. Not in the exuberant bear style, but with a feline subtlety that was no less sincere. It was there in the invitations to pack events, in the fact that a young Mercant with an interest in construction was now interning at DarkRiver HQ, and undeniably so in how Sascha and Lucas had permitted Arwen to babysit their cub.

The latter had been a disaster of epic proportions, Arwen the worst babysitter on the planet when it came to discipline. Naya had played hide-and-seek with him—emphasis on the *hide*—until he admitted defeat and promised her chocolate cake for dinner if she revealed her-self. After which, he'd allowed her to watch cartoons till she fell asleep on a besotted Arwen, a tiny black panther with a rounded stomach.

Of course, Arwen was now Naya's all-time favorite babysitter.

As for Ivan's grandmother, she'd formed an unexpected friendship with Yariela, who'd gained a new lease on life in the past months.

It wasn't unusual for Ena to visit with her over a cup of tea.

"We're not so very different, Ivan," Ena had said when Ivan mentioned it. "Yariela wears her heart on her sleeve, while my heart is reinforced with steel and barricaded by ice, but we'd both gut anyone who came after those under our care. She'd cry about it. I wouldn't. Our enemies would still be as dead."

Ivan, too, had formed friendships in the pack—including with Mercy's calm and grounded wolf mate as well as with the sentinel Vaughn. Ivan might not have learned to laugh yet, but he got the feline sense of humor, liked their sly wit and wicked asides.

The one other major shift in his life had been in how he dealt with Jax dealers. Since discovering that Soleil would feel it through their bond if he killed anyone, her soft healer's heart taking brutal hit after brutal hit, he'd begun to work with DarkRiver and the authorities to clear out the trash.

It wasn't as satisfying, but it got the job done—and it protected this woman who was his world.

Today, she hooked her arm through his, the bangles at her wrists a beautiful confusion of color, and looked up. "Ready?"

Jaw clenched, he gave a short nod. *This is just closing a too-long-open door*, he told himself. *I'll be in and out in a matter of minutes, my questions about my genetic inheritance answered.*

They walked quietly up the wide and shallow steps to the locked front door. A sign to one side asked visitors to contact the front desk using the intercom provided, and if buzzed in, to make sure to close the door behind themselves to "protect residents who can no longer protect themselves."

Soleil was the one who made the call. "Hi, we're here to see Tabor Novak."

The response was kind but firm. "We're not supposed to have visitors while we're working. Standard rule, I'm afraid."

Ivan's hand clenched convulsively on Soleil's.

"Oh," she said after shooting him a wide-eyed look. "I apologize. We were told he was a resident here."

The receptionist paused a beat, then laughed. "Oh dear, it looks like there's been a misunderstanding. He is resident here, but he isn't *a* resident. He's one of our live-in care staff. Hold on a sec, honey." The sound of tapping. "Schedule says he's on break in thirty minutes. Can you wait that long?"

"Yes. Shall we wait here?"

"Why don't you head on over to the park? Tabor usually takes his break there anyway. I'll tell him to meet you under the old oak tree. Oh wait, who should I say is visiting?"

Crushed stones on his chest, in his voice, Ivan said, "He knew my mother once. Her name was Norah."

"Oh, how nice. I'll tell him. Half an hour." The receptionist hung up.

He and Soleil walked in silence to the park. It wasn't hard to find the tree—it dominated the right side of the entrance to the park, a large wooden seat underneath.

While Soleil sat, Ivan paced like a caged tiger.

She wanted to say something, anything, to make things better, but she knew that there was no way to make this better. He had to speak to his father, had to figure out what to do with the knowledge.

All she could do was be there for him.

"Hey, you," she murmured when he finally stopped pacing. Rising, she put her arms around him. As always, he put his arms around her at once, his cheek brushing her hair.

No more words. Just this touch, this warmth.

Until his head lifted and she knew. Stepping away, she said, "I'll go for a walk so you two can talk."

"No." He gripped her wrist. "Stay."

She could almost think he was afraid, this man who was the most dangerous predator on this quiet suburban street. Overwhelmed by tenderness, she shifted to stand by his side, his hand still around her wrist, and watched a man in blue scrubs walk toward them.

It was like seeing a too-thin and far older version of Ivan—an Ivan who'd lived a hard life, but who'd laughed, too. Lines marked his face, and the backs of his hands bore a number of scars—such as those created by addicts who picked compulsively at their bodies. Tabor Novak was lucky he'd chosen his hands.

Many went for the face.

The man who was Ivan's father came to stand opposite Ivan, and just stared at him with eyes of a familiar ice blue. They were softer than Ivan's, less piercing, but the shape of the eyes, his nose, the way all his features knit together . . . there was no question they were kin.

"Norah's son?" Emotion-laden eyes, his voice unexpectedly shallow and reedy.

Voicebox damage, she diagnosed. Likely from an untreated injury.

"Yes. According to DNA testing, you're my father."

No shock in Tabor's expression. It was clear he'd already seen that truth in the younger mirror of his own face that was Ivan. "Is your mother alive?" A whisper of hope.

"No."

Trembling, Tabor collapsed onto the bench like a puppet with its strings cut, his hands gripping the edge of the wood smoothed by thousands of hands over the years. "God, she was so beautiful." It came out a rasp. "I was like a puppy dog, would've done anything for her. All she wanted from me was 'fertilization'—that's how she put it."

A laugh that could as well have been a sob. "I got all excited, thought I was going to get lucky, but she didn't want the physical, just . . . well, you know." He blew out a ragged breath, looked up. "I became lost in my poison of choice in the months afterward, and she was gone from our hangouts by the time I'd gathered up enough clarity to remember her, look for her."

Ivan was a stone statue beside Soleil.

"But you do remember her?" she murmured.

"Norah was unforgettable." Sorrow, such sorrow in his voice. Shoving both hands through black hair heavy with threads of gray, he looked once more at Ivan. "A son. I have a son." This time, the tremor in his voice was joy, not sorrow. "I thought I had a good life after I finally crawled out of that pit of poison, but I never expected that it could become a million times better."

Ivan didn't react to the wet shine in Tabor's eyes, but he did speak. "How did you two meet?"

It was as if Tabor had been waiting all these years to tell the story, because he opened his mouth and began to speak. Of a beautiful Psy woman with eyes of vivid blue and dreams of a life lived in wild freedom, and a young human man who'd been broken by life before he ever had a chance to grow into adulthood. Of drugs that provided an illusionary peace, and of months, then years lost in the lying mirages they offered.

"How did you get out?" Soleil asked.

"Got really sick, was picked up by a Human Alliance group that was out to help addicts. They nursed me back to health—and it was enough of a long process that they were able to wean me off. I could think for the first time in a long, long while, and I *hated* it."

He smiled, sorrow in human form. "I began to do drugs because I didn't want to see clearly, didn't want to remember the ugliness of my childhood. I would've walked out and gone right back to that life, but the woman in charge of the clinic—so damn clever, she was—said I had to pay them back by helping to care for someone else, and that person was a young boy—sixteen, maybe. I saw him and knew he was where I'd once been."

A shrug. "I couldn't leave him. I wanted a better life for him. So I stayed. And after he was better, I looked after someone else . . . and then it was a year and I had enough hours as an aide to actually get the start of a qualification, and here I am. Turns out I like taking care of people, like helping them."

Soleil could see why; there was a patience in Tabor that meant he didn't push at Ivan to speak, to share himself. This man understood wounds of the soul, and he understood that people would only speak when they wanted to speak.

And Ivan didn't want to speak.

So when Tabor's break ended, he rose and said, "Thank you for coming, for showing me that a piece of Norah remains. She was a gift, an artist who never got to make her art. But she made you. Please never forget that." He swallowed. "I'd like to see you again. I can give you my call code."

When Ivan nodded, Tabor gave it to them before turning to leave. "She used to make these tiny drawings at the bottom of city walls. They're all over, hidden in corners and in the shadows. I look for them to this day, even in cities where I know she likely never went."

As he began to walk away, his shoulders bowed inward, Ivan said, "I have no memories of her art."

Tabor turned, and it was a little wobbly. "I don't have any pictures, but I remember them. I could tell you if you want?" A quiet plea in the words.

"I would appreciate that." Digging into his pocket, Ivan pulled out his mother's ring. "Did she ever tell you anything about this?"

"Just that it was a family ring." Tabor traced the swirling shape of the etching in the air. "An *S* for their family name."

Now that Tabor had pointed it out, Soleil could see the resemblance. It was extremely stylized but present.

"Not a ring anyone would miss, she said," Tabor continued. "Not one that would be remembered. She said she'd taken it to remind herself where she came from—so she would never be tempted to go back."

Soleil could feel Ivan's stillness as he debated whether to ask the next question, betray the extent of his lack of knowledge about his mother and her family. But then Tabor took the decision out of his hands.

"Scott," he said with a sudden smile. "That was it. One time, when we were both sober, she said she was a Scott, and I asked her if she had a kilt, and she laughed so hard and said no, not that kind of Scot. A Scott with two *T*s. But you must know that."

"Thank you, Tabor." Ivan's voice was difficult to read. "For remembering my mother. I'll call to arrange another meeting between us."

Shoulders rising, Tabor gave a shaky smile before turning to continue on his way back to work.

"I think the tall, dark, and quiet thing might be a little genetic," Soleil joked, though her throat was choked up at the idea of an artist forced to live a lie. It didn't change the fact that Norah's choices had so badly affected her child, but Soleil couldn't help but feel sympathy for her. If Soleil hadn't been allowed to be a healer, it would've surely driven her mad.

Ivan gave her a speaking look, but his next words made it clear that his attention was on another matter. "Scott is a common enough surname."

"True. But there's a famous Psy Scott family, right? I remember— oh—what was her name?" She clicked her fingers. "Shoshanna Scott, the Councilor. I used to see her on the news comms sometimes. But her husband was a Scott, too, wasn't he? Was the name his?"

Ivan dug through the PsyNet before shaking his head. "No, it's hers. He was older, but she had the more prestigious family line, so he took her name when they decided to work as a political unit."

"If I'm remembering right, she had the same coloring as you and your mother, too," Soleil said with a frown. "Blue eyes, dark hair, fair skin. You see any harm in checking if there's a connection?"

"No." Ivan slid away the ring. "I'll see if we can dig up her DNA profile."

"Spies R Us activate!" She grinned, unrepentant, when he said, "Stop talking to bears," in a stern tone. "They're a bad influence."

Still grinning, sparkles over her eyelids and dusted onto her cheeks, she pressed her lips to his jaw. He didn't move, didn't react . . . except to bend a little, so that she could reach him more easily.

And her heart, it melted all over again.

"Te amo, Ivan Mercant," she told him. "Forever and always and back again."

Killer blue eyes looking into her own, a love so vast that it encompassed her in flame-shot silver . . . and a smile so subtle that only she would ever know it. "Forever and always and back again, Soleil Bijoux Garcia."

Revelations

Kaleb, I have a request for a piece of classified information.

—Ena Mercant to Kaleb Krychek

KALEB KRYCHEK LOOKED out at the ocean that crashed at the foot of the Sea House, while Ena sat in an armchair to his right, a cup of herbal tea lifted to her lips. "You're sure?" he asked her.

"We did the run using the DNA print you provided to us."

Kaleb had retrieved that print from an old Council medical archive, where such things had been kept to verify the identities of the Councilors for various access requirements. "What's the relationship?"

"Shoshanna Scott's genetics intersect with Ivan's on such a level that it's likely she's his aunt." Ena dropped the bombshell with elegant grace. "Our research has also revealed an N. Scott who is listed as having died at age twenty-nine. Interestingly, Shoshanna came on the scene twelve years after her sister's birth, which might point to the family unit deciding the elder sister was unsuitable to be their heir."

"The Scotts are extremely proud of their genetic line." Kaleb had always considered them one of the most ruthless in the Net when it came to the "purity" of their genetics.

NALINI SINGH

"Exactly so," Ena agreed. "We could find nothing on Shoshanna's sister past the date noted as being of her death, but Ivan's father has confirmed that Norah was at least thirty when Ivan was conceived. She might've been wiped off the family tree at twenty-nine, but she wasn't dead except to the Scotts."

That was the way of the Psy in the time of the Council, Kaleb thought. Problems just disappeared. "Ivan's mother must've been extremely intelligent to have survived." The Scotts would've surely sent out a death squad to take care of a problematic member.

"It appears so." Ena placed her cup down on its saucer. "Pity she chose drugs over a defection into another family more suited to her."

Putting the cup and saucer on the side table beside her, she said, "Ivan has given me permission to be transparent with you in terms of this information. With the DNA link confirmed, he's certain that the Scarab Queen is either Shoshanna Scott or another intimate blood relation.

"He says the psychic resonance was too powerful for it not to be a direct familial connection, and there aren't that many Scotts in the running. It's a small line. Shoshanna has a daughter, does she not?"

"Not one she chose to raise." His sense was that Shoshanna had only agreed to the conception deal as part of her agreement with Henry; focused on her own power, she'd never appeared concerned with leaving a genetic legacy. "I believe the daughter was brought up as a member of Henry's family group. She's barely twenty-three."

"Strange, how some cherish their children and others see them as nothing but pieces on a chessboard."

And then there were those who were simply monsters who should've never sired a child, Kaleb thought. "It should be easy enough to get an indication of the likelihood that it's a Scott—per my understanding, Ivan did significant damage to the individual concerned. Significant enough that they should be nowhere close to recovered."

"I'll wait to hear back."

The news Kaleb discovered was unexpected to say the least. "According to all sources, Shoshanna is dead," he told Ena the next day. "Catastrophic neural failure that her family is explaining away as the result of a genetic disease. Her body has already been cremated, and the daughter we spoke of—Auden Scott—is now in charge."

"I have no real knowledge of her."

"Neither did I before this meeting. She's either been kept—or been careful to remain—out of view."

Kaleb thought of those intense blue eyes looking out of an ebony-skinned face with Henry's aristocratically masculine features made softer and more rounded, and felt his instincts stir. Despite her clear beauty, there was something . . . unusual about Auden; physically, she'd inherited only her stature and eyes from the maternal side of her line, but in every other way, she was very much Shoshanna's progeny.

As cold and unblinking as a cobra.

"Do we believe that Shoshanna is dead?" Ena petted the black cat in her arms.

"I believe nothing when it comes to the Scotts, but Shoshanna isn't a woman to give up power unless she had to." She'd fought to the end to hold on to her position as a Councilor.

"Still . . . keep the Mercant network listening for her name. Even a whisper, and I want to know." It wasn't an order but a request; Kaleb knew better than to give Ena an order, and he felt no compulsion to do so.

Theirs was an alliance of equals.

"We will listen," Ena murmured before turning to look at him. "Let us be wrong, Kaleb. Let us hope that Shoshanna is dust in the air, the PsyNet no longer under threat from her evil."

Kaleb had never believed in hope, but Sahara, the woman who was his light in the darkness, did. So he would let her believe for both of them—while he watched for the creeping malevolence that hid in the open and crawled in the shadows.

This was war and the Scarabs had only fired their first shot.

DEEP underground, in a remote Scott stronghold, machines beeped and hummed, keeping alive a brain in a body that was nothing but a fleshy adjunct. The patient's eyes were closed, her face appearing peaceful—but her neural activity spiked on the screen, showing massive surges and dips.

As she slept, a near inaudible whisper crept through the PsyNet: *Scarab. Queen. Scarab. Queen. Mother. We wait.*